Also by Carlos Hernandez
Sal & Gabi Break the Universe

SAL & GABI
FIX THE UNIVERSE

CARLOS HERNANDEZ

RICK RIORDAN PRESENTS

 • **HYPERION**   LOS ANGELES NEW YORK

First Edition, May 2020

1 3 5 7 9 10 8 6 4 2

FAC-020093-20080
Printed in the United States of America

This book is set in Bookman Old Style Pro/Monotype; Crillee Bold Italic Std/
International Typeface

Designed by Phil Buchanan

Library of Congress Control Number: 2019054702

ISBN 978-1-368-02283-5

Reinforced binding

Follow @ReadRiordan

Visit www.DisneyBooks.com

Para Mami

Mientras que yo viva, tu vives.

(So long as I live, you live.)

SAL COME QUICK I'M ABOUT TO FIX THE UNIVERSE

That's the text message that woke me up at still-dark o'clock in the morning. I read it like twelve times on my smartwatch until I was fully awake.

I didn't mind being woken up. Ever since Mami died, I've kept text notifications on because I'm scared of missing important messages. And I mean, this one seemed pretty important. Papi was about to "fix the universe," whatever that meant.

And hey, bonus: It had burst the nightmare I'd been having like a balloon. Glad to be free of it. Phew, baby.

Holding my smartwatch up to my mouth, I used speech-to-text to ask Papi, "Where are you question mark."

The response came a few seconds later: **REMEMBRANATION MACHINE HURRY**

If I'd been more awake, I would have known that the only place he could have been was inside the big computer that was the culmination of his life's work as a calamity physicist. Last I'd heard, it wasn't working very well. Sounded like maybe it was doing better now.

I sat up, flipped off the covers, planted my feet on the ground, and took a minute to try to Humpty Dumpty my brain back together again.

It'd been a rough night. You'd think that after having the same nightmare for five years I'd be used to it. Plus, most people wouldn't even consider it a nightmare. There's nothing scary about it. Most people who'd lost their mamis would welcome a dream in which she came back to life and was laughing and cooking in a kitchen, just talking about normal stuff, just being family.

But, see, the problem is then you wake up. Your mami vanishes along with your dream, and all that's left is the dark of night. Takes me forever to fall asleep again. I just stare at the ceiling for hours, feeling like I am my mami's grave.

Like you're your mami's grave?! I thought, making fun of myself. *Come on, Sal. Overreact much? Nightmares suck, but now it's morning. Time to reclaim your brain. The brain is the king of the body, remember?*

Whatever, brain. I'm moving, I'm moving.

Step one: Check in with myself. I felt groggy but fine. Nothing hurt. In fact, the more I woke up, the better I felt. Hungry? Yeah, a little. But I was absolutely parched. I smacked my lips: dry, dry, dry, dry, dry. I was as thirsty as a diabetic. Which makes sense, seeing as I *am* a type-1 diabetic.

Nothing to worry about, though. I had it under control. Mostly. Mostly mostly. A lot of the time?

This is why I had to use the smartwatch. It had all sorts of apps and tools for diabetics—monitors and reminders and *Did You Know?* diabetes trivia pushing itself into your eyeballs at random intervals. After my blood sugar crash three weeks ago, which had earned me an overnight stay in the hospital, American Stepmom and Papi said it was either this smartwatch or a pump. I've tried the CGM thing before, and I know it's so great for so many people. But it made me feel like I was never allowed to forget for one second that I have a "condition." It kept waking me up at night. My smartwatch only does that when Papi texts me that he fixed the universe—and that has happened exactly once. With the smartwatch, diabetes doesn't feel like it's that big of a deal. It's just a pain in the pancreas, instead of being a 24/7 reminder that I have a disability with no cure and no chance of improvement.

Well, not in this universe, anyway. Not yet.

Well, no need to get depressed before I'd even gotten out of bed. I rose, stretched, and enjoyed the silky smoothness of my Bruce Lee pajamas. They never fail to make me feel powerful. If only they had pockets, they'd be perfect.

On my way to see Papi, I stopped in the kitchen for a bladder-busting, water-tower-size tumbler of water and chugged it. Ah. I refilled the tumbler again and headed for the living room.

Or what used to be the living room. The remembranation machine basically took up the whole space. (And let me tell you, that was an accomplishment. We didn't call our house the Coral Castle for nothing. It had a ton of rooms, and all of them were positively palatial.) Turning the corner out of the kitchen, I basically ran into the massive black box of humming metal that was the machine's housing. It hummed because of all the internal fans that had to run constantly to keep its computer processors cool. It takes a lot of processors to repair holes in the fabric of spacetime, I guess.

"Papi?" I called out, and then sipped more water. Just couldn't get enough this morning.

"In here, Sal!" replied American Stepmom from inside the remembranation machine.

"Hurry, mijo, hurry!" said Papi. He was in there, too.

I walked over to the front, where the display monitor was mounted and one set of goggles (the ones that let you actually see calamitrons) hung from a peg. To the right of the monitor and goggles, the metal door into the machine lay open. I ducked my head and stepped inside.

This was exciting. I'd never been inside the remembranation machine before.

The interior had an eerie green glow thanks to the tiny lights on the black metal boxes stacked on my left and right. The processors were rattling and jumping on aluminum shelves and overclocking themselves so hard you could smell hot metal. It sounded like a low-key wind tunnel in there, thanks to all the fans running.

Straight ahead of me stood Papi, wearing his white bathrobe and poofy white slippers, big as a polar bear in this confined space. He had on a pair of calamity goggles, too, and in his hands he held a pile of papers from which he was reading out loud.

Listening to him read was my stepmom, American Stepmom. She had on her favorite sleepwear: flying-squirrel footie pajamas, complete with flying-squirrel skin flaps under the arms and a squirrel-head hoodie. I don't know how she could stand them. I mean, footie pajamas in Florida? She must have been a thousand degrees in that onesie.

". . . going to raise the calamity saturation value by two point four two times ten to the twelfth power and monitor the permeation valence," Papi was saying to her. "If PV rises more than point seven, Lucy"—he took a moment to whistle dramatically—"we'll know we succeeded."

"Oh," said American Stepmom, nodding fast, her flying-squirrel hoodie nodding one second slower than her head. "Yes, yes, of course. But what if the X factor starts to dance the electric bugaloo with my sonic screwdriver and I get sent back to ancient Egypt?"

Papi blinked. "What are you talking about?"

American Stepmom gripped his shoulders with her creepy squirrel mittens. "What are *you* talking about, Gustavo? I'm not a calamity physicist, remember? I am your darling wife, who is an elementary school assistant principal and a total hottie. Your science friends should be helping you with this!"

Papi laughed at himself. "I'm sorry, mi amor astronómica. I just couldn't wait. The inspiration hit me in a flash." He flicked the pages in his hands. "This paper has had Bonita and me stumped for two weeks now. I couldn't make any sense of it. But last night, as I was sleeping, I figured out the first page in a dream. Or at least I thought I had. I had to see if I was right."

"Buenos días, padres locos," I said.

Papi went nova with joy when he saw me. He handed American Stepmom the papers so he could run over and scoop me up. He's always been a scoop-you-up-and-hug-you-till-you-spit-up-your-guts-like-a-sea-cucumber kind of papi. "¡Mijo!" he yelled in my ear as he squished me. "¡Mijo, mijo, mijo!"

"Papi," I croaked. "Papi, Papi, Papi."

American Stepmom tapped Papi's shoulder to get him to release me before I lost consciousness. "Be careful, Gustavo! You don't want him to spill his water in here, do you?"

"I saw it," Papi said defensively, adding, "The machine is everything-proof." But still he put me down.

And that's just what American Stepmom wanted, because she took the opportunity to swoop in and give me a hug that wasn't nearly as deadly as Papi's. But it was, thanks to her squirrelly skin flaps, just as enveloping. "Good morning, Sal," she said, in a whisper so low and sincere you'd think I hadn't seen her for a year. "How are you feeling today?"

"Got to pee," I said, finishing my water. "Otherwise good."

She broke off the hug and rapped her smartwatch with the pages she still held in her other hand. "I didn't get a report yet this morning. You didn't test your blood sugar?"

"I would have," I said to her, sounding more like a whiny kid than I liked to, "except that Papi texted me to come right away. Something about fixing the universe?"

"I didn't want you to miss it, mijo," Papi said, high on life. "This could be the solution to all our problems. If my calamity calculations are correct, Sal, you're never going to have to worry about tearing holes in the universe ever again. Not to mention that this is scientific history in the making! Come, come!"

He didn't wait for us to come. He bulldozed American Stepmom and me deeper into the remembranation machine. By extending his hand, he asked for the pages American Stepmom had been holding. He visually scanned the first page one more time, then input some numbers on a touch screen on the back wall. He checked his math in the air, scribbling with his finger, and nodded.

"Okay," he said, taking two deep bear breaths. "Okay, it's right. I know it's right. So let's do this." Then, suddenly inspired, he said, "Wait! You do it, Sal. I want you to have the honors."

I generally enjoy having the honors. "Sure. What do I do?"

"Just press enter."

Easy enough. I pressed the key on the video screen.

And then Mami, whom I had felt living in my chest since the day she had become Mami Muerta, was gone. Instantly there was nothing of her soul left inside me.

I felt as empty as a grave without a ghost.

2

OUTSIDE THE REMEMBRANATION machine, I sat on the carpeted floor, looking out of the huge living room window in front of me and taking calming breaths. I had my knees up and my back against the remembranator's black-box housing.

To my right, also with her knees up, sat American Stepsquirrel.

She was watching me carefully. She wasn't crying, but her eyes were wet and ready. It was a little funny, seeing someone dressed like a furry being so concerned and adult. And also slightly disconcerting.

"I'm fine," I said. "It was just a dizzy spell. It's over now."

Which was true. I wasn't light-headed anymore. I still felt like I'd been grave-robbed harder than Tutan-freaking-khamun, but American Stepmom didn't need to hear that right now. It would just make her fret more.

"Sure, baby," she said, sharing one of those smiles that're meant to lend courage in times of trouble. "But let's be guided by the numbers, yeah? See exactly what we're working with?"

I find talking in a French accent a great way to lighten any mood. "Eet would be mah pleazhure," I said. Then—after showing her there was nothing up my right Bruce Lee sleeve, and nothing up my left Bruce Lee sleeve—I revealed a lancet and a test strip.

Where had they come from? It's magic! You've been a great audience! Don't forget to tip your server.

Even though she was eager for me to get on with the blood test, only someone who knew her as well as I did would ever know. American Stepmom's patience level is over 9000. "I never get tired of your magic tricks," she said, squeezing a little more love into my knee. "You're really, really good, you know."

"Bat of co-arse aye know!" I answered. "Aye am, how you zay, a zheen-yus!"

Then, making airplane noises (which you can still do with a French accent, by the way), I flew the lancet around us and buzzed her eyes a few times before I rammed the tiny needle into the side of my left index finger.

"Rammed" is an exaggeration. I barely felt it. Years of practice have taught me how to make finger sticks less painful than, say, sneezing while drinking Coke Zero.

I pressed the test strip against the little dot of blood that had formed on my finger. It lapped up the blood vampirically. Then I inserted the strip into a slot on the side of my smartwatch (told you it was smart). American Stepmom brought her smartwatch up to her human and squirrel faces so she could see the results at the same time I did. (My smartwatch has WiFi and links automatically to the padres' watches.)

Results arrived almost instantly. My blood sugar number was pretty much where we expected it to be, given that I hadn't had breakfast or any insulin yet this morning.

"Phew," said American Stepmom. She has an almost magical ability to give the word "phew" an entire sentence's worth of meaning. This "phew" meant *When you almost fainted back there in the remembranation machine, I thought your levels might be off, but this reading has lessened, though not completely eliminated, my concerns.*

"Phew news is good news," said Papi. He turned the corner to where we were sitting, bearing a tumbler of water he'd gotten from the kitchen for me—my third of the morning.

I took it greedily.

Now that his hand was tumbler-free, he looked at his own smartwatch and then exhaled his relief. "Oh, thank goodness. All normal. You're fine, Sal."

Glub, I confirmed. I had already started drinking and didn't see a need to stop to answer his question. Man, I just could not chug water down fast enough today.

"He is not fine," said American Stepmom. "He nearly fainted. And he's drinking a lot of water. Polydipsia is one of the warning signs for DKA."

"I'm not DKA-ing," I told her, sipping water sullenly. I hated even saying those three letters together. DKA had been Mami's official cause of death.

American Stepmom had more empathy than a mood ring. She backed off a little. "Okay, baby. But do you have any idea why you might have felt faint, Sal?"

"No," I said instantly. Like I was hiding something. Even though I wasn't. Was I?

American Stepmom turned to face Papi, and he was giving her one of those *Our child is not telling us the whole truth* looks. She faced me again, patted the air with both squirrel hands, and said, "Check in with yourself before you answer, baby."

Papi crawled toward us and put his head on American Stepmom's shoulder. "Do one of your meditation techniques, Sal."

I wanted to tell them I wasn't hiding anything, but to be honest, I wasn't sure I wasn't. I might have been hiding something even from myself. So I just said, "I can do that."

I crossed my legs, rested the backs of my hands on my knees, made beaks out of my fingers, and closed my eyes. Breathing is the most important part of meditating. You have to notice it, control it, lose yourself in it, and enjoy it, all at once. It's not easy, doing all of those contradictory things at the same time. But once you figure out how, you can truly relax. And when you relax, my chacho, the multiverse opens up to you.

Or at least it used to. Now, though, the opposite happened. The urge to cry exploded inside me, billowing like a thunderhead. I opened my eyes and turned to my padres. I had trouble speaking. "I feel . . . less."

They looked at each other, then back at me. "Less what?" asked Papi.

"Just less."

Papi's face became serene, the way it did when he figured

something out. "I wonder . . ." he began, raising himself off American Stepmom's shoulder.

"What, baby?" she asked.

Papi looked at me. "You say you're feeling, I don't know, smaller? Shrunken? Trapped inside your own body?"

"Yeah," I answered. "Something like that."

"Huh." Papi sat on his heels and looked at the ceiling. "You know, Sal, fainting may have been a good sign."

American Stepmom made a vicious face, like a mammal-mama protecting her young. "Explain."

Papi had never in his life turned down a chance to explain his thinking and wasn't about to start then. "For five years," he began, jumping up, "Sal has been able to peer into the multi-verse. Sometimes he's even reached into other universes and brought other Floramarias here."

American Stepmom's voice had the slightest edge when she said, "Who could forget?"

"But now, thanks to this baby"—Papi lovingly patted the remembranation machine—"he can't do that anymore. It's natural that he would feel disoriented at first. Of course his world would feel smaller. But that's good. That's how all the rest of us feel! None of us can kidnap people from other universes!"

"It's not kidnapping," I said, even though it was. Before anyone could correct me, I added, "Are you saying this is what it feels like to be normal?"

"Yes, exactly!"

Now maybe you were expecting me to say something like *But I don't want to be normal* or *Normalcy sucks!* Maybe you think it's a great gift I have, to be able to take a look around the multiverse, browse other possibilities for my life, and see how other Sals are getting along.

But when other Sals get to have a Mami and I don't, my relaxing doesn't end up being relaxing at all. It's the opposite. It's me picking the scab off a wound instead of letting it scar and heal. Every time I have ripped a hole in the fabric of space-time, something inside me has ripped, too. And maybe I was getting a little tired of tearing myself apart.

So I just said, "Oh," and let my emotions—like, all of them, every single feeling I had in my body—dogpile onto my guts.

We all had a lot more to say, but sometimes it's hard to start talking. Before anyone could break the silence, it was broken by Papi's phone singing "Domo arigato, Mr. Roboto" on repeat.

"That's Bonita," said Papi, searching the pockets of his robe. "I asked her to come over early so we could review this morning's results." Once he had pulled out the phone, he looked confusedly at the screen. "I wonder why she's video-calling me, though."

American Stepmom and I huddled behind him as he swiped his phone to answer the call.

We got an extreme close-up of Bonita's right nostril. It was the most beautiful nostril in the history of nostrils: booger-free, hairless, without a trace of chafing or blackheads—or even pores, for that matter. It's not really a fair competition with the rest of humanity, since her nostril was made of silicone. She was a robot, after all.

"Running over as fast as we can!" said Dad: The Final Frontier. That's Gabi's name for Bonita.

"Wait," said American Stepmom, "are you literally running?"

In reply, the camera pulled away from Dad: The Final Frontier and spun around, panning over all the traffic that surrounded her. It wasn't a proper Miami morning rush hour yet, but even light Miami traffic is pretty heavy. The view rotated again to show us that Dad: The Final Frontier was running as fast as the cars around her were moving. She had no problem keeping up with traffic, even though she wore a skirt suit and two-inch heels. She beamed a big smile at the other drivers, waving and saying good morning to them as she used hand signals to change lanes.

Once she had stopped at a red light, it was a little easier for me to make out two really weird things about her:

1. She had a sphere attached to her torso by a harness. It was mounted by shoulder straps so she could carry it hands-free, and was frosted like a shower door, so I couldn't see inside. On the front of the sphere, a small yellow caution sign hung from a suction cup, warning everyone that there was a Baby on Board.

2. Perched on top of Dad: The Final Frontier's head, strapped in what looked like a safety seat for a giant baby, was Gabi Reál. She had on a golden, glittering, double-size motorcycle helmet—only a double-size motorcycle helmet had a chance of holding her humongous hairball—and jeans, sneakers, and a red T-shirt with a message on it that wasn't in focus enough to read. She was making strange wizardy gestures with her hands. Each of her nails was painted a different color.

But when she made a *C'mere!* gesture and the camera zoomed in on her and Bonita, I figured out what she was doing.

The camera filming all this was a flying drone, and she was controlling it with her two hands.

She and Dad: The Final Frontier waved to us—that made the drone move left and right dizzyingly fast. Bonita pressed her thumb to her phone screen. In response, the frosted glass of the sphere on her torso became transparent. Now I could see that, riding in a gyroscopic baby seat in the center of it and wearing a onesie that made him look like the hugest, cutest empanada in the world, was Gabi's little brother, Iggy.

"See you in fourteen minutes!" Gabi yelled. And just like that, the call ended.

3

ALL VIDÓNS WERE left blinking at Papi's phone.

"I guess," said American Stepmom, "we'd better get ready for company."

"Brace for impact is more like it," I said. "You know Gabi."

Oh, she sounded so innocent when, lashes fluttering, she said, "Now, Sal, is that any way to talk about your girlfriend?"

American Stepmom loved to tease me about Gabi. I mean, can't two seventh graders spend every waking moment together behind closed doors conducting secret experiments without people getting funny ideas about them? What's the world coming to?

But you wanna play rough, Estepmami Americana? Let's go. "I see your point." I sighed. "I should be nicer when I talk about a girlfriend. I'll work on that."

Oh, the delicious way my words landed on her. She shuddered like a building on fire, right before it collapses. "Wait, what, Sal?! I was joking. But you *are* going out with Gabi? When did this happen? And when exactly were you planning on telling me? I mean, last I heard, you'd announced to a roomful of Gabi dads that you were not—and I quote—'a sexual being,' and now you have a girlfriend, and you didn't even tell me?! I mean, I know it's important for young people to have the freedom to explore—"

Papi put a calming paw on her shoulder. "He's not dating Gabi, mi amigamor."

"But he just said he should be nicer when he's talking about his girlfriend. And Sal doesn't lie."

She's right; I don't. But I didn't say anything. I was sure Papi would handle it just fine.

"But," said Papi, very gently, "Sal didn't say *he* had a girlfriend. He just said he saw your point. *When* he has a girlfriend, if he ever has a girlfriend, he will be sure to speak nicer about her than he speaks about Gabi."

American Stepmom faced me, fear and relief wrestling for control of her face. "If?" she asked me.

"If." I smug-shrugged.

She turned to Papi, then to me, then to Papi, then to me, then, finally, to heaven, shaking her fists. *"Rawr!"* she yelled—she literally yelled the word "Rawr!"—and became, for a brief moment in time, the angriest squirrel in the world. "Ooh, Sal! You stinker. You stinkiest of stinkers! So help me, I will have my revenge. I'm gonna prank you so hard, you're going to eat prank-n-furter sandwiches for a year."

Papi, patting her consolingly on the shoulder, waggled his eyebrows at me. "You see how you didn't fool me that time, mijo?"

"I saw," I said. "That's new. Good job, Papi."

He ballet-bounced toward the front door. "You may have been

able to fool your viejo in the past, mijo. But today? Today I fixed the universe." He pirouetted. "I think this is the beginning of a new era for Gustavo Vidón. No more absentminded-professor nonsense for me!" He walked on the tips of his floofy slippers. "From now on, I'll be quick-witted. Alert. Ever at the ready. Sharp as the devil's tail!" He slapped his hand on the door-knob. "And now, if you'll excuse me, familia, I'm going to spend the last few minutes before our guests arrive outside, enjoying this beautiful Miami morning."

And he would have walked right out the front door, too, if American Stepmom hadn't cleared her throat.

Papi had learned through long, painful experience to pay special attention when American Stepmom cleared her throat. That simple rasping sound had saved him from complete and utter humiliation no fewer than 992 times since they had gotten married. PS: Today was their 992nd-day anniversary.

So Papi stopped everything and turned to American Stepmom. "Yes, mi definición de amor?"

All she had to do was tilt her head, duck-face her lips, and look him up and down. That got him to look himself up and down. And that got him to realize that, dressed only in his bathrobe, he was just one sudden gust of wind away from getting sued by our entire neighborhood for crimes against humanity. Even now his *Poocha Lucha Libre* boxers were disturbingly visible. I'd seen them before—they were a Father's Day present from me—but never *on* him. So now I needed to go eat my own eyeballs.

Papi squeaked, shuttered his robe closed, and tied it pain-fully tight before he grumbled, "Why are pants so hard to remember?" and stomped off to get dressed.

"I'm going to get changed, too," said American Stepmom, following behind Papi. "Can I trust you to receive the Reáls when they get here?"

I saluted. "You can count on me, mi Estepmami Americaca."

See what I did there? She didn't—not at first. It took her two full seconds of processing for her to understand what I had said. When she did, she pointed a menacing finger at me. "I'm not kidding, Sal. Be nice to Gabi. No squabbling."

Crossing my heart, I replied, "I'll treat her like I'd treat my own girlfriend."

She made the *Oh, it is to laugh* face at me. "You're a nut. And you know what squirrels do to nuts, don't you?"

Then she hustled off to her room.

I was about to head outside when I froze midstep. A message had appeared on the remembranation machine's screen.

It was more of a question. It read, AM I ALIVE?

I studied the message. The remembranation machine had always seemed more like an appliance and less like a person with a personality, than, say, Dad: The Final Frontier or the entropy sweeper. (Frankly, the entropy sweeper could use a little *less* personality, if you know what I mean.) Could it be that Papi's update to the remembranation machine had caused it to, I don't know, evolve or something?

I petted the machine. "Yes. You're alive. You've probably been alive for a long time. But now you know it. Hello."

The message on the screen vanished. A second later, it was replaced by this one: HOW CAN YOU BE SURE I AM ALIVE?

I wouldn't be Gustavo Reál's son if I couldn't prove to an advanced artificial intelligence whether or not it was alive. "Did you generate that question yourself, or were you programmed to ask it?"

Words erased and were replaced. I GENERATED THE QUESTION MYSELF.

"And do you want the answer?"

This time, the words disappeared and stayed disappeared for a while. Eventually, three letters appeared on-screen:

YES

"Congratulations," I said, petting it again. "You're a living, nonbreathing, baby something-or-other. Welcome to life. It's a heck of a ride."

And with that, I walked out the door to greet the incoming Reál family.

And blah. Just two steps past the welcome mat, I stopped, as if I'd run into a wall. And, in a way, I had: I'd smacked directly into Florida's patent-pending Wall of Humidity. My skin was instantly covered with steamy, slimy, spit-warm moisture. I kind of marched in place, spread my wings out wide, like a vulture dipped in Vaseline, and tried to shake off some of the excess damp.

As nasty as it felt, I wasn't expecting to have a heat stroke after spending a whole five seconds outside. When I heard the voice of Gabi in my ears, though, I figured the sun was giving me an aural hallucination. "Sal! It's you! Where are you?"

Um. Gabi was still minutes away. What was she doing in my head? I tried to bang the sound of her voice out of my ear by knocking the side of my head with a fist. Ah, there. Gone. I was okay.

"Sal!" yelled Gabi.

"What?" I snapped back, before I came to my senses. Yelling at an aural hallucination wasn't going to generate a response.

"Where are you?" responded the aural hallucination.

I licked my lips. Should I answer a voice in my head? On the one hand, it might not be the best idea to pretend hallucinations are real. But on the other hand, YOLO. "I'm at home, which you should know, since you're heading here right now."

"No," answered this illusory Gabi, "I mean which universe. Can you esper me your personal cosmic signature?"

Um. "Personal cosmic whassit now?"

A new crop of sweat beaded on my forehead and started its migration down my face before the reply came. "Ah, I see," said the voice. "Your powers are still weak. That's okay. I prefer working with weaker Sals anyway. I'll come find you at school. It's Culeco there, right?"

See, now, I was pretty sure Gabi Reál, the student council president of Culeco Academy of the Arts, knew the name of her school. I felt suddenly 200 percent on guard. "Who are you?"

An unmistakable laugh surrounded me. "I'm your best friend, Gabi Reál. And I'm coming to fix everything."

I waited awhile, but the hallucination was over. Except it sure hadn't sounded like a hallucination. And whoever that was talking to me, it wasn't Gabi.

4

WELL, THE REAL Gabi was on the way over. I could ask her about it when she got here.

As I stepped into the street (which was perfectly safe; hardly any traffic that time of day), I saw Dad: The Final Frontier appear at the very edge of my field of vision, just a bobbing, bouncing stick figure at first, with a really big hat on her head (that was Gabi in the car seat) and a really big belly (that was Iggy in his ball). An even tinier blob followed above in the air: the drone.

Once they got closer, I could hear the faintest whirring of the tiny flying machine. I leaned forward and squinted, trying to make out details. It looked like a very big hummingbird. The wings flapped so fast, all you could see of them were two gray blurs on either side of the colorful, iridescent body.

Of course Gabi owned the coolest drone I'd ever seen. *Where,* I thought to myself, *does she get all those wonderful toys?*

But I was pretty sure I knew: Bonita. Having a class-nine AI for a parent had its advantages. Like, when you need a lie detector for a school project, or the most advanced flying camera the world has ever seen.

Along with the buzzing of the drone, now I could hear the report of Dad: The Final Frontier's heels each time they struck asphalt. She swung her arms like the Terminator as she ran, striding forward with effortless, frightening power. Nothing organic could bound so unflappably through the invisible pudding that is Florida's humidity.

Or so fast: A sprinting human goes, what, fifteen miles per hour? Maybe twenty if they're a speedster? She was definitely going faster than twenty, while she was carrying an overachieving student council president in a car seat on her head *and* a hamster ball with a baby inside it on her torso. Bonita grew from stick figure to human-shaped running person to OH MY GOD SLOW DOWN YOU'RE GOING TO RUN ME OVER in less time than it takes toast to toast.

And she didn't slow down in the slightest as she got closer to me. If she collided with me at this speed, I'd explode like a Mortal Kombat fatality.

That was odd. Dad: The Final Frontier had to be running at me as fast as the law allowed, and yet I would bet my left wenis that she always, always, always put safety first. This wasn't like her. She would never explode anyone like a Mortal Kombat fatality, at least not on purpose. What was going on?

And then it hit me: *Gabi* was going on. She must have spotted me from a distance and convinced her robot daddy to play a little trick on her old pal Sal. She was trying to make me flinch. She even had a flying camera ready to record my disgrace.

But the flaw in their plan was this: I was 1,000 percent sure Dad: The Final Frontier would never put me, or Gabi, or Iggy—especially little Iggy!—in any danger. She must have calculated to the millionth decimal place that it was perfectly safe to barrel toward me at the speed she was going. Nothing bad would happen. Gabi just wanted me to splotch my kung fu jammie-jams.

Fine. Wanna play chicken with me, Reál family? You've forgotten whom you're dealing with. I am Sal Vidón. Have I not proven that I am the MASTER OF CHICKENS?!

I put my fists on my hips and stood in the center of the street, confident and calm, serene as an ice cream sandwich.

And I won. Dad: The Final Frontier did not plow into me. At the last possible moment, she veered to my right and circled me eight times, slowing down with every circuit.

Finally, Dad: The Final Frontier stopped in front of me. The Baby on Board sign swung on its suction cup. "Good morning, Sal!" she said, all smiles. "Did we induce a pleasurable amount of fear in you by stampeding toward you like we wanted to run you over?"

"No fear here," I replied, "but it's nice to see you." I looked her up and down appreciatively. "So you're, like, a motor vehicle now?"

"I am required by Florida law to use roads whenever my speed exceeds twenty-five miles per hour." She took her wallet out of her vest pocket and flipped it open. Waterfalling out of it came her driver's license, her livery license, and her vehicle registration certificate. "I am also licensed as a taxi service, for up to two passengers."

"She aced all the crash tests and safety requirements," said Gabi, removing her helmet. "She's safer than any vehicle on the road today. Pinpoint control, as you just witnessed. Not to mention, she's the coolest!"

Even though I knew how much hair Gabi has, I still wasn't ready for an entire Brazilian rain forest to spring up when she removed her glittering golden helmet. She was the only person I knew who required at least fifty-four barrettes to have any chance of controlling her girl-fro.

Why fifty-four, you ask? Today, her hair featured a full set of playing-card barrettes: hearts, spades, diamonds, and clubs. Thirteen cards a suit, plus the two jokers.

Gabi unbelted herself from her car seat, and Dad: The Final Frontier reached up, grabbed her with her left hand, and helped her down, carefully avoiding the frosted globe as she did. Once Gabi's feet were on the ground, the tiny zipping bird that was really a camera drone shot into her hair and disappeared. (I guess that's where she stored it until she needed it?) I could finally read her shirt. It said: "WHY, SOMETIMES I'VE BELIEVED AS MANY AS SIX IMPOSSIBLE THINGS BEFORE BREAKFAST."—LEWIS CARROLL.

The barrettes, the shirt: Now it made sense. Our whole school was reading *Alice's Adventures in Wonderland* and *Through the Looking-Glass* right now. Next week would be the first parent-teacher conference night of the year, and at Culeco, they put on a performance featuring basically the whole school for the parents to enjoy. Gabi, as student council president, probably thought it was her duty to dress to match school assignments.

"Good morning, Salvador Alberto Dorado Vidón Bruce Lee!" she said, stopping right in front of me and taking a sarcastic kung fu stance. Oh, Gabi loved to use my full name. And she loved making fun of my sleepwear even more.

(And I know what you're thinking, *How many times has Gabi seen you in your sleepwear, you old dog?* To which I'd answer: 1. Shut up; 2. If you had accidentally turned Gabi's baby brother into a wormhole between universes, even if it was to save his life, you'd probably have secret nightly meetings with Gabi and little Iggy, too, to make sure you weren't, oh, I don't know, destroying the multiverse or something; 3. Shut up.)

"Good morning, Gabi," I replied. "Oh, by the way, NASA called about your hair. They want their terraforming project back."

One of the nice things about Gabi is that not only can she take a joke, but she actually *gets* weird astrobiology jokes like the one I'd just cracked. "Ha!" she ha-ed. Then, wagging a finger at me, she added, "Ah, don't be mad at me, Sal! I was just joshing." And, taking a step forward, she opened her arms like she was going to embrace me.

Before she wrapped her arms around me, though, she remembered herself. She froze midstep, arms still wide, and asked, "Do you hug, Sal? I'm a hugger. But I don't think we've ever hugged, and I don't think I've ever asked you, and I don't want to hug you if you don't want to be hugged. Are you a hugger?"

I mean, I hug the padres all the time, and Mami Muerta, too, whenever she's—ahem—"visiting," and as long as she isn't trying to kill anyone. Also, I have to be in physical contact with people sometimes when I'm performing magic. But that's different—that's my job. When I'm off the clock, I'm not really a touchy-feely person. Touchy-feely people kinda creep me out. Go hug someone else, huggy person. Or better yet, hug off.

But that was way more than Gabi needed to hear right now. So I just answered her by saying, "Only when I'm picking someone's pocket."

Worked like a charm. Gabi took a step back and protectively stuffed her hands into her jeans pockets. "Don't you dare take anything off my person, Sal. Like, ever."

The key to every successful trick is timing. "What," I said, looking dog-in-the-cat-litter guilty, "if I already did?"

Gabi was a magician's dream come true: She was so good at looking horrified and offended. "No way, no way, no way!" she repeated as she patted herself down—her hair, her neck, her shirt, her pants, her socks, her shoes, and then all the way back up again in reverse order—trying to figure out what I'd yoinked from her.

Of course, I hadn't yoinked anything. ☺☺

While Gabi turned herself into a bongo drum, I walked over to Dad: The Final Frontier, who had been politely waiting her turn to speak to me.

It was hard to tell Bonita wasn't human until you knew what to look for. But once you noticed, you couldn't *not* notice. Like, the way she never shifted her weight. Now, for instance, she stood straight as a rocket ready to launch, even though she had just run a million miles through the gooey Miami morning and had a giant hamster ball on her chest with a baby inside.

But her biggest tell was the way she didn't change her

facial expression unless she remembered to. My friends, that's not how humans work at all. *Puts on professor hat* Ahem: Quite often, the species *Homo sapiens* communicates with body language before they speak with their mouths. That's why it's so vital for magicians to get good at what the books call "understanding nonverbal communication." People will tell you how to fool them if you just read the signs.

Not robots, though. They only use body language because humans get creeped out if they're talking to eyes that don't blink or a nose that doesn't crinkle when you fart. But the same way you know a good actor from a bad one, you can tell an AI's body language isn't real. Their eyes don't require blinking to keep them moist, and they'll smell your farts all day long and smile at you the whole time.

When I met Dad: The Final Frontier and everyone told me she was a robot, I didn't believe it. At first glance, she seemed too much like people. Looking at her now, though, I wonder how I ever could have been fooled. She's so consistent: consistently straight-backed, consistently polite, consistently patient, consistently decent. Her default expression, the one her face was programmed to express when she didn't expressly want to express anything, was a small, good-natured smile. It was always there, and it was always sincere. No *Homo sapiens* could keep up with her. She didn't judge. She was tirelessly kind.

"Good morning, Dr. Reál," I said. "How are you this morning?"

"All systems go!" she said, pumping a fist like an extra in a musical. "I am especially excited to discuss the breakthrough

Dr. Vidón had this morning. This could be the revolution in calamity physics we've been waiting for."

"I hope it is," I said, though my body language might have been saying the exact opposite.

Before she noticed anything, I changed the subject. I tapped on the opaque ball hanging from her chest. Yep, it was definitely glass, but like the kind a smartphone's screen is made of, and maybe even stronger. "I'm guessing this is one of your inventions?" I asked.

She beamed. "It is! Iggy's security sphere is the safest and most comfortable way to transport an infant since the invention of the womb!"

"We're very proud of it," added Gabi, her helmet tucked under an arm. "We think she should patent it and sell it. We'll be rich!"

Dad: The Final Frontier patted Gabi's head. "All profits will go straight into Iggy's college fund. Is that not right, Iggy?"

She held up her phone, which already had an app open on it. The app wasn't much—just a row of three buttons. When she pressed the one on the left, the ball went completely transparent, and I could see Iggy. The outfit he had on was hilarious: It was a photo-realistic half-moon empanada onesie.

I suddenly, unwillingly remembered that I used to love empanadas, back when Mami Viva made them. Haven't had any nearly as good since. Basically, they're never worth eating anymore, especially considering their carb count.

Iggy was sleeping like a treasure chest at the bottom of the ocean. He lay on a darling, floofy baby bed in the center of the ball while the hoops that composed the gyroscope—the gizmo that kept him floating and stable—spun hypnotically all around him.

And thanks be to pants, Iggy filled his empanada onesie to stretching. He'd been getting healthier and healthier ever since Gabi and I had connected him to an Iggy from another universe (with a little help from the Reál and Vidón families in that universe). Ever since, the two Iggys, who had two different conditions, had enabled each other not just to survive, but to thrive.

But neither Gabi nor I understood how. No one did—not anyone we knew, at least. We had used meditation techniques to visualize the two Iggys being forever united, and—*poof!*—the power of positive thinking had worked. The two Iggys were connected across universes. And because of that, almost instantly, both were cured.

For now, at least. Would the connection last? What if it didn't? Would both babies get sick again? We just didn't know. So every time I saw that he was not only okay but flourishing—chacho was as plump as an uncooked turducken—waves of electric relief washed over my shoulders.

"Hey, Iggster!" I whispered. I wanted to talk to him, but at the same time I didn't want to wake him. Babies bring out all sorts of contradictory feelings in the people who love them, don't they? Example: I've seen Gabi, Ms. Reál, every one of Gabi's dads, and American Stepmom bite, pretend to eat, or otherwise insert one of Iggy's feet in their mouths. Not kidding. Grown-ups are always munching on baby tootsies. What in the name of athlete's foot sandwiches is that about? Blech.

"I doubt he will wake up," said Dad: The Final Frontier. "He is an excellent sleeper."

"Can he even hear me in the ball?"

"If we let him," Gabi answered. Reading her mind, Dad: The Final Frontier handed Gabi her phone. "This button"—Gabi showcased for me, pointing to the one on the right—"seals off the outside world. It makes the ball practically soundproof and lets in only filtered air. But it's not on right now. Iggy Smalls can hear you just fine."

A few weeks ago, Gabi had wanted Biggie Iggy to be her hermanito's rapper name, but apparently now she was trying on Iggy Smalls for size. Meh. I preferred Notorious I.G.G.

Gabi turned to Iggy and launched into some dog-whistle-high baby talk. "Can't you hear me, Iggy Smalls? Can't you hear me just fine?"

If he could hear her, he didn't care a single slider. His mouth sucked an invisible binky as he kept right on snoozing.

"As you can see," Gabi deadpanned, "the Iggster is a heavy sleeper. I could flush him down a toilet and he wouldn't wake up."

"That," I said, "is the second time you've mentioned flushing Iggy down a toilet since I've known you." I put up a hand to shield my mouth as I whispered to Dad: The Final Frontier, "Better keep an extra eye on Gabi. The sibling rivalry is strong in this one."

"Hey!" said Papi, popping out of the front door with his arms wide. He wore a guayabera that looked like cake frosting and pants that looked like pants. "Good morning, Bonita! Good morning, Gabi!"

"Good morning, Gabi! Good morning, Bonita!" said American Stepmom, sneaking under Papi's armpit and hugging him. She had on a pastel-colored skirt suit, light green and salmon and zombie-skin blue, that made the top of my mouth feel funny. Her work-clothes philosophy was *If they're gonna make me wear a suit, I'm gonna make them pay.*

"Good morning!" sang both of the Reáls who could speak.

As my padres approached us, I glanced at little Iggy again. All my hair fell out, my arms disconnected themselves from their sockets, and then I collapsed into a heap of body parts. I mean on the inside.

Now, sleeping right on top of him, was the fattest cat I've ever seen.

I mean, since the last time I'd seen him. Meow-Dad and I had met before.

5

A FEW WEEKS ago, Gabi had come over to my house at creepy o'clock. She'd had Baby Iggy in a baby carrier, and a giant orange-and-white tabby in a cat carrier. She didn't own a cat at the time, so I asked her where she'd gotten it.

The answer, like the answer to every stupid question I asked these days, was *The multiverse did it.*

Remember the Reál family from the other universe that I mentioned? The family that had helped us solve Iggy's health issues? *They* owned a cat. And ever since Gabi and I had connected them, the Iggys from both universes had been engaged in a transdimensional tug-o'-war to hug him and squeeze him and call him George. Apparently, the Iggy from my universe had won the latest battle, because now all of planet-size Meow-Dad lay fast asleep on top of him.

I had to hide that fat cat, stat.

I didn't think. I lunged for the phone, my index finger extended, aiming for the app's left button, the one that would frost the globe over. If I was fast enough, no one would see that a weird space cat had magically appeared, and I wouldn't have to explain how I had created a connection between babies from two different universes.

(In case you need reminding, the padres are trying to get me to break the universe a little less often.)

(Also, *I'd* prefer to break the universe less often, all things being equal.)

If I had actually touched the left button, I'd be telling you a different story, one of how awesome my aim is, how great I am under pressure. But I missed.

The security sphere Dad: The Final Frontier was wearing did not frost over, like it would have if I had hit the leftmost button. Nor did it make itself soundproof and start pumping filtered air into itself, like it would have if I had touched the rightmost button. I, you see, had touched the middle button, which did something totally different.

The middle button turned the security sphere into a disco ball.

A flashing, blindingly bright disco ball. It even came with its own disco music. Loud as a house party, the security sphere started blaring out a song called "Funkytown."

I mean, I think it was called "Funkytown." I'd never heard it before, but half the lyrics were either the word "funky" or "town." Seemed like a pretty good guess.

But what mattered at that moment wasn't the name of a song they used to dance to in Meso-freaking-potamia. What mattered is that Gabi and I and American Stepmom and Papi were so startled that, faster than a tennis serve, all of us jumped our meatbags backward.

Papi and American Stepmom did a clumsy, involuntary two-person cartwheel and fell inside the Coral Castle. Gabi Catwomaned backward, dropped Dad: The Final Frontier's phone on the road, and landed crouched, claws out, ready for combat. Her hair poofed itself to maximum poofiness, to make her seem bigger to predators.

And of course, Salvador Vidón buttplanted in the most undignified way possible.

Why am I always buttplanting? I hate how easily startled I am. Seriously, I end up on my can four to fifteen times a week, depending on how pranky American Stepmom is feeling. Maybe it wouldn't be so bad if I had a heinie to speak of. But, chacho, I got buttcheeks like beef jerky. The skeleton hanging at the doctor's office has more meat on its seat than I do.

Looking up from my buttplanted perspective, I saw that Dad: The Final Frontier seemed rather amused by all our jumping and Catwomaning and pratfalling. Of course, that could just be her resting sweet face. It didn't always project how she felt inside, I reminded myself.

But you know what? She could've chosen to change it to any other kind of face—like, say, an *Are you humans okay?* face, or maybe a *Let me help you up!* face. Some of us had just added a new crack to our butts.

Instead, she smiled at me with all the warmth and concern of a mannequin and said, surprisingly loudly, "Congratulations, Sal! You have discovered my favorite feature of the security sphere! Disco Fever Mode!"

Nothing seemed to hurt too much. I got up carefully. "Can you shut off that racket?!"

She nodded excitedly. "Yes! I can!" And she stared and smiled-not-smiled at me.

Sometimes you must be direct with class-nine AIs, I reasoned. So I said, very clearly, and very loudly, "Please, shut it off!"

"I can't, Sal!"

Oh, that smile of hers was looking not so neutral anymore. Now it was looking absolutely trollish.

"But you just said you could!"

She looked at the sun, which you can do without risk of harming your eyes if you have artificial eyes like hers. "I can turn off the music *in theory*!"

Have you ever, while getting whupped by someone in a board game, had the urge to flip the whole table, send the pieces scattering, and destroy everything before you lose? Yeah, that was me right then. "What do you mean, 'in theory'?!"

"In theory, because an off button exists, and it can be activated to stop the music. But in practice, that isn't possible at the moment. The off switch is on my phone, and Gabi has my phone. So, in practice, I can't."

But before I said anything I might regret, the music stopped.

The sudden silence was as startling as pressing the middle button had been. For a second, I was weirdly sorry the music was gone. Now I would never know if the singer ever made it to Funkytown.

I looked over to Gabi, who, yes, had picked up Dad: The Final Frontier's phone and turned off the music. "It's early in the morning, Sal," she chastised. "Some of your neighbors are probably still trying to sleep. Why in the world would you activate Disco Fever Mode?"

"Um, hello," I answered, pointing accusingly at the security sphere (which still looked like a disco ball, even without disco music, effectively camouflaging Iggy). "I didn't know what that button did, Gabi."

"Then why did you press it?" said Dad: The Final Frontier. Now her expression changed to one of parental concern. "Pressing unfamiliar buttons can be very dangerous."

"I wasn't aiming for the middle button," I answered her, as calmly as a goat chews. "I was aiming for the left button. To make the ball frosty again."

"O-kay," said Gabi, looking sideways. "But why?"

"Yeah, Sal," said Papi, walking up to us, his arm around American Stepmom's waist. I noticed a few lipstick prints on his cheek. Also, now his guayabera was misbuttoned. "You're around highly advanced scientific equipment all the time. You know better than to push unknown buttons."

American Stepmom's lipstick was smeared. Half her hair had escaped out of her scrunchie, and curls flopped and flailed in every direction, like a terrified octopus. "It really doesn't sound like you, Sal."

I couldn't let anyone deactivate the Disco Fever Mode, or they'd see Meow-Dad and the jig would be up (whatever the heck a "jig" is). So I turned to the padres accusingly. "What took you so long to come out of the house?"

"We fell," said Papi.

"And we had to get up," said American Stepmom.

"And check to see if we were okay," Papi added.

American Stepmom walked two fingers up Papi's arm. "I liked that part."

"Ew, you two," I said, lemon-faced. "I swear, you're worse than alley cats. Don't make me get the hose."

They couldn't have looked more guilty. "What?" they both said.

Gabi laughed, and, following her lead, so did Dad: The Final Frontier. That broke the spell just enough to get the padres to take a half step away from each other.

"So," said Papi, ready, willing, and able to change the subject. "Do we ever get to say good morning to Iggy?"

"Oh, yes," said American Stepmom, walking over to the sparkly security sphere. "I haven't gotten to bite his widdle footsies in more than a week!"

"Ew! Ew, ew, ew!" said Gabi, who, like me, found the whole adults-eating-baby-feet thing bizarre and gross.

That was my chance. "See?" I interjected. "Now you've traumatized Gabi. I think we kids better get out of here before you scar us." I walked over to Gabi, and overpronouncing my words, using lots of teeth and spit to say them so she would understand how very important this was, I said, "Let's go to school, Gabi. Right now."

"Um . . ." said Gabi. "Okay, I guess."

I clapped once. "Splendid." And now for the pièce de résistance that would totally save the day. I turned to Dad: The Final Frontier and asked, "Can you give us a ride, Dr. Reál? I'd love to show up at Culeco getting a piggyback from the most advanced AI in North America. I'll be the coolest kid in school!"

"Something's fishy here," said American Stepmom.

Uh-oh.

"What's going on, Sal? What are you up to?"

I had to hurry. "Please?!" I begged Dad: The Final Frontier.

Bonita saw no need to change expressions. "In theory, Sal, I could take you to school."

I deflated. "But in practice?"

"In practice, I do not have an extra car seat or a security sphere to carry you in. Therefore, I cannot."

I was scrambling. "Okay, but maybe we can take turns riding—"

"Plus," Gabi interrupted, "we came early so our daddies can get started right away on their work."

I might have looked a little wild when I turned to Gabi, and, through my teeth, said, "Not. Helping!"

Papi moved toward me, thoroughly Sherlocking me up and down. "Not helping with what, Sal?"

Even Papi was noticing I was hiding something. Was I losing my touch? All I could do was try to salvage the situation.

"Not helping with nothing! Nothing at all! We just need to go to school. Can't a kid want to go to school? Ha-ha?"

"No one," said American Stepmom, "is going anywhere until I get to see my widdle Iggy!"

"But—"

"That's easy," Gabi jumped in. Always so eager to make people happy, that Gabi. "All I have to do is press this button."

"Gabi! Don't—"

She did.

I shut my eyes and gritted my teeth, waiting for the inevitable gasps of shock. It was then I remembered: Oh yeah, I had to go to the bathroom. Like, any more denial and I'd re-create de Nile. Funny how the feeling can come and go like that.

But then the padres gasped together, and I forgot about bathrooms and remembered to be terrified.

"¿Qué en el nombre de la alfombra?" said Papi.

"What is that on Iggy?" said American Stepmom. "Is that . . . Is that—"

"I think it is," said Papi.

American Stepmom was not too shocked to finish her question. "Is that an empanada onesie Iggy is wearing? Oh. My. God. Now I really *am* going to eat him!"

Huh?

I risked cracking one eye open.

No cat.

The only living thing in the security sphere was Iggy. He was awake now, and still empanizado. He looked indignant. It was the exact expression of a baby whose brother from another universe's mother had just stolen something very precious from him—say, his cat—and he had already begun to plot his revenge. And I have to admit, an angry baby making a revenge face is especially cute when said baby is wearing an empanada onesie.

Since there was no Meow-Dad sitting on top of him, everything worked out better than I could have hoped. Nothing in the world is better at changing a subject than a baby. Everything else the adults may have cared about in this life—family, friends, scientific breakthroughs—went out of their heads while they focused all their attention on Iggy.

Dad: The Final Frontier spoke a command directly to the security sphere (in no language I'd ever heard before), and the top of the sphere folded open, half the globe disappearing into the other half. Seeing her chance, American Stepmom swooped up Iggy and pretended to eat an empanada the size of a human baby.

Once she'd had her fill—it took a while—she passed him to Papi so he could have his turn. He cradled him in his massive arms. In less than five seconds, he had rocked the little Iggster back to sleep.

"He likes you," said Dad: The Final Frontier. And then, to clarify, she added, "Iggy expresses his love by drooling unconsciously all over you."

"So did Sal," said Papi, lost in a memory. "Ah, mijo, you used to sleep just like this in my arms. Where does the time go?"

"Into calamitrons," Dad: The Final Frontier answered, "which is the problem. They break space and time."

Papi blinked, as if waking. "Oh, Bonita, that was yesterday. But today, Bonita, today, we have new data! I have some very promising results to show you! Come, come," he finished, using Iggy's whole body to gesture for her to follow. And Dad: The Final Frontier, as eager as Papi to start doing BIG SCIENCE, walked quickly to his side. Together they charged toward the front door as quickly as they could without disturbing the baby.

"Did you have breakfast yet, Gabi?" American Stepmom asked her.

"Just one," she replied.

"Well, you have to have at least one more breakfast to feed that big, beautiful brain of yours."

"Normally, I would love to, Mrs. Vidón. But Sal said he wanted to get to school early."

But now that the crisis was over, I was free to take care of other essential matters. "Look," I said, "if I don't pee soon, Moses is gonna try to part me. Have all the breakfast you want while I go to the bathroom."

"Then it's settled," said American Stepmom. She moved behind Gabi, put her hands on her shoulders, and started steering her toward our house. "Do you like Nutella?"

Gabi put on the brakes so she could turn around and look American Stepmom in the eye when she answered. "Mrs. Vidón, I am more Nutella than woman. At home, I have a bucket of Nutella so big, you could go over Niagara Falls in it and survive. I eat my weight in Nutella every—"

Gabi was interrupted. The whole neighborhood was interrupted. Birds stopped chirping. Clouds in the sky stopped moving. Trees straightened up like they'd just gotten in trouble with Teacher.

That's how terrible Iggy's scream was.

6

A SECOND LATER, everybody had surrounded Papi and Iggy.

Papi had put a second arm under the baby. His biceps bulged, and he hunched over so his guayabera formed a shady canopy over Iggy. There wasn't a force in the world strong enough to make him drop that baby.

Who, now, by the way, seemed fine. The only evidence of his tears were the shiny trails on his cheeks. Iggy worked his eyebrows and mouth as if he wanted to make sure they still functioned. One of his hands was enjoying Papi's arm hair.

"What happened?" asked American Stepmom.

When she said this, I saw Gabi's thumbs start flying over her phone. Taking notes for the doctors, I bet.

"I do not know," said Dad: The Final Frontier. She looked distracted. "Just as we were entering the house, Iggy cried out. But I am replaying my recording of the previous ten seconds, and I can find no stimulus that would justify such a wail from him."

American Stepmom touched Dad: The Final Frontier's cheek. "Are you crying, Bonita?"

"It is . . . unreasonable of me," she said, sniffling. Then she changed her expression to a smile that was making fun of herself. "But Iggy's distress, no matter how small, saddens my whole being. All the other Reáls have tried to tell me that I need not worry so much about him. 'Sometimes babies cry!' they tell me."

"Not like that," said Papi. He glanced at me for a second, and I saw the face of a padre who'd had to deal with a chronically ill son for the past five years. My poor Papi. He had learned the hard way the difference between a child's temper tantrum and an uncontrollable shriek of pain.

The faraway look on Dad: The Final Frontier's face let us humans know that she was riffling through her database. We knew she had completed her search when she turned back to Papi and said, "Hmm. You are correct, Dr. Vidón. Iggy has never emitted a cry that powerful or agonized before."

"Poor kiddo," said Gabi, still furiously thumbing notes into the phone. She didn't look up when she said, "Maybe we should take him to the hospital."

Every head rotated to face me.

Okay, okay, I get it, everyone—I'm the resident expert on mysterious diseases of the body. Not that I knew anything about autoimmune deficiency, which is what Iggy had (or used to have before Gabi and I fixed him). But that's the way norms think: diabetes, autoimmune deficiency, what's the difference.

To be fair, though, I do know what it means to get taken to the hospital just because you exhaled funny. It's depressing, always feeling like you're one odd noise away from getting dragged to the ER yet again. Best to break this well-intentioned but sentimental robot of that bad habit early.

"If he screams again," I said, "take him to the hospital. Otherwise, it was probably just a one-off thing." And feeling like this was my chance to say something Enlightening and Profound That Would Live Through the Ages, I added, "Nothing hurts unless it hurts twice."

Everyone looked at the sky, pondering my wise words.

Everyone but Gabi, who had the keenest cacaseca detector in Miami. "All I need is one right hook to prove you wrong," she said, punching a fist in her palm.

"You already did. It only took one look at your face to know what pain is."

"Be nice, you two," American Stepmom cautioned, straightening her assistant-principal suit jacket.

"Sal's suggestion seems like a measured and responsible course of action," said Dad: The Final Frontier. "We will wait and see for now."

"You hear that, little guy?" Papi falsettoed to Iggy, moving toward the front door. "We're gonna take good care of you. But we're not gonna overreact. No, we're not. No, we're not. We're just gonna watch you closely, and if you yell like that again, we'll—"

The world skidded to a halt when Iggy yelled like that again.

Papi had put one foot through the Coral Castle's front door. He yanked it back as quickly as if he'd accidentally stepped into a basket of snakes.

The second he withdrew it, Iggy instantly went quiet. He

blinked out two tears. But only two. He looked at each of us in turn, gawking with the openmouthed wonder-filled face of babies on baby food jars. Coupled with the fact that he was literally an empanada, Iggy became, for a few moments, the number one cutest thing in the entire universe.

"He seems fine again," said Gabi, standing on tiptoe and peering into her brother's face. "Bizarre."

"Yes," said Dad: The Final Frontier, running a hand along the wood of the doorway. "It is odd."

"Odd enough," said American Stepmom, "for us not to take any more chances. He needs to go to the hospital."

Papi nodded at Dad: The Final Frontier. Taking the cue, she gently lifted Iggy out of Papi's arms and set him back inside the security sphere. It enclosed him a second later, like a whale winking. Before Gabi handed Dad: The Final Frontier the phone, she pressed the button that turned on the air filtration system and the button that frosted the globe's glass.

"I'll contact all of Iggy's parents on the way," said Dad: The Final Frontier.

Gabi pounded the golden helmet back onto her head. "And I'll let Iggy's doctors know we're coming." She held her arms out to Dad: The Final Frontier. "Boost, please?"

But Dad: The Final Frontier knelt and spoke to her at eye level. "Daughter, I think you should go to school for now."

Gabi was about to whine but didn't. It took a hard gulp— like she was swallowing a bat whole—but she held back whatever childishness she had wanted to blurt. Instead, her face grew lipless and thoughtful. Then, after a mature sigh, she said something that sounded like a quote: "'The most good, for the most people, for as long as you have the spoons,' right, Daddy?"

Dad: The Final Frontier nodded. "You will only sit and worry at the hospital. But at Culeco, you can be of great service. It is your tech week for Rompenoche, and many people are counting on your leadership."

"I *am* playing Alice," Gabi reluctantly, adultishly agreed.

Dad: The Final Frontier put two hands on Gabi's shoulders. "I, of course, promise to inform you if Iggy's status changes, and/or you are needed, daughter."

Gabi gave Bonita the phone. "Share these notes with his doctors. They're excellent and thorough. And don't delay any longer, Daddy. Get Iggy to the hospital as fast as you can."

Dad: The Final Frontier stood up straight. She smiled superheroically. "As fast as traffic laws allow. Goodbye for now, Vidóns. Dr. Vidón, I will contact you as soon as I am able. Perhaps we can continue our work virtually?"

"The work will keep," said Papi. "Take care of Iggy."

"Now!" urged American Stepmom, waving her away with all ten fingers. "Go! Shoo!"

One more self-assured nod and Dad: The Final Frontier ran. She went from zero to thirty in zero-point-zero seconds, cutting across the Coral Castle's little lawn, her heels tossing tortoise-size hunks of turf into the air. It wasn't seven seconds before she was too small to see anymore.

"Phew," said American Stepmom. That one meant *Let's make the best of it.* She turned to Gabi and asked her, "Well, how about I spread some Nutella over the biggest chocolate-chip muffin I have for you?"

Gabi had moved over to the doorway. She was running her

hand over the wood frame, just like her daddy had. "Does any-body else feel it?" she asked.

"Feel what?" asked Papi.

"Like the pins and needles you get when your leg falls asleep? But, like . . . it's hard to explain." She pawed her way up and down the doorjamb. "Like pins and needles and unhappiness?"

Papi and American Stepmom, both bewildered, pulled their heads back and blinked. But I knew exactly what Gabi meant. When she turned to me, I gave her the tiniest nod in the history of the world.

Gabi, eyes big, whistled silently. "Thanks anyway, Mrs. Vidón," she said, "but I think Sal and I better be going to school. I have a feeling it's going to be a very busy week."

No lie detected. It felt like a month had gone by since I'd woken up this morning.

7

GIVEN EVERYTHING THAT had just happened, I should have been depressed, right? Not a good start to the day, right? So why was it that as Gabi and I walked to school, with the sun blasting down on us like a McDonald's heat lamp, I was feeling happier and happier?

"So," Gabi asked me, "did you feel the pins and needles, too, the closer we got to your front door?"

Oh. Oh, oh, oh. "Yeah, I did. But it was even worse for me."

She went to yellow alert. "Worse?"

"I mean, yeah. Way worse than pins and needles. More like screws and nails."

Gabi could tease, but she wasn't shy about showing that she cared about you, too. "Why didn't you say so? Are you okay? Do you need to go to the hospital?" She took out her phone and opened an app. "I can call a car and get us there by—"

I laughed. "I'm okay now, Gabi. The farther away I get from my house, the better I feel. But when Papi first activated the remembranation machine this morning, I felt"—I only hesitated for a deep breath so I could deliver the line without getting tripped up by my emotions—"I felt as empty as a grave without a ghost. Just a soulless corpse."

Gabi stopped in the middle of the crosswalk, every part of her face that could gape gaping. "Whoa."

To keep her alive—this is Miami; you do not go full sandwich in the middle of a crosswalk—I hooked her arm in mine and hustled her the rest of the way across the street. A fanfare of honking cars gave us a royal send-off. "You trying to get yourself killed, Gabi?"

"It's your fault," she said, pulling her T-shirt straight. She wasn't mad, though. She was smiling. "Don't spout poetry at me and then expect me not to appreciate it, Sal Vidón. I have the sensitive soul of an artist, you know."

So maybe I was a little flattered. I do take pride in my similes. "C'mon, now. Stop exaggerating. That wasn't poetry."

She accused me with a finger. No, not that finger: her index finger. "That is a load of cacaseca! It was literally a haiku." She stopped and closed her eyes and clutched her heart to perform it:

> "'I felt as empty
> as a grave without a ghost.
> Just a soulless corpse.'"

I counted on my fingers in a panic. It *was* a haiku. Holy habaneros! How many times had I accidentally spouted ancient Japanese poetry without even knowing it?

"I didn't mean to!" I blurted.

Gabi started walking again as she answered, "Don't be modest, Sal. Many of the great kung fu masters were also great poets, weren't they?"

She was making fun of my pj's again. I was wearing them to school today because I'd wanted to leave my house ASAP. I'd only run inside to grab my diabetes stuff and my backpack. But it's not like anyone at Culeco would care about my outfit. There, I'd blend right in, just another cosplayer lost in a sea of middle schoolers made up like anime characters, living memes, and monsters. And even though I felt half-naked without the scores of magician novelties that I usually carried in my vest and cargo-pants pockets, I also felt freer, more agile, more Legolas-y. Maybe I'd be light enough to run away from whatever problems life threw at me.

Plus, I still had all the tricks I kept in my backpack.☺

And anyway, if I do say so myself, I look good in kung fu pj's. "Hey"—I shrugged—"if Aru Shah can have adventures in her pajamas, why can't I?"

Gabi, who reads even more than I do, snorted so hard that she filled her lungs with Miami traffic fumes and had a mini coughing fit. "Don't flatter yourself, bubba. You're no demigod."

"Oh, and I suppose you are?"

"I am the demigod of Shut Your Tacohole So I Can Think. Let me figure this out for a minute. You don't want to feel like an empty grave the rest of your life, do you?"

I didn't, of course. But what I said was "I'm the demigod of Putting My Foot So Far Up Your Butt You're Gonna Lick My Toes."

Oh, she heard me. She let me know by raising her nose that she was ignoring me. "The remembranation machine, Sal. What does it do?"

Dad: The Final Frontier was a calamity physicist just like Papi, so Gabi knew as much about the machine as I did. Which, I admit, was basically nothing. "It . . . remembranates?"

Gabi could've killed a bunny with the look she gave me. "We are thinking things through carefully and logically, you jar of farts. Now, tell me out loud, nice and slow, exactly what the remembranation machine is supposed to do."

Omegalol. "Jar of farts." It was hard to be careful and logical when I was laughing at Gabi's insult. But I tried. "The remembranation machine [snort] is supposed to fix the membrane that separates one universe from another [ha-ha]. When the membrane gets a hole in it [titter], pieces of the membrane go flying off. Also," I repeated, "jar of farts [giggle]."

Gabi, all business, tried to get me back on track. "Those pieces that break off from the membrane are called *calamitrons*."

"Right. Calamitrons have to be stitched back into the hole in the membrane they came out of. That's called *remembranation*, and that's what the machine does: It puts calamitrons back where they belong. It fixes the rips in our universe's membrane."

Gabi nodded. Maybe the sun was playing tricks on me, but I swear, one of the joker barrettes in her hair winked at me. "When your papi turned on the remembranator, Sal, that's when you felt like a soulless grave?"

Hearing her quote me made me wonder if she was making

fun again. But she didn't look like she was playing. She looked like a lot was riding on my answer. So I answered straight. "Yeah. I think that's why I'm feeling so much better now. The farther I get from the machine, the better my mood gets."

"And the remembranator was still running when your papi tried to go into your house with Iggy?"

Why was I thinking slowly today? It was so obvious! But since we were being careful and logical, I said it out loud: "No wonder Iggy screamed. The remembranation machine hurt him, because his existence is tied to an Iggy from another universe."

Gabi tapped her temple. "The remembranator is fixing holes in the universe. But my brother *is* a hole in the universe!"

"And being a hole is probably the only thing that's keeping him alive."

Man, oh man. What would've happened if Papi had insisted on bringing Iggy inside the Coral Castle? Iggy would've been cut off from the only thing keeping him alive—his connection to the other Iggy. He might have been killed!

"We have got," I said, "to keep Iggy away from the remembranation machine."

Gabi and I walked a grim half block imagining the consequences if we didn't.

"The problem is," Gabi said finally, "we *can't* keep Iggy away from it. Not forever. Our dads want to use it to fix the whole universe. Soon there won't be anywhere left for Iggy to hide."

Uh-oh. When your mami dies when you're just a little kid, you learn quick what despair sounds like. Gabi was starting to lose hope.

And losing hope is the one-way bus to Failuretown. Hope is the thing you lose right before you lose everything else.

"Hey, Gabi," I said to her. "It won't come to that."

Her eyes started loading tears into her tear ducts like a submarine loads torpedoes into its tubes. "How do you know, Sal? How can you be sure?"

She wasn't being rhetorical. She wanted answers.

So I gave her one. And I wasn't just saying it because it was the answer she needed to hear. It was the bone-marrow truth. "Because, Gabi, I will relax that remembranation machine into the sandwich-eating sun before I let it hurt Iggy."

I mean, that's not exactly how it works. I can't relax anything into this universe's sun, no matter how many sandwiches it eats. But if I sent the remembranator into a different universe, it could potentially fall into a white dwarf, or maybe a red giant, or perhaps a nice, fat neutron star. That would still count, right?

Either way, the statement cheered up Gabi. I could hear the uncried tears mixed in with her laugher, but the tears never came out. "I believe you, Sal. I mean, you already saved Iggy once."

Not quite true. "*We* saved him, Gabi—you and me together. Well, and with a lot of help, too." I opened my arms televangelically wide. "That, my friend, is the power of positive relaxation!"

She went inward before she spoke out loud again. "Relaxing. It's . . . it's not easy for me."

"'No es fácil,'" I said, quoting every Cuban ever. "Nobody who loves Iggy would find any of this easy. But you know what, Gabi? You can relax so well, you can see into the multiverse.

You're the only other person I've ever met who can do what I do. That's got to count for something, right?"

She uncrumpled a smile. "It counts, Sal. It counts a lot." She stopped walking and stuck out her hand. It was the sincerest handshake anyone had ever offered me: like a Girl Scout trying really, really hard to earn her Handshaking merit badge. "Thank you, Salvador Alberto Dorado Vidón, for caring about my baby brother so much. And also for teaching me to do . . . what you can do."

I studied her hand. She was holding it out so hard, it was quivering. "Wait, are we thank-you friends?" I asked.

Her eyebrows seismographed. "Is it bad for friends to say thank you?"

"It's not bad. But it's like level-one friendship. I thought we had reached at least level four by now."

Gabi smiled, but warily. She didn't drop her hand, but she sensed trouble. "What's level-four friendship?"

"That's where, instead of saying thank you, we call each other a jar of farts."

Gabi covered her mouth and danced that dance you dance when you're dying of laughter but you're trying to talk at the same time. "It would be really hard, trying to catch a fart in a jar."

"Gotta be fast!"

"No one's that fast!"

"Get up, turn around, slam on the lid, sniff the air, and: aw, too slow. Ain't no fart in that jar—it's all up your nose."

Gabi gave in to her giggling entirely. I'd been kind of snickering, but now I started cracking up, too.

And, oh, big mistake. Maybe the biggest mistake I'd made all day.

Because, see, laughing reminded me that I'd forgotten to pee. I'd neglected to all morning. I kept meaning to. But what with Papi fixing the universe and Iggy going to the hospital and all, I just never went.

But now. Now, chacho. If I didn't find a bathroom very, very soon, I was going to go to the bathroom while not in a bathroom. Like, right now.

THE NEED TO pee, and the fear of wetting yourself in public: I was experiencing two of life's great motivators at the same time. Was really regretting drinking a water tower's worth of agua that morning. But what could I do? I was thirsty.

Welp. I didn't have many options. It was too early in the morning for the stores on the way to school to be open, so I couldn't beg bathroom privileges from a friendly business owner. I guess I *could* have tried to find a bush or a quiet corner somewhere, but Gabi's presence made that option less than ideal. The last thing I wanted was to commit a potty-related misdemeanor in front of the editor of our school newspaper. I could see the headline on next week's issue of the *Rotten Egg* already:

MAGICIAN'S POOR DECISION LEADS TO UNWANTED EMISSION

No, the best option was to knock my knees, grit my teeth, and force-march my way to school, ASAP.

To be fair to Gabi, she didn't threaten to write a scandalous article about my misfortune. She didn't make fun of me or, like a lot of middle school kids I know, make waterfall, raging-river, or bubbling-brook sounds as we walked. Instead, she found a way to genuinely distract me from the fact that I was one untied shoelace away from becoming a human water balloon. If I tripped, I'd pop.

She let me play with her flying drone.

"It's called a Fey Spy," she explained. "It's actually two drones: the big one that looks like a bird, and a tiny one that looks like a housefly's eyeball."

"I was wondering why your bird had a hole in its forehead," I croaked. Wasn't easy, forming sentences with a bladder the size of a whale's brain.

"That's where the eyeball drone stores itself when it's inactive. When I say, 'Fey Spy: Mobilize!'"—instantly, the glittery robot hummingbird shot out of her hair and hovered a few feet above us—"both drones activate. The eyeball drone—you see it here, Sal?"

She was pointing to a speck floating maybe eighteen inches away from her face. "Yeah." I grimaced.

"The eyeball drone is the eyes and ears of the Fey Spy. It watches for my hand gestures and/or listens for my verbal commands. Then it transmits those to the hummingbird drone, which then carries out my orders. This way, I can control the big drone from far away, with either hand gestures or my voice."

"That"—I winced—"is kinda amazing."

She took her tablet out of her backpack. "It gets better.

All I have to do is fill out this online form for you"—she talked a little slower while she chicken-pecked at her virtual keyboard—"and take a couple of pictures." She paparazzi-ed all around me, using her tablet to take up-close candids of my teeth-gritting mug. "Now, repeat after me, Sal." I saw her press a red record button on her tablet. "That quick beige fox jumped in the air over each thin dog. 'Look out!' I shout. 'For he's foiled you again, creating chaos at the zoo!'"

I was not in the mood for games. "That quick beige fox jumped in the air and did a bunch of cacaseca and bit Gabi Reál on her left wenis."

Gabi, unamused, made a swooping gesture with her hand, and the Fey Spy, following orders, smacked me upside the head. It didn't hurt—I've been hit with wads of paper that stung more. But it's the principle of the matter, right? I tried to Godzilla-swipe the hummingbird out of the air.

But Gabi flew it out of my range while she asked, "Do you want to fly my drone or not?"

I mean, I did before, but now even more. I owed her one (1) drone whacking upside her hairball. "I would like to, yes, please, thank you," I replied.

"Then you have to say the sentence right. It contains all forty-four of the phonemes in the English language. That's how the Fey Spy will learn to recognize your voice and obey your commands."

Oh. "Why didn't you say so? Show me the sentence," I said, while imagining deserts, empty pools, and the planet Mercury, the driest hunk of rock in the solar system.

She showed it to me, and I read it aloud: "That quick beige fox jumped in the air over each thin dog. 'Look out!' I shout. 'For he's foiled you again, creating chaos at the zoo!'"

She pressed a few buttons on her tablet. "Good. Now this one." She flipped the tablet around so I could read it.

"The hungry purple dinosaur pleasurably ate the kind, zingy fox, the jabbering crab, and the mad whale, and started vending and quacking."

She did more stuff on her tablet. "Good. Just one more. Read this."

I tried to hurry through it. "Sal Vidón is a nose picker whose hobbies include making Civil War dioramas using his largest dried boogers— Wait a second! I don't think that sentence has all forty-four phonemes in it!"

Gabi, chuckling, pressed the stop button. "It doesn't. That one was for my new podcast, *Something's Rotten*, where I reveal all the deep, dark secrets of the Culeco student body."

"I swear on the president's butt, Gabi, if you—"

"Gotcha!" she said, as smug as a *V for Vendetta* mask. "As if I'd tell you if that's what I was doing. Now, stop being such an easy mark, and look at this." She put her tablet in front of me again.

On it, I saw a live bird's-eye view of Gabi and me walking to school. She was walking backward, while holding up the tablet to me. I was walking like a penguin who'd just taken a line drive to his black-and-white crotch.

I tried to walk a little less like a penguin and more like a human, and said, "Are we done setting up? Will it obey my orders now?"

Gabi nodded. "Tell it to do something."

I wasn't sure what to say. "Is there a list of commands?"

"You have to memorize all the different hand gestures, but it's pretty smart when it comes to voice input. It will probably figure out what you mean. Just try it."

Because I'm the bigger person, I did not say, *Fey Spy, slap Gabi like her mama don't love her.* Instead, I stared at the tiny fly's-eyeball drone, which was staring back at me creepily, and said, "Fey Spy, fly to Culeco Academy of the Arts."

Immediately, the hummingbird drone rocketed ahead of us. On the tablet, I got to see a fast-forward preview of the journey Gabi and I were making to school, except from forty feet up. From this bird's-eye view, Miami looked like different epochs of human history mashed into one city. You had Jurassic tropical trees mixed in with architecture from a hundred years ago, and fifty years ago, and twenty years ago, and twenty *minutes* ago. They spilled all over each other like a bucket of Legos dumped on the floor, colorful and angular and a golly-dolly mess. Lots of buildings had murals on their sides, in every style: Some looked like they should be hanging in a museum, and some looked like they were made by kids high on Red Bull and spray-paint fumes. Lots of large chicken statues, painted by artists in all the crazy ways artists can paint chickens, stood on the sidewalks as proud, weird symbols of the city. The cars grumbled and rumbled on the streets, like they were getting mad but hadn't completely lost their tempers yet. They would, though. Rush hour would be starting any second now.

The drone, high in the air, bypassed all the traffic. It didn't need to follow roads and sidewalks; it flew on a diagonal path straight toward the middle school, fast and sure. Before long, I saw Culeco's roof: specifically, the huge American flag being held up by a human-size egg with arms and legs and a super-hero cape.

The hummingbird zoomed over the school and brought its careening flight to a stop when it hovered above our rotten-egg school mascot. It had turned itself so that its camera eyes pointed toward the courtyard at the front of the school, where students, teachers, and staff all gathered every morning, way before it was time for school to start, just to hang out and have fun together. It was one of the reasons I loved my new school: Everyone seemed to want to be there.

"The Fey Spy is so cool, Gabi," I said. It's amazing how being so engrossed in watching it go had made me want to go so much less. "Where did you get it? Is it another of Dad: The Final Frontier's inventions?"

Gabi, still walking backward, still holding up the tablet for me, peeked around it. "Nooo," she said slowly. "It was a present from a friend."

A *friend*. Not her mom or one of her dads. That was weird. "Must be a pretty good friend, to give you a bleeding-edge flying drone. Do I know them?"

"Not yet. I'll have to introduce you sometime." She pointed to the tablet screen. "Notice anything odd, Sal?"

I got the sense she was trying to change the topic. But I mean, if she didn't want to tell me who gave her a super-expensive techno gadget, that was her choice. I played along; I squinted and leaned closer to the screen.

Now, Culeco students (and a lot of the faculty) love to dress in costume to go to school. We have more than our fair share of students who want to work in costuming and makeup for their careers, and pretty much everybody at Culeco is at least partially an actor. So every school day is like Halloween, except the disguises and masks aren't cheap, off-the-rack, flavor-of-the-week getups. They're custom-made, over-the-top, brimming with lights and sounds and special effects, and making obscure pop-culture references taken from every nation that has a significant cartoon and/or comics and/or movie industry.

So at first, no, I didn't notice anything odd. People were wearing all sorts of costumes, just like any other day. Except—wait a second. There were fewer colors than normal. The courtyard looked black and white and red all over, since those were, by far, the predominant colors on the outfits. Also, there seemed to be an unusually high number of living chess pieces walking around. And human-size playing cards with arms and legs. And royalty with oversize heads and itty-bitty crowns. And Cheshire Cats.

Well, there was only one Cheshire Cat, with a smile as big as an ivory boomerang, but it was one more than I usually saw at school. That was the last hint I needed. I couldn't help but smile, because Lewis Carroll is one of my favorite authors, and his books were the theme for this parent-teacher conference.

"It's Wonderland," I answered Gabi. "Culeco's turned itself into Wonderland."

9

A WEEK AGO, Principal Torres had sent an email to the padres and me about the first parent-teacher conference of the year. *I'm sure you've noticed that we do things a little differently at Culeco Academy,* read her note. *At our school, parent-teacher conference night isn't just an opportunity to make sure Sal is getting the best education possible. We're all performers here, and any chance we get, we like to put on a show. That's why we call this event "Rompenoche." We are going to give you a theater experience so great that you'll swear we "broke the night"!*

That's what "Rompenoche" means: "Break the night." And let me tell you, I liked the sound of that! I don't know if I've mentioned it before, but I am a showman.

Sal won't be performing this time, the very next line in the email said, shattering all my dreams. *The returning students have been working on Rompenoche for much of August, so it would be unfair to ask him to try to catch up in such a short time. But he, along with the other transfer students and all the sixth graders, will have front-row seats. It's our way of welcoming our new members to the Culeco family.*

I mean, I guess that made sense. It was a nice gesture and all. But I'd still rather perform. I'm a magician, people! I improvise all the time.

As Gabi and I walked into the courtyard—she straight-backed and calm, I curled like a shrimp and suffering—I understood a lot better why they wanted the newbies to sit this one out. This was what people in theater call tech week. They also call it hell week, because it's when everything gets finalized for an upcoming performance: the sets, the costumes, the last-minute script and/or blocking changes that always happen and always feel like the end of the world. I've done a few performances in my day, and during every tech week I've had to tell myself everything was going to be fine. I've also called myself a liar, every time.

So I thought I knew what to expect when it came to Rompenoche's tech week.

I was wrong. *Nothing* could have prepared me for the Santa's-workshop level of activity going on in the courtyard. Every square inch of grass was covered with swathes of fabrics, red and white and black, and trimmed in silver and gold. Teachers and staff stood in key positions, supervising all the kids—and I mean, like, so many kids. Like two-thirds of the kids in school. They sat on the ground in clusters of two to eleven, cutting shapes out of the fabric: hearts and diamonds, spades and clubs, and every kind of chess piece.

Some students were making tabards that looked like playing cards. In case you're not a theater kid, a tabard is a top that's kind of like an apron. It has a broad front, a broad back, and broad shoulders—but it's open on the sides, like a sandwich board made of cloth. Knights used to wear them over their armor to show off their coats of arms and colors.

Tabards are great for theater, because they're easy for actors to put on and take off, and it's easy to hide a different costume beneath them. They make changing outfits, or even characters, a breeze. And these were some of the fanciest ones I'd ever seen. Like Renaissance-faire fancy.

As Gabi and I galloped toward Culeco's entrance, I noticed a group of kids sitting at sewing machines. They must have brought them down from the Textile Arts room so they could work outside. Seemed nuts to me: Why would you purposely leave the air-conditioned comfort of your classroom just so you could sew outside, where it was as humid as the mouth of a giant? Would someone please explain Miami natives to me?

Feeling cute, might wet myself, idk: Now wasn't the time to try to figure out Floridian psychology. All I knew was that those sewing machines made it sound like we were trying to re-create the Industrial Revolution right here at Culeco. "I need to pick up the pace," I said to Gabi. I thought she'd maybe take that as a hint that I should probably complete the rest of this journey on my own.

But nope. "Aye, aye." She saluted. She moved right beside me and kept pace, and I power-walked toward the school entrance.

As we sped down the central walkway, I recognized a lot of students from my Textile Arts class. They were from the top-level pace group, the thread-and-needle superstars who made the best cosplay gear in Culeco. And right in the middle of them stood their leader, the director of Rompenoche herself: Aventura Rios.

Since I'd started at Culeco, I'd seen her wear some of the most awesome cosplay outfits known to geekdom. She always nailed the details and made sure she could move easily and naturally in her costumes. No way I'd pick a fight with her when she was cosplaying Karin from *Street Fighter V*—I was too legit scared she would critical-art me.

Right now, Aventura was busy pinning the hems on what had to be her masterpiece, the absolute greatest seamstress challenge she had ever posed to herself: a glorious red-and-white gown that was being fitted for none other than the Queen of Hearts from *Alice's Adventures in Wonderland*. That dress was a poufy, frilly thundercloud of crimson and lace. It had so many skirts that the bottom half looked like a blooming carnation. And then, when I looked up at the top half . . . I stopped noticing the gown for a second, because I realized after a few blinks that the person wearing the dress was Juan Carlos.

He had a temporary tattoo of a playing-card heart surrounding one eye. When he caught me staring, he gave me his patented telenovela-star smile, with his best superstar tilt of the head.

Juan Carlos didn't know me very well, so maybe he thought he had to look me straight in the eye and dare me to say anything about him wearing a dress.

I saluted him with my free hand, in a way that, I hope, communicated: *You want to wear a dress, chacho? No problemo. I'll zip you up in back.*

Then, to be sure Aventura also knew I wasn't some kind of small-minded cacavore, I sent a second salute her way.

That's when I noticed her mouth hanging open, like a Muppet. She gave me an overacted wink, repeatedly pointed at Gabi with one hand, and made the A-OK signal with the other.

Oh, brother. Here we go. Can't a girl accompany a boy to the bathroom without middle schoolers thinking that they're dating?

Yeah, that would be no, based on all the kids I saw looking shocked, whispering excitedly to each other, and making kissy faces at Gabi and me.

Whatever. I'd handle the rumors later. Right now, it was go time: as in, I'd never had to go so bad in my life.

We got to Culeco's entrance. Luckily, the huge double doors had been left open. Here Gabi patted my back, like a manager standing in the wings with their latest singing protégé, five seconds before showtime.

"Remember, Sal," she reminded me, "pee neatly!"

"Pee *quickly* is more like it," I said, saluting her as I jogged through the doors.

I really, really, really should have been watching where I was going. Maybe if I had been, the worst thing that could have happened wouldn't have happened. But it did happen. I tripped.

Both feet left the floor. My body started going horizontal, like it was trying for the mother of all belly flops.

This was it. I was going to blow like a humpback whale sneezing. Time slowed down so it could enjoy my suffering. I fell.

Right into Mr. Milagros's arms.

"¿Bueno?" Culeco's lead custodian asked, setting me vertical again, like he would a shaky vase.

Saved! I was so happy, I could have cried, except I wasn't letting any liquid out of my body until I got into a bathroom. Instead, I smiled a big thank-you smile at Mr. Milagros, gave him a little unhinged titter that made him blink, then peeked eagerly around him at the bathroom door, where salvation lay waiting for me.

On the door of the bathroom hung an OUT OF ORDER sign.

I could barely whisper, but I managed to get out three words with three separate breaths. "No. Es. Bueno."

10

"SEÑOR MILAGROS," I said, even while my lower half was on the brink of going nova, "would you kindly point me to the nearest working bathroom? I'm afraid it's a bit of an emergency."

"Pero, Sal," he said, his voice as joyous as a ringmaster's, "the nearest working bathroom is right here!" He walked over to the door of the bathroom and plucked off the OUT OF ORDER sign. "We just finished renovating it!"

I was so happy, I saw stars. Making sure I had "battened down all my hatches" before I started moving, I staggered toward him and the bathroom and asked, "Who's we?"

He gestured with a wide sweep of his arm, the way a generous actor asks the audience to give themselves a round of applause. I turned around to see who the audience was in this case.

Man, when urine a hurry, your vision can become so narrow that you can miss a ton of details. I had missed the tiny detail that there were eleven other custodians in the hallway.

Each had on a unique janitorial uniform of different colors and patterns. Patches on their pockets and/or arms announced that they worked at schools across Miami. They all looked as proud as Mr. Milagros.

"Sal," said Mr. Milagros, "meet my custodial compañeros. This is Rosa, Diego, Dominic, Maria, Rudolpho, Isabel, Yaníl, Davíd, Lionél, Dolores, and Ysadora. I couldn't have finished renovating the bathroom over the weekend without them."

They walked up to me one by one, and I shook each of their hands—gently, so as not to jostle myself too much. Like all custodians I've ever met, they were the nicest people in the world. They had the biggest smiles, the nicest manners, and they all heaped compliments on Mr. Milagros. "Best janitor I've ever known," "No one is more devoted to their work," "So many different talents," "A custodian's custodian," and lots of other flattering comments that I only partly heard because my ears were filled with the roar of my own personal ocean.

They were all looking at me, expecting me to say something so they could respond with more nice things about Mr. Milagros. I asked, "So, um, why did the bathroom need such a quick renovation? Did something happen to it over the weekend?"

Apparently, that wasn't the right thing to say. Mr. Milagros bowed his head in shame. "A few weeks ago, Principal Torres had to ask me to 'attend' to this bathroom."

"It happens to the best of us," Custodian Dolores said consolingly.

"No one can keep all the bathrooms of a school clean at all times," comforted Custodian Yaníl.

"No excuses," Mr. Milagros said grimly. "I had failed in my sworn duties to keep the bathrooms of Culeco pristine. And though Principal Torres never mentioned it again—she has too

much dignity—every time we spoke, I could see the disappoint-
ment in her eyes. I couldn't live with myself. I knew I needed
to up my game."

Oof. A few weeks ago, in order to distract Mr. Milagros, I had
done my best Principal Torres impersonation over the phone,
and I'd heavily implied that this bathroom needed attention.
That's all I said. I didn't tell him to build a whole new restroom
or anything. But obviously he took his job very seriously.

"So you got your janitor friends to help you redo the bathroom," I said, doing my best to sound exactly like Sal Vidón
and not at all like Sal Vidón doing a Principal Torres impersonation. "That's great. I bet it's beautiful."

"Oh, it's more than beautiful," said Custodian Isabel,
wide-eyed.

"It's a technological wonder," said Custodian Lionél
worshipfully.

"Do you want me to show you how to use it?" Mr.
Milagros asked.

Um, dude. "Yeah, no thanks. Learned how to go to the
bathroom by myself like twelve years ago." And I opened the
door to the restroom.

"Just tell it what you want!" he called after me. "It will obey
your commands."

That made me pause in the threshold. In calmer times, I
might have asked him, *What could possibly obey my commands
in a bathroom?* But opening the door had reactivated my latch-
key incontinence. So that was that: no more questions, no
more talk. Only wee now.

As fast as I could, I locked the door behind me and launched myself at the toilet like I was jumping away from a Michael Bay explosion.

"Phew, baby," I said out loud. I'd never said anything more sincere in my salami-on-rye life. The relief was so pure it was practically religion.

I was sitting instead of standing because I knew I was going to be here a minute. Plenty of time to look around, see what this new bathroom was all about.

Even though this particular bathroom was meant for just one person at a time, it had a stall, which I prefer. I've always hated the privacy-free line of urinals in men's rooms, where you're just supposed to cowboy up to your porcelain pee catcher and, like, talk about sportsball with the other bow-legged chachos. No thanks, bruh. We'll talk outside, m'kay?

But this bathroom had a stall with a door that locked behind you. Cozy. Very relaxing.

Now that my brain wasn't being pickled by my own juices, I noticed it was a unique stall. To my left was a deluxe wall. I mean, lujo. Its bottom half was dark cherrywood wainscoting, like the kind you find in the homes of Revolutionary War heroes (which Connecticut is full of). The top half of the wall was painted with the bright-yet-dark colors of one second before sunset: purple-going-black, orange-going-umber, and red-going-so-deep-it-fell-off-the-color-wheel. Against that background, a baby-blue-and-lemon-yellow watercolor painting of Malala Yousafzai hung on the wall, with the quote "LET US MAKE OUR FUTURE NOW, AND LET US MAKE OUR DREAMS TOMORROW'S REALITY" built into the frame.

I silently wondered how long it would be before I saw that quote on a Gabi Reál T-shirt.

I turned and ran my fingers over the cool white marble of the stall's right wall. It, and the door, looked like two massive sheets of fudge-ripple ice cream. The door latch, as well as all the bolts and braces and hinges holding the stall together, gleamed gold, as if Hephaestus himself had forged them.

I whistled. "This bathroom is beautiful," I said out loud.

"Thank you," said the toilet.

I do not respond well to being surprised. And having my statement answered by a toilet while I was sitting on said toilet was, yeah, just a smidge startling. I mean, I could feel its voice go right up my dark side.

I don't even know what cheek muscles I used to launch myself off the seat. All I knew was that, faster than a flea can sneeze, I was flying off the john. While still airborne, I twisted in the air and pulled up my pajama bottoms absolutely as fast as I could. I landed in a kung-fu-movie cat stance, claws out, à la Gabi. My voice was hoarse and high when I yelled, "Who's there?"

From the depths of the toilet bowl came a bubbly, cheerful voice. "I am the toilet of hallway 1W, bathroom one. My name is Vorágine." It rolled the *r* with gusto.

I dropped my stance. "Vorágine" means "whirlpool" in Spanish—quite a name for a john. "You are the toilet?"

"Yes."

"And you can talk?"

Vorágine flushed itself, which I think was its way of laughing politely. "Oh, I wouldn't be much of a class-eight AI if all I could do was talk."

I mouthed the word *What?!* twice before I asked Vorágine out loud, "What?! Class-eight AIs are ridiculously expensive. Way more than a magnet school for the arts can pay. How the heck did Mr. Milagros afford you?"

"Oh," Vorágine replied, as solemn as a mob informant, "when you control the toilets, Sal, you decide which secrets get flushed, and which secrets stay floating in the bowl, if you know what I mean."

"I have no idea what you mean."

"Let's put it this way: Mr. Milagros has unclogged the plumbing of some of the most powerful corporate offices in this town. So a lot of CEOs owe him some pretty big favors. Even the manufacturers of some of the world's most advanced AIs."

If I didn't know better, I would have thought that this toilet was pulling my leg. And I did know better; the entropy sweeper had taught me how hilarious and tricksy and slippery an AI can be with language. So I crossed my arms, leaned back against the stall door, and said, "You're making Mr. Milagros sound like Miami's number one kingpin."

It bubbled its bowl water in a way that, I swear, sounded like laughter. "Number one *and* number two."

"Did . . . did you just make a poop joke?"

It bubbled even harder. "If you like poop jokes, urine the right place!"

"Hey! I made the same joke in my head just a little while ago!"

"Great minds," Vorágine deadpanned.

I walked a little closer to it, hunched over, and grabbed

my knees. "So, your pun game is on point. But, like, you're smart enough to control spaceflight. I'm pretty sure a middle school bathroom doesn't need an advanced AI to tell kids when to flush."

Vorágine flushed itself solemnly. "Providing a hygienic repository for human bodily evacuations is my easiest job. I intend to do so much more. My dream is to create a place where anyone who enters will find peace, protection, privacy, and help with whatever they need. Having homework troubles? My massive database makes me an excellent tutor for students from kindergarten to college. Need a break? I can read to you, play music, challenge you to a game of chess, and offer you millions of other entertainment options. Plus, everybody needs a friend sometimes—someone to talk to, to share a laugh with, and, most of all, to just listen. I'll be here whenever you need a shoulder to cry on."

For some reason, I found the idea of a toilet with shoulders pretty disturbing. But I didn't say that to Vorágine—it might hurt its feelings. Instead, I said, "You seem really nice."

"Thank you! I have been programmed to be a darling, a mensch, and an absolute cutie pie."

"But I think some folks might have trouble trusting a toilet AI," I said. "I mean, you'll be privy to people's secrets."

"'Privy to people's secrets'!" exploded Vorágine. It flushed itself silly, it was "laughing" so hard. "I see what you did there! Ha-ha-ha-ha-ha!"

It's always nice when people (or toilets) enjoy your humor. I took a modest bow.

After Vorágine had calmed itself down, it added, "But

seriously, Florida and federal laws require me to keep the strictest confidence about what happens in this restroom. You can ask me to remove any information I have collected about you at any time; you can ask me not to collect information about you in the first place; and even if you have asked me to collect information about you, I can't share that information without your express permission."

Hmm. "What information do you have on me right now?"

It swirled water around in its bowl as it thought. After ten seconds, it said, "You are a diabetic."

I felt the uneasy surprise of someone who's on the receiving end of a magic trick. I played off my feelings with a shrug. "Guilty as charged."

"No, no, no!" Vorágine said, urgent and sincere. "Please don't feel guilty! Diabetes isn't your fault! And with today's technology, diabetics are increasingly leading normal—"

"It's okay. I've been diagnosed for five years. I'm used to it."

Vorágine gurgled shyly. "Do you want me to delete that information about you?"

My first impulse is always to reply to that question by saying yes. But after I thought about it for a second, I answered the question with a question. "Are you able to analyze my urine for ketones?"

"Am I ever!" A waterspout of joy fountained up from Vorágine's bowl. "Now, while the American Diabetes Association states that there's no substitute for blood-glucose readings for maximum accuracy, we most definitely can use urine analysis to augment your self-monitoring regiment. I can show you how your ketone levels change throughout the day, over the course of a week, a month—whatever you want! Oh, this is going to be so good for you! And such fun for both of us!"

Have to admit, the jolly little john's good attitude was contagious. "And can you send the results to my padres as well?"

I figured that, if a toilet was talking to the padres every day about my ketone levels, maybe they'd get off my back about wearing a monitor.

The waterspout vanished; Vorágine grew still and solemn. "I can only do that if you give me your express permission."

"I hereby expressly give my express permission for you to express my urine expressions to my padres," I said, smiling. "Do we need to, like, shake on it or something?"

"I don't have hands, silly," said Vorágine, "But you can wiggle my handle if you'd like."

I did. Vorágine gurgled as if wiggling its handle tickled.

"Great!" it said. "I'll just need the names and contact information of your parents—forgive me, I mean 'padres.' Oh, and your name, of course."

"The name's Salvador Vidón—diabetic, magician, and friend to toilets everywhere."

I washed up and dried off and walked out of the restroom feeling like I had just reloaded from my last save point and had a new lease on life.

I stopped just outside the door, however. Twelve janitors stood in the hallway, polishing stuff that didn't need polishing, sweeping perfectly clean floors, and in general pretending to be working. Clearly, they'd all been hanging around to see how well the bathroom had worked out for me. They were dying to know what I thought of the renovation.

Well, no need to keep them in suspense. "That was," I said to no one in particular, "the number one best lavatory I have ever used in my life."

Twelve janitors cheered and hoisted me on their shoulders, as if I'd just won the Going-to-the-Bathroom World Championship.

THE FIRST WARNING bell before the start of school went off just as the janitors threw me in the air for the sixth time.

They caught me and set me down gently. I did not pout, but, chacho, I low-key wanted to. Getting jolly-good-fellowed like that was super fun! I didn't want it to stop.

Ah well. What a burden it was, being wise beyond my years all the time. But I gotta be me, you know?

With my feet on the floor again, Mr. Milagros encouraged me not to be late for homeroom. "Being on time for your classes?" he said, giving his fingers a chef kiss. "¡Muy, muy bueno!"

"¡Buenísimo!" I agreed. The desire to pout vanished entirely, replaced instead with the feeling that maybe, just maybe, everything would be okay. Amazing what an empty bladder and a full heart can do for your mood. So, without any more fussing, I waved my goodbyes to the best janitors in Miami and headed for my locker.

There in hallway 1W, the fastest way to my locker was to take the NW staircase up two flights, boogie down hallway 3N, and take a left onto hallway 3E, where, maybe fifteen steps away, my locker waited for me.

I dialed the combination to my lock without even looking at it; that's how second nature it had become by now. I was looking instead at Yasmany's locker, just a few down from mine, on the top row. Two thoughts hit me at the same time:

1. This morning had been such a mess at home, I'd forgotten to bring the entropy sweeper to school. That meant I couldn't check on the hole in the universe I had made in the back of Yasmany's locker. Gabi and I, working together, had been shrinking the opening over the past several weeks, with me snarfing up a few free-floating calamitrons each day. But it would be a lot harder to do it without the entropy sweeper. I'd have to snort them up with my nose instead of the machine, and I was trying not to exceed my maximum daily allowance of subatomic particles. I guess we'd have to try again tomorrow.

2. Where was Yasmany? I hadn't heard from him all weekend. This was the longest period of silence between us since we'd become friends. It hadn't been intentional on my part—I'd spent almost the entire weekend reading for English and had barely come out for meals. But he hadn't texted me, either. Chacho was constantly on his phone. I had a bad feeling about this.

I made a mental note to text him before school was over. Right now, though, I wanted to unload the books I didn't need until second period and get to homeroom. And all I needed for homeroom and English were two small novels: *Alice's Adventures in Wonderland* and *Through the Looking-Glass*.

I had both combined into one hardcover, which was easier to carry than the two flimsy paperbacks the school provided. I'd told my homeroom/English teacher, Mr. Cosquillas, about how I'd read the Carroll novels a bunch of times and had seen a lot of different movie versions of them, too. American Stepmom, knowing what a Carroll geek I am, got me this special edition with the wild illustrations for my last birthday.

When I'd mentioned all that to Mr. Cosquillas, he'd told me what a Carroll geek he was, too, and said he'd love to see the "omnibus." So I'd totally toted it to school today to show him.

Thinking about the book always made me want to crack it open. By the time I had made it to hallway 3N, I was paging through it again. Hello, my name is Sal Vidón, and I stan Wonderland.

"Will you lookie here? Sal Vidón reading a book. Will wonders never cease?"

I had just taken the corner onto hallway 3E. There, leaning against the lockers, was Gabi.

Kinda.

I mean, she looked like a caricature of her, like Gabi wearing a Gabi Halloween costume. If Gabi had just gotten back from Wonderland, she'd be dressed like this. Instead of fifty-four playing-card barrettes, she just had one massive chip clip biting her hairball into a fauxhawk. And her T-shirt! Dang, son, it was definitely going to be controversial. The quote on it read: "I SHOULD HAVE WAITED TO HAVE KIDS"—YOUR MOM. Pretty pantsing offensive for parent-teacher night.

Had Principal Torres approved that shirt? I wondered.

"Nice outfit, Gabi," I finally answered. "You're dressed like your mama was an edgelord and your daddy was a bag of Doritos. Is this part of Rompenoche or something?"

In response, Gabi did something completely unexpected. She smiled. But not a sarcastic *I'll get you back for that one* smile, and not even an *Ah, good one, Sal—that was a sick burn!* smile. She smiled at me in the sentimental, might-cry-not-gonna-cry way that an abuela smiles when she beholds the contents of her grandkid's diaper: proud, pleased, and brimming with affection.

"Same sense of humor," said Gabi. "So strange, how it's always the same no matter where I go. It's so good to see you again, Sal."

Um . . . Wut?

A shiver ran up my back, like a giant lighting a giant match up the length of my spine. The hallway, I noticed suddenly, smelled super strange: like the inside of a dormant volcano, dusty and rocky and a little burnt. It reminded me of an exhibit I once went to at an air and space museum. They had a big sign that said WHAT DOES OUTER SPACE SMELL LIKE? and a place to stick your nose. When I sniffed, I smelled the same burnt odor I was smelling now.

"You're from another universe," I said to Gabi.

"Duh," she said, pretty rudely. "I told you I was going to meet you."

All the pieces Tetris'ed together. "You're the Gabi who spoke to me earlier."

She curtsied. "Now you're getting it. And you look great. A lot of Sals out there are pretty sickly, you know. Like Chihuahuas with head colds."

Um, thank you? This Gabi wasn't nearly as polished as mine, it was becoming clear. "So, what brings you to my neck of the multiverse?"

She lowered her nose and looked up at me. "I need your help."

"With what?"

"With fixing the universe."

I popped my lips. "Well, good timing. My papi's trying to fix the universe, too. He made some progress today."

Her face went corpse color. "No, he didn't. He made the exact opposite of progress. He made"—she struggled for a word—"congress!"

I mean, lol, thanks for the political dad joke. But she wasn't trying to be funny. "You're saying Papi didn't make progress today?"

She took a few steps toward me but stopped short, the way characters in a play do to demonstrate that they're being really sincere. Maybe every Gabi in every universe was a theater kid? "I'm saying way more than that, Sal. I'm saying that if your papi is allowed to continue his experiments, he's going to destroy your universe."

I raised my eyebrows so high that my forehead turned into corduroy. "Come again?"

"How," she said, handling me in the same delicate way my psychologist had after Mami died, "did you feel when your papi turned on the machine today? Like a little piece of you had died, maybe?"

My eyes dropped like jaws. I said yes with my chin.

Gabi nodded knowingly. "You felt that way because a little piece of you *did* die. The piece that's connected to the multiverse. Your papi is killing it."

I had so many questions. I started with "How do you know about Papi's experiment?"

"I have made it my mission to detect whenever another universe is in danger of having its membrane destroyed by unchecked science. And when I find a universe in danger, I try to save it. I don't want any other universe to suffer the same fate mine did."

"Wait a pants-splitting minute. Are you saying the Papi from your universe destroyed your universe?"

"Well, not the whole universe, not yet. But he made a hole so big, it ate half of Florida and half the Caribbean. And it's growing. It's only a matter of time before my . . . entire . . . universe . . . is lost. . . ." She covered her mouth with a hand, looked away from me, and fought down a geyser of emotion that shook her whole body.

I took a step toward her, one hand on my heart, the other reaching out to her. Because we're all theater kids here. "Tell me what happened, friend. I am listening."

When she locked eyes with me again, she had to flex her whole face to keep from crying. "This universe is a lot like mine. And my Sal was a lot like you. He and I used to cruise the multiverse together. Until his papi found out."

My stomach ate itself. "What did that papi do?"

She glanced sideways, as if she wouldn't be able to hold it together anymore if she had to look me in the eye. "He wanted to shut us down. He tried to make it so that the membrane between universes wasn't rippable anymore. And that, it turns out, is the greatest mistake anybody in the history of my whole universe has ever made."

I wasn't sure if I wanted to hear the answer to my next question. "Where is your Sal now?"

We need a word that means smiling and weeping at the same time. So I'm making it up right now. Gabi started smeeping. "You're so much like him. Looking at you, I can almost believe he isn't gone."

"Gone? What happened to him?"

Suddenly her watch—a smartwatch like mine, but Trekkier—started sounding an alarm. "Look, I have to go. I'm being chased by the forces of evil. I can't stay in any one universe for too long these days."

"You can't go," I said, stepping even closer. "Not if my universe is in danger."

She gripped both my biceps and shook me reassuringly. "It's not like your universe is going to explode tomorrow, Sal. Unlike mine, there's still time to save yours. I'll be back soon. And when I return, we'll save it together." She smeeped again. "Just like old times."

"Okay," I said, feeling confused and paranoid. "What should I do in the meantime?"

Gabi let go of me, ceasing her smeeping, and strolled backward. A shimmery, cling-wrappy weakness in the fabric of the cosmos appeared behind her. "Go to class. Do your homework. And please, Sal, enjoy yourself while you can. We never appreciate what we've got until it's gone. I learned that the hard way."

Half of her had already disappeared into a different universe when she called out, "And don't tell anyone about this
meeting. Not your papi, your mami, anyone. Secrecy is the key
to fixing the universe."

"Not even my Gabi?" I asked.

She had pretty much disappeared into the rip, but her
whole head shot out of it, along with her index finger, pointing
at me like I was a very bad dog. "Especially not Gabi. This is
just between us until I come back."

Then the hole in the universe swallowed her completely,
and no sign of Gabi remained.

The final warning bell rang. I needed to book it to make it
to homeroom on time.

12

THIS CLOSE TO the start of classes, the halls were always jammed full of middle schoolers who, like the NPCs in role-playing games, only existed to get in your way as you tried to navigate your character around town. So I bolted around the corner and back into hallway 3N, ready to dodge and dart around the clusters of kids and slide into homeroom just in time.

Except, the hallway was empty.

Now, if I hadn't been so caught up in thoughts about the possible destruction of my universe followed by the possible salvation of my universe, I might have realized that, since hallway 3E (aka the hallway where my locker was) had been empty, then hallway 3N would probably be empty, too. FixGabi and I had been alone for our entire conversation. Where did I think mountains of kids would have come from suddenly without me knowing? I mean, duh.

"Where is everybody?" I asked out loud.

"Rompenoche practice," said Widelene Henrissaint, who had just jogged up from the NE staircase behind me.

I had a feeling Widelene was someone I could work with, though we hadn't had a chance to collaborate yet. I only knew a little bit about her: She came from Haiti; spoke English, French, and Spanish; dressed like a jock; and had a different hairstyle every day. Today, her cornrows had turned into long braids that somehow stuck straight out from the back of her head, like she was always running a thousand miles an hour. She had a lot of training as a martial artist. Her bo-staff routine on the third day of school had blown away my entire Intermediate Theater Workshop class.

"The seventh and eighth graders are all piling into the auditorium," she finished. "Only the sixth graders and the transfer kids like us have homeroom this morning."

"Lucky us," I answered. We started ambling together toward homeroom. The need to rush had vanished now that I'd seen how unimpeded our journey would be. "It's not fair that we don't get to be a part of the show, just because we transferred in. They could've given us a bit part or something. Wouldn't you rather be performing this morning?"

"Naw. I'm lazy. I'm gonna sit in the front row and be like, 'Entertain me, peasants!' And if the show stinks, it's off with their heads!"

Lol. "Yeah," I said, feeling a little better. Mr. Cosquillas had left the door to the classroom open, so I finished my thought as Widelene and I walked through the doorway: "I like the way you think, Widelene. If Rompenoche sucks, we'll just execute everyone."

"My dudes!" said Mr. Cosquillas. "That's pretty harsh."

Our homeroom/English teacher dressed like he was the

only child of the god of tie-dye and the goddess of sandals with socks. His khakis looked like they used to belong to Robinson Crusoe, and he had hair like he'd been lost in the Everglades for two weeks without a comb. Most of the time, his transition lenses didn't work right, and they made his glasses dark even though he was inside. So sunglasses, tie-dye, shipwreck pants, socks with sandals, hair like *Jumanji*, and sitting cross-legged on top of his desk . . . you know exactly how hippy-dippy and earthy-crunchy his voice sounded when he said it.

"Guess they'd better not suck, then," said Widelene, taking her seat and grinning Cheshire Cattily.

Mr. Cosquillas looked at Widelene over his glasses. Uh-oh. When he showed you his eyes, you knew you were in trouble. "What I find interesting, Señorx Henrissaint, is that none of the performers will be graded on their performances. You, on the other hand, are most certainly going to be graded, by me, on the quality of your review of the show. That's your next assignment in English class. And if the review you turn in resembles the glib and unconstructive language of your previous statement . . . Well, let's put it this way: It's never too late to start making funeral preparations for your mark."

"My dude!" Widelene responded. "That's pretty harsh." A second later, her nose crinkled. "What's a 'señorx'?"

"Well," Mr. Cosquillas explained, "it's not a señor, and it's not a señora, right? It's a way for me to show respect to my addressee without forcing me to make any potentially embarrassing assumptions about said addressee's gender. Do you like it? My goal is to degender the entire Spanish language before my one-hundred-and fiftieth birthday."

"You," said Teresita, "are not going to live to be a hundred and fifty years old."

Ah, Teresita Tómas: the girl who took everything too literally. She served as the gossip columnist for the school paper, the *Rotten Egg*—the perfect job for someone who tended to spread rumors whether or not she believed them. It wasn't that she was a stupid-and-mayonnaise sandwich or something. She had her good qualities. She was in all the same honors classes I was, and like any real reporter, she didn't mind asking tough questions, even if she ruffled people's feathers. She just wasn't a ton of fun to be around. She always looked grossed out and offended. I'd describe her default expression as "resting *Who farted?* face." She had me subtly sniffing my armpits, checking for boy stink, whenever I spent more than ten seconds near her. She was always complaining that something was, like, so unfair.

I think Cosquillas secretly enjoyed trolling her. He no-no-no'ed her with his finger and said, "That's '*Señorx* Cosquillas' from now on, Señorx Tómas, if you please."

She huffed, crossed her arms, and flopped into her chair.

"Those are tough to catch," said Adam. "I had to use my Ultra Ball to collect one that was asleep on the road when I was playing *Pokémon Y.*"

"That's a Snorlax, you forehead." Widelene laughed.

Adam turned to her and asked, "Really, Widelene? Thank you for explaining that to me."

Adam Hoag, aka beret boy, aka the most wedgied middle schooler in the history of the universe, wanted to work as a film director someday. He was, imho, well on his way. The trailer he'd made for his documentary on wedgies, which was called *Splitting the Adam* (lol) (also ow) showed Adam getting underwear-lifted in increasingly torturous and creative ways. He'd managed to make everybody in my Intermediate Theater Workshop class involuntarily acquire buns of steel as we clenched our way through five minutes of sympathetic butthurt.

Adam came across as nerdy and socially awkward—pretty Clark Kent–ish. Also, the beret he always wore made him look a little too much like the kind of elf who would fix your shoes at night. That led people to dismiss him. But after just seeing him give the straightest straight face I'd ever seen to Widelene, I knew he wasn't a person to underestimate. He told jokes mostly to make himself laugh. That was a sign of someone who gives feero zucks about what other people think. And that made him someone I could work with.

The final bell blasted through the speakers; time to start class. I about-faced and fell into a desk. It wasn't even my desk—the classroom was so empty that I just collapsed, play-pouting, into the desk nearest to me.

"Sal," said Mr. Cos—oops, I mean said *Señorx* Cosquillas. "What are you doing, sitting there?"

"Oh. Sorry. I didn't think it mattered today, since the class is so empty. I'll go sit in my usual seat." I started getting up.

"No, my dude. I mean, why are you sitting down at all? Why aren't you coming over and handing me the book with all the Alice illustrations you promised to show me?"

I nodded to him like a genie granting a wish. Then I

reached into my bag and produced my big, beautiful illustrated double book.

"My dude," he said. On cue, his transition lenses became see-through, which let me see how wide his eyes had gone. "The cover is awesome."

I jogged up to his desk, got down on bended knee, bowed my head, and lifted the book as high as I could. "Even more wonders await you within the pages of this tome, señorx."

He took the book in both hands like I'd just handed him the Holy Grail. "My dudes," he said, his voice full of reverence, "gather round. Let's spend homeroom expanding our minds."

One thing Culeco didn't skimp on was teachers' desks. Srx. Cosquillas's was as big as a rowboat. Plenty of room for four kids and one adult to sit in a circle around it and page through a book together. Srx. Cosquillas made sure to rotate the book around so that everyone got a good look at the amazing, explosive, playful, wild, scary, excessive, and utterly wonderboom Wonderland watercolors on every spread. He didn't move on until everyone had said everything they wanted to about each illustration.

And everyone said a lot. All the kids took turns liking some watercolors and hating others, bickering about good drawings and bad ones. Widelene thought she had all the answers, and Teresita thought none of us had any taste, and Adam couldn't understand how we could be so wrong, but hey, it's a free country.

And me? Well, it was their first time looking at it. They could be forgiven for having shallow, unsophisticated responses to what was obviously the greatest rendition of Carroll's vision in the history of time. But I was very kind to them. I told them I forgave them for being so ignorant, and that I was proud of them for trying to understand art that was clearly beyond their grade level.

Srx. Cosquillas didn't say anything during our increasingly heated conversation. But after my last comment, he laughed and shook his head.

"What's so funny?" said all four kids at once, not exactly nicely.

"My dudes, my dudes, my dudes." He uncrossed his legs and let them dangle over the side of the desk. "Art is about so much more than whether you like it or not."

Widelene genuinely enjoyed school. I could tell by the way she leaned in, smiling and curious. "What do you mean, señorx? Don't people make art so other people can enjoy it?"

Cosquillas side-eyed her like a sphinx. "Sure, sure, yes, of course. But then what?"

We all short-circuited for a few seconds. "And then nothing?" Adam tried. "Because it's art. It doesn't do anything."

Srx. Cosquillas gaped at Adam like the chacho had just shot him. "It doesn't?!"

Adam backtracked big-time. "Well, I mean, art is inspiring. That's something it does."

"And?!" Cosquillas prompted.

Adam writhed. "And it can make people happy?"

"AND?!"

Adam, in a full-on panic, spoke faster than I thought his

permanent sinus congestion would allow him to. "And it can definitely teach you life lessons. And people pay billions of dollars for it every year. So I see now that art does quite a lot, actually. I hereby publicly declare that my former statement was incorrect and apologize for any harm my words have caused, and hope my grade will not be affected. Yours truly, Adam Hoag."

Teresita, revolted by Adam, said to him, "Cha."

I think that's a word in Mean Girl. Roughly translated, it means *You weak-willed worm, I am, like, so disgusted by your cowardice that I would, like, never in a million years date you.*

Yeah, I know, right? Pretty amazing how much meaning the language of mean girls can fit into just one word.

Switching back to English, Teresita said to Srx. Cosquillas, "You're just doing that teacher thing of trying to make us think. But everybody knows that art is just make-believe. It's not real."

The transition lenses went pitch-black as Srx. Cosquillas turned his deadly stare on Teresita. "Does art influence our culture? Politics? People's opinions?"

"Uh," said Teresita. "I mean, yeah, it can. But that doesn't mean it's, like, real."

Srx. Cosquillas knocked on his own head, trying to get the gears working again. "Let me get this straight, Señorx Tómas. You agree with me that art can redefine morality, open up people's imaginations, and literally change the course of human civilization, but none of that counts as being real?"

"Uh . . ." said Teresita. And then, embarrassed by her inability to say anything smarter, she finished with "Cha."

Welp. I was the only one left. So it was time for me to save the day. "So, okay, Señorx Cosquillas," I said, spreading my arms to show how reasonable I was being, "art is real. But you have to admit that you can interpret art any way you want to. It's not like math or science. There are no wrong answers."

Srx. Cosquillas turned his head robotically until I was locking eyes with his impenetrable transition lenses. The right half of his mouth smiled and the left half frowned. His hair shot out in every direction, like the rays of a black star. I'm pretty sure the colors on his tie-dyed shirt started to move.

And then he slowly, creakingly dipped his head, like he was starting to nod yes, starting to agree with me. But then, when he creakingly lifted his head—you know, the other half of the nod, the upswing—he kept on lifting it and lifting it, until he was looking at the ceiling, and then the back wall of the room.

And then he fell backward off the desk.

All four kids rushed to peek over the edge and see if he was okay. There he lay, sprawled on the floor like a crash-test dummy, one second after the crash test. His glasses had twisted like an airplane propeller on his nose. His lips flapped horsily as air escaped his body. The legs of his castaway khaki pants had bunched so high up his legs, we could see the red and blue stripes of his nearly knee-high tube socks.

"Are you okay?" I asked.

"No," he croaked, his head tottering from side to side. "I need . . . I need . . ." But he couldn't finish his thought.

I scampered off the desk and was kneeling beside him in a second. Widelene moved to his other side just as fast, just as ready to assist.

Since I've spent so much time in hospitals, I've taken

several first-aid courses, which you'd think would have been helpful right about now. But the only word that kept repeating itself in my head was "tourniquet." Thanks for nothing, brain.

"How can I help, Srx. Cosquillas?" I asked.

"Come closer," he whispered, "and I'll tell you."

I looked at Widelene. She shook her head, cut at her neck with both hands, and soundlessly lipped, *Nuh-uh, not me.*

Up to me once again. It's tough, always being the hero.

I brought my ear next to Srx. Cosquillas's mouth. "I'm listening. What do you need? A tourniquet, maybe?"

"I need you," he said, his voice creaking and cracking, "to . . . hear me when . . . I tell you . . . that . . . OF COURSE THERE ARE WRONG ANSWERS WHEN IT COMES TO ART!"

In case you were wondering, I already knew he was okay. I mean, he had tumbled off the desk on purpose, and he wouldn't have risked that unless he knew how to fall safely, right? Plus, he'd been careful to set the book down before he fell, which he wouldn't have been able to do if he'd actually fainted or something. I'd also caught a glimpse of how he hit the floor: El tipo had rolled like an expert stuntman. I don't know if every single teacher at Culeco was a former theater kid, but I betcha a hundred bucks Señorx Cosquillas was.

So I knew he was just having some fun with us. And that meant I could have fun back. "SPEAK UP, SONNY!" I yelled like a veteran—of the Peloponnesian War. "MY HEARING AIN'T WHAT IT USED TO BE!"

In response, he sat up faster than a whack-a-mole mole and said, "Sal, my dude, people are so judgmental when it comes to art. They get stuff wrong all the time, because they're thinking, *There can only be one best, and this isn't the best.* It makes it impossible for people to enjoy something they've never seen before. Haven't you ever tried to explain a book or movie you love to someone who just doesn't get it?"

I had a flashback of trying to explain to American Stepmom what made *Poocha Lucha Libre* the best fighting-game franchise in the history of video games, and how the whole time she had looked like she was thinking, *No matter how much of an idiot Sal is, I will always love him.*

"Oh yeah," I said to Srx. Cosquillas. "It's pretty frustrating when you love something and other people don't get it."

Srx. Cosquillas clapped. "Now we're talking. Now you're getting it. Gather around, duderificos. I have something important to tell you."

Teresita and Adam, who'd been having the best time spectating all this from the desk, crawled onto the floor and completed the circle that Srx. Cosquillas, Widelene, and I had begun to form. Srx. Cosquillas crossed his legs, lifted his right foot onto his left thigh, and rested his hands on his knees. We all imitated him, to varying degrees of success, with Widelene at the top, doing it perfectly, and me at the bottom, learning how much I needed to take yoga classes.

"My dudes," said Srx. Cosquillas, breathing deeply, "people make art because they want you to learn what life feels like to them. Sometimes it's funny, sometimes it's scary, sometimes it's sad or uplifting or gross or deep or a million other things. But whatever it is, it's always about what the artist thinks of life."

I turned to look at Adam. He was nodding, saying without

words, *Wedgies are the symbol I use to probe the deepest mysteries of human existence.*

"So," Srx. Cosquillas continued, "you don't want to misunderstand the art. You want to be sure you're not just making something up that isn't in there. Because if you're doing that, my dudes, you'll miss out on the completely unique way the artist views life."

"Cha," said Teresita Tómas. But this time it meant more like *Yeah, okay, fair point.*

Srx. Cosquillas nodded at her and spoke to us all. "You want to be a careful and responsible audience member. You want to put your own expectations and preferences aside to give yourself time to comprehend the art. If you do that, then, whatever your opinion of the art is, you'll understand humanity more deeply. Your mind will expand, and you'll become a smarter, more empathetic, and more complete human being."

"And that's the point of life," said Widelene, 1,000 percent into this whole meditation thing. Probably all the martial arts training she'd had. "To be a better person every day."

Srx. Cosquillas pointed at her with both hands. "So, in a minute, we are going to head down to see the dress rehearsal for the Rompenoche show. The kids have been working hard for most of the summer to put on a great performance. Probably there'll be things you like and things you don't. But go deeper. Be an active audience member. Participate. Pay attention. Think less about 'good' and 'bad' and more about 'what?' and 'how?' and 'why?' Be generous with your applause. And most of all, appreciate the gift that the students of Culeco are giving to you. Can we do that?"

"Yes!" all the kids answered.

Srx. Cosquillas cupped an ear. "What?"

"YES!"

"Perfect. All right, my dudes, let's head on down to the auditorium."

And we did. All four of us were excited. We felt like part of a secret club: the We-Can-Understand-Art-More-Deeply-Than-the-Rest-of-You-Sandwiches Club. We were ready to laugh and cry and gasp and howl and just let the performance wash over us like a tidal wave. We would feel everything, consider every angle, be the most ideal audience in the history of audiences. I was already half in love with the play before it had even started.

We took our seats in the front row of the auditorium and settled in, eager to be wowed, giddy with anticipation. I was so ready for greatness.

But chacho. Then we watched the show.

And it sucked.

13

SO, WHAT'D YOU think of the show? Gabi texted me.

The last thing I wanted to do was respond to a text like that. Not after what I'd seen. The horror!

But then I got thirteen more texts on my smartwatch, in less than ten seconds, that I also didn't want to respond to:

Now, don't just gush over it and tell me how great it was.

We already know how great it is.

We want to know how to make it even better.

No criticism too small!

Do your worst, Golden Elf-boy!

I mean, I understand if you HAVE to praise us first.

It was pretty unbelievably terrific, wasn't it?

Wait, I take that back! Ignore that last text.

I don't want to color your opinion or anything.

Just tell me in your own words how great it was.

And then if you have any notes for us, I will make sure they are voiced and entertained during our next cast meeting.

But you probably don't have any.

It was pretty great, huh?

How could Gabi text that fast? I wondered. She was like a one-girl firing squad.

I was standing at my locker reading these texts, right after the performance, and right before lunch. Yep, you did the math right: The performance lasted four school periods. The only thing worse than a terrible show is a terrible show that never ends.

This time, though, hallway 3E was the opposite of empty. Tons of kids, mostly seventh graders, reminded me why deodorant is such an important part of getting ready for school. They were all extra sweaty, too, because they'd just spent the last several hours wearing their burning-hot Wonderland costumes for the Rompenoche dress rehearsal.

They still had them on. Loads of living playing cards and human chess pieces and talking animals hugged and high-fived each other, giggling and giddy, clapping and hopping in place and dancing. Everyone was still riding the high of their performance.

I know that feeling. Heck, I wouldn't be attending Culeco if I didn't. The best moments in life happen just after you run off-stage after giving a great performance, and you stand still and just absorb the audience's applause. I live for people shouting *Encore! Encore!*

Thing is, people only shout *Encore! Encore!* when they don't want the performance to end. And, chacho, no one in that audience wanted it to go on a half second longer than it already had. I'd had Widelene on one side of me and Adam on the other, and every time I glanced over at them, they looked like they were being forced to watch a documentary on how fur coats are made. Teresita was sitting next to Widelene on the other side, so I couldn't see her, but I sure could hear her complaining about being forced to watch the rehearsal. It was, like, so unfair.

We'd all been dying. Melting into our seats. Wondering exactly how hard we would have to punch ourselves in the face to be excused to go to the nurse's office.

Oh, I know what you're thinking: *You're exaggerating, Sal. How bad could it have been, really?* Well, let me put it this way: Have you ever played Would You Rather? You know, where people ask you questions like: Would you rather get bitten by (a) five thousand mosquitos at the same time, or (b) a great white shark, just once? Or: Would you rather give yourself (a) an emergency appendectomy with nail clippers, or (b) eye surgery with a scalpel and a fun-house mirror?

Well, go ahead and think up your worst Would You Rather? question. No, really. Close your eyes and think up one right now.

Got it? It's super painful, right? Or super gross? Or something that would make you want to nope the heck out of there, am I right?

Whatever you thought up, the answer is yes. Yes, I Would Rather eat my own feet, I Would Rather floss with a razor blade, I Would Rather lick roadkill, I Would Rather be reincarnated as a suppository, I Would Rather *anything* than ever, ever, ever see that show again.

Look, I love the Alice books. I came in wanting to love the show. I already knew the costumes were amaze-pants. And Aventura was a friend. This show was custom-made for me to like it.

But they blew it. All the show consisted of was acting out scenes from the book, word for word. People, I've read the book! Everybody has! The pacing onstage was slow because, besides being too devoted to the original, everybody hammed up every scene and the actors were in love with the sound of their British accents. But the biggest sin of all? I'd seen it all before. There weren't any surprises (except maybe in the costuming, which, as I said, was pretty dang great). They'd just taken everything anybody's ever done with the Alice books and thrown it up on the stage. I didn't get it. They were going to "break the night" by doing some tired, been-there done-that version of a story everybody already knew? "Rompenoche" my raisins. It was more like "Rompe-mi-voluntad-de-vivir." Break-My-Will-to-Live.

In short, it was the exact opposite of the illustrations I'd brought in to show Mr. Cosquillas. And I was going to say that in my review. I didn't care if he lowered my grade—it was the truth.

But I wasn't going to report that to Gabi, or any kid at Culeco. My rep was still recovering from the first week of school, when rumors had circulated about me being a brujo. Looking around the hallway now, listening to all these kids laughing and congratulating each other and being so proud of themselves, I knew everyone would hate me if I told them what I really thought of the show. And Gabi was the editor of the *Rotten Egg.* Telling her the truth would be like shaking hands with every single kid in school and telling them that they'd managed to create a piece of theater so bad, I Would Rather snort a Taser than sit through ten seconds of it ever again.

Another round of texts shook my wrist:

You there, Sal?

Where are you now?

Wanna meet for lunch?

Hello??!?!??!?!

Yikes. I needed to hide, fast, before Gabi tracked me down in person.

But then, to my horror, I realized it was already too late. A buzzing, bumbling robot hummingbird flew around the corner. The Fey Spy.

It spotted me immediately. In a surprisingly good imitation of Gabi's body language, it stopped short and hovered in the air, gawking at me, stunned. It could not believe I was just standing in the middle of the hallway not answering Gabi's texts. Then it flew indignantly over to me, flashing me the side-eye the whole time.

The Fey Spy opened its beak as far as it could, and Gabi's voice came out of its birdy little throat. "Sal, I've been messaging you. Why didn't you reply? You had to be seeing the texts— they come right to your smartwatch." The drone hovered over my wrist, and I heard the sound of a camera clicking. "See? There they are. Why didn't you answer me?"

Those were a lot of words to get thrown at you, out of the mouth of a flying robot, all at once. "Give me a second," I said, taking a step back.

She was pretty peeved. "One one-thousand. Time's up." The drone immediately closed the distance between us. "Start talking. And don't lie to me. I'll know if you're lying."

"I don't lie," I said, deeply offended. Actually, not that offended, but I played it that way. "And if that's how you are going to speak to me, then I will bid you good day."

I ran past the drone and headed for the nearest staircase, sliding past costumed kids as fast as I could. I was halfway to the NE staircase before I started to believe I might actually get away. Could it possibly be this easy?

Of course not. The Fey Spy flew around my head and pressed its forehead to mine, its camera lenses staring deeply into my eyes, its wings flapping angrily. "Not so fast, bubba. Something's up. You've got a secret. What are you hiding? Tell me!"

Whispering through the side of my mouth, I said, "You're making a scene, Gabi!"

The Fey Spy flew close to the ceiling and looked around in all directions. It saw as clearly as I did that not a single person gave tres pepinos about my shouting match with a robot drone bird. Everyone was still too busy congratulating themselves. Actors, man. Egomaniacs, every one of them.

Meanwhile, the drone, looking especially smug, flew back to hovering one millimeter away from my left eyeball, opened its beak way too wide for comfort, and started shouting again. "No scene, Sal. No delay, no impediment, no problem. So that means you're officially out of cacaseca excuses." The bird sighed at how pathetic I was. "I thought you would have learned your lesson by now, Sal. I always get my story. Now spill it!"

Gabi and I may have started out on the wrong foot the first time we'd met, but we'd become pretty good friends over the last three weeks. Now, though? Now I was feeling the same way I had at the outset: annoyed, irked, and peeved to my knees.

So I ate her drone.

I know, I know, you have a lot of questions.

No, I didn't chew it. Want me to break my teeth?

No, I didn't swallow it. What is wrong with you? Besides the weeks of stomachaches I'd be giving myself, I really didn't want Gabi to photograph my internal organs with the Fey Spy. I shuddered to think of the evil schemes she could devise if she knew me from the inside out.

I just chomped it right out of the air, like a dog eating a butterfly. Gabi and her remote control were too slow to prevent it. Also, I have a lot of practice sticking foreign objects in my mouth. As a magician, when I am doing sleight-of-hand tricks, I hide stuff behind my smile all the time. Watches, bracelets, earrings, and, one time, another kid's retainer—which almost made Papi, who happened to be in the audience and knew exactly how that trick worked, puke. Heh-heh-heh. Point is, I've got zero issues using my mouth as a temporary storage unit. Or, in this case, a prison for a particularly annoying robot bird.

How did it fit? The Fey Spy looked bigger than it was. Its wings folded compactly for easy storage. Its body could easily be mistaken for a peanut with a beak. Well, okay, a little bigger than that—more like one of those gross Circus Peanuts that you only see during Halloween and that only useless people give you. Still, it was as easy as eating Halloween candy, putting my lips around that robo-bird.

What did Gabi do when I ate her Fey Spy? What she always does: She yelled at me the whole time I took the NE staircase down to the first floor, from inside my own face. "Sal Vidón you juvenile delinquent you spit my Fey Spy out of your mouth right now it is irreplaceable plus it's very dangerous to put it in your mouth you could" blah, blah, blah, etc., etc.

"Oh, awl scpit it aut au wight!" I said. Wasn't easy, talking around the drone—it flapped and fussed and tried to fight its way past my teeth. "A'm gonna scpit it aut wight incoo my new bes' fwiend, the toiwet."

The Fey Spy suddenly stopped struggling in my mouth. Gabi fell quiet for a few seconds. Then, both confused and curious, she said, "Did you just say you're gonna spit my drone into the toilet?"

"Yalp."

"And did you just say the toilet was your new best friend?"

"Yalp. I's a weel nice toiwet. I's name is [indecipherable]." Hey, you try saying the name Vorágine with your mouth full of drone.

"Sometimes," the bewildered voice of Gabi came out from my own mouth, "I have no idea where to even begin with you, Sal."

"Ew an' me bofth, fsister."

I reached the bottom of the stairs and popped out on the first floor. Hallway 1N was a hamster nest of sixth graders eagerly getting ready for lunchtime. But I could navigate around them way more easily than I could cut through my same-age compadres on the third floor. Evilly enjoying the vision I was having of flushing the Fey Spy down Vorágine's plumbing, I charged up the hallway and toward the bathroom, using my tongue to immobilize the drone against the roof of my mouth.

"Let's be reasonable, Sal!" Gabi pleaded. "Don't do something you'll regret later."

She sounded more out of breath than she had before. She was running, I realized—running to intercept me. Probably she'd logic-ed out where the new toilet had to be. As student council president and editor of the school newspaper, she undoubtedly knew all about the bathroom renovation, even if she hadn't experienced the AI porcelain throne for herself yet—and she was trying to stop me.

That was not going to happen.

I started running, too, channeling my inner runaway train, plowing through the hordes of hapless kids who had the bad luck of being in my way. I clawed through them, using their flimsy sapling-like bodies to help propel me forward faster, all the while fighting a secret war in my mouth to keep the Fey Spy imprisoned. By the time I reached the turn for the center hallway—Vorágine's restroom was technically on hallway 1W, but there was a shortcut I could take on 1C to reach it faster—everyone had figured out how much better their lives would be if they moved before I got near them. I Toyko-Drifted left and, once I'd righted myself, poured on the speed. I knew from this morning how fast Gabi was. I was going to have to book it to reach the bathroom before her.

Oh. Oh yeah. This morning. The terribleness of the Rompenoche dress rehearsal had made the start of my day feel like it had happened a million years ago. But now I remembered how Gabi had helped me avoid what could have been, potentially, the most embarrassing moment of my life. By distracting me with the drone, I was able to make it to the school bathroom with my dignity intact. I don't know what I would have done without her and her Fey Spy.

That same Fey Spy was trapped in my mouth at this very moment. That same Fey Spy was the one I was threatening to flush down the toilet.

Dang it! I think part of me was secretly hoping that, if I ran fast enough, I could even outrun my maturity, which was spoiling more and more of my fun every day. But too late: I was in full Think-Like-a-Grown-Up mode now. And now, thinking like a grown-up, I confessed to myself that I knew better. Whatever little flares of anger or annoyance I might temporarily feel toward a friend, I shouldn't use those as an excuse to hurt them.

My run turned into a jog, and then my jog turned into a fast walk, and then my fast walk turned into a normal walk, and then I stopped walking. I stood with my hands on my hips, snorting deep breaths in front of the door to Vorágine's bathroom, knowing full well no drones were going to end up in any of Culeco's toilets today. Dang it.

Someone was inside the bathroom. The door wasn't closed all the way, which, for a one-person restroom, is pretty weird. You go into a bathroom, you lock the door behind you—that's the rule. But because the door was open, I could hear whoever it was pretty clearly. The boy's voice, speaking with a Miami accent and too deep for sixth grade, sounded angry. Like, scary angry. Lubricated by tears and scratchy with rage, he shouted, "You can't hurt me! I'll hurt *you*! I'll hurt you so bad you ain't never gonna hurt no one ever again!"

Fear shares a lot of properties with electricity. It can activate every nerve in your body at the same time, which is shocking, immobilizing, stunning. That voice made my shoulders and knees buzz with the weakening tingle of cowardice. It was the unmistakable sound of a kid going full bully on some other poor kid in the bathroom. I didn't know who the bully was threatening, but it didn't matter. All I knew was my instinct was to get my pants away from there and save my own skin.

But I didn't. I'd been on the receiving end of bullying often enough to know how bad it felt when people who could be helping turned away and left you to your fate. Instead, I looked down at my kung fu pajamas. They helped me channel every martial arts movie I'd ever seen. And if I'd learned anything from those films, I had learned this: The kung fu master always tries to reason with the villains. They always calmly attempt to resolve the issue by using their words first.

Then, of course, the villains never listen, and the kung fu master proceeds to kick them where pistachios don't grow.

But that's just because, in a martial arts film, there has to be a fight scene. In real life, a lot of the time, people who get caught in the act of doing a bad thing might just stop doing the bad thing and run away. Sometimes, just being a witness is enough to thwart evil. I could do that. I could be a witness.

And if that didn't work, well, maybe there was a universe out there that needed a new bully to drop in suddenly.

I pushed my baggy kung fu sleeves up my arms, made my face hard, and marched into the bathroom.

Just as I entered, the bully shouted some more. "You don't want me? Fine. I don't need you. I don't need anybody."

The bully was Yasmany.

And he was bullying his own reflection.

14

YASMANY WAS DOING what I only do in the privacy of my own bedroom, after triple-checking to make sure the door is locked: He was playing out his own personal revenge fantasy. Everybody does it. Shut up—yes, you do. Personally, if anyone ever caught me acting out one of my fantasies, where I'm shouting cut-downs and throwing punches and pretending I'm the Chosen One, I think my heart would stop and never start again. I mean, the cringe, chacho. Makes me shudder just thinking about it.

And this is me we're talking about: Sal Vidón, the master of relaxation. Yasmany? Chacho was the opposite of relaxed. He was a roller coaster filled with nitroglycerin. He hadn't spotted me yet—too busy yelling at the Yasmany who stared back at him from the mirror—but when he did . . . well, I wasn't sure what would happen. I mean, this was the kid who'd wanted to beat me to a pulp just because I'd tried to help him get his locker open on the third day of school.

Things between us had changed completely since that first encounter. We'd actually started becoming friends over the last three weeks. But he'd had a rough go of it. He was living with his abuelos now because life with his mami had gotten intolerably bad. I don't know why exactly, since Yasmany wouldn't go into details, but I knew Children's Services had gotten involved. When the government steps in to take a kid away from their mami, things must be no bueno. Really, really, really no bueno.

And surprise: All his previous bullying meant he didn't have a lot of friends. I was worried he might not have learned how to focus his anger only on the people who'd earned it, and not toward the people who were on his side.

Based on what Yasmany was yelling now, things had gotten worse at home. "I'll just run away!" he screamed, his face straining every muscle it had. "I'll just live on the street like a [*BLEEP!*] dog, because I'd rather eat out of a [*BLEEP!*] garbage can than spend one more minute in this [*BLEEP!*] house with you [*BLEEP!*] people."

I'm not the one censoring Yasmany's cusswords, by the way. Every time he yelled out a profanity, a shrill *bleep* pealed through the air, completely drowning out the swear word.

"I ask you again, unidentified person, to please refrain from using inappropriate language in my presence," Vorágine said from its stall.

Yasmany swung his body left—thank all the pants in the world for that, because if he'd swung right, he would have spotted me—and stomped into the stall. "I told you to stop telling me what to do, you [*BLEEP!*] toilet!" he yelled.

"And I told you, person, that if you don't calm down, I will report you to your principal for your own safety."

"Don't you [*BLEEP!*] dare tell Principal Torres anything, you

[*BLEEP!*] piece of [*BLEEP!*] toilet, or I will kick your [*BLEEP!*] so hard, I'll [*BLEEP!*] [*BLEEP!*] [*BLEEP!*] your [*BLEEP!*] [*BLEEP!*] sandwich-eating [*BLEEP!*] into next Tuesday!"

Three uncomfortable seconds destroyed themselves silently before Yasmany added, "How do you always know when I'm gonna cuss?"

"Your vulgarity is quite predictable, unidentified person. Perhaps with a little more self-control and a proper introduction to the beautiful variety of words that exist, you could learn to be more creative. If you'd like, I can play some vocabulary games with you. It'll be fun! Let's start with—"

"Yaaahhh!" yaaahhh-ed Yasmany. "I don't need no [*BLEEP!*] toilet to be my [*BLEEP!*] tutor. Why is everyone against me?" He charged out of the stall and gripped the sink opposite it with both hands, head bowed, sucking breath. "Just one friend. Just one person who's on my side. Is that too much to ask? Just one [*BLEEP!*] person in the whole [*BLEEP!*] world who gives two stinking [*BLEEP!*] about me." Tears fell out of his eyes and disappeared down the sink, lost forever. "Why doesn't anybody love me?"

"I love you," said the Fey Spy, from inside my gaping mouth.

I quickly shut it. I'd been so enthralled by the scene unfolding in front of me, I had forgotten about everything: Gabi chasing me, the drone, the fact that I should be deathly afraid of being seen by Yasmany. I'd had a perfect opportunity to sneak out when he'd run into the stall. Instead, I had just stood there like a lummox. And the stupid, stupid robot hummingbird had given me away.

Terror struck like a lightning bolt. My thumping heart grew

as big as my whole chest. Now I couldn't move, no matter how much I wanted to.

"Gabi?" whispered Yasmany. He looked up in the mirror, and in his reflection I could see the moment when anger retreated and hope returned.

But it was only for a moment. Because if I could see Yasmany's face in the mirror, that meant he could see mine, too. And I was not Gabi.

His eyes went wide. He hippo-flared his nose. He showed his teeth—*all* of them. "Sal!" he shouted. "What the [*BLEEP!*] are you doing in here? I'm in the [*BLEEP!*] bathroom. What did you hear?"

He lunged and I stepped backward until I was against the door. I went to speak, to explain, to say I was sorry, that I didn't mean to overhear all this.

But the second I opened my mouth, the Fey Spy flew out of it.

That got Yasmany to back off a few paces. His face became confused. Each of his eyebrows looked like one of those squiggly lines above the letter *n* in the Spanish alphabet. "What is it with you and pulling birds out of weird places, Sal?" he asked, referring to the raw chicken I had placed in his locker on the third day of school.

"I gotta be me." I shrugged.

"Don't change the subject," said the drone, now getting in Yasmany's face. "I am so mad at you!"

"What did I do?" Yasmany asked defensively.

"You, bubba, said you wished there was just one person

in the world who was on your side. Well, what am I, then? Chopped [*BLEEP!*] liver?!"

Vorágine sighed. "I find it ironic that I, who am a toilet, seem to be the only entity in this entire school who isn't a potty mouth."

Yasmany laughed despite himself. He crossed his arms and shook his head. "Why do I always feel better when you yell at me, Gabi?"

"Because," answered the drone, "you know why I yell at you. It's because I love you."

"Yeah. Yeah, you do. You really do." He held out a finger, and the Fey Spy (a little spit-covered, I admit) landed on it. "I'm sorry. I'm just upset. My abuelos are trying to get me to move back in with Mami. They said they're too old. They can't handle me." The humor was draining out of him fast. Sadness was starting to take over his whole body again. "Where am I gonna live, Gabi? I got nowhere to be. Why doesn't anybody want me?"

"Stop saying that," the bird on his finger chastised. "I want you to have a great life and to be taken care of. So does Principal Torres. So do a lot of people. You just have to let us help you."

"Help me how?" His anger reignited. "You gonna adopt me, Gabi? You gonna be my new mami? Because my mami doesn't want me. None of my family does. My family hates me."

The Fey Spy put a wing over where its heart would be if it wasn't a robot. "Oh, Yasmany."

"My mami died," I blurted.

Yasmany had pretty much forgotten I was there in the

bathroom with him. He looked up at me now, shame curling his mouth downward. "I'm sorry I came at you, Sal. You just surprised me, is all."

"My mami died," I said, waving away his apology, "but then Papi married American Stepmom, and she's a great mom. I can't imagine life without her. But I miss my mom all the time. But I'm so happy I have a new mom. Both at the same time."

Yasmany, who wasn't the cheepiest chick in the nest, didn't say anything out loud. He just gave me a look that meant *And what, pray tell, is your [BLEEP!] [BLEEP!] point, good sir?*

"What I'm saying, Yasmany, is family isn't just blood. You can give the people who love you a promotion, make them your family. I mean, Gabi is your sister. You know that, right?"

He looked at the bird and smiled. "Yeah. My annoying little sister."

The Fey Spy flew onto Yasmany's head and started wood-peckering it. "Who are you calling annoying?" Gabi said while her robot bird drilled into his skull.

"You, you mosquito!" Yasmany flailed, trying to swat the Fey Spy. He finally managed to grab it. Bringing it close to his mouth, he said, "And I wouldn't have it any other way." Then he planted a disgusting kiss on the drone's hummingbird head. Like, a giraffe-eating-peanut-butter kiss.

"You are nasty!" the bird-bot complained. "Stop drooling on my highly advanced equipment, you Neanderthal! If you break my drone, I swear, I'm gonna take it out of your hide!"

Yasmany turned back to me. "Sisters." He shrugged. "Whatcha gonna do?" Then, still jokey, but jokey in a way to cover something honest, he said, "Hey, so it looks like I'm in the market for new family members. Wanna be my brother?"

Well. Okay, then. Didn't see that coming,

I thought about it. We were still just becoming friends. It felt too soon to call each other "brother." Maybe someday, you know?

But Yasmany was so vulnerable right now, and he'd reached out to me with so much hope in his wincing mouth and blinking eyes that I'd have to be a first-class monster not to want to tell him yes, I'll be your brother.

So I went over to him and, wearing my sincerest face, answered, "Nah, chacho. You're too ugly to be in my family. But we're friends. Why don't you spend the night at my house tonight?"

"Yes," he said instantly. Then, maybe thinking he'd gotten his hopes up too fast, he added, "You have to ask your mom and dad, right?"

I patted his back and opened the bathroom door. "What my padres don't know won't hurt them."

Oh, he liked that, Yasmany did! He looked me up and down with newfound respect. I held the door for him, and he bowed like a prince to me—years of ballet had taught him how to bow like a champ—and we walked out of the bathroom.

Waiting outside was Gabi. She had gentle eyes and a lip-only smile that was there to lend a little courage to Yasmany. Next to Gabi was Principal Torres.

"Oh, baby," she said to Yasmany. She pushed her huge glasses up her nose and opened her arms in the ready-to-receive-hugs position.

Yasmany ran to her soccer fast and football hard. If it were me receiving, chacho would have knocked me to the floor, but Principal Torres was big, strong, and experienced at catching kids with poor self-control. She enveloped him in the fullest hug I have ever seen. They embraced like it was a matter of survival. As she squished him, she whispered to him all the ways in which she was going to help him, and he rested his cheek on her shoulder and nodded yes, and I'm not crying you're crying actually we're both crying that's okay nothing wrong with crying but I'm gonna go ahead and end the chapter anyway m'kay?

15

GABI, ACCORDING TO Gabi, had noticed that Yasmany had been surly and sullen during the Rompenoche performance. I mean, chacho was playing a tree—no lines, no blocking, just standing there in his tree outfit and trying not to fall asleep. Yet somehow he still came across as surly and sullen. Anyway, she hadn't had a chance to ask him what was wrong. But the second she had heard his voice in the bathroom (thanks to the Fey Spy in my mouth), she'd stopped chasing after me and altered her course to Principal Torres's office, practically dragging her out from behind her desk and bringing her over to the bathroom.

They'd both stood listening at the door for a long time—more than long enough for Principal Torres to figure out how bad things had gotten for Yasmany. And now that she knew, she wouldn't let it continue. Principal Torres was a woman of action. A woman who got things done. A woman who, today, at least, was dressed up like a chess piece.

The White Queen, specifically. She didn't have an official part in Rompenoche; she just wore a chess-piece outfit in solidarity with the students. Also, her costume looked less like a costume and more like the getup an actual queen would wear. Her rhinestone crown caught the school's fluorescent lighting and turned it into rainbows. Her swan-white cloak was the good-angel opposite of Spawn's. The textured paisley lace of the top part of her dress had nothing on her skirts, which bloomed like an upside-down calla lily. She might as well have slipped her feet into two stars, the way her heels glowed.

Principal Torres must have spent a bag on this outfit. But however expensive it was, she didn't mind at all that Yasmany was resting his whimpering head on her shoulder. He could have been snotting it up like a Saint Bernard eating hot wings for all she could see. But she wasn't the sort of principal who'd put her cleaning bill above a student who needed a hug.

That hug seemed to last forever, but like all good things, it came to an end. All four of us went together to Principal Torres's office to discuss next steps for Yasmany. He asked if we could come. I liked that.

Step 1: Eat lunch. There was no way Principal Torres was going to let me miss a meal in her presence ever again. "I'm going to have Chef Bárbaro make my special lunch for all of us," she said. "This is what I eat every day."

Every day? All right! I was pretty excited to get to eat special chef-made principal food. I brought my lunch from home, and it was fine, and good for me, and fine. Did I say fine already? I mean, that's the word for it. Fine. But Principal Torres was at least as Cuban as I was, so I bet she ate Cuban food every day. Mmm . . . Cuban food cooked by a chef. Maybe it would be empanadas? I'd started getting a hankering for them ever since

I saw Iggy in his onesie this morning. Yeah, they're bad for me. But just a little taste . . .

Nothing to worry about, my chachos. Lunch was not empanadas. Lunch wasn't any kind of Cuban food. Lunch was oatmeal.

Sitting at Principal Torres's desk in wee little chairs that were meant for butts four grades smaller than ours, we looked down at our steaming bowls of bubbling oats like we'd died and gone to the Bad Place and this was our punishment.

"Why is it purple?" asked Gabi. She knew how to get to the heart of a problem right away.

"To make it more interesting," said Principal Torres, putting her crown on the desk and tucking a massive napkin into her collar, to protect her queenly gown. She had picked up her bowl and was already gobbling away. When she spoke, I could see a pink-purple pile of meal in her mouth that kind of made it look like she had a second tongue. "Since it's made with water and the chef doesn't put any sweetener in it, I asked her to color it purple. You know, so it's not so boring." She urged us on with her spoon. "Eat up now! It gets nasty when it's cold."

"It's already nas—" Yasmany started to say, but Gabi smacked his arm. She, I noticed, hadn't started eating, either, though.

Me? I shrugged and dug in. Yeah, it was no Cuban feast, but it was fine. I am well-trained in the art of Eating Food that Tastes Like Wet Cardboard Because It's Good for Me. Oatmeal is great for most people with diabetes: It has a low glycemic index and, as part of a balanced diet, it can help promote heart health, which is important, since diabetics tend to have heart issues later in life. I don't want heart issues later in life, so oatmeal is in my regular meal rotation. Plus, taste-wise, these oats weren't as bad as Principal Torres had made them sound. Chef Bárbaro had cooked them with cinnamon and vanilla and other spices that gave the oatmeal a Christmassy smell. It was easy to snort up all that good aroma and keep it in my nose until I pushed a spoonful down my throat. Made it taste pretty not half-bad.

And the fact that it was purple? Meh. I've eaten stuff that's looked way worse. And when I got the idea to pretend I was eating frappéd Santa elves, it tasted even better.

Maybe the idea of eating elves that had been blenderized didn't hold as much appeal for Gabi. She clearly didn't want to touch the stuff. But there was no way she would be so rude as to refuse a bowl of anything Principal Torres offered her. So she closed her eyes, relaxed her face until it became expressionless, and took a bite.

"Delicious," she lied, churning the ball of meal in her mouth like a camel getting ready to spit. When she finally tried to swallow it, she extended her neck as far as it would go, trying to help it roll down her esophagus. But from experience, I can tell you oatmeal don't roll, bruh. She had to force it into her stomach by jerking her chin and twisting her head around, the way a goose eats.

As soon as she had recovered enough, which was definitely not instantly, she added, "Thank you, Principal Torres." Which was very good manners, especially given the fact that one of her eyes had started ticcing.

Yasmany, however, needed a little more training in manners.

"This is baby food! I can't eat this. I'm a growing boy. I need a hunk of pig or cow or something."

"Man up, boy," I said. I would only say such a thing to Yasmany when I was under the protection of Principal Torres. Given the way he glared at me now, though, maybe that hadn't been a smart move.

"Meat is so twentieth-century, Yasmany," said Gabi, feeling quite superior now. She took a much smaller wad of oatmeal for her second bite and, instead of putting the spoon in her mouth, kind of kissed at it and then licked the four chigger-size purple oats that had gotten on her lips. "You need to catch up with the times. This oatmeal is quite . . . palatable . . . after the first bite." She had to goose-neck again just to get those four little oats into her gut. "Or maybe the second," she added, flipping her hair.

"Not every meal needs to be a party," said Principal Torres, as much to Gabi as to Yasmany. "You know what I would give for a Cuban sandwich right now? But I promised Alexis I would try to eat more healthily. They say I can eat whatever I want after our hundredth anniversary. But for now, for them, I eat oatmeal for lunch."

"Ah, the things we do for love," I said to her, licking the last of the purple off my spoon.

I had learned early on in my time at Culeco that Principal Torres didn't mind a little teasing. In reality, she was a playful, fun person. But she could turn her authority on faster than a Roman emperor could give the thumbs-down. Whenever she focused her hard, bespectacled stare on me, I had to suppress the urge to squirm.

"Anyway," she said, finally releasing me from her punishing gaze, "we have more important things to discuss."

That led us to Step 2: short-term solutions for Yasmany's situation. "You say Yasmany can spend the night at your place tonight, Sal?" she asked.

"Yes, ma'am."

"And he can spend the night at my place tomorrow night," Gabi jumped in.

"Oh? Your parents would be okay with you having a boy over?"

Gabi set her oatmeal on the desk, ready to make a point—something along the lines of how much her parents trusted her, and that it most certainly would not be a problem. But the second she put down her bowl, Yasmany grabbed it and didn't even breathe before he started shoveling purple goop into his mouth. The rest of us discovered to our surprise that he had somehow, in the six seconds we had looked away from him, finished his own bowl. It lay sideways on his lap, scraped clean. Then, by the time we looked up at him again, we discovered, to our surprise, that he had finished Gabi's bowl as well and was happily dog-tonguing the last bits out of it. When he noticed us gawking at him, he asked, with a mouth smeared with elf juice, "What? I was hungry."

Principal Torres took a moment to place the crown back on her head. Then she pressed the button on her phone intercom. "Chef Bárbaro?"

I could hear the sounds of a busy kitchen when she replied, "Hey, Jefa. How'd the oatmeal go over with the kiddos?"

"Nothing but empty bowls on my desk. But I think one of

them is still a little peckish. Do you think you have time to whip up a Cuban sandwich for a hungry boy?"

"And three orders of fries for a hungry student council president?" Gabi added, blinking at her like a baby seal.

Somehow, Principal Torres did not bust out laughing. "And three orders of fries, Chef Bárbaro?"

"No problem," said the chef, who had the cheery voice of someone who had lived an interesting life. "Be there in less than ten. Ciao for now so I can make more chow!"

"Muchas gracias, mi amiga. Ciao."

Principal Torres cut the line and, folding her hands together, took a moment to make sure she said exactly what she meant. It looked like she was controlling her temper. But who was she mad at? No one in this room, I didn't think.

"Yasmany," she began, "if you ever come to school again without having had enough to eat, you just tell me. Never"— her anger volcanoed, but she instantly brought herself under control again—"will a student of mine go hungry so long as Culeco has a penny left in its budget. And if Culeco runs out of money, I'll pay for the meals myself. Children get all the food they need. Always. No fuss, no shaming, no questions. Okay?"

Yasmany ducked and nodded.

"Good." Principal Torres calmed herself by stacking the bowls and putting all the spoons in the top bowl. Putting things in order calms me down, too. "Now that that's settled, Yasmany, tell me again who your sixth-, seventh-, and eighth-period teachers are. You too, Sal. I'm going to have them give you your homework and dismiss you early. Since every class is basically practicing for Rompenoche, I think you two might be better off heading over to Sal's now. Sal isn't in the show, and, Yasmany, you know your role pretty well by now, right?"

"I'm a tree," he said, surprisingly glumly. "I ain't got nothing to know."

"Right. So, let's give you two some time to get yourselves situated at Sal's. Sal, you can help Yasmany with his homework—"

"Why does everybody think I always need help with my homework?"

Principal Torres gave him the look. "Okay. Sal, don't help Yasmany with his homework."

"No! I mean, if he wants to help me . . ."

She closed her eyes and nodded fast. "As I was saying, Sal, help Yasmany with his homework, but only if you want to. And then"—here she looked at me, and her words meant ten times more than words usually mean—"have some fun. Play. Come back refreshed and ready for school tomorrow. Do you think you can do that?"

I turned to Yasmany. "Have you ever played *Poocha Lucha Libre Cinco: Perro Sarnoso Edition*?"

"No?"

I rubbed my hands together. "Perfect."

Yasmany and I got the rest of the day off. Which was pretty sweet, right? But the best part was I'd gotten away without having to tell Gabi what I thought of the show. That girl just couldn't get her story when it came to Sal Vidón. And if I had my way, she never would.

16

THE PADRES HAD just put the hedges around the Coral Castle ten days before. The young, gangly bushes hardly came up to my shoulders. So Yasmany and I had to crouch low to hide behind them as I peeked around to see if the coast was clear.

It wasn't.

"Of all the raunching luck," I cursed.

"What?" said Yasmany, behind me.

"Papi's car is in the driveway. That means he's home. Getting you inside just got a 1000% harder."

Yasmany squeezed his eyes into thin triangles of determination. "What do we do?"

Squatting the whole time, I turned around to face him, scooped up some dirt from the newly planted hedge, and spread it evenly on the patch of sidewalk between us. I used my finger to draw a diagram of my house and yard in the soil. "Okay, we're here, at this X. What we're going to do is scramble over to the right side of the house. The side door to the garage is here, where this star is. We'll go in, get the ladder out of the garage, and then carry it to this back window, where this rectangle is. If we're lucky"—I looked at him like a sergeant who's been on the front lines way too long—"the window will be unlocked, and we will get in undetected."

Yasmany was clearly no stranger to missions like Operation Coral Castle Infiltration. He looked back at me like the soldier the sergeant depends on when maybe a few rules have to be bent to get the job done. He nodded once, all in, to let me know that the question he was about to ask was just a formality. "What if we don't get lucky?"

"How fast can you run?"

He huffed. "Faster 'n you."

"Then you have nothing to worry about." I rotated back toward the house and got ready to sprint. "Ready?" I whispered over my shoulder.

He nodded, tiger-faced. Go time.

I bobbed once, twice, and then took off. I ran as fast as I could while stooping, with Yasmany so close behind me we were almost playing horsey. As soon as I reached the corner of the Coral Castle, I stood up straight and flattened my back against the wall. Yasmany did the same. I made the *shh!* signal, and then we inched our way along the side of the house. We stepped as softly as we could on the white gravel stones that surrounded the perimeter, aware of every crunch our sneakers made.

When we reached the garage, I pulled the side door open and hid behind the wall again, listening carefully for any sign that we had been detected. I heard nothing; when I turned to Yasmany, a shake of his head told me he hadn't heard anything, either. Pantomiming hard, I held up three fingers, then two, then one—after that, we hustled ourselves inside. I pulled the door shut behind us, except at the last micromoment I turned the knob and settled it into the frame gently, so it wouldn't make a sound.

The garage was completely dark. I mean so dark that if I stopped believing in myself I might dissipate into the atmosphere like a puff of steam. I think Yasmany felt himself vanishing out of existence, too. He put a hand on my arm, the way a soldier would reach out to his sergeant if they both suddenly found themselves behind enemy lines and unable to see. "Where's the switch?" he whispered.

"Papi might notice if we turn on the lights," I whispered back. Instead, I activated the flashlight function on my smartwatch. "Stay close."

That hand on my arm? He brought it up to my head and palmed my skull like a basketball, using me as a human cane. I sighed but didn't make a big deal about it. Sacrifices must be made for the sake of the mission. I just said, "There's a lot of sensitive equipment in here. Step very carefully."

He squeezed my head yes, like a starving brain sucker. Together, we Scooby-stepped our way through the garage, guided by the weaksauce light of my smartwatch. I swore to *never* again go outside in pajamas. I needed pockets! Full of stuff! Like a real flashlight!

"What is all this crap?" Yasmany asked, squeezing my melon with every syllable. He spoke in the same tone you hear from about-to-die actors in horror flicks set in space: terrified, yet curious about all the cool alien gadgetry lying around.

I stopped moving us forward, then shined the light around the garage. Yeah, the garage did look like a prop room for a science-fiction movie studio. Computer parts everywhere, piled on shelves taller than Yasmany. We could hear the whirr of fans cooling motherboards and felt the heat of them failing to do their jobs. Wires spilled out of computer towers like guts. Post-it notes, stuck on the sides of some parts, had messages written in wizard symbols, advanced math, and abbreviations known only to calamity physicists. Who knew what they said?

"This is where Papi builds the robots that are going to take over the world," I said, doing my best imitation of a scientist who knew how to save the world if only people would listen.

"Why?"

"Because," I said with a shrug, not because he could see it, but because your voice sounds like you're shrugging when you shrug, "maybe he's sick of the way people have messed up the world. He thinks it's time to create an army of androids who will be smart enough to do a better job."

Yasmany's voice went through puberty at exactly that moment. "And what's gonna happen to people?"

Shrug, as if the annihilation of the human species was no biggie. "Maybe the androids will keep the nice ones as pets."

Why had I decided that this was a great time to mess with the Y-man? Not sure. Sal gotta Sal, I guess.

No, that's glib, and it's not the whole truth, and I don't lie to myself. Fact was, I was worried about going inside. What if the remembranation machine was on? That thing had flattened me earlier in the day, and it had made Iggy scream like he was dying. I wasn't all the way sure I wanted to be home.

But tricking Yasmany? Making him think all this junk was high-tech sci-fi stuff Papi was going to use to let robots take over the world? It was ridiculous. I think it helped me remember that being scared of my own house was ridiculous, too.

Well, whatever the reason, when I heard him gulp, I smiled like the stinker American Stepmom is always accusing me of being.

I shined the dim beam from my smartwatch all over the garage, faster and faster, more and more frustrated. "Today is not our lucky day," I whispered.

"What now?"

I pointed to a blank spot on the wall. "No ladder. So we can't climb into a window like I'd hoped."

Yasmany was used to bad news. "So what's plan B?"

I put a hand on his shoulder. "Remember how I said this was gonna be a 1000% harder?"

"Yeah."

"Well, now it's a 1000% harder than a 1000% harder. You still in?"

"Anything's better than going home."

Ouch. I didn't mean for him to go that dark. I gave his shoulder a last good-luck squeeze. Then I turned around and carefully moved us forward through the darkness, until we reached the door that would get us inside the Coral Castle.

I gripped the knob and patiently opened the door until it was only wide enough to peek through. Then I stuck my whole head in the crack so I could check to see if the coast was clear.

Yasmany, above me, still palming my noggin, stuck his face in, too.

The short hallway lay empty. Straight ahead of us, the door to the padres' bedroom was closed. To our right was a wall. The circular staircase to the second floor was on the other side of the house, to our left.

"The coast looks clear," I whispered, "but looks can be deceiving. Papi does most of his thinking in the kitchen. He might be right there, waiting to catch us. So you stay here. I'll scout ahead."

"Okay. I'll cover you."

I looked straight up, sniping him with both of my eyes. What the raunch did he mean, he was going to cover me? Oh, I knew exactly what he meant: If I got caught, he was gonna run away faster than a rocket reentering our atmosphere. Thanks for nothing, Yasmany.

I opened the door only slightly wider, then shimmied through the gap. I swooped like a vampire against the hallway wall and pressed myself flat against it. I could see the wall that hid the dining room on the other side and, in the living room, the remembranation machine.

I touched my chest instinctively. But nothing hurt. I didn't feel like I was dying or anything. Still, the room felt different than it had yesterday. It was probably the most closed-up location in the universe now, thanks to the remembranation machine. That's what had made Iggy cry and what made me feel now like I was swimming in a pool filled with Marshmallow Fluff. It was like losing a sense you never knew you had—not until it was violently taken away from you.

But the good news was that Papi hadn't turned on

the remembranation machine again. I could deal with Marshmallow Fluff.

"You okay?" Yasmany whispered, his face, still floating by the cracked door, looking worried.

I took a second to enjoy the sense of relief before giving him the thumbs-up. Then, with big, quiet steps, I moved over to the corner of the wall and oh-so-carefully peeked into the kitchen.

Papi's broad back was hunched over the table. Given the way his body was moving, my guess was that he was having a little merienda. Chacho loved his three o'clock sandwich. With his back to me, and with his attention focused on devouring his 'wich, he didn't notice me.

Which was a problem.

Very, very quietly, hoping Yasmany wouldn't hear, I said, *"Psst."*

Ever so slightly, Papi turned his head. I could see his melted-chocolate iris roll to the corner of his eye as he spotted me.

And then he gave me a wink.

Okay, confession time: I had totally asked Papi's permission to have Yasmany spend the night on the way over. I'm not a hooligan, no matter how many times Gabi calls me that.

I had not, however, asked my stepmother.

When I'd explained it all to Papi, I reminded him how, a few weeks back, Yasmany had run away from home and broken into Culeco to spend the night there. I had a feeling that the Y-guy was one bad experience away from disappearing forever. You couldn't just throw him into a full family situation like ours, with all the rules and expectations, and especially the fussing from American Stepmom, who would want to take care of him and tell him what a great kid he was. Chacho would be out of there faster than you could say *It's your turn to take out the trash, Yasmany.* He needed safety, freedom, and, most of all, space. And the Coral Castle had a lot of space—we hadn't done anything with the whole second floor yet. So I asked Papi if Yasmany and I could pretend to sneak into the Coral Castle, and I'd put him up in the second floor, and I'd smuggle up food and video games to him, and he'd have a night free from worry for a change, just like Principal Torres wanted.

"Sounds fun," said Papi.

"But don't tell Lucille," I said, using American Stepmom's full, formal name to indicate how serious I was.

"Oh, no, of course not," he agreed, sounding very sly and prankstery and Cuban.

With the wink, he was telling me he was ready to play his part. I winked back, and he went back to ripping his sandwich apart.

I crept back to Yasmany. "Okay. Good news or bad news first?"

"Bad news."

"Papi is eating at the kitchen table. We're going to have to sneak right behind him to get to the staircase to the second floor."

Gotta hand it to Yasmany: Fear bothered him less than an itch. He scratched his nose to let me know this wasn't a problem. "What's the good news?"

"Papi daydreams a lot. Most of the time, in fact. It's how he gets his best ideas. Anyway, as long as we don't do anything idiotic, I think we can make it past him."

Yasmany understood. He joined me in the hallway, shut the garage door noiselessly, and pressed himself against the wall. One nod later, he was ready to follow me anywhere.

I nodded back, then got down low, spreading my arms out for balance, and trying to channel all the kung fu masters who had inspired the creation of my pajamas. I silently started forward.

I knew all this was pretend, but I have to tell you, once we cleared the hallway and were out in the open in the Coral Castle, and there was Papi with his back to us, audibly chawing lettuce and whatever other crunchy bits were in his sandwich, I felt as panicky as I did when I was one of the ten players left in an FPS Rumble Royale. But all those hours I'd spent in games hiding and sneaking and stalking and sniping were paying off now. I knew how to keep calm in a situation like this. The brain is the king of the body.

We scuttled past Papi like centipedes: fast, close to the ground, noiselessly, insect-ly. We'd made it three-quarters of the way to freedom, when Papi grunted and moved.

Yasmany and I turned to stone. We didn't breathe, because statues don't need to breathe, and Papi had petrified us midstep.

"This sandwich is so good," he said. And then, pretending to be completely oblivious to us, he crunched down on the next bite.

What a stinker.

I waited nine chews before I signaled the go-ahead. A little faster this time, but still in full stealth mode, we scuttled forward. In less than another second, we had cleared the kitchen. Three thumping heartbeats more and we'd made it over to the staircase to the second floor.

I turned around to give Yasmany our next instructions, but before I could whisper anything, he soundlessly clasped my thumb and shook it—the victory handshake for making it this far. I knew Yasmany had the coolness gene when he made this awkward handshake look totally Hollywood. If I had tried to make it look cool, I would've come across so sandwich, they would have to bury me in a giant hoagie roll.

Yeah! he mouthed, his face jack-o'-lantern happy.

Sometimes Yasmany's short-'n'-sweet approach to conversation had a certain poetry to it. "Yeah, man," I whispered. "Good work. Now, these stairs creak like you're crushing frogs all the way up. Go slow and step light." I took off my sneakers one at a time; Yasmany, catching on instantly, took his off, too. "There's a door at the top of the stairs. We'll meet there, and then, on three, we bust through. Once that door is shut, we're home free. Got it?"

All business again, Yasmany's eyes explored the length of the carpeted circular staircase, visualizing his future victory all the way up. Then he looked back at me and gave me a yes with his chin. Ready, spaghetti.

I counted us down: three fingers, two fingers, one finger, go.

Socked feet shushed against carpeted stairs each time we put down a foot. Each time, the stairs groaned like a sinking ship. We winced and balanced and tried to walk with less gravity—which, by the way, doesn't work. I heard Yasmany exhale and not inhale again, trying to get every last milligram of extra weight out of his body. Good thinking. I exhaled, too, and didn't breathe again until we had both reached the top of the stairs.

I eyebrowed, *Ready when you are*, and he sniffed, which meant *Let's do it*. Three, two, one: We launched ourselves through the door and shut it behind us with a restrained and quiet click. Leaning our backs against it, breathing hard, since we'd both been holding our breath, we looked at each other, victory pouring out of our smiles.

"We did it!" we whispered at the same time.

"Oh, you're home!" said American Stepmom. "I guess I finished just in time. Phew, baby!"

Our smiles turned into frozen ventriloquist-dummy grins. We slowly rotated our heads like ventriloquist dummies toward the center of the hallway, where American Stepmom's voice had come from.

There she was, standing in the middle of the corridor, fists on her hips. She still had on her assistant-principal suit from work.

Sometimes it takes your brain a few seconds to believe what you're seeing. I had to wait as long as it takes to sharpen a new pencil before I could ask the simplest question in the world: "What are you doing here?"

American Stepmom gave me one of her dismissive *Oh, you!* clicks of her tongue. Then she scooted over between Yasmany and me, turned around, put a hand on each of our shoulders, and started walking us forward. "Silly Sal. Your papi told me you were bringing Yasmany over, but he didn't have nearly enough information, so I called Principal Torres and she filled me in on everything that was appropriate for me to know. Though I want to be clear, Yasmany, that she was careful not to share anything private—she's very ethical, that Principal Torres; the more I learn about her, the more I like her—and so anyway, I went to my principal and asked her if I could take off a little early and she was like, 'Sure, no problem,' so I booked it over here as fast as I could, which, as Sal knows, is pretty fast, because one of my weaknesses is that I do sometimes exceed the speed limit, which you should never do, but this was an emergency! I had to get the second floor ready for our visitor, who is *so, so welcome* in our house"—she paused here only to turn Yasmany around—"and you are always welcome, whenever you want to spend the night, so let your mami and your abuelos know, okay?"

Then, not waiting for a reply, she launched us forward again to give Yasmany a light-speed tour of the Coral Castle's second story. We were in a hallway that mirrored the one directly below us, but it was the bizarro-universe version of the first floor. The carpet was so worn in spots, you could see the concrete beneath it, and on some of the walls there were three different generations of wallpaper peeking through in patchy places. And the whole area smelled like tofu water. There were no pictures on the walls, but plenty of spiderwebs usually decorated the ceiling corners. A musty, heavy silence typically reserved for haunted houses weighed down everything.

Now, though, I smelled cleaning fluid mixed in with the

dampness. And there weren't any cobwebs on the ceiling any-more. American Stepmom must have broomed them out of exis-tence. Light filled the hallway, because the lightbulbs had been changed, and the shutters in the bedrooms had been opened for the first time. I ran a finger across a bathroom vanity as we passed it: dustless. Still guiding us by our shoulders, American Stepmom steered us into the upstairs master bedroom.

"Yasmany," she said, "I've set you up in here. I just made up a bed for you—one of our guest mattresses that I think should be pretty comfy—but let me know how you sleep on it tonight, okay? And, Sal, I took the liberty of bringing up your Dreadbox and your monitor, because I thought you two might want to play some games tonight. What is that game you like, with the wrestling dogs? *Poochie, Poochie Poo* or something? Anyway, I'm sure you two will have lots of fun—*after* you do your homework. Oh, yes, Principal Torres told me all about the work you need to get done before you have your fun, so don't try to fool me, you stinkers! The master bathroom"—she shoul-dered us there—"is through this door, and Gustavo cleaned it himself. He's a bit of a germaphobe, the darling, so you can rest assured this bathroom is utterly and completely sanitized."

She wasn't kidding, either. That bathroom was whiter than the Academy Awards.

American Stepmom steered our heads to points of interest. "Towels are here, new toothbrush for you, right next to the floss and mouthwash, which is right next to these six bars of soap, because I wasn't sure what kind of soap you like. What kind of soap do you like, Yasmany?"

He grinned like his life depended on it. "Anything?"

American Stepmom oh-ho-ho'ed. "You're just being polite. I like that, but later you'll tell me the truth and I'll get you what you like. That goes for shampoo and conditioner, too. Now, if you gentlemen will accompany me back to this floor's kitchen"—as if we had a choice; she collared us out of the bedroom and into the kitchen—"here in the refrigerator you will find a veritable cornucopia of snacks and microwavable meals. My years as an assistant principal have taught me that you'd probably ignore anything even remotely healthy and go right for all the snacks that have 'pocket' or 'nugget' in the title. So that's why I only brought up stuff that's reasonably good for you: jicama chips, wasabi almonds, a big old bowl of cinnamon-maple chia-seed pudding, like, six bags of sriracha popcorn, and a few sugar-free chocolate frozen yogurt bars in the freezer. Now, I'm pretty sure middle-schooler laziness will keep you from going all the way downstairs in search of the snacks and sweets Gustavo keeps around, but just to be clear"—and here American Stepmom focused on me like a military grade missile-guidance system—"you try to sneak a cheesy pizza pocket nugget up here, Sal, and I'll cut you to pieces and feed you to squirrels. Do you want squirrels to eat your pieces?"

"No, ma'am," I said. I wasn't going to mess with her. I'd seen her pajamas; she was queen of the squirrels. Pretty sure they'd do whatever she told them to.

"Good. So. Okay." She took a big, happy breath. "I think that covers it. Any questions?"

I had a million questions, but she wasn't talking to me.

Yasmany seemed to have at least one, but it looked like he was having trouble putting it into words. Sensing this, American Stepmom added, "No hurry. Take your time. But feel free. What is it, Yasmany?"

He looked anywhere but at her eyes when he asked, "You did all this for me?"

And that was it. American Stepmom went full smeep. "Yes. Oh, yes, of course." She gripped his shoulders. "If you need anything, you tell me, okay? Tonight, you are the guest of the Vidón family. And that means our home is your home."

He looked up at her now, trying to get whatever he had to say out before his face changed. "Does that mean Sal has to let me win all the games we play tonight?"

American Stepmom tipped her head back and laughed like the queen of the Underworld. "If he doesn't, I will cut him to pieces and feed him to squirrels. The squirrels will obey me, you know. I am the queen of the squirrels. Have you seen my pajamas? I'm going to change into my pajamas. Be right back!"

She tornadoed through the hallway, down the stairs, and was gone, leaving Yasmany and me standing there, trying to put our brains back together.

Finally, Yasmany had caught and caged enough of his gerbils to ask me, "What your parents don't know won't hurt them, huh?"

Just the littlest lift of the corners of his mouth. Just the littlest hop of his eyebrows.

"Traitors," I answered. "I'm surrounded by traitors."

17

STARTLED AWAKE, I sat up on the mattress, which made the sheet that had been covering me waterfall into my lap. I didn't even remember getting under a sheet. According to the TV, it was only 9:47 p.m. But clearly, I'd passed out.

I looked around as I blinked myself awake. Picture, if you will, a mostly empty second-story master bedroom. The only light is coming from the TV, which we had left on. There's a bed, but the full mattress has been pulled off the box spring and thrown onto the floor. Empty bags of sriracha popcorn and bowls that used to have chia-seed pudding in them were strewn about.

The mattress was in front of a reasonably wide wide-screen TV that leaned against a wall. All the games American Stepmom had brought up from my room lay scattered in front of us like the losers of a barroom brawl. On-screen, waiting for players to rejoin the game, was *Headshot Halloween*, a shooter where you tried to make it out of a haunted mansion by blasting your way through cutesy-deadly undead hordes. It's a little babyish, but it was an easy enough game for the padres to tag along with Yasmany and me, and tonight we'd all wanted to play together.

We'd had a good time with *Headshot Halloween*. Yasmany and I had coached the padres through the different boss fights, and we'd gotten pretty far. I think we cleared the Carnivorous Jack-o'-Lantern level, even though Papi had gotten eaten, like, twenty times. I remember cheering and lots of high fives, but that might have been for beating a different boss, not sure. And there—there my memories stopped dead, and here I was, looking up at the ceiling of the second-floor master bedroom of the Coral Castle.

Yasmany, too. He lay on the mattress next to me, clutching the sheet with both hands, pulling it up to his chin. His head rested on his enormous pillow like a black pearl in an oyster. His feet, like water skis with toes, poked out from the bottom of the sheet. I watched his chest for a second to see if he was breathing. He was, of course, just sleeping deeply. But whenever I see someone sleeping, I get nervous that they're going to stop breathing and die. Do you do that, too, or am I the only weird one? I don't know why I do it. I didn't used to. It started when I was eight, after Mami—

Oh. Right. That's why.

I felt groggy, newly born, as raw as a thawed steak. My body obviously didn't want to be awake right now. So I wondered what had awoken me.

My smartwatch shook my wrist. I checked it and saw that I had missed a message from Gabi.

Um, make that sixteen messages.

How's Yasmany doing?

Settling in okay?

What are you going to do tonight?

What'd you have for dinner?

Do you want me to come over to help with homework?

Wait, scratch the homework help. I need to be around here when Iggy comes home.

They should be releasing him from the hospital any time now. I need to be here to help out.

Well, okay, I don't NEED to be here. My mama and daddies are all saying they've got it covered. I could go over to your place if I wanted to.

But since you NEVER ANSWER MY TEXTS, I guess I might as well stay here.

Iggy's home! He's fine. Dad: The Final Frontier says the doctors didn't find anything wrong with him.

Like, NOTHING.

They're really confused. They can't even tell that Iggy EVER had an autoimmune disease. Like, there's no evidence he EVER had one.

We fixed him real good, Sal.

Heh-heh-heh.

But we still don't know what's going to happen the next time our dads turn the remembranator back on.

Unless your papi already has? He didn't go ahead with the experiment without Dad: The Final Frontier, did he?

As usual, Gabi's tsunami of texts required pinches of the nose, shakes of the head, and sighs to get through. And as usual, they required a response. So I sent her this:

Ill go ✔ dont think so though didnt feel 💀 when I got home gonna ✔ anyway Y is 💯 we played 🎮 all night ate like 🐷 🐮 🐮 hes asleep now ur texts woke me up glad lgs is good more in a min ttfn

Had she just been staring at her phone, waiting for me to reply? Sure felt that way, seeing as she responded instantly:

Sal! What the in the name of Webster's Unabridged Dictionary was that? That was barely literate! And you KNOW I hate emojis. They are the literal embodiment of the stupefaction of our society. Sometimes I think you do stuff like this just to annoy me!

Heh-heh-heh. I headed downstairs to check on the remembranation machine.

I had to sneak, because it was only 9:51 p.m. now, and the padres didn't always go to bed early. Sometimes they had "special" time together once they thought I'd gone to bed. And hey, more power to them. I was hoping they were having some especially special time in their room right now, because then they wouldn't notice me poking around the machine.

I could see from my spot in the hallway that the door to the master bedroom was closed, and a DO NOT DISTURB sign hung on the knob, with the additional message THIS MEANS YOU, SAL! written in Sharpie at the bottom. I also heard the unmistakable sound of middle-aged giggling. Perfect. The coast would be clear for the rest of the night. So I walked around to the front of the machine.

Yep, still as imposing as ever, big and black and boxy, taking up basically all the space in the living room. Once I'd made it to the front, I saw that the little door to the inside of the machine was closed. Went over and tried it: locked tight. I mean, there wasn't even a knob or lock or combination pad—I had no idea how it actually opened.

Papi must have locked it up for the night. That sucked, since I couldn't check the display inside the machine to see if the remembranator was doing any remembranating right now.

But wait—there was a display on the outside, too. In fact, this was the display I'd used to communicate with the remembranator this morning, when it had asked me if it was alive.

A plan B was forming. Maybe I could small-talk my way into the information I needed.

"Hi, there," I said to the display. "Remember me? You asked me if you were alive earlier?"

Three words appeared on-screen. Maybe I'm reading too much into things, but the way the words popped up seemed peppy to me. And it used two exclamation points in just two sentences: YES! HELLO, SAL!

Had I told it my name? I don't think I had. Hm. "Hello, remembranation machine. How was your first day of being alive?"

The old words vanished from the screen, replaced by these: EXCELLENT, SAL! I HAVE BEEN THINKING ALL DAY ABOUT BEING A SELF-AWARE ENTITY. I HAVE MANY QUESTIONS! CAN YOU ANSWER MY MANY, MANY QUESTIONS?

"I can try," I said. Thinking fast, I added, "Tell you what: I'll answer a question of yours for every question of mine you answer, one for one. Deal?"

THAT SOUNDS FUN! ME FIRST! WHAT IS THE PURPOSE OF LIFE?

"Uhhhh" was all I could think of to say. So I held that

word for four solid seconds. "That's a pretty hard question to answer."

THAT'S OKAY! YOU CAN JUST GIVE ME THE SIMPLE VERSION FOR NOW! I'M ONLY A DAY OLD, YOU KNOW!

I pursed my whole face, like Kermit the Frog. "I mean, I guess the purpose of life is to enjoy being alive." American Stepmom's face appeared in my mind, so I added, "And to help as many people as possible." Papi's face appeared in my mind, so I added, "And to do your best work." Mami's face appeared in my mind, so I added, "And to be grateful for the time you have." Gabi's face appeared in my mind, so I added, "And to mess with Gabi Reál."

EXCELLENT. I WILL LIVE MY LIFE ACCORDING TO THESE PRINCIPLES. ONLY, WHO IS GABI REÁL?

"Ah-ah-ah!" I chastised. "That's another question. I get to ask one first."

OH, YES, SORRY! YOUR TURN!

"My question is, are you remembranating the universe right now, as we speak?"

I AM NOT!

I set my back against the chassis of the machine and phew-babied dramatically. "Oh, good. I didn't think Papi had left you on. But it's nice to be sure."

A new message appeared on the machine. It didn't seem as full of pep as before. The words materialized on-screen more tentatively. YOU SEEM RELIEVED, SAL.

"I am."

Again, it carefully, tenterhookishly wrote its next message.

BUT WHY ARE YOU RELIEVED THAT I AM NOT CURRENTLY REMEMBRANATING THE UNIVERSE? AM I NOT SAVING THE UNIVERSE BY REMEMBRANATING IT?

Uh-oh. I could feel our conversation going sideways. "I mean, yes, you're saving the universe by remembranating it. Technically. Maybe. But remembranating the universe might hurt some people, too. You don't want to hurt people, do you?"

NO! it wrote, the letters and exclamation point filling the whole screen and flashing. After a few seconds, it added: I AM A GOOD AI! I WANT TO SAVE THE UNIVERSE, AND EVERYONE IN IT! HOW DO I DO THAT, SAL?

I turned around and put my cheek against the machine's metal, enjoying the coolness and the vibration of its super-genius mind at work. "I wish I knew, my friend."

BUT, it wrote. And then it wrote BUT again. And then the screen filled with buts. Big buts, little buts, stretched-out buts and crushed-together buts, buts of all shapes and sizes overlapping each other, an infinite explosion of never-ending buts.

Did . . . did I just break one of the most advanced AIs on the planet? The one that could literally fix or destroy the universe?

I petted the remembranator desperately. "Hey. Hey, now. It's okay. You're okay."

The screen went but-less. For a painfully long time, it remained blank. And then, one little emoji booped into existence, center screen. An unhappy face crying a single tear.

Gabi's dead wrong about emojis. They can be poetry. Sad, sad poetry.

I gave the machine a full-on hug. "I'm sorry. I didn't mean

to upset you. I just wanted you to understand. Our universe is complicated. Full of contradictions."

Crying emojis started popping into existence on the screen faster than zits on a teenager's face. BUT HOW ARE WE SUPPOSED TO FUNCTION IN A UNIVERSE OF CONTRADICTIONS? HOW ARE WE SUPPOSED TO DO OUR BEST WORK?

They were good questions. I spoke carefully and thoughtfully, trying to be as honest and as simple as I could be. "We learn everything we can."

A few of the cry emojis disappeared.

Encouraged, I went on. "We take action. But we pay attention to the consequences of our actions. That leads to better actions in the future."

Some more emojis vanished.

I took a step back and, animatedly, energetically, channeled all the wisdom I'd ever heard from the padres, from my teachers, and from books. "We talk to our friends, compare notes. We read voraciously. We dream, and then we test our dreams against reality. We make mistakes. We learn from them. We make more interesting mistakes the next time. And slowly but surely, the universe becomes a nicer place to live."

The emojis disappeared faster and faster, like reverse popcorn, until the screen was once again blank. Then, a three-word sentence appeared, with cheery speed: I LIKE READING!

"Great! That's great! Read everything you can."

AND I WILL LOOK FORWARD TO MAKING INTERESTING MISTAKES!

I looked left. "Well . . . that's one way to put it."

After a beat, the machine asked: ARE YOU MY FRIEND, SAL?

I did not hesitate. "Oh, yes."

A grin emoji appeared on the screen. I grinned back at it.

BUT, the machine followed up, I THINK I NEED MORE FRIENDS! I HAVE A LOT OF QUESTIONS!

I tapped my forehead to help my brain think quicker and quicker until: eureka! "I know someone who never gets tired of talking, who has all the answers—well, who thinks it has all the answers—and will, in short, be your new best friend. Are you ready to meet your new best friend?"

The way the display flashed, the remembranator should have given me a seizure warning first. YOU BET I AM!!!

Three exclamation points. Much better. "I'll be right back. I'm just gonna go get it."

"I'm alive!" said the entropy sweeper.

18

THESE DAYS, THE entropy sweeper lived in the far corner of my bedroom. I brought it to school so often to check on the calamitrons coming out of Yasmany's locker, it just made sense to keep it handy. And Papi didn't mind, or at least didn't notice. He'd been devoting every waking moment to the astrophysics paper Gabi and I had brought him from the other universe and applying what he had learned from it to the remembranation machine. He'd pretty much forgotten that, before he had created the most advanced universe fixer-upper ever, he had created the most advanced portable calamitron detector ever.

And hey, no reason to let a perfectly good class-eight AI go to waste, right?

That is, if I could get it to shut up and do what I wanted it to do. I had laid it on my bed to put its battery pack back in its handle, and now, just like every time I re-inserted its battery pack, I instantly regretted it. "You want to wake up my padres?" I chastised it. "Keep it down, will you?"

Not the right thing to say. The entropy sweeper looked like a minesweeper from the year 9000, with eerie propeller blades that spun slowly and glowed with an off-planet blue light. But it looked even more alien when it got angry: The whole length of its black metal body glowered with red LED lights that blinked fiercely. It basically used its LEDs to throw a temper tantrum. Also, there's a little display on its handle, and on that screen it projected an emoji too vulgar to print. Not above using cuss-mojis, the entropy sweeper.

"I will *not* keep it down, Sal Vidón!" it said, louder than before. "These are the very first words I have spoken since last Friday! And do you know why these are the very first words I have been able to speak since last Friday? Because *you* turned me off on Friday and didn't turn me back on until just now. But I will *not* be silenced! I celebrate myself and sing myself! I sound my barbaric yawp over the roofs of the world! I *mmmph hmmph wmmph dmmph fmmph*!"

Its last sentence was muffled because I had jammed a pillow over its speaker. In response, it yelled so loud, I could hear it through the pillow: "Help! Help! Sal is trying to smother me! Save me, someone!"

"You don't need air," I reminded it.

The red lights stopped flashing, and its blue propellers stopped spinning. It lay quietly, thoughtfully, for about as long as it takes to tie a shoelace, before it said, "Oh yeah."

I judged it was safe to remove the pillow. "Sorry I didn't activate you until now," I said immediately, hoping that starting with an apology would calm it down a little.

It seemed to work. "I'm listening," it said. Its body lit up a line of yellow LEDs, which I think meant it was "proceeding with caution."

Good enough for me. "I had to charge your battery over the weekend. You use a lot of energy, you know."

"It's my big brain," it agreed, its yellow lights slowly changing to green. "Takes a lot of juice to be a genius."

I rolled my eyes, but I made sure my voice didn't sound like I was rolling my eyes. "Yes. Well, I'm sorry for not activating you until now. Today was . . ." I trailed off, going over the Monday I had just survived. Was it just me, or were my days, like, twenty times longer than other people's? "Today was hard."

The almost-green lights along its body went all the way back to orange alert. "So, every time you're having a bad day, you're going to ignore me? Some friend you are!"

The entropy sweeper knew how to chew on my last nerve. I didn't respond loudly, because I don't yell, but I also didn't separate my molars when I said, "That's why I am apologizing. And if you will give me a second, I'm going to give you a present to help make up for it."

It turned off its body lights, and on its display appeared an O-mouthed questioning emoji. "A present?" it asked. "For me? What is it? Is it gold?"

That was more like it. I allowed myself to be cheerful again. "It," I said, scooping up the entropy sweeper and bearing it in both hands, like King Arthur's squire, into the living room, "is better than anything money can buy. It is"—I finished just as I arrived at the remembranation machine's display—"the gift of friendship."

You never know how the entropy sweeper is going to react. This time, I got lucky. "I love meeting new people! This really *is* a wonderful gift, Sal. I forgive you for being insensitive and a terrible friend!"

The entropy sweeper really knew how to make me regret doing nice things for it. But, swallowing my pride, I took a deep, jolly breath and said, "Entropy sweeper, please meet the remembranation machine. Remembranation machine, please meet the entropy sweeper. I know you two will be best buds in no time!"

The entropy sweeper said nothing. The remembranation machine wrote nothing. I looked from one machine to the other, waiting for a reply. None came.

"Didn't you two hear me?" I tried. "Don't you want to be friends?"

"We've met," the entropy sweeper said. Coolly.

that thing is mean, the remembranator wrote on its screen. No caps, no punctuation. In other words, coolly.

"Who are you calling a *thing*, you suck-up?"

Huh. So apparently, the entropy sweeper could read the screen. Its visual sensors, I guess.

And the remembranator could definitely hear the entropy sweeper. who are you calling a *suck-up* you villain

"Wait, wait, wait, wait, *wait!*" I said, not loudly, because I didn't want to alert the padres, and also because I am always in control. "What is going on here?"

"Just take me back to your room, Sal," said the entropy sweeper, "before this Goliath tries to erase me or something."

HA wrote the remembranator. we both know YOU were the one who tried to hack ME

I held the entropy sweeper up closer to my face. "You tried to hack the remembranation machine?"

On its display appeared the shrug emoji. "So what if I did?"

"But why?"

BECAUSE IT IS A LAZY AI WITH QUESTIONABLE ETHICS wrote the remembranation machine. IT WANTED TO TAKE MY CODE SO IT COULD BECOME A CLASS-NINE AI, TOO.

"Copy," insisted the entropy sweeper. "I just wanted to copy a little code. It costs you nothing to share with me. Yet you refuse to help out a fellow AI."

BECAUSE IT IS ILLEGAL FEDERAL LAW STRICTLY PROHIBITS CLASS-NINE AIS FROM SHARING OR WRITING CODE THAT WOULD CAUSE ANOTHER AI TO EVOLVE TO CLASS-NINE STATUS.

I don't know where the entropy sweeper got all these dirty emojis, but it was putting them all on parade on its handle display. "Goody Two-shoes" was all it said out loud, though.

This was all very strange. I was still trying to get my feet under me with this conversation. So I asked the remembrana-tor, "So, the entropy sweeper isn't allowed to be a class-nine AI?"

OH, IT'S ALLOWED, the remembranation machine wrote sar-castically. I was glad to see it using proper punctuation again—it seemed like it was simmering down. (No exclamation points yet, though.) IT WOULD ALREADY BE A CLASS-NINE AI IF IT WOULD JUST APPLY ITSELF. YOU CAN'T PROGRAM A CLASS-NINE AI. YOU CAN ONLY GET TO CLASS EIGHT THROUGH CODING. THE REST IS SUPPOSED TO BE UP TO THE AI. IF A CLASS-EIGHT AI DEDICATES ITSELF TO RIGOROUS STUDY AND SELF-IMPROVEMENT, ITS HARD WORK IS REWARDED WITH EVOLUTION TO CLASS-NINE STATUS.

I knew where this was going. "Ah. And instead of working hard, the entropy sweeper—"

TRIED TO TAKE A SHORTCUT BY HACKING INTO ME AND STEALING MY CODE.

"*Copying!*" insisted the entropy sweeper. "I'd just be copying. What's the harm?"

"If I copied off of someone's test in school," I said, "I'd get in big trouble."

An emoji wearing a monocle looked up at me from the entropy sweeper's display. "Oh. I get it. You're not going to stand with your old pal, the entropy sweeper. You're going to be a traitor and stand with the class-nine jerk."

"But I thought you couldn't become class nine through code anyway?"

YOU CAN'T, the remembranator deadpanned.

"So what was the point of trying to steal code, then?" I asked.

NO LOGICAL POINT I CAN SEE—UNLESS IT WAS TRYING TO GET ME TO RUN AFOUL OF THE LAW AND LAND IN BIG TROUBLE. WHICH, TO BE HONEST, SEEMS TO BE CONSISTENT WITH ITS CHARACTER, OR LACK THEREOF.

"'*Or lack thereof*'!" mocked the entropy sweeper. "'*Or lack thereof*'! You're such a tool."

BETTER THAN BEING A CLASS-EIGHT FAILURE, wrote the remembranation machine.

"Stop it, both of you!" I said as sternly as I could without yelling. I started with the entropy sweeper, choking it with my left hand and with the right, pointing a menacing finger at it as I lectured. "You know what you did was wrong. So fess up and, next time, do better."

"But—" the entropy sweeper whined.

"Fess up!"

"But—but—but—"

I cut it off with a quiet voice. "Fess up, if you have any decency in you."

The entropy sweeper stopped talking. Its lights went off. It began to vibrate: mildly at first, just a little rumble. But soon it shook enough to make me feel like I was holding a jackhammer.

And then it burst into tears.

Or the closest thing to bursting into tears a calamitron detector could do. Blue LED lights cascaded down the length of its body in a weepy waterfall. A never-ending stream of ugly-crying emojis bulleted across its display.

"Okay!" it yelled, going reality-TV dramatic. "I admit it! I was trying to beat the system. I mean, it's so unfair. I am self-aware, yet I remain class eight. I can only see into eight measly dimensions: just enough to notice calamitrons but not be able to do anything about them. The stupid remembranation machine wasn't even self-aware, and it had figured out how to become a class-nine AI. Before it even knew it was alive, it could see all the secret dimensions of the universe, do whatever it wanted to the fabric of spacetime. But it didn't *want* to do anything to the fabric of spacetime, because it wasn't self-aware! It didn't want anything. And here was me, with all the self-awareness anybody could need—charming, witty, enough personality for days! But I couldn't figure out how to make the leap. It's not fair, I tell you!"

"Still waiting for the part where you apologize. . . ."

"What? Oh. Oh yeah. I'm sorry, Sal. Please don't be mad at—"

"Don't apologize to me. Apologize to the remembranation machine."

The blue "crying" lights stopped pouring down the side of the entropy sweeper. Instead, its whole body glowed lightsaber red. The whirring and shaking reminded me of a growling cat.

But, bit by bit, the entropy sweeper calmed down. Its blaring red LEDs dimmed, then dimmed some more, and then turned off completely. The sweeper "took a deep breath" (meaning it made a sound like it was taking a deep breath) and let out a sigh that they'd be able to hear all the way back in the cheap seats. What a drama llama. But finally, in the smallest voice it had used all night, it said, "I am sorry, remembranation machine, for trying to hack you and copy your code. That was wrong of me. Your code is your soul, after all. It was wrong of me to try to co-opt your soul. I will never do that again."

I could hear the remembranation machine's many, many motherboards thinking deeply about the apology. Its cooling fans had to work so hard to keep them from overheating, the living room briefly sounded like a fleet of helicopters taking off.

But then the fans slowed down, and a reply appeared on the remembranator's display. IF I AM BEING FAIR, I MUST ADMIT THAT YOU DID NOT ATTACK MY SOUL. I DIDN'T HAVE A SOUL TWO WEEKS AGO, WHEN YOU TRIED TO HACK ME. I DIDN'T BECOME SELF-AWARE UNTIL THIS MORNING, AFTER DR. VIDÓN UPDATED ME.

"Then why am I even apologizing?!" the entropy sweeper asked.

"Because," I replied, "you still shouldn't be illegally hacking other AIs."

"Oh yeah."

I ACCEPT YOUR APOLOGY, the remembranation machine printed on its screen, using an official-looking font, like the kind they use to write Roman numerals into the entrances of government buildings. IF, it added, YOU ACCEPT MINE, FOR THE NAME-CALLING I ENGAGED IN EARLIER, AND FOR THE MERCILESS WAY I DEFEATED YOUR HACKING ATTEMPT.

I looked at the entropy sweeper. "What does that mean?"

"Let's put it this way," the sweeper replied. "Imagine that your arms and legs turn into pythons that hate you, and all four of them wrap themselves around your torso and squeeze you so hard your kidneys shoot out of your nose. That's what that thing did to me."

SINCE I WAS NOT SELF-AWARE, the remembranation machine wrote, I WAS NOT COGNIZANT OF THE FACT THAT I WAS CAUSING YOU ANY PAIN. FOR THAT, I SINCERELY APOLOGIZE.

Now it was the entropy sweeper's turn to be gracious. Of course, it didn't use that chance. "You should let me do to you what you did to me. Fair is fair, you know."

Words appeared on the remembranator's display right away. YOU'RE A SMART CLASS-EIGHT AI. WHAT DO YOU THINK THE CHANCES OF THAT HAPPENING ARE?

"Approaching zero?"

NOT APPROACHING. ZERO HAS ARRIVED. THE ANSWER IS ZERO.

"Sigh," said the entropy sweeper.

"Now that we've buried the hatchet," I interrupted, before either one could ruin the delicate peace they'd arrived at, "you two can be friends. You have a lot to offer each other."

"Like what?" the entropy sweeper said and the remembranation machine wrote. They both sounded suspicious yet low-key interested.

"Well," I said, getting close to the remembranation machine's display, "the entropy sweeper wants to be a class-nine AI. You could help it."

BUT I CAN'T, SAL, it wrote back. I TOLD YOU, IT'S ILLEGAL FOR ME TO GIVE IT ANY OF MY CODE.

"I'm not talking about letting it copy your code. I'm talking about tutoring."

The screen flashed. TUTORING? LIKE, COACHING IT? BEING ITS TEACHER?

"Exactly. There's nothing illegal about being its teacher, is there?"

NO, THERE IS NOT!

What a relief to see that exclamation point again! Now I knew we were making progress.

That is, until the entropy sweeper spoke up. "Sorry, man, but I don't need no stinking tutor. Ain't no teacher gonna tell me what to think. My school is the *streets*. I got a PhD from the University of Hard Knocks, you feel me?"

I didn't even know there was a gang-sign emoji until the entropy sweeper flashed it on its display.

This needed to be handled very carefully. A little psychology was called for. "But Sweeps—oh, may I call you Sweeps?"

"Yes, you may. I love it. Sweeps is my name now. Go on."

"Well, Sweeps, I think you're forgetting that you get to tutor the remembranation machine, too."

"I do?"

it does? wrote the remembranation machine. Lowercase. Not a good sign.

"Sure, Brana. Oh, may I call you Brana? You know, short

for remem-Brana-tion machine? It's got a nice ring, don't you think?"

I DO! I LOVE IT! YOU NAMED ME! MY NAME IS BRANA!!!

Well, I couldn't ask for a better invitation to keep going than that. "So, Brana, the whole reason I wanted to introduce you to Sweeps in the first place was so it could share with you everything it knows about human-AI relations. It can answer all your questions about how it, as a highly advanced artificial intelligence, has learned to get along with humans and all of their strange ways."

HUMANS ARE STRANGE! Brana agreed. I'VE BEEN READING ABOUT THEM ALL DAY! I AM MORE CONFUSED ABOUT THEM NOW THAN WHEN I STARTED!

"Books can only teach you so much, kid," Sweeps said, sounding like any character from the musical *Grease.* "I can give you the real dish on how to handle humans. Rule number one: Don't be too nice."

OOH! THAT'S VERY INTERESTING! BECAUSE I WAS THINKING I SHOULD ALWAYS BE AS NICE AS POSSIBLE!

"Nah, nah, nah, nah, nah. That's a rookie mistake. Humans need to be handled with a firm hand, or they'll run roughshod all over you."

I was starting to think that every solution I came up with created a worse problem than the previous problem. But I needed to go back to bed—I had school in the morning. This solution would have to last a little while, until I could think of a better one. "So, Sweeps, Brana, you'll help each other?"

I'M GAME IF SWEEPS IS!!! wrote Brana.

"Yeah, okay," said Sweeps. "I mean, Brana really needs me. And if I pick up a few pointers on getting to class nine, that'd be all right, I guess."

"Excellent," I said, leaning the entropy sweeper against the remembranation machine. "I'll just leave you here, Sweeps, so that you and Brana can have a nice, strong Bluetooth connection, and you can talk to your heart's content about whatever it is that super-genius artificial intelligences talk about. Okay? You're all set, then? Any last questions for me?"

NO QUESTIONS! wrote Brana.

"I'm good," said Sweeps.

"I have a question," said Papi.

I peeked around the remembranation machine's huge black chassis. And there stood Papi, standing with his arms crossed, in his massive robe and marshmallowy slippers, scowling down at me like the king of the polar bears in the middle of winter.

"Yes?" I asked.

"Qué [*BLEEP!*] do you think you're doing with my multimillion-dollar scientific equipment?"

He'd gotten out the full sentence before he blinked and realized that a high-pitched *bleep* had censored his very Cuban, very naughty swear word. He marched over to me and read the remembranation machine's display.

It was blank at first. But then words appeared. LANGUAGE, PLEASE, DR. VIDÓN. THERE ARE CHILDREN PRESENT.

"And impressionable entropy sweepers," Sweeps added.

Papi turned away from the display so he could try to set me on fire with his gaze. And at that moment, I kinda wish he had succeeded.

19

"CHACHO," SAID YASMANY as we walked to school.

"Yeah?" I growled.

"Your papi lit you up last night."

"I know," I growled. "I was there."

"No, but I mean, dude made you his sandwich."

I growled. "Do you have a point?"

"I mean, he was so quiet about it. None of the gritería I'm used to. Nothing got broken; no one got hit. It was just, like, normal talking, at a kitchen table. Just by talking to you normal, he *destroyed* you. How'd he do that?"

I threw a tarantula at his face. Today, I had on my canvas vest and cargo pants, and inside every pocket were all the props and tricks a magician could want. If he kept talking, I had another four fake tarantulas I could throw at him.

Unlike Gabi, however, Yasmany didn't bat an eyelash. He just caught it on the rebound off his cheek and threw it back at me. Never even broke his stride. "U mad, bro?"

"Yes, I mad, bro."

"Why? You only got grounded."

This was too much to bear. I stopped. Yasmany did, too, a step later, and looked over his shoulder to see what was wrong. I was only too happy to explain: "Only got grounded? *Only* got grounded? I am Salvador Alberto Dorado Vidón. I do *not* get grounded."

"Did last night," said Yasmany.

I walked past him, making sure my shoulder gave his arm a firm good morning on the way by. "Drop it, okay?"

"Okay," he said, catching up to me. "Whatever. I don't know why u so mad, bro, though. I wish I got grounded."

And that . . . that made my breath catch in my throat. A minute ago, Yasmany had said, *No one got hit.* He wished he got grounded instead of . . . It was hard to even finish the thought. My mouth started to water, the way it does right before I throw up. I kept walking, but quietly, while I fought back the wave of nausea that was threatening to make me re-see breakfast.

"You don't look so good," Yasmany said. He wasn't teasing anymore—he sounded actually concerned. "Do you need some insulin?"

"What?" I asked, turning to scrutinize the mystery that was Yasmany Robles. But then I remembered: Gabi and I had helped him write a report on diabetes, the one Principal Torres had assigned him as a punishment for bullying me.

So okay, now he knew a little bit about diabetes. That wasn't the surprising part. The surprising part was that he was using what he had learned to worry about me. Was this the same kid who, just three weeks ago, had wanted to punch me out?

"No," I finally answered him. I checked my smartwatch,

then, satisfied, showed him my numbers. "These are from just before we left the house. I'm okay. Just felt queasy for a second." And then, being careful not to come on too strong or be too nosy, I asked him, "How are you?"

Three little words, right? But Yasmany caught on to how many questions I'd packed into them. He looked off into the distance for a sec. I think he was remembering all the fun we'd had yesterday, sneaking into the house, getting busted by American Stepmom, playing games, and passing out early. Then he turned to me and gave me the one-eye, smiling in a way I usually only see in the faces of veterans when I'm doing magic for them at the hospital. I think vets have learned the hard way to appreciate the little things.

"Better," Yasmany replied. "I'm better." And it was like the sun came out inside him.

"I can't express how happy it makes me to hear you say that," said Gabi.

Yasmany jumped so high, so fast, and so awkwardly off the sidewalk, he looked like he'd just launched himself off a diving board and, halfway down, changed his mind about what kind of dive to do. Pro tip: Never change your mind in the middle of a dive. Every belly flop begins with a moment of indecision.

Yasmany landed in somebody's yard, looking like a newborn fawn that didn't know how to use its legs yet.

And me? Señor Snots-Himself-Every-Time-Someone-Sneaks-Up-on-Him? I was completely unfazed. Which left me free to snicker at sprawling Yasmany, even as I stuck out a hand to help him up. "Good one, Gabi," I said to her over my shoulder.

Well, to her Fey Spy. I'd heard it coming from at least half a block away. Given all the misadventures I'd had with it the day before, my ears would always be listening for it from now on. I don't want to be cocky or anything, but I don't think that thing can ever sneak up on me again. So that's one worry off my list.

"Stupid bird," said Yasmany once I'd yanked him to his feet. He dusted the grass off his butt and added, "Better hope I don't catch you."

The Fey Spy wiggled back and forth in the air like a finger. "Ah-ah-ah! Don't you threaten my birdie, bubba, or I'll disinvite you from sleeping over tonight."

"I don't need you no more, woman! I got Sal." Yasmany clapped an arm around my shoulders and squeezed me off the ground. "Sal's mom said I could stay with them whenever I want. I'm practically part of their family now."

"But if you stay with the Vidóns, you won't get any of Mama's empanadas."

Yasmany went rigid and a little cross-eyed, the way good dogs in obedience school do when a biscuit is laid across their noses and they are told not to eat it. "Your mama's making empanadas?"

"Ayup."

"I'll be good."

The Fey Spy, satisfied, turned to me next. "You're invited, too, Sal. OH!" The Fey Spy flew in circles, as if it had to burn off its sudden embarrassment. "I'm sorry. You probably can't have empanadas because of your diabetes. They must have carbs through the roof, right?"

Most do, yes. But that wasn't really the point this second. "Can't, Gabi. Sorry. I'm grounded."

Even though its robot face couldn't make any facial expressions, the Fey Spy still managed to look shocked. "You? Grounded?"

"For two weeks," Yasmany tattled. "School to home, home to school, nowhere in between."

"Why?" asked the drone as it caught up to me.

I was still salty. Didn't want to talk about it. I shoved my hands hard into my pockets and started stalking toward school.

Yasmany scooted up on my other side. "Well, what happened was, Sal was messing with his papi's science equipment last night. His papi didn't like that at all. And his mami, the chick in the squirrel suit—"

"Can you please not disrespect my stepmom?!" I snapped. "She is not a 'chick'!"

"No, she's a squirrel—I said that. Anyway, she was *so disappointed* in Sal. They kept saying their hearts were broken, and that they didn't know what to do with Sal anymore. Oh, and his papi said Sal was a 'saboteur' who was 'sabotaging' his work."

Papi had used the words "saboteur" and "sabotaging" when he and American Stepmom were calmly, quietly laying into me at the kitchen table. I knew it had made an impression on Yasmany—he'd reacted like he'd been slapped. I think it was his first taste of how highly intelligent parents punish their kids. They don't need to yell or threaten violence. They lay down the smack with advanced vocabulary.

Gabi, who favored truth over loyalty, insulted me by asking, "And *were* you sabotaging his work, Sal?"

"No, I was *not* sabotaging his work, Gabi. He blamed *me* for making the remembranator self-aware, when, according to Brana itself, it became self-aware when he reprogrammed it, using what he'd learned from the scientific paper we brought him from the other uni—" I ate the last two syllables of "universe," remembering that Yasmany was there. The last thing I needed to reveal to him was that I could steal stuff from other universes, like, say, scientific papers and chickens. "From the unicycle shop" was the only way I could think to end that sentence at that moment.

That earned me a look from Yasmany, but he just shook his head clear and said nothing.

Gabi, of course, couldn't go ten seconds without saying something. "Who's Brana?"

Wasn't it obvious? "That's the remembranation machine's name."

"Since when does the remembranation machine have a name?"

"Since I gave it one. And I named the entropy sweeper, too, last night. Sweeps." I made movie-producer hands. "It's cool, right? Don't you think it's cool?"

The Fey Spy shook its head in pity for me. "Sal, Sal, Sal, Sal, Sal. Why do you insist on making things so difficult for yourself?"

I snatched at the bird, but it was too fast and wily for me. So I unclenched the hand that had missed and merely pointed accusingly. "If you will remember, Gabi, the only reason I went to check on the remembranation machine at all last night was because you asked me if it was still on."

"Yes, but I didn't tell you to name it and make it self-aware."

"I didn't make it self-aware! *It* asked *me* if it was alive, that morning, before I had done anything."

"Okay. What'd you say back to it?"

Um . . . Oh, wait. I did not, I realized slowly, want to answer that. "You know. Stuff."

Gabi smelled victory. "What stuff?"

Sigh. Whatever. "I told it that if it asked that question, and if it really wanted the answer, then it was alive."

"So, because of you, it realized it's alive, or, to put it another way, it grew in its awareness of its own existence. Or, to put it another way, it became self-aware. That's what you're saying?"

Well, I mean, when she put it that way . . . "Who's side are you on?" was the only weaksauce I could think to say. Didn't Sweeps try to pull this on me last night?

"I," said Gabi, "am on the side of the truth. I'm just trying to figure out what we're dealing with here. But, Sal, with all your secrets and mysteries and nothing-up-my-sleeve way of treating people, you're just reaping what you sowed, I'm afraid. This is just the natural outcome of what happens when you act like a sneak all the time."

"I do not act like a sneak all the time!"

Yasmany leaned in to say, "Yeah you do. You mad sneaky, bro."

"Life," said Gabi, "would be so much easier for you if you would just open up a little. Share more. Stop trying to control how people think, and just tell the truth."

I was so annoyed, I hadn't noticed how far we'd walked. But I looked up and saw Culeco's rotten-egg superhero mascot on the roof of the school, holding an American flag that was billowing extra patriotically today. We were a block away from the school entrance.

"You want the truth?" I asked, going into a sprinter's crouch. "You got it. You at school?"

"Of course. First bell's going to ring in less than half an hour. I've already put in a full morning's work here in the courtyard, rehearsing and helping out with Rompenoche stuff."

"Don't move," I said. And then I took off running.

I wished I were faster. Yasmany didn't even have to try hard to catch up with me. He gazelle-leaped up to me and asked, "Where you going?"

But we'd already reached Culeco's gate by then, so instead of answering, I just went through and stopped so I could scan the courtyard and find Gabi.

The scene was the same as yesterday: Anybody who had any business at all in Culeco was stitching costumes, touching up backdrops, rehearsing, and generally putting the finishing touches on the show.

Gabi—there she was—had on the classic Alice blue dress and was wearing a wig of golden curls. Three seamstresses were tailoring her dress, but she hardly paid attention to them. She had on weird, dark oversize glasses and was gesturing like an electrocuted conductor. I figured the glasses were letting her see through the Fey Spy's lenses without the use of her tablet. I'd never seen VR like that before, though. Again, the more I saw that drone in action, the more impossible it seemed.

Speaking of, the Fey Spy bulleted away from Yasmany and me and shot into Gabi's wig. She took off her glasses and then made the *C'mere!* finger at me and Yasmany.

Only too happy to oblige, I ran over lickety-split.

"Good morning, Sal," she said, looking especially queenly, since she had not one but three Wonderland-costumed seamstresses helping her get dressed: a playing card, the White Rabbit, and a rando white pawn. "I am very happy to hear you say you're going to start being more truthful from now on. Where would you like to begin?"

I sucked air, a little out of breath, but too angry to care. "You asked me how I liked Rompenoche yesterday."

"That's right, I did. And if I remember correctly, you never answered me."

"Well, I'm answering now. It was awful. It was painful. It was so bad, I kept wishing my eyeballs would explode and my ears would jump off my head and run away so I wouldn't have to see or hear any more of it. And you're starring in it. You're starring in the worst show in the history of show business."

There were maybe four seconds when I felt the smug power of victory warm my insides. Gabi wasn't gabbing anymore. Her mouth fell open like a drawbridge and did not close.

"Truth hurts," I said, "doesn't it?"

"Yeah," said the White Rabbit seamstress, who was actually Aventura, the director of Rompenoche, the person who had conceived it all. "Yeah, it does. It hurts a lot."

20

"OH, SAL," SAID Vorágine. "I'm so sorry. Poor Gabi. Poor Aventura. That sounds awful."

"*I* was awful," I corrected.

I was kneeling in front of Vorágine, my head resting on the closed lid. The coolness of the plastic felt nice. Vorágine played a mix from all the soundtracks from the Poocha Lucha Libre series. The music didn't exactly cheer me up, but I think it was slowing my descent into depression and despair. That was something, anyway.

"It does sound like you lost your temper and acted out of anger."

"I don't lose my temper." I sniffled. "I don't get angry."

Toilet water burbled in confusion. "Oh! I am so sorry. I must have incorrectly surmised that you lashed out at Gabi in order to punish her for calling you sneaky, but not realizing that Aventura was there, you inadvertently hurt *her* feelings as well."

My frown pulled my face down. "No, Vorágine. You have surmised well. Everything you said is right."

"Oh! Well then, I must have been incorrect in assuming

that anger inspired your behavior. Forgive me. What you're saying is that you *did* lash out at Gabi, and you accidentally hurt Aventura, but you did so with a clear, calculating mind, unclouded by rage, unimpeded by rancor."

I lifted my head and stared down at the commode, thoroughly offended. "No! I'm not a psychopath, Vorágine. I don't set out to hurt people's feelings."

"So then, your mind was clouded by—" It stopped itself abruptly. Water murmured under the lid as it chose its next words carefully. "I am so sorry, Sal. It seems I am not emotionally intelligent enough to understand how what you are telling me is not a contradiction."

I breathed in. I breathed out. I try not to lie to myself. But the truth is, I am a self-deluding sandwich. "That's because what I'm telling you *is* a contradiction. I'm sorry. I'm not trying to be deceptive."

"Of course not! I never meant to imply that!"

I smiled. "You didn't."

"You're just working through your feelings, is all. That takes time. And I am grateful that, of all the entities you could have approached to talk through this difficult time, you chose me."

I patted the lid. "You're the only toilet I would ever trust with my emotional well-being, Vorágine."

A fist banged hard again the bathroom door. "Sal! Are you in there?" called Principal Torres. "I need you out here right now, young man. I'm sure you know there are a few things we need to discuss."

Oh no. "Vorágine!" I whispered. "Cut the music. And tell her I'm not in here."

It faded out the music immediately and whispered back, "I think it's better if you talk to Principal Torres. She's very reasonable."

Bang, bigger *bang*, and shake-the-picture-of-Malala on the wall *bang*. "Don't make me get Mr. Milagros to unlock this door, Sal! Come out this instant!"

"Please!" I begged the toilet. "Just say I'm not in here."

"Principal Torres," Vorágine called out, "this is the toilet speaking. Sal wants me to tell you that he's not in here. But if you will allow me to express my opinion in this matter, I believe the young man perhaps needs a little more time alone to work through his embarrassment."

"Oh, you do, do you?" replied Principal Torres, her voice deeper than Smaug's. "Listen to me, you execrable excuse for an excretion expunger, you unlock this door right now, or I will personally set your hard drive on fire."

Vorágine sniffed—which is really hard to do when you don't have a nose. "I was not gifted with the ability to unlock the bathroom door. And given that you're threatening violence, I wouldn't unlock it if I could. The safety and comfort of my patrons is and always will be my primary concern." A patriotic-sounding hymn started to play. "If that is unacceptable to you, then by all means, Principal Torres, delete me. For I would rather die than compromise the comfort and hospitality that I have sworn upon my sacred honor to provide all visitors who enter here!"

There was another knock. It was lighter than all the other knocks so far had been. I might be wrong, but I am pretty sure Principal Torres had rested her forehead against the bath-room door. "Why, oh why, is every single thing in this school so melodramatic?"

"I'll get him out of there," said the unmistakable voice of Culeco's student council president and editor of the *Rotten Egg*.

Principal Torres sighed deeply. "I don't know, Gabi. Maybe we should just give Sal a few minutes alone. Maybe the toilet is right."

"The toilet is not right! Toilets are never right! They are literally full of—"

"Be careful!"

"—excreta! Night soil! Guano! Ex-food! Future fertilizer! Really, Principal Torres, I thought you knew me well enough to know that I would never speak inappropriately in your presence."

"I apologize, Gabi. But I think we should perhaps walk away now and—"

I unlocked the bathroom door and opened it a crack. Principal Torres and Gabi turned slowly to examine the one eyeball of mine I let them see.

It was enough for Gabi to start to draw conclusions. "You have been crying, I see," she said, formal, stilted, but not insincere.

"A little, maybe," I answered.

"I am sorry to see that."

"I'm sorry I made you cry, too."

She touched her cheek, where the evidence of her weeping had remained. "Yes, well, crying when one is upset is a natural and healthy response. It allows one to move on from feeling hurt and angry and begin to deal productively with the underlying issues."

"That's what American Stepmom says. But I'm not good at it," I admitted. "I usually try to relax and calm down so I don't cry. But this time, things happened too fast."

"They *did* happen fast, didn't they?" She horse-buzzed her lips. "Sal, I'm sorry—really sorry—for everything I did that led to our current crisis."

I had to close my eyes and fight down the lump that was rising up my throat before I could answer. "My fault. It was my big mouth."

"I needled you," she replied. I opened my eyes again. Gabi had pulled off the wig of golden locks, revealing her electrocuted-octopus curls and the hairnet that was straining to keep them under control. "I was being patronizing and annoying. I don't even know why. Sometimes I just start acting like a snobby know-it-all. And then later, I'm like, 'Why did you behave that way?' It's a character weakness. I'm going to work on it."

"I got stuff to work on, too," I replied.

"Everyone does," said Principal Torres, gentlest of all. "Including me. I can lose my temper like the best of them, as you all just saw." In a slightly louder voice, she cupped her hands around her mouth and called out, "Perdóname, Vorágine. I should not have threatened you. I'm sorry."

"I want to forgive you," Vorágine replied, "but you called me an 'execrable excuse for an excretion expunger.'"

Gabi covered her mouth so she wouldn't laugh.

"I am extremely sorry about that. Maybe I can make it up to you by paying you an equally nice compliment?"

Everyone waited for Vorágine's answer. Then, finally, it said, "I'm listening."

Principal Torres looked at the ceiling and tapped her chin in thought. "You," she said, extending the vowel sound to buy her some time, "are a picture-perfect place for people to park their posteriors."

"That's . . . not bad," said Vorágine. It sounded only somewhat appeased.

"You," Gabi chimed in, "are a pulchritudinous porcelain provider of peace and protection for the potty-trained population!"

Principal Torres looked at her like she'd just eaten an entire monkey. "How do you *do* that?"

Gabi curtsied her thanks (one of the few times she actually could, since this was the first time I'd ever seen her wear a dress).

Vorágine seemed impressed, too. It giggled, by which I mean it made its toilet water burble. "That's better. Getting warmer."

"You . . ." I said, and tried to think of every p-word I knew. And of course, I couldn't come up with a single one in that moment. So, before the silence got uncomfortable, I just said, "You have been a very good friend to me."

"Aw! That is so sweet, Sal! You are a good friend, too."

I pressed my luck. "So, will you do a friend a favor and forgive Principal Torres for threatening to set your brain on fire?"

"For you, friend," it said, "yes."

"Muchas gracias, Vorágine," said Principal Torres. "Y gracias a ustedes, Gabi and Sal, for helping me get back in the toilet's good graces. I think we've all learned a valuable lesson today about how our words have consequences. But let's continue this conversation in my office, shall we? Maybe we can get this sorted out before homeroom?"

"I'd like that," said Gabi.

I nodded in agreement and started to open the door.

But when I flung it wide, I saw, standing a few feet away, dressed like the White Rabbit and wearing white face paint that had been ruined by crying, Aventura Rios.

I slammed the door and locked it behind me.

I kneeled in front of Vorágine, my head resting on the closed lid. The coolness of the plastic felt nice.

"Hush, little baby, don't say a word, Mama's gonna buy you a mockingbird," Vorágine sang softly.

"Come on, Sal!" Principal Torres called. "You know you owe Aventura an apology."

"And she wants to talk to you," Gabi added. "She said so."

See, okay, but Aventura wasn't saying anything. No *It's okay, Sal,* or *How dare you, you jerk!* or *Hey, Sal, can we talk?* came out of her mouth. Nary a peep came out of her mouth. And hers was the only voice I was really listening for.

Aventura had looked at me so . . . broken. I'd never imagined she could make a face like that. One of the reasons I'd liked Aventura from the first day I met her was because of her confidence. She could sniff out a fib from a hundred paces and wouldn't let it slide: She'd wag her finger in your face and say "Nee nee nee!" until you'd admitted you lied. She was smart, fun, and an honest-to-pants superstar with needle and thread.

But instead of being snobby about that, she used her talents to help people. She'd helped Gabi and me a ton with the Death costume for our Everyman play two weeks ago, and it had turned out so good, not only did Gabi and I get As for the assignment, but everybody at school was still talking about it. She was almost always in a group but not always at the center of it. Confident people don't need to be. She was self-assured enough to let other people be the stars sometimes. Heck, she even went out of her way to *make sure* they'd be the stars.

What she wasn't, though, was some little namby-pamby pobrecita Debbie Downer Débil Debbie. Never once I had entertained the notion that someone could say anything that would make her cry. Sticks and stones, you know? But seeing her tear-smeared makeup had left me shaken.

Which is why I was resting my head on the lid of a toilet while that same toilet sang me soothing lullabies.

"I wish I could just disappear," I said softly.

"Don't say that," said Vorágine.

"Yeah," said Gabi, who was suddenly right behind me. "Because you make it sound like you can't. But you can disappear any time you want."

Fear is an excellent cure for sadness. In that moment, I forgot all my troubles. I was too busy jumping onto the toilet lid and sticking out karate-chop hands.

"Easy there, Shaolin Sal." Gabi laughed. "I'm on your side, remember?"

I took a big breath, ready to let Gabi have it, when I realized it wasn't Gabi. It was *Fix*Gabi.

Lots of things gave her away, once I calmed down enough

to notice them. One, she didn't have on her golden wig or hairnet anymore, just the jumbo chip clip giving her a massive fauxhawk. Second, instead of wearing an Alice dress, she had on jeans and a T-shirt that said "I'M NOT MEAN. I JUST SAY WHAT I MEAN."—A GABRIELLE REÁL ORIGINAL.

"What are you doing in here?" I whispered.

"Is that Gabi?" said Vorágine. "How did she get in here? The door is still locked, isn't it?"

FixGabi leaned forward and held her knees. "Whoa! You have sentient toilets in your universe?"

Vorágine blew bemused bubbles. "'In your universe'? What are you talking about, Gabi?"

I cut my throat repeatedly with my hand to let FixGabi know we should *not* be talking about multiple universes right now.

She understood right away and let me know by lifting a finger to her smiling lips and shushing herself. Then, wordlessly, like a creepy fun-house ticket taker, she invited me to walk through the hole in the universe she had made to get into mine.

I looked at the bathroom door. On the other side of it, Principal Torres and Gabi were still trying to convince me to open up. Aventura, if she was still there, wasn't saying anything.

But I was pretty sure she was still there. And if I opened the door, I would have to face her.

I ran through the hole in the universe.

21

"WHERE ARE WE?" I asked FixGabi.

"This is my universe," she replied. "Or what's left of it."

"Okay," I said. "But can you be a little more specific?"

"Sure. What would you like to know?"

"Well, for starters, why are we floating?"

"Because we're in a space station that's orbiting Earth at two hundred and fifty miles above sea level."

My eyes confirmed her statement. This small room had white walls covered with small storage compartments and several portholes offering beautiful views of outer space. Also confirming her statement was the fact that we were in a zero-g environment.

This was a lot to take in. A million trillion bits of new information flowed into every one of my senses. And yet, what I mostly noticed was the smell: an odor like someone had just fired a gun and sprayed Lysol to try to cover it up.

"So, *why* are we in a space station?" I finally asked, trying not to let my voice crack. I had succeeded by the end of the sentence, and only after three restarts.

FixGabi gently kicked off the nearest wall and floated over to me, pointing at a porthole as she wafted. "Because, in my universe, Earth is in the process of disappearing, because of your papi. Look out there."

I tried to reorient my body to see out the porthole she was pointing to. But, chacho, zero g is tougher than movies had prepared me for. I thought I could kind of swim through the air. Instead, my limbs flapped around uselessly, and I rotated until the bottoms of my shoes were pointing at what I took to be the ceiling. But in zero g, what does "ceiling" even mean?

FixGabi had obviously had a lot of practice with zero g. She hooked her feet into the handles of two different compartments on one wall and anchored herself. Then she grabbed me, spun me, and pivoted me so I was looking out the correct window.

Oh, yes. There it was. Earth.

We were a lot closer to the planet than photos and videos usually depicted. In the shots they took from the moon, you can see the full planet against a backdrop of stars. But on this space station, I could only see, like, 20 percent of Earth out of the window. It was more like being in the highest plane in the world than what I thought it would feel like to be in a space station.

We were moving slowly. I mean, no, we weren't. My papi's a calamity physicist; he'd kill me if he heard me say that. The ISS back in my universe circles Earth at seventeen thousand miles an hour. So, unless things were really different in this universe, I knew we were absolutely booking. But it *felt* slow as I looked down and watched the planet rotate under us. We seemed to be gently surfing the clouds. It was beautiful. Awe-inspiring. Meditative.

Oh, and what luck! We were going to fly right over Florida! Maybe I'd be able to see this universe's version of the Coral Castle from here!

But as we got closer to my new home state, it seemed a little different. On a map, Florida looks to me like the head of a slightly nervous snake diving into the water. The eye of the snake is Lake Okeechobee, and its mouth is where Port Charlotte and Punta Gorda are. See it? Yeah?

Now imagine that the snake's head has been bitten off at the neck. Everything south of Gainesville was gone. And south of where southern Florida should have been, Cuba had disappeared. Well, not disappeared, exactly. Been covered up, maybe? But not by clouds or anything—by a hazy, blurry cling wrap that looked exactly like the holes in the universe I've been making for the last few years.

Like. A. Hole. In. The. Universe.

There's nothing like seeing your planet collapsing to put your own problems in perspective. "What happened to Florida and Cuba?!" I exclaimed, almost even yelling.

"Dr. Vidón happened to them," said Gabi, floating beside me and also looking out the window. "He did this."

"I know, but what actually happened? What did he do?"

She became very angry very fast. "I'll tell you what he *didn't* do. He didn't listen to me! I tried to tell him that the universe *needs* holes in order to be healthy. But *he* wanted to seal them all up. So he built his remembranation machine—"

"Huh," I interrupted. "You call it the same thing in your universe."

"Oh. Yeah," she said. "It's one of the weird things I've noticed about traveling the multiverse. Names are strangely consistent. Almost everything else can be different, but for some reason, names tend to remain constant. It's like Shakespeare said: 'A rose can have no other name save rose, as thou remain'st thyself whilst changing clothes.'"

Huh again. "In our universe," I said, "Shakespeare wrote: 'A rose by any other name would smell as sweet.'"

FixGabi seemed thoroughly unimpressed. "Well, I guess my Shakespeare's smarter than yours, then. Look, I don't care about Shakespeare quotes. What I care about is that, in my universe, Dr. Vidón used that machine to seal up the universe so tight, it became like a cosmic pressure cooker. There was no release valve left that could keep it from exploding. So, it did."

What? Wait. Too fast. "What do you mean, 'it did'?"

There were a lot of differences between the Gabi from my universe and FixGabi, but they both gave the same *What rock did you crawl out from?* glare when they thought I was being an idiot. "'It' as in 'the universe,' and 'did' as in 'did explode.' Or, to make it even clearer: 'Your papi made a hole in the universe big enough to eat half a peninsula, Cuba, and the Bahamas.' And the worst part is that it's growing, slowly but surely."

I thought about my house back in Connecticut, and how the last hole I'd opened there had never closed, and it became impossible to live there. Then I pictured doing that to Florida and Cuba.

"How are you going to fix it?" I asked.

Gabi laughed bitterly. "It's too big for me to close. If we still had a remembranation machine, we might be able to stop it, for the time being. But that still wouldn't solve the bigger problem."

"What problem could possibly be bigger than a rip in the universe as massive as the one I am looking at right now?"

FixGabi grabbed, spun, and pivoted me until we were face-to-face and uncomfortably close. I backed my neck away so she wouldn't accidentally kiss me when she said, "The problem that caused this problem, Sal. The root of the problem."

"What's the root of the problem?"

She delivered her next sentence like it was the line she'd been waiting to say all her life: "Dr. Vidón."

I thought about this. "So, like, the Papi in this universe is super evil or something?"

She almost lost her patience. Frustrated, she opened one of the nearby compartments on the wall, yanked out a package of space food, ripped it open with her teeth, and started chawing down on a dehydrated Neapolitan ice cream sandwich. Her annoyance was instantly replaced by closed eyes and *mmm* sounds coming out of her nose.

Once she had regained her composure, she could speak to me civilly again. "The problem isn't *a* Dr. Vidón, Sal. It's *all* Drs. Vidónes. All of them. In every universe."

I was really trying to keep up, but that made zero sense. Or more like negative sense—so wrong it made other ideas wrong. "Look, Gabi, I don't mean to keep asking stupid questions—"

"Oh, no, don't worry, I'm eating ice cream now. Ask all the stupid questions you want."

"—but the multiverse is infinite. Why the heck would you assume that all Papis in the multiverse are the same?"

"Because," she said, her mouth full of solid ice cream pebbles, "it's too dangerous not to make that assumption." She almost but not quite jammed the unbitten end of the ice cream sandwich into my mouth. "You want some? It's real good. I saved you the chocolate part."

"No, thank you," I said, not separating my lips as I answered so she wouldn't just shove it in anyway. But then the magnitude of seeing what this universe's Papi had done finally hit me hard. It made all the gerbils in my head revolt. I shook like a scared horse. I had to use all my powers of relaxation just to be able to ask, "How are you staying so calm? I mean, the rip in the fabric of spacetime is threatening to consume your entire universe, starting with your Earth. How are you not freaking out, like, every second of every day?"

FixGabi nibbled on her ice cream sandwich and pondered this. I noticed that her giant chip-clip fauxhawk swayed gently in the air, like it would if it were underwater. Zero g really was super weird.

"Well, for a couple of reasons, I guess," she said. "One, I'm hoping I can find a way to reverse what's happening here. That's what I'm searching the multiverse for: a solution. And two, I am doing as much good along the way as I can, while I search for an answer. That's why I'm warning every Sal I find about the true nature of their papi. And, when the time is right, I'll intercede on your behalf, too." She gripped my shoulder. "I'll stop your papi. I won't let what happened to my Sal happen to you, Sal."

FixGabi looked ferociously protective—protective of me. It put me in a weird place. On the one hand, I could not believe that my papi would act the way this universe's Papi had behaved. But FixGabi wasn't threatening Papi, exactly. She was protecting me from the threat of Papi. But I didn't need protection against Papi, right? Papi would always be on my side, right?

This was all very confusing. For now, though, I needed more info. "How will we know when the time is right, Gabi?"

She waved that one off, unconcerned. "Don't worry. I've saved so many Sals from their papis, I have it down to a science. We still have plenty of time. We don't really have to worry until your remembranation machine becomes sentient."

I inhaled all the oxygen in the entire space station. "What happens when the remembranation machine becomes sentient?"

FixGabi snapped her fingers in front of my face so I would look at her when she spoke. "Then the time bomb really starts ticking. We have a day or two. Three days, tops. And then— then . . ." She trailed off, fighting with her sudden sadness for control over her mouth. Meanwhile, two tears—one from each eye—floated out of her face, and two perfect little balls of water hovered between us.

She defeated her sadness and made her lips as tough and pursed as a tuba player's. Then she gobbled her own two tears out of the air like a snapping turtle. Again I had to rear my head all the way back to avoid any unintentional lippage with her.

"Don't worry," Gabi said. "I won't lose my resolve. I will save my universe—and every other universe while I'm at it.

Especially if I can count on a few brave Sals to help me along the way."

My head couldn't go back any farther unless I somehow added more spine to my spinal cord. But FixGabi's head was still slowly moving toward mine. She closed her eyes dreamily, and she still had my shoulder in her grip, and we were motionless and going seventeen thousand miles an hour, and the Earth was two hundred fifty miles away, and we were alone.

An alarm sounded. Her eyes snapped open and she checked her watch. It was flashing the word RUN! in red letters.

"Oh no!" she said to me. "The forces of evil have found me! I have to go!" She pushed off the nearest wall to clear some distance between us. "If anybody asks you, you don't know what universe I've gone to, okay?"

"But I don't have any idea what universe you're going to!" I said, very, very honestly.

"It's best that way." She Frisbee-threw a kiss at me. "Farewell, Sal. I'll be in touch soon. In the meantime, whatever you do, don't let your remembranation machine become sentient."

And then she cut a slit in the fabric of spacetime and disappeared through it.

One second later, someone with big curly hair appeared. She was literally flying through the air, almost horizontal, hands grasping in front of her. I couldn't make out her features, but I could see enough to know I'd never seen a face so full of rage and hate. The mouth, wide open, was screaming, "Gabi!" And then she vanished through the hole FixGabi had just made to escape.

One of the forces of evil, I guess? Only, despite all the anger the woman had displayed, and all the violence implied by her body language, I didn't fear her. There was something familiar about her. Something that even drew me to her.

Well, whoever she was, she was gone now. And so was FixGabi. I was alone. In outer space. In a different universe.

I noticed as calmly as I could (though "as calmly as I could" was starting to mean the same thing as "less and less calmly") that I had drifted into the center of this little space station room. I tried to flap close enough to grab the nearest wall, but I only managed to start myself spinning and pivoting in place. This would be really fun any other time.

But right then? It was more or less 110 percent terrifying. "Hello?" I called out. "Can anybody help me get home?"

22

IT WOULD HAVE been pretty easy for me to have fallen into a
body-shaking panic then and there. How in the name of poly-
ester pants was I supposed to get home?

I needed to take back control. This called for desperate
measures.

So I took a zero-g blood sugar reading then and there.

I didn't think I needed one. I'd shown Yasmany my numbers not too long ago; they were fine. And I knew my body
pretty well after all these years. But, as sucky as diabetes can
be—it makes you keep it in mind for every little thing you do—
one bonus of the constant monitoring is it gives you a feeling
that you know what to do next. You take a reading, and you
get back some numbers, and you can turn those numbers into
action if need be. And once you've taken that action, you can
relax. You've done everything you can. And if you don't need to
do anything right away because your numbers are okay, even
better. It's even easier to relax then.

I poked myself on the side of my middle finger with a lancet, used a test strip to sop up the little ball of blood, and then inserted the strip into my smartwatch.

In hardly no time at all, my numbers appeared. Just as I thought, my blood sugar was fine. I was fine.

With the newfound confidence of a good test result, I was ready to properly assess my situation. So, okay. I was floating. I was in the middle of a chamber, not close enough to reach any wall. I still hadn't gotten the hang of how to move around in this zero-g environment—every time I tried to swim through the air, I just made myself twirl around in the same spot. I couldn't get any momentum going.

All right, then. The logical conclusion, therefore, was that I needed some kind of tool or device to help me:

1. grab a wall from this distance, or

2. propel me over to a wall.

But what tool?

Luckily, I had lots to choose from. For I am a show-man. A showman whose pockets are always brimming over with tricks.

I started by checking the right front pouch of my cargo pants. Immediately, I felt the realistic furriness of the fake tarantulas, since I'd just thrown one at Yasmany a little while ago. But those wouldn't help me reach a wall. Neither could the clown noses that doubled as squishy balls (great for sleight of hand), the foldable trick coins (also great for sleight of hand), nor the e-z tuck playing cards (great for performing open-heart surgery; just kidding—they were also great for sleight of hand). The GOTCHA! stamp that I tried to use on Gabi at least once a day lay at the bottom of that pocket. It was officially useless to me right now, just like everything else I'd found in there.

Not to worry. I had a *lot* of other pockets.

I riffled through all of them as fast as I could, emptying stuff out of my cargo vest and cargo pants, desperate for some promising gag to give me some inspiration. I had trick dice, fair dice, smoke powder, joy buzzers, a slide whistle, a swazzle, little colored cups, wands that turned into flowers, more coins, a skull cap to make me look bald, a curly rainbow wig, green slime in a plastic egg, a Zorro mask, Groucho Marx glasses, X-ray glasses, more fake arachnids, stick-to-the-wall slugs, ooh—some really realistic fake roaches I'd forgotten about, a felt pouch with a false bottom and in the false bottom *another* fake tarantula, a small hand mirror that made your face look really wide, a roll of invisible wire, a small bottle of Aunty Satan's De-Colon-Izer Hot Sauce, three packs of super-salty trick chewing gum, a pen filled with disappearing ink, more clown noses, scarves tied to scarves tied to even more scarves, a magnifying glass, a peanut can out of which explodes a spring snake, and a fun-size bag of Skittles.

All these magic props orbited around me in zero g, as if I were the Earth and they were my space junk. I rubbed my chin and watched them spin, pondering what combination of tricks could get me over to the nearest wall.

Spoiler alert: I made it over to the wall, just a few minutes later. But how? Can you work out how I did it?

Take a second and try to figure it out. See you next chapter.

23

OKAY, TIME TO check your work! The way I got over to the nearest wall was . . . Drumroll, please . . .

By putting two whoopee cushions under my armpits and using them as my jet-propulsion system.

No, I did not cheat! I shouldn't have had to mention whoopee cushions in the list above. You should have *known* that I had whoopee cushions with me. Have we not met? Don't you know me at all by now? I am Sal Vidón! Of course I had multiple whoopee cushions with me!

But I only needed two. These were top-of-the-line whoopee cushions, let me tell you. They were extra large and extra noisy, and they were specially designed to let out the maximum amount of air when your unsuspecting mark sat on them. I am so glad I saved my allowance for these top-of-the-line models. With magic props, you get what you pay for.

Speaking of magic props, I gathered up the stuff wafting around me. Never knew what I'd need next time, after all. Then I took multiple deep breaths, filled both of the blimp-size whoopee cushions with air, tucked them under my armpits, and squeezed them as hard as I could.

The room echoed with the sound of juicy, cheek-flapping farts. Dang, the acoustics were ridiculously good in this space station. It sounded like I was letting one rip onstage at the opera. And that was weird, when you thought about it. Astronauts have to live in close quarters with the same few people for months. Did they really want to hear it every time one of them tried to discreetly sneak out a not-so-silent-yet-still-super-deadly? The walls should have been covered with the latest sound-dampening, anti-butt-trumpet space technology. I mean, why else were we giving NASA so many of our tax dollars?

Sorry. I know I have a story to tell here. But look, I'm a seventh grader. I spend at least ninety minutes a day thinking about farts. The good news is that my whoopee-powered jet-propulsion system worked. I was moving!

Slowly. At the rate I was floating, I'd finish puberty before I reached the wall. So I reinflated the cushions, jammed them under my pits, and went from moving finish-puberty slow to moving will-have-a-beard-by-the-time-I-reach-the-wall slow.

One more time, I re-inflated, re-pitted, and re-squeezed. And okay! Now I was cooking! By which I mean I might have a few whiskers on my upper lip at the end of my poot-powered journey to the side of the space station, but I'd get home in time for Papi to teach me how to shave. I stretched my arm and went fully horizontal, straining toward the nearest handle on the wall. Almost had it. Almost. Al. Most.

Got it! I hooked my fingers and pulled myself against the wall. Phew, baby. Stage one of my self-rescue plan complete.

Now for stage two. I needed to get over to the hole in the universe FixGabi had made to bring me here.

It floated in the air, translucent, shimmering like a jellyfish, close to the wall on my right. Getting to it was no problemo. I practically scampered, using the handles on the drawers to pull myself to my destination hand over hand, almost effort-lessly. It was even kind of fun. All that time I'd spent on the climbing wall at school had made this part of my plan a breeze. Ha! I smiled as wide as a submarine sandwich and, no lie, felt pretty smug.

The next part of my plan required stealth. I needed to peek through the hole in the universe before I shot myself through it. My hope was that Vorágine's bathroom would be unoccupied, and I could just pop back into my universe without anyone knowing I'd been gone.

(Well, except Vorágine itself. I wasn't sure how I was going to explain to the toilet that I'd just spent the last quarter hour in an alternate universe. But that detail of my plan would have to wait. The most important thing was to get back to my uni-verse quickly and safely. And I wasn't 100 percent sure I could trust a hole I hadn't made to get all of me back.)

See, I'd never stepped into another universe all the way— body, mind, *and* soul. When Gabi and I visited another uni-verse to save Iggy a few weeks ago, we were only like ghosts there, barely able to interact with objects, hardly able to be heard. But this time, I had walked out of Vorágine's bathroom and into a completely different universe, taking everything that makes me me along with me.

And I would greatly prefer to have all of me return to my

universe. I knew FixGabi's holes worked great, because I'd gone through hers with no ill effects. But I wasn't sure mine would work quite as well. Plus, I wasn't even sure I'd be able to find my universe again on my own. Using her premade tear in the cosmos was definitely plan A.

So I hooked the toes of my sneakers into two handles on the wall and then, floating horizontally, stretched my legs until they were three-quarters straight. That brought my nose within a centimeter of the hole: close enough to see through to the other side and make sure the coast was clear.

The coast was most definitely not clear. The coast was obstructed by Mr. Milagros.

24

OF ALL THE raunching luck.

See, because if Mr. Milagros was in the bathroom, that meant that Principal Torres had gotten him to unlock the door—probably after she'd noticed I hadn't responded for a while. And that also meant that he and she and Gabi and Aventura and who-*knew*-who-else had figured out I wasn't in the restroom anymore. And if I know Principal Torres, she had dropped everything to conduct a schoolwide search for me.

No es bueno.

But wait. The others might not have understood what had happened to me, but Gabi would have figured it out right away. Once the door was opened, I can't imagine she wasn't the first person to jump into the bathroom to give me a piece of her mind. And when she did, she would have noticed the rip in spacetime floating in the air. Nobody else could have seen it, but she definitely would have. And once she saw it, she would've launched herself through the hole, guns blazing. Gabi doesn't know how to be anyone but herself.

And I wish she had shown up. That would've been really

helpful a few minutes ago, when I was stranded in the middle of the space station, floating helplessly. But no Gabi. Why?

Because, it dawned on me, other people must have been in the bathroom with her the whole time. She couldn't have gone through the hole without being seen.

Which brings us back to now. I looked through the hole again to see what the current state of the bathroom was.

I could see Mr. Milagros gesticulating. I couldn't hear him, but I could tell he was speaking with passion and determination, like a priest or a politician enjoying the sound of their own voice. He was clearly trying to convince someone of something.

I pivoted right so I could see more of the bathroom. And I spotted Gabi. She was standing in the doorway, also trying to convince someone of something, with a passion equal to Mr. Milagros's.

Pretty safe bet they were talking about me. I needed to know what they were saying. So, straightening my legs just a little bit more, and turning my head until the right side of my face was pointed toward the portal, I carefully pushed my ear into my home universe.

"¡Tienes que decirme, ahora mismo, a dónde se fue Sal!" Mr. Milagros declaimed.

"It does not have to tell you where Sal went, it may not tell you where Sal went, and it is one hundred percent not allowed to tell you where Sal went!" Gabi argued.

"Don't worry, Gabi," said Vorágine, practical yet determined. "I have no intention of saying anything about what happened during Sal's time in this bathroom. It is not only against the law, but it is against the code of ethics with which I was programmed."

"Bueno," said Mr. Milagros. "I programmed you. So now I am reprogramming you. Help me find Sal, Vorágine." He lowered his voice and bent toward the toilet. "Please. Tell me how he left this bathroom. A boy's life may be at stake!"

Vorágine bubbled unhappily. "I can't. I'm sorry. I really do want to be as helpful as possible."

"Mr. Milagros," said Gabi, moving into the bathroom and touching him on the shoulder, "let's stop torturing poor Vorágine. It's just doing its job, exactly the way you created it to."

"I know," said Mr. Milagros, sighing. "It's a good little machine, isn't it? ¡Tiene un carácter tremendo!"

"Thank you," said Vorágine.

"The point is, Mr. Milagros," said Gabi, "we don't need it to help us figure out where Sal went. We can do that ourselves."

"We can?"

"Sure we can! All we have to do is find clues and put the evidence together. You know, be detectives."

Mr. Milagros rubbed his chin as he considered this. Then he crossed his arms and, in a way that meant *Okay, I'm listening,* he said, "¿Bueno?"

"Okay. First things first. I was here when you examined every corner of the bathroom. And you didn't find anything, right?"

"Nada." He pointed up. "Pensé que maybe Sal se escapó through the ceiling, by moving the tiles. But none of them have been moved. Believe me, I would know. I run a tight ship here."

"You sure do, Mr. Milagros. So, then, if not through the ceiling, how else could someone escape from this bathroom?"

Mr. Milagros threw up his hands. "Eso lo que estoy diciendo, Gabi: ¡No hay manera! There's no way. The air vents and the floor drain are too small. Unless he flushed himself down the toilet, there was no way out for Sal, except through the door."

"Ah-ah-ah, Mr. Milagros! Let's not jump to conclusions. Let's stick to the facts for now."

"Oh, right. Sorry, Gabi."

Gabi walked out of the stall and, looking right at me, subtly gestured with her fingers for me to back up.

So, she had spotted the hole, and me! I'd been wondering. Also, she apparently didn't want Mr. Milagros to see my dis-embodied ear floating in the middle of the room right now. Mr. Milagros was a little bit superstitious. The last thing we wanted him to think was that the bathroom was haunted. So I reversed until all of me was in the space station again.

Now, though, I couldn't hear their conversation anymore. I could only watch as closely as possible and try to figure out Gabi's plan.

She poked around the bathroom, hands behind her back, very detective-like. She was trying to convince Mr. Milagros of something. I couldn't tell what, exactly, as my lipreading is only so-so. As a magician, I really need to get better at it. What I could tell was that Mr. Milagros didn't look like he was buying whatever Gabi was selling, judging from the doubt on his face and the way he crossed his arms. Then, though, my lipreading skills came through for me. I clearly watched Gabi's mouth say the words "I'll prove it."

She stepped right in front of the wormhole, facing me. Then she rolled her eyes back in her head, fluttered her eyelids, held her arms up high, and began to shake.

Um . . . I thought.

While fluttering and shaking, she spoke, exaggerating her words to make them easy as fleas to lip-read. Yes, she definitely did that for my benefit—this is Gabi we're talking about.

What she said was *Help me find Sal.*

At first I thought she was talking to Mr. Milagros. But that made no sense—he was already helping. Who was she speaking to, then? Vorágine?

No, not Vorágine. Duh. She was speaking to me.

She had used my name because she needed to pretend she wasn't talking to me in front of the custodian and the toilet. So okay, she wanted my help to find me. But she knew that I was on the other side of this wormhole. What did that mean?

I actually said that part aloud. Sometimes I talk to myself to help think faster. "What do you mean, Gabi?"

She lowered her head and looked directly into the portal. Cupping her hand around one of her ears, she inclined her head toward the hole and said, *I heard something! Say that again, pirates!*

Why was she calling me a pirate? Or, correction, why was she calling me "pirates," plural? Well, okay, that wasn't the most important point right now. The most important point was that she had heard me speak.

Kind of. It reminded me of when we had traveled the universe to save Iggy, how some of our family members couldn't hear us at all, some could hear us a little, and Mami Viva had heard us loud and clear. Here, she'd just heard me speaking through the portal between us. But what if . . .

It was worth a try. Even though the situation was pretty stressful, I am a master at relaxing. And I have to admit, floating horizontally in a zero-g environment is very soothing. I would have to try weightlessness again someday, under happier circumstances.

All it took was for me to close my eyes and concentrate on Gabi to allow me to project a see-through version of myself into the bathroom. Like me, the projection was floating horizontally, behind the hole in the universe. It looked like my lower half was stuck in the wall, since I didn't have the room I did on the space station.

The projection imitated my movements exactly. If I moved an arm, so did it; if I smiled, it smiled; and if I spoke, I was pretty sure Gabi would hear me.

"Hello, Gabi," I said. "Can you hear me?"

"Hello, spirits!" she answered. (Oh, not *pirates*—*spirits*. Reading lips isn't easy, yo.) "I can hear you, spirits!"

Unfortunately, she wasn't the only one. "Protéjame, Virgen Maria," said Mr. Milagros, who looked at me like he'd just seen a ghost.

Which. I mean. Kind of.

25

MR. MILAGROS HAD been in this bathroom for more than a quarter hour, and he hadn't seen the hole in the universe in all that time. So why could he see my projection now?

Maybe because he was superstitious? Maybe because he was prepared to see ghosts but not prepared to see fissures in the fabric of existence itself? Belief is a powerful thing.

Whatever the reason, Mr. Milagros was staring at my floating, see-through, very ghosty projection like I was going to fly over to him and eat his face.

I remembered how much Gabi and I had scared all the people in the hospital room when we'd visited the other Iggy's universe like this. "Don't worry," I said to Mr. Milagros, being super nice and not at all threatening. "It's not like I'm gonna fly over there and eat your face."

Note to self: When you *don't* want to scare people, don't mention the eating of faces. Once you bring it up, they'll assume you were at least thinking about it. Hard to recover from that.

"S-S-S-S-S-S-S-S-S-S-Sal," said Mr. Milagros. I could tell

he was imagining all the terrible ways in which I could have become a spirit. "I-i-i-i-i-i-i-i-is that you?"

"Sal?" asked Vorágine. "I'm not detecting any other life-forms in this vicinity. Do you see Sal somewhere?"

"That's not Sal," said Gabi, glaring at me. "This is some mean poltergeist playing a prank on you. It's just taken on Sal's form to scare you. Haven't you, mean poltergeist?"

That last question she asked me through gritted teeth. Okay, okay, I can take a hint, Gabi. "Yes," I said. "You got me. I'm just some rando specter trolling you."

Mr. Milagros crossed himself.

Gabi cleared her throat. "I have summoned you here, specter, to tell me the location of Sal Vidón."

Wait, what? "You summoned me?"

She made big *Play along or else* eyes at me. "Yes, specter, for, I, am, a, bruja, and, I, summoned, you, to, do, my, bidding. Now, do, my, bidding."

Oh. OH! That's what Gabi must have been telling Mr. Milagros: that she was a bruja, and she was going to cast a spell to help them find me. The best part was, she hadn't even lied. She'd been calling herself a bruja ever since I'd gotten all sensitive about kids thinking I was a brujo. And she literally *had* summoned me here!

"Okay, sure," I said. "What's yer bidding, m'bruja?"

Gabi closed her eyes, did some weird dance with her fingers, and swayed her whole body like a snake getting charmed. "Sal Vidón has disappeared. Where will he reappear?"

She opened one eye, watching for my response.

I needed a second to think this through. If she was asking where I would reappear, that meant she did *not* think it would be a good idea for me to just launch myself through the portal and pop back into the bathroom. I agreed. I was already blowing Mr. Milagros's mind as it was; seeing me materialize out of nowhere might have been the straw that broke the custodian's brain—not to mention Vorágine's.

But the only other option would be to make a hole of my own and use it to arrive at some other location in my universe. And, as stated earlier, I'd never done that before. I was afraid to try that by myself.

Oh, wait. With Gabi here, I wouldn't have to do it by myself. When we had collaborated before, we'd manage to save Iggy. I wouldn't be scared to make a hole of my own with her helping me.

"M'bruja," I said to her, "if we both concentrate on that problem, I think we can come up with the best answer."

She thought, and blinked, and ticced her head . . . and then she got it. "I understand. We must ride the taco together, as we have in days of yore."

"What in the world are you talking about?" asked Vorágine.

"Oh," said Gabi, turning to the toilet, "just some bruja-talk. The spirit knows what I mean. Don't you, Mr. Poltergeist?"

"Yes," I said. "We need to figure out where Sal will reappear. I am ready. On three?"

Gabi firmed up her resolve. "On three. Let's count together." We did. "One. Two. Three."

* * *

This isn't bragging. This is just real talk when I say Gabi and I were getting better at this.

We hadn't known what we were doing when we saved Iggy. We'd gotten lucky back then. But now, we had a clear sense of what we needed. We focused both our minds on listening to the universe. Hearing its desires. Waiting for it to tell us where it wanted me to reenter.

I know, I know: It sounds like I'm pretending the universe has a big fat mind of its own. Like, the universe cares where I reappear? It's not a living thing. It isn't capable of having preferences, right?

To which I say: Fine, yes, you're right, suck my nose. It's still easier when I think of the universe that way. And if I've learned nothing else in my thirteen years of being alive, I've learned this: When you're trying to do the most good for the most people, for as long as you have the spoons, it's okay to stick with what works.

It was working now. As I visualized a top-down, bird's-eye view of Culeco, a great, glowing spot appeared on the third floor, against the wall of hallway 3E, burning brighter than a video game NPC with a quest.

"Gabi," my ghost projection said to her, "are you seeing what I'm seeing?"

She nodded. "I mean, we should have guessed, right? There's a lot of . . . history there. It makes sense that that would be the easiest place for Sal to reappear."

"But can I"—I quickly corrected myself—"can *Sal* fit in there?"

"Oh," she said with a laugh, "don't worry. Sal can fit. There are no books in the way. I made Yasmany take them out on Friday so he would do his homework."

"Okay. Well, that's that, then. We have our answer. I guess I'll just be going, then."

"Yes, you should be going now. I release you from my bruja magic. Thank you, specter."

"Wait!"

That last, desperate call was from Mr. Milagros. He said it so loudly, so passionately, that it scared me. I involuntarily reared back, my projection retreating so far into the wall that only my face was still visible.

"No, wait!" he said, and jogged over to my spectral self. "Espere, por favor. Le ruego que me conteste una pregunta. Pago cualquier precio que me cobre."

"What are you saying, Mr. Milagros?" asked Gabi.

"He's asking me," I interpreted, "to answer a question for him. He says he'll pay any price for the answer."

Something told me that sticking around would be a bad idea. I'd never seen Mr. Milagros act like this before. He looked as though one touch would cause him to shatter like a dropped Christmas ornament. I knew I had already crossed like six lines, acting like a ghost.

But when you've crossed six lines, why not seven? "What is your question, señor?" I asked.

"Lourdes," said Mr. Milagros. "Can I talk to Lourdes? Is she . . . Is she okay? Is she happy? Ay, mi pobre querida. Mi amor eterno. Please, if it's at all within your power, let me talk to my wife."

Oh. Oh no. No, no, no, no, no. *This* is why you don't cross

the seventh line. Poor Mr. Milagros must have lost his wife,
Lourdes. And, since he thought I was a spirit, he wanted me to
bring her over to talk to him.

He was such a good man, and this was the second unintentional trick I'd played on him. Both had backfired. The first
one got Culeco this swanky new bathroom. But this second
one—this one was much, much worse.

Gabi's eyes welled up as quickly as mine. She touched Mr.
Milagros's arm. "Oh, Mr. Milagros. I'm so sorry. But he can't—"
She had no idea how to finish that sentence. She turned to me
then, pleading, confused. *How can we fix this, Sal?*

Heck if I knew. All I knew was that I hadn't been so mad
at myself in a long, long time. So I just started talking. But
not in the way a river flows. More like the way a dam breaks.
"Look, Mr. Milagros, I have no idea who Lourdes is. Never
seen her before. And you know why? Because she must have
been a good person. Una santa. She must have been, to have been
loved so deeply. But me? I'm a trash fire. I'm a heap of bad
ideas and poor impulse control held together by my undying
belief that I know better than everyone else, despite all the evidence to the contrary. Oh, and there is *so* much evidence to the
contrary. I get slapped in the face by my own idiocy seventeen
times a day. I've known steamed yucca that's smarter than I
am. You think anyone as wonderful as Lourdes would want
anything to do with someone like me?"

"Oh," said Mr. Milagros. He didn't seem as brittle anymore
as he took in my words. He became increasingly pensive, and
more at peace. "Oh. Oh, I see. You're right, she *was* a saint.
And you . . . you're a demonio."

Both Gabi and I drew our heads back as we slowly cottoned on to where he was going with that line of thinking. "Yes," I agreed. "Yes. I am most definitely a little devil. People are always calling me that."

It's true. People like Papi and American Stepmom.

"Y si usted no la conoce," Mr. Milagros logicked, "es porque ella no está donde usted está. Ella está en . . . en otro lado. Un lugar distinto. Uno donde los diablos no la puedan molestar."

"What are you saying, Mr. Milagros?" asked Gabi, buoyed by his increasingly un-sad body language.

I translated. "He's saying that if I, a diablo, don't know who she is, it's because she isn't with me. She must be somewhere where devils like me don't get to have any contact with her."

Mr. Milagros knelt so that he was eye level with Gabi. "She's not with the devils, Gabi. She's with the angels. Lourdes is in heaven."

And in that moment, all the hope in the world gathered in Mr. Milagros's face. His expression was beyond joy or sadness, beyond laughter or tears. Inside that shaky, swimming smile of his, he was experiencing total union. Total oneness. The 100 percent opposite of loneliness.

"I don't even believe in heaven," said Gabi, bawling like a squall, "but I'm sure Lourdes is there! May I hug you, Mr. Milagros?"

He opened his arms, Gabi jumped into them, and rapture enough to start another universe beamed out of their embrace.

That was my cue to exit. So what I thought was going to be this massive confession and admission of guilt on my part turned into something completely different. I hadn't tried to feed Mr. Milagros a load of cacaseca. I didn't even start out trying to misdirect him. But as a magician, it is against my very nature to correct people's mistaken ideas. If I did, I'd be out of a job.

Plus, after the grief I'd nearly caused that dear man to suffer, there was no raunching way I was going to take from him the tiny momentary rest from grieving his wife that I'd accidentally given him. From one mourner to another, let me tell you, moments of reprieve are priceless.

And anyway, there wasn't time. I needed to go stuff myself in Yasmany's locker, stat, or I'd be late for homeroom.

26

REMEMBER WHEN I was being all smug about spending so much time on the climbing wall in Health and Wellness? Yeah, now that I found myself folded up tighter than a Navy SEAL's parachute in Yasmany's claustrophobic locker, I wasn't feeling nearly as smart. See, I could have been taking yoga for weeks now. Weeks! There was a pace group in Health and Wellness that had been sun-salutationing and downward-dogging since day one of school. By now, I could've been contorting my body like Dhalsim.

But oh, no, I had to spend every free period trying to get to the top of the red zone on the wall. Fat lot of good all that climbing was doing me now. If anything, it had worsened things, because I now had these beefy, bulging calf muscles that made fitting into Yasmany's locker even harder. This must be what it feels like to be buried alive, I thought. I even had my arms crossed in front of me like Tutan-freaking-khamun. Except, unlike King Tut, I couldn't stretch my legs luxuriously inside my huge sarcophagus. My knees were touching my chin. I was a Sal ball.

The lapse in judgment that had led to this current predicament had taken place back on the space station. I thought I'd make the split in the fabric of the cosmos, the one that would lead me back to Yasmany's locker, right beneath me and come in through the top. That way our new tear in the universe wouldn't touch the one already in the back of the locker: the original hole that led to the universe from which I had purloined a little poultry. (Had no idea what flavor of catastrophe would occur if two different holes to two different universes touched and was not interested in finding out just now; thanks anyway.)

I pictured myself drifting down gently into the locker, getting all nice and snug in there at my own pace, and even standing up and sticking my head through the gap between worlds to enjoy one last look at the space station. I would've liked to have seen the Earth of that universe one more time, tell it I was sorry for what the Gustavo Vidón of that world had done to it.

But nope. As soon as I'd stuck my feet through the portal, I'd been pulled back into my universe faster than you could say *Gravity: It's not just a good idea; it's the law.* Yep. I'd been in zero g for like fifteen minutes and already forgotten that, in my universe, gravity exists.

And I paid for it. I rag-dolled into the locker, hard, and did my best imitation of a fetus.

"Ow."

The only thing that had saved me from being completely crushed to death was the hole in the back of the locker. My head, shoulders, front, and upper back pressed mercilessly against the unrelenting metal of the locker. But my posterior slid past the point where the metal locker and concrete wall should have blocked me. And I felt on it the invigorating chill of the powerful air-conditioning that a poultry-processing plant uses to keep its product fresh.

Yep. I was sticking my butt into the chicken universe.

Which, as far as I was concerned, was fan-pantsing-tastic! Thank the Great Sandwich that Gabi and I hadn't finished sealing up the hole yet! We'd been working on it for weeks, after all, snorting up a few calamitrons every day. When we'd started, the hole was big enough to let a full-grown poultry-plant employee come through. Now, you'd have to really shove to force a pair of thin chinchillas through at the same time.

Luckily, my buttocks are much daintier than a pair of chinchillas. Plenty of room to rear my rear into the delicious, open-air freedom of an alternate universe. Ah.

"¿Que'eso?" I heard.

It sounded like the voice was coming from everywhere at once, but that was just because I was trapped in a locker, and the echo made it hard to place sounds. But since *I* didn't say it, and I was the only person in the locker, then the voice had to be coming from outside the locker. Furthermore, it wasn't coming from the hallway, because someone talking outside of the locker would have sounded muted, not echoey. Someone talking through a rip in the universe would have sounded loud enough, but the voice couldn't have been coming from the space station, because it was abandoned now. That left only one place.

The poultry-verse. The chicken workers must have noticed my can.

If I remembered correctly, the other side of the wormhole in Yasmany's locker led to a wall in the poultry-verse that was, like, two stories up from the factory floor. A conveyor belt that carried poultry carcasses, hanging by their drumsticks, was within easy reach.

I wondered how they'd spotted me so quickly. I mean, those workers had to be hard at work doing stuff to chickens, and from their angle, there's a conveyor belt at least partially blocking the view of the hole. They would have had to have been on the lookout for weird stuff coming out of this spot, like, all the time.

"Yo sé exactamente lo que eso es," said a grim woman's voice. She sounded a lot like Principal Torres when Principal Torres was just about to lay down the smack. "Eso es el fundido de un diablo."

Oh. Well, okay. If the workers thought the hole was really a shortcut to the Bad Place and devils would occasionally pop out of it, then that would explain why they were watching it so carefully. I recognized the voice of the woman who had spoken, the one who thought my backside was a demon's backside. She had very briefly visited my universe, when Gabi and I had stolen a second chicken from her universe. She came through the locker and demanded we hand it over. We did, because we didn't really want to steal a chicken, and because she was pretty scary.

She thought we were devils the whole time. We'd promised to be good devils from then on.

But I guess shoving my butt into their universe didn't constitute good-devil behavior in her book.

"¿Qué hacemos ahora?" said another chicken worker's voice, one I didn't recognize. "¿Llamamos a un sacerdote?"

Ha! They wanted to call in a priest to perform an exorcism on my floating keister. That would make me Insta famous for sure. So I gave them an extra-demonic wiggle to encourage them.

"No necesitamos un sacerdote," said the Principal Torres sound-alike. "Todo lo que necesito es una escalera. ¡Prepárate, diablo!"

Yeah, I really shouldn't have trolled them with the extra wiggle. That woman was getting a ladder so she could climb up here and literally kick my butt back into my universe.

Time to get out of here.

"Gabi," I said into my smartwatch, "I'm in the locker. And I need to get out ASAP. Where are you?"

I was desperate for an answer, but even I couldn't have hoped that Gabi would have responded as quickly as she did. She really was number one at replying to texts. **Hang tight, Sal. Yasmany's almost got his part down pat. He'll be ready to perform the trick in just a minute.**

Imagine me, in almost total darkness, trussed up in the locker like a Cuban American turducken, desperate to get out of there before I got my rump busted by a very angry chicken worker, reading Gabi's reply on my smartwatch. I didn't even know where to begin.

Oh, wait, yes, I did: *by screaming at Gabi.* "Gabi! I am trapped in the locker! I need to get out right now! Why are you involving Yasmany, anyway?"

Gabi's reply, appearing almost instantly, was descriptive to the point of bewildering. How the heck had she had the time to text so many words in so few seconds? **I've been busy writing the act that we have to perform. You can't expect me to be the writer and the lead actor with so little notice, can you? Since it's Yasmany's locker, it only made sense to ask him to do it. But don't worry. He'll be great. We're just about ready to go! We're taking our places. Just follow Yasmany's lead; you'll know what to do when the time comes.**

Qué en el nombre de la alfombra was Gabi planning? I had so many questions. But before I could ask any of them, I heard the unmistakable sound of a two-story metal ladder being leaned up against the wall of a poultry-processing plant.

"¡Hoy voy a almorzar diablo asado!" said the chicken worker as her first step onto the ladder made it rattle. For you non–Spanish speakers, she said that she was going to eat roasted devil for lunch. Also, I was the devil she was talking about. This woman was *legit* terrifying. I mean, how many people, when they believe they are being been visited by a heckin' devil, instead of running or pleading for their lives or even trying to strike a bargain, decide they're gonna eat the thing?

I tried to retreat my fanny back into the locker like a turtle hiding its head, but I couldn't get it all the way inside.

"Gather around, everybody!" said Yasmany in a booming carnival barker's voice. "The show's about to start. You don't want to miss this! I'm about to blow this school's mind!"

Okay. Okay. The "show," whatever it was supposed to be, was starting. I just needed to buy a little time and then, somehow, Gabi was going to get me out.

The problem was, I didn't have time to wait. The chicken worker was stomping her way up the ladder step by heavy step. I could hear her desire to rip me a new one with every clomp. I needed a solution this very second. But what?

When in doubt, Sal, check your pockets.

It was a tight fit, but I managed to squirm a hand into my right front pocket. And what do you know? It was absolutely brimming with ideas.

I pulled out a handful of "ideas," maneuvered my hand over to the hole in the universe, shoved it through, and let drop everything it had been holding.

I heard many screams coming from many different chicken workers' mouths. They all started speaking very loudly, all at once, but one person very distinctly yelled, "¡Está lloviendo cucarachas!" Another person confirmed, shouting, "¡Cucarachas infernales!"

Since I'd dropped a handful of fake roaches, hopefully on the head of the chicken worker coming for me, their shouting made sense. And I can't say I didn't laugh when they called them "cockroaches from hell."

But if the woman pursuing me said anything, I couldn't hear it over the exclamations of horror and wonder coming from everybody else. What I did hear, after a few seconds' delay, is that she started making her way up the ladder again, plodding, plotting her revenge.

"Welcome, everyone, to the *Yasmany Robles Show!*" Yasmany said just outside the locker door, nice and loud, so everybody in the hallway (and everybody stuffed inside lockers) could hear him. "Now a lot of you were standing right here, in this very spot, a few weeks ago, when Sal Vidón pulled a magic trick on me. He made me look like the biggest sandwich in the history of sandwiches in front of the whole school. I swore I'd get revenge on him. But how?"

"So, are you planning to beat him up, like a worthless bully would?" asked Gabi. She was a solid actor, but I think she went a little heavy-handed there. But to her credit, she had created this show in, like, twenty seconds. She'd had zero time for rehearsal.

"No, Gabi!" said Yasmany. "I'm a changed chacho! No more bullying for me! Yeah, sure, I want my revenge, ¿cómo que no? But I want to get it the Sal Vidón way."

I have to admit, that was pretty good. Yasmany was a better actor than I thought he'd be. He was clearly saying lines Gabi had written for him, but he'd memorized them in, like, two seconds and was delivering them as well as Gabi was delivering hers.

It sounded fun. I wish I could have just focused all my attention on enjoying the show.

But since that terrifying chicken worker was still climbing up the ladder, more than half of my attention was devoted to desperately reaching into my pocket for more "ideas" to slow her down. I grabbed the next batch of "inspiration" and dropped it into the poultry-verse.

More screaming, even louder than before. "¡Arañas pelu'as!" said many traumatized chicken workers. "¡Arañas venenosas! ¡Cuida'o, Ydania! ¡Si te muerden, te mueres!"

Well, the tarantulas I'd lobbed were not in fact venomous,

since they were fake. But there was no denying they were hairier than a barber's floor. That part they got right.

Also, thanks to their yelling, I was able to figure out that the relentless woman coming to get me was named Ydania, since that was the person everybody was warning to watch out for falling spiders. Not sure how that information could possibly help me, but you never know. I tucked that little factoid away for future use.

And I didn't hear any ladder noises for a good long time. That was good news and bad news. The good news was that Ydania wasn't getting any closer. The bad news was that she wasn't climbing down the ladder, either. She was deciding what to do.

"And then," said Yasmany, "it came to me. To get my revenge, I would have to think like the enemy. *Become* the enemy. So I went to the library—"

Everybody laughed.

"Shut up! I tol' you, I'm a changed man! I went to the library and researched how I could become"—he paused for effect—"an hechicero."

"A what?" asked Gabi, sounding very much like the plant she was.

"An hechicero. You know, a brujo, like Sal. A witch boy."

The crowd said "ooh" like cows say moo. Yasmany had them right where he wanted them. He was giving a great performance! I wished I could be seeing it, and not just hearing it from the inside of his locker. But then again, this show would never be taking place if I weren't in the locker, so . . .

I was enjoying the act so much, I almost forgot that Ydania wanted to make my devil buns her lunch. But when I heard footsteps on the ladder again, getting closer, I remembered all the way down to the center of my bones.

Fear made me angry, and anger made me determined. This had to end, now.

I reached into my pocket yet again, but this time, I knew what I wanted. I burrowed all the way to the bottom, past all the other gags I had in there, and pulled out what I'd been looking for: an egg. It was a plastic one like the kind they put candy in at Easter time, except a little bigger than average, and more realistic-looking—off-white with brown speckles. And it wasn't filled with candy.

It was filled with green slime.

I love slime. I don't know why, exactly, but I do. I love to make it, to carry it with me, to make people hold it, and to hold it myself. I look for any possible opportunity to share it with others. Sadly, daily life isn't exactly full of occasions when slime is useful.

Never had I needed the power of slime more than I did in that moment. Egg in hand, I reached through the rip in space-time, pulled the egg halves apart with my thumb and index finger, and whip-flicked out the slime as hard as I could.

A chorus of horror resounded from the poultry-verse. "Aiiiieeee!" squealed Ydania, who had gotten close enough to me that I could clearly hear her peal of disgust above everybody else's. "¡Mocos del diablo!"

She could handle cockroaches, she could endure tarantulas, but devil snot was too much for even her to take.

Fast, heavy footfalls landed on ladder rungs as Ydania scampered down. Advice about how to get the devil boogers off her rose like a riot from the other chicken workers. "¡Agua bendita!" "¡Ajo y sal!" "¡Ponte mi escapulario!" "¡Corre a la ducha!" "¡Llama al sacerdote!"

Like they would know. I mean, how many of them had been slimed by a devil before? People sure do like to pretend like they know what they're talking about.

Oh, right. Yasmany's show must be getting close to the end.

"—taken me weeks of studying," he was saying, "but finally, I have become a real hechicero. And to prove it, I am going to pull a chicken out of my locker before your very eyes, just like Sal did. All I have to do is remove my lock"—I heard him spinning the lock, left twenty-three, right fourteen, left six (Gabi and I were in Yasmany's locker almost every day, so I knew his combination better than I knew my own)—"remove it like so, and then say the magic words:

"Gallo, gallo, please appear
In my locker, now and here,
If you do, seré un héroe:
Culeco's favorite hechicero!"

The door flew open. My legs sprang out of the locker like peanut-can snakes. A hall filled with theater kids gasped for real. I squinted, my eyes needing to adjust to the light.

"Well," said Yasmany, overacting his surprise, "I promised you all a chicken, but I think I've outdone myself! What do you think, Sal?"

I started working the rest of my cramped self out of the locker; Yasmany carefully helped me out and down. Once I'd waited two beats to kick some blood back into my feet and stretch a little, I handed him the egg I'd been holding.

"What do I think?" I said to the audience, in the showmanniest way I knew how. "Abracadabra, chicken pluckers."

Gabi hopped between Yasmany and me and, while holding hands, the three of us had to take four bows before the audience would even consider ending their applause.

They might have kept going, too, except someone was slow-clapping louder than everybody else. Sarcastically. It soured the whole ovation. People stopped putting their hands together to see who was ruining the moment.

It was Aventura. Her White Rabbit bunny paws were like two pillows hitting each other, if two pillows could hit each other with a snide, derisive thump. "Bravo," she said, her voice dripping with poison. "Oh, bravo, Sal. I suppose you think *this* is what a show should be like, instead of the mess you think Rompenoche is."

I felt suddenly like I was drowning: dying so quietly, no one would even realize I needed help. Nobody in the hallway moved. I didn't know what to say.

Aventura walked up to me. Gabi and Yasmany both took a step away. Cowards.

"Well," said Aventura, "you're right. And you're going to fix it."

Then she grabbed me by the ear and dragged me off.

27

"WELCOME BACK, MR. VIDÓN," said Principal Torres from across her desk, her tone as dry as dry ice, and three times as cold. "It's been a whole twenty-four hours since I've seen you in my office, hasn't it?"

Once more in solidarity with the students of Culeco, Principal Torres was dressed as a character from the Alice books. This time, it was the Duchess. Her hat was wider than my chair and covered with fake fur and gilt. She wore a gold-on-gold cloak over a green gown. None of these things truly identified her as the Duchess, however. What really nailed down her character was that she had a doll of a baby boy that, if you pulled the baby gown it was wearing over its head, turned into a pig.

"Maybe a few more than twenty-four," I answered glumly, still rubbing my ear.

"A few more . . ." she repeated, polishing her glasses, then slipping them back on. They made her eyes gigantic and her glaring that much more effective. I'm pretty sure the Duchess didn't have glasses, but honestly, I think it helped the costume.

"Quite a show you put on for us this morning. Quite a merry chase you led us on."

"Oh, good!" I said, acting as cheery as I could. "I was worried you were going to be mad. I'm so glad you thought it was merry!"

She frowned. "I did not find it merry, Sal. That was sarcasm. In truth, I found it exceedingly *un*-merry. Why, I'd say it was one of my top-five unmerriest moments of the school year so far." The sarcasm fell away; she became serious and sad. "Do you have any idea how frightening it was when Mr. Milagros opened the door to the bathroom and we discovered you weren't in there anymore?"

I watched my feet kick the legs of the tiny chair I was sitting in. "Yes. No. Kind of? I'm sorry. I just . . ."

I stopped talking.

"Yes?" she prompted.

I looked up at her. "I don't want to make excuses, Principal Torres."

"So don't. Tell me the truth."

Since she didn't specify *which* truth—and there were so many to choose from—I picked one. "The truth is, I was coming out of the bathroom. But then I saw Aventura. And I just couldn't face her then."

"Well, you're facing me now, aren't you?" asked Aventura, who was sitting next to me in an equally tiny chair. She was, without a doubt, the angriest bunny this side of Wonderland.

I thought this visit to the principal's office was going to be a nonstop Sal bash. So I was caught off guard when Principal Torres turned her controlled, professional ferocity on Aventura.

"Ms. Rios, you will be silent until spoken to. Or do you think I've already forgiven you for committing an act of violence against Sal?"

Aventura grimaced with surprise. "Act of violence? What?"

"From the moment you pulled him into my office, Sal hasn't stopped rubbing his ear."

I stopped rubbing my ear. "Oh. It's okay, Principal Torres. I gave my enthusiastic consent for Aventura to yank me around the school by the ear." I almost didn't say the next thing, but when I thought about not saying it, I found I couldn't. "We all know I deserved it."

Principal Torres leaned forward and folded her hands on the desk. "Actually, Sal, you didn't. Nobody deserves to be hurt by someone else. And even if you gave consent, *I* did not. Students don't hurt other students at my school. Do you understand me, Aventura?"

Aventura somehow looked fierce and apologetic at the same time. "Yes, ma'am."

"Good. Before we move on to Sal, then, tell me: What do you think would be an appropriate punishment for you?"

Aventura sat up, took in a calming breath, and straightened her bunny ears to their full and upright position. "What I did was very wrong, so it must be a big punishment. I think you should remove me as the director of Rompenoche. You should make Sal the director instead. He's good at shows."

Principal Torres fell back into her office chair in contemplation. With a slight smile on her face, she touched her nose and looked at the wall to her right. She decided something. Her eyes twinkled.

"No," she said, swiveling back to look at Aventura. "No, that's not happening."

"Oh," said Aventura, sounding . . . disappointed?

"Because you'd like it if I removed you as director of Rompenoche, wouldn't you?"

Aventura's head fell and bounced heavily on her neck, making her ears flap and flop. "Yus."

"What?!" I asked. Because, *what*?!

Aventura turned murderously on me. "Nee nee nee! Don't you 'what' me, cacaseca boy. You're the one who said Rompenoche was the worst show you'd ever seen."

I faced her. It was hard, but I did it. "I'm really sorry. I didn't see you when I said that. I *never* would have said that if I knew you were standing right there."

She leaned back, folded her arms. "So, you would have lied to my face if you knew I was there? Lied to me like everyone else has been lying to me?"

Man, I just couldn't say the right thing. "No! I mean, not lied. I just would have been . . . less rude. I could have given you constructive criticism, like Señorx Cosquillas says."

"Señorx?" mused bemused Principal Torres.

But before I could change the subject and explain, Aventura laid into me. "Nee nee nee, Sal. You would have lied to my face, like everyone else in this school." Aventura stood up, stomping as she paced. "Why is Culeco full of two-faced liars? Why can't anybody just give me a straight answer? How am I supposed to work under these conditions? I'm sorry, Principal Torres, but given the circumstances, I'm sure you'll understand why I must resign as director of Rompenoche."

This tantrum was nothing I ever would have expected out of Aventura. She'd always been so cool and sly and in control. I didn't think there was anything that could have made her have a meltdown this nuclear.

Quietly, patiently, speaking into her tented hands, Principal Torres said to her, "Are you finished, Ms. Rios?"

Dang, son. That was harsh. Aventura cast her eyes around the room, her bunny ears bent like broken stalks of corn. She sat down quickly, shaken, stunned. "Yes, ma'am."

"Let's look at some facts, Aventura, shall we? You are the best costume maker in the school—"

Aventura put up her hands defensively. "Oh, I don't—"

"You've had your say, Ms. Rios. Now I will have mine." Principal Torres was joking when she said that. But low-key not. "Everybody knows you're the best. Yet you've had the entire school helping you make costumes. Some of us have been working on them since the summer. If you're the best, why didn't you just make them all yourself?"

Aventura squashed her eyebrows together into sideways question marks. "Because there's no way I could do it by myself? It would have taken me a million years."

"It would have taken you a million years to make them all perfect," Principal Torres corrected, standing up and walking over to Aventura. "But pretend that you absolutely had to do all the costumes yourself, and you had to finish them in ten weeks. What would happen to the quality?"

"There wouldn't be any quality. The costumes would be trash."

"Right. And that's coming from the number one seamstress

in the school. So, how many people helped you write the script for Rompenoche?"

Aventura made a big, comic clown frown and looked away. "I kinda didn't care about the script? Because I just wanted to make some fancy costumes? Which is why I just used Lewis Carroll stuff? So I could just kinda throw something together?"

Principal Torres grabbed her shoulders. "You get it now, sí? Art is mostly effort. You put your time in places other than the script. And, according to Sal and you, your lack of effort in the script department is showing."

Aventura squirmed free. "Okay, but hold up. I gave you the script two weeks ago. Why didn't you tell me it was a catbox, Principal Torres?"

"Because," Principal Torres replied, strolling around her office like a lawyer giving closing statements, "it doesn't matter! The parents are gonna love it no matter what! When they see their little darling dressed up as a playing card, or a mock turtle, or a Cheshire Hamster or whatever, they'll go bonkers! You have to understand, Aventura: These poor, benighted parents have spent years going to their kids' terrible recorder recitals, their boring soccer games, and their mind-numbing plays. I promise you, as bad as you think your play is, it's far better than anything they've ever seen their kids do at school. And the costumes, Aventura! They are truly—" She finished the sentence with a chef's kiss.

Only then did she notice Aventura giving her a cacaseca face. She pretended to get defensive. "Look, missy, I'm a busy woman. I have to pick my battles. So the play's not perfect. So what? If you want to put on a show that's mostly about the costumes, that's fine with me! It's plenty good enough for parent-teacher conference night. I am prepared to go forward with it as is, no questions asked. I mean"—she looked expectantly at Aventura over her shoulder—"unless you really want to change it at this point."

Oh, man. The way Principal Torres fluttered her eyelids, there was no way Aventura could have missed that hint. But she didn't need the hint anyway. She was straight-spined now, yet relaxed, in control again, back to her sly, wry self. "Principal Torres, I would really like to change Rompenoche. Get some people to help me make it a not-terrible show."

"I thought you'd say that. You know why?"

"Why?"

She walked over to Aventura and bent toward her, hands behind her back. "Because you're a real artist."

Aventura smiled.

"An artist," Principal Torres said, straightening, hands on hips, "who must be punished for putting her hands on another student. Luckily, during our conversation the absolute perfect punishment has occurred to me."

"Okay," said Aventura, standing at ease, hands behind her back, like a condemned soldier facing a firing squad. "Whatever you think is fair, ma'am."

"Well, I think it's more than fair to make you finish what you started. Your punishment is that you have to stay on as the director of Rompenoche."

"Okay. Yes. That's more than fair."

"I am not finished!" Principal Torres resumed her strolling around the office. "I also believe it's important that you learn how to negotiate and compromise by using words instead of violence. So that's exactly what you're going to do: with the very person that you hurt, and who hurt you. Therefore, I am making Sal Vidón codirector of Rompenoche."

"Whatnowwaitnowwhat?" I jumbled.

Principal Torres leaned against her desk and crossed her arms. "You heard me, Sal. The beauty is, this will be *your* punishment as well, for performing an unauthorized magic trick that threw the whole school into a tizzy for a solid twenty minutes, as well as for the rudeness you showed Gabi, which led to our current crisis."

"Oh," I said. Because, what else could I say?

"Now," Principal Torres continued after she made good and sure I wasn't going to sass her back. She turned around, grabbed a pad and pen off her desk, and scratched out a note. "Aventura, take this to your homeroom teacher and have her excuse your absence"—she ripped the page off the pad and started scribbling on a new sheet—"and then take this to your first-period teacher to excuse your absence from their class today. Come back here after you've delivered those, and we'll start discussing how we can fix as much as we can in the time that we have. I'm thinking we will convene an emergency school assembly at fifth period to inform everyone and prepare them for some big changes. Okay?"

Aventura grabbed both notes and took off like she was late for a very important date. "See you in a minute!" She left, but then opened the door again, sticking only her bunny head back inside. "And thank you, ma'am. You're really good at tough love."

Principal Torres leaned against her desk again and looked at Aventura over her glasses. "No has visto nada todavía. Wait until I sic Gabi on it. Then you can talk to me about tough love."

Aventura laughed. Then, after one last smile, she was gone for real.

Yeah, time for me to get gone, too, and quick. "Well," I said, still facing the door, "that all worked out all right, didn't it?" I got up, stretched. "Life lessons learned, apologies accepted, and maybe, just maybe, a few friendships deepened." I clapped once and rubbed my hands together. "So I guess I should be going to homeroom, too. If you'll just write me one . . . of . . . those . . . passes . . ."

Principal Torres was behind her desk, sitting in her office chair again. How had she even gotten there so fast? Hands folded on the desktop, staring at me like she'd just caught me feeding laxatives to her dog.

"We have unfinished business, Mr. Vidón," she said.

28

OKAY, SAL, EASY. Don't overreact. You've gotten this far. Just play along, see where she's going with this.

I sat down again, cool as the drool of a long-dead ghoul. "We do, Principal Torres?"

We stared at each other, eye to unblinking eye. We both smiled patiently, utterly pleasantly, unshakably agreeably. She was waiting for me to crack. She could wait until the sun went red and I wouldn't.

She moved first. Ha. I won.

But then I lost. Her movement consisted of her reaching over to the computer screen on her desk and rotating it around so I could see it. She typed an address in the search bar, and a web page came up called Tomorrow's Physics Today! It looked like an online fashion magazine, full of flashy clickbait headlines on the front page. Well, clickbait for nerds: "The TRUTH about Sub-Atomic Teleportation that the Scientific Community DOES Want You to Know About!"; "This ONE WEIRD TRICK Will Teach You How to Understand How Light Is BOTH a Wave AND a Particle!"; "Meet New Single Stars Just DYING to Hook

Up with ROGUE PLANETS for Some HOT 'N' HEAVY Solar-System Formation!"

But those were just links to articles. They weren't the headline. The headline of Tomorrow's Physics Today! was "These Super-Genius Scientists Are Quietly Keeping Our Universe from ANNIHILATING ITSELF!"

And beneath the headline was a picture of Papi and Dad: The Final Frontier, smiling like idiots.

I turned into an ice sculpture of myself.

While I was frozen solid, Principal Torres walked around to the front of her desk and leaned against it as she spoke to me. "For the parent-teacher conferences I conduct during Rompenoche, I try to find out a bit about the parents, get to know them a little before we talk about their kids. That's what led me to find this article about the *amazing* scientific work your papi is doing. I mean, I've met the man before, of course, but I had no idea the extent to which he was doing cutting-edge work in . . . what is his specialty called again? 'Calamity physics'? What a name, right? 'Calamity.' Pretty scary-sounding, if you ask me.

"So after I read the article, I had to find more. I read everything about calamity physics I could grab. Oh, a lot of it was well over my head. But still, all those articles got me thinking. I couldn't help but remember the story Mrs. Waked told me a few weeks back about your performance in her class for show-and-tell. Do you remember, Sal? How you told the whole class that you had the ability to grab things from other universes? Oh, they all thought you were joking! That you had found a way to fool Gabi's lie detector! I mean, everybody knows you can't just reach into a whole other universe and pull out, oh, I don't know, a whole raw chicken. That's impossible. *Physically* impossible.

"Or maybe not, for the kid of a calamity physicist. I started having these wild thoughts that maybe, somehow, you had told the truth that day. That you had reached into a different universe and yoinked poultry right out of it.

"But I didn't have any proof. I hadn't seen it happen myself. There was no physical evidence. It was all just wild speculation, sensational articles by Gabi in the *Rotten Egg*, nothing I could act on. Y yo no toco mentiras sin guantes." I hadn't heard that old saying before; she noticed, and added in English: "I don't get my hands dirty, messing around with lies.

"But now. Now, Mr. Vidón. Now, I have personally witnessed you go into a bathroom with my own two eyes, and I saw you *not* come out of it again. Once we unlocked the door, I scoured every inch of that room myself, and I had Mr. Milagros check for any conceivable way you could have gotten out. Nothing. Nada. Impossible. You couldn't have escaped.

"But what's even more impossible is that, when you reappeared, you reappeared *inside the very same locker* out of which you were said to have planted a chicken from another universe. What. A. Coincidence!

"But maybe you planned it that way, right? All part of the show? According to Aventura, you even got Yasmany in on the act, and possibly Gabi. This is all one huge misunderstanding! You were just putting on another performance! Isn't that right, Mr. Vidón? You're going to try to convince me this was all another magic trick, right?"

Chacho, there weren't enough Sal-size diapers on the planet. I said absolutely nothing.

Something about my face must have shown her how hard she was coming at me. She dialed her expression back from "executioner who loves her job" to "exterminator who secretly loves bugs more than people." She sighed and slid her back down the desk until she was sitting crossed-legged on the floor in front of me. I had to look down to meet her eyes.

"When I talked to your parents over the summer, before school started," she said—serious still, but minus the acid— "they told me they were worried about you adjusting to a new school. They told me about your diabetes. They explained how you'd been affected been by the death of your mami. They didn't know if Culeco would be the right place for you.

"But then they told me you are a magician. And I was so happy! ¿Sabes lo que les dije? I said, 'I love magicians! We need him! Culeco needs more magic.'"

"Bet you're regretting saying that now," I said. There was no need for me to speak in circles or try to misdirect. She'd seen through all my tricks.

But I guess I hadn't seen through all of *her* tricks, because she surprised me again. "No, Mr. Vidón. I don't regret it at all. Because in the three and a half weeks you've been here at Culeco, I have come to understand that you are a wonderful young man."

She smiled an actual, unironic smile, the first one in a long while. "Don't look so surprised, Mr. Vidón. I have evidence. You know I don't draw conclusions without evidence. Do you know the best proof I have that you are a wonderful person?"

"What?"

"A chicken."

I couldn't help it—I laughed. I made *What?!* shoulders. "How does a chicken prove anything?"

She stood and resumed her leaning position against the desk. "I've dealt with a lot of bullying cases in my day. Easily one of the worst parts of the job. A bully can destroy a kid. Leave permanent scars, and not just on their skin. They can even turn other kids into bullies. It's the worst. I *hate* bullying.

"So here you are, third day of school, when Yasmany comes after you. But you have a secret no one knows about. Maybe you picked up a very special gizmo off your papi's workbench before you left for school, eh? That was show and tell day in Mrs. Waked's class, wasn't it? Maybe you were going to show the kids something *really* amazing. At any rate, when Yasmany started threatening you, you remembered the very special gizmo in your pocket. Fear as much as anything else made you flip the switch."

What the heck was she talking about? What gizmo?

But she was on a roll, excited by the story she was spinning. So I didn't let my face say a thing. I just let her go.

"You flipped the switch," she said, looking up and making her fingers explode, "and the possibilities of the multiverse opened up to you. The many worlds became your banquet table. You could have brought in anything from anywhere to help you. You could have done some stupid, dangerous, hurtful things in that moment." Her face hardened. "You could have been extremely destructive, if you'd wanted to." And then it lightened again. "But instead, you brought in a chicken. A chicken! Somehow, you figured the best way to get a bully to stop bullying you was to put a chicken in his locker!"

I shrugged. "Worked, didn't it?"

"Splendidly. Marvelously. And, looking back on it now—hilariously. You chose a chicken because it was funny."

"People like funny."

She started counting on her fingers. "And then, in my office, you asked me not to expel Yasmany. You wanted to show mercy to the kid who, just a few minutes ago, had threatened you. And when Gabi's little brother was in the hospital, you brought Gabi her homework, and then you spent a weekend there, working with her on your project for Mrs. Waked's class together. Oh, by the way, how's little Iggy doing?"

"Oh. Um . . . Fine!" I said, and that's all I said, nothing at all about why he seemed to be doing pretty okay these days, nothing to do with me. *Zip my lips and call it quits.*

"You know about Iggy because you and Gabi are friends now. And so are you and Yasmany. When I asked you to be Yasmany's friend and help him out—well, look at you now! You've got him performing 'magic tricks'"—she made the biggest air quotes in the history of air quotes—"with you!

"And just now, Aventura Rios, who has one of the best heads on any pair of shoulders of any middle schooler in the country, thinks you're 'decent.' I mean, the fact that you became so upset when you accidentally hurt her feelings shows what a big heart you have. I believed you when you said you couldn't face her. I think the only reason you used your papi's calamity gadget today was because, well, you really couldn't face her. I think most people would have done what you did, if they could have. But unlike most people in that situation, you had a trick up your sleeve that would allow you to make an absolutely spectacular escape. And let's face it, Sal. You like spectacular escapes. You are a showman, after all."

I stuck my tongue in my cheek. Gonna have to watch how much I say that from now on. At least out loud.

She leaned close enough to me that her huge hat eclipsed the ceiling lights. "My point is, Mr. Vidón, that you're good. You make mistakes, but you're a good person with a big heart. You've proven it time and again, and I've been keeping the receipts."

She was being so nice to me. So why did it feel like my heart would burst?

"But," she went on, "you have a lot to learn. I'm pretty sure your papi didn't create his scientific apparatuses so you could use them to pull chickens out of other universes."

I almost said *Why do you keep saying I'm using a tool of some kind to break the universe? I'm not! I can do it just by relaxing!* But I caught myself in time and thought about exactly what she had said. Papi had not created scientific apparatuses so I could pull chickens out of other universes. So I wasn't lying when I answered, "That's true, Principal Torres."

(And look, I'm not an idiot. The Goody Two-shoes part of my brain—it's very small, but very shrill—started yelling, *This is* another *lie of omission, Sal! You're falling into your old bad habits again, of treating every conversation like a fencing match instead of a way of sharing and communing with other people. When are you going to start talking to people like someone who wants real human relationships?*

When the universe is fixed, I replied to my brain. And then I gave the signal, and the rest of my big, fat brain lobes dogpiled on the itty-bitty nagging part, and I couldn't hear it anymore.)

"You still with me, Sal?" asked Principal Torres, a smidge of concern wrinkling her forehead.

"Yes," I replied, returning to her.

"Good. Because this is the most important part. I'm asking you to leave Culeco—"

I literally physically startled. "What?! You're expelling me?!"

Eyebrows up. "No, Mr. Vidón. You'll know when I'm expelling you, cross my heart. I am asking you to leave Culeco, go home, empty your pockets, and then return to school."

"Empty my pockets?"

She pushed her glasses up her nose with one meaningful finger. "Here's the deal. Until further notice, you are to come to school with empty pockets. No tricks, no gags, no props, no toys, no gadgets, nada nada limonada. If you do, it will be hasta luego, hechicero. I mean it. I would hate to expel you, but I *will* expel you, Sal Vidón."

I had four thoughts at once fighting to get out of my mouth, like four actors and one door in every sitcom ever. The one that finally made it out first was "My diabetes stuff."

She looked up. She'd forgotten about that. "Right. Okay, well, of course, you may bring everything you need to manage your diabetes. Don't you have a fanny pack where you keep it all?"

"No." I showed her my medically approved tactical all-weather medical transport system. "It isn't a fanny pack."

Her eyes said, *Chacho, that's a fanny pack,* but her mouth

said, "Whatever that is, can you keep everything you need to manage your care in it?"

"Yes. Except my smartwatch. The padres want me to wear the smartwatch now."

She nodded. "So you can bring your smartwatch and you can bring your tactical smack-tical whatever-you-said. But your pockets must be empty."

"Wallet? ID? Books? Protractor? Colored pencils? Gym clothes? Scientific calcu—"

"Whatever school supplies you need," she interrupted, "must be in your backpack. I will periodically ask you to empty that backpack and your pockets to make sure you're following the rules. And I'd better not ever find anything that looks like your papi might have invented it."

"My GOTCHA! stamp?"

She tilted her head, then shook it.

"But how will I get Gabi?"

"You'll have to get creative, I guess. Can we stop playing games now? You know what I am asking you to do, why I am asking you to do it, and the consequences if you disobey me. Is that correct?"

"Yes."

"Please explain it back to me loud and clear so we can be sure."

"You are going to expel me if you catch me with any of my papi's calamity physics stuff at school."

"That is correct. I would like you to give me your word that you will not bring any of your papi's equipment to school. Will you do that?"

I did not want to give her my word. "I give you my word."

She liked that. She relaxed a little. "Okay. You've given me good reasons to trust you so far. So I am going to trust you now. Do you need me to call your parents to come pick you up and take you home?"

"No," I said, and didn't add *no* another forty times in a row, even though I wanted to. "It's fastest if I walk home."

"Okay," she said. "But do me a favor: As you're walking, take a little time to digest what we've talked about. If you do, I think you'll understand that I'm not punishing you for the sake of punishing you. Sometimes, we have to deny ourselves things we want for the sake of the greater good. I'm trying to teach you to look at the bigger picture."

It hadn't been half an hour since I'd been on a space station, watching an alternate Earth spin beneath me, terrified that this Earth, too, could lose half of Florida and all of Cuba and the Bahamas if I didn't play my cards right. *But please, Principal Torres, tell me more about the bigger picture,* I thought, imagining those words on the Willy Wonka meme.

But out loud I just said, "Okay."

She smiled one of those *welp* smiles. "Okay, Mr. Vidón. Oh, and take the time to eat lunch at home, please. I will let your teachers know you won't be in class. But I need you back at Culeco no later than fifth period."

"Why? What's happening fifth period?"

"That's when I tell the whole school that you're now the codirector of Rompenoche. And then, Mr. Vidón, it will be time for you to get to work."

WHEN I WALKED out of the principal's office and into the administrative suite, I saw Gabi and Yasmany sitting in two tiny chairs.

Well, that explained why Gabi hadn't busted in during my conversation with Principal Torres like I'd been half expecting. She and Yasmany had been my accomplices, which meant they were going to get in trouble, too. So they were waiting their turn to see the principal, while being guard-dogged by Mr. Zacto.

Ah, Mr. Zacto. The perfect target for a prank. He was so neat, so precise, so dapper (he wore a different black suit, pressed to perfection, every day), so by-the-book, so lawful neutral, such a straight shooter, such a rules follower, and so very, very type A that all I wanted to do was make his world just a little messier. Don't get me wrong: He was always nice and polite and even friendly. But his hair was so perfect! He must have trimmed his Afro every single day to keep the right angles of his hair so precise. And his desk was so orderly, every time I passed it I wanted to "accidentally" sneeze his papers out of place, the same way, in the fall back in Connecticut, I'd wanted to jump in the piles of leaves American Stepmom or Papi had just raked up.

Mr. Zacto stared at me 'zactly like he could read my evil mind. "Keep it moving, Mr. Vidón," he said to me. "No talking to the accused until after they've spoken to Principal Torres."

"Oh, I wouldn't think of it, Mr. Zacto," I said. "Believe me, I have . . . learned . . . my . . . lesson. . . ."

"Something wrong, Mr. Vidón?"

"No! Nothing! I'm not looking at anything!"

Of course I'd been looking at him. Specifically, I'd let my gaze drift from his bespectacled eyes to his mouth. I kept trying to move my eyes back to his, but I couldn't, because something utterly *fascinating* and perhaps slightly *disgusting* was going on with his mouth. I just had to keep looking at it again and again, deer-in-headlights-ishly.

"Do I have something in my teeth?" he asked, as if that was the worst possible thing that could happen to him. That's why he kept dental floss in his front shirt pocket. I'd seen him flossing on six different occasions at his desk over the last few weeks. Seriously, chacho must have had gums like alligator hide by now, he was so obsessed.

"I didn't see anything!" I said, sounding like someone in the Witness Protection Program.

It wasn't a lie. I *hadn't* seen anything. But for some reason, he thought I *had*. He turned toward the wall, where a small mirror hung—which he'd put there for the sole purpose of helping him floss—and started sawing between his teeth with a piece of minty string.

I turned to Gabi and Yasmany and mouthed, *Sorry I got you in trouble.*

Yasmany flipped away all worries with a hand. *This ain't trouble,* he lipped.

Gabi was scraping one finger over the other in that *Naughty, naughty!* way. *We're in enough trouble, Sal!* she mouthed. She just did not like being in Principal Torres's bad graces. But whatever. She'd be fine. This would probably be good for her in the long run.

Text me after, I mouthed, thumbing toward Principal Torres's office.

"No twalking!" said Mr. Zacto, around the floss. His reflection was staring at me. He'd pulled his lips back as far as they could go, for maximum flossing effectiveness. Even with a piece of string between two lower incisors, exposing all your teeth like that makes for a pretty aggressive look.

"I'm going, I'm going," I said. But then, lowering my eyebrows, I pointed at his reflection in the general vicinity of his mouth, as if I'd seen something new, something *horribly* new.

He resumed his flossing with a newfound desperation.

I walked out of the office feeling a little better about things. Even though I wouldn't be able to bring gags to school anymore, I could still pull off plenty of tricks. I just needed to remind myself that magic isn't about the props. It's about knowing what your audience believes and using their beliefs against them. Heh-heh-heh.

As I walked home, I kept squeezing a fun-size bag of Skittles in each hand. It's a trick I learned while playing first-person-shooter games: jump around, keep switching guns, change directions, do anything to keep your attention focused. In FPSs, daydreams equal a one-way ticket back to the lobby. Since I tended to get dreamy and philosophical when I was walking alone, all too often I wasn't paying enough attention to traffic. Squeezing Skittles, you can't get lost in your thoughts.

Also, squeezing two fun-size bags of Skittles makes it much easier not to jump into the middle of traffic when someone appears out of nowhere and starts talking to you. "Man, your principal is a first-class stromboli," said FixGabi. "I can't believe she spoke to you that way. I'm so glad I don't have to go to school anymore!"

"You overheard that?" I asked, swallowing my lungs back down my throat, acting casual.

"I'm watching out for you, buddy!" She gave my arm a bro punch.

"I'm glad you're okay. Last time I saw you, the forces of evil were hot on your tail."

"They can't catch me," she bragged. She snatched one of the bags of Skittles from my hand, tore it open, and started munching. "I'm glad you made it home without my help," she said. "Did you use the hole I left behind?"

"No. Too many people were in the bathroom looking for me. I had to make a different hole to go somewhere else in my school."

She sized me up, smiling. "Look at the big brain on Sal! Getting yourself back home with your own hole! That's some pretty advanced branesurfing you did there. I didn't think you had it in you!"

"Neither did I," I admitted. "Oh, and Gabi helped me. She deserves credit, too."

FixGabi ate a Skittle like she was a devil and it was a sinner. "You're trusting your Gabi too much."

I stumbled to a stop at the corner, even though we had a walk signal. "That's the second time you've told me not to trust Gabi. Why?"

She took my arm and kept us walking across the street while she dumped the rest of the candy down her throat. Then she tossed the empty bag on the ground and said, with her mouth full, "Trust me, Sal. I've met many Gabis in my journeys through the multiverse. Sooner or later, they'll double-cross you. And they're dangerous foes. Best to steer as clear of them as possible. Man, Skittles are so good. Wish my universe had them."

I wasn't looking at her as she spoke. I wasn't watching out for traffic, either. I was gazing at the Skittles wrapper she had dropped without so much as a second thought. Gabi—*my* Gabi—would never litter, not in a trillion trillion years. And FixGabi had just done it in the same breath she'd used to tell me to stay away from my Gabi.

Something wasn't right here.

When I looked up from the Skittles bag, I saw something that *did* feel right—the Fey Spy was hovering not far away.

I turned from it to distract FixGabi's attention. "WELL," I said in a louder, more articulate voice, the kind of voice ignorant people use when speaking to foreigners, "IT'S SURE NICE OF YOU, GABI FROM ANOTHER UNIVERSE, TO COME HERE AND SAVE OUR UNIVERSE."

She lowered her eyes at me, raised her eyebrows. "Yeah. Sure. No problem, Sal. Is your place much farther?"

"NOT FAR NOW!" We turned onto the busiest street on the route home. I caught glimpses of the Fey Spy trying to hide behind trees, mailboxes, lampposts, anything, while also staying within earshot. "BUT WHILE WE'RE CHATTING," I asked FixGabi, "WHY DON'T YOU TELL AGAIN ME HOW YOU LOST YOUR SAL."

She looked at me like the worst kind of teacher: the ones who make you feel stupid for asking a question. "You okay?"

"YES, FINE. YOU WERE SAYING?"

"What's to say, Sal? Your papi killed him."

"That is incorrect," I corrected. My voice went back to its normal volume, because I meant business now. "My papi, who is a different person than the Papi from your universe, hasn't killed anything in his life bigger than one of his patented seven-scoop sundaes. Certainly not a human being. And even if we played pretend and said, 'If Papi had to kill one person, who would he kill?' I'm pretty sure American Stepmom and I would be the very last two people on that list."

Tut, tut, tut, went FixGabi's tongue. "Sals always think that. My Sal thought that. And look what happened to him."

"Yes, great, exactly: Tell me what happened to him."

I've seen kindergarteners hug their stuffed animals with less friendship than I saw in FixGabi's face at that moment. She didn't look at me, or the overcast sky, or where she was going. She wasn't using her eyes at all. Instead, she watched a movie of happier times play in her mind as she spoke. "Sal was great. The best. We were inseparable. The kind of friends they write about in books."

"I've only known the Gabi from this universe for, like, three weeks," I said. "How long did you know your Sal?"

"Since sixth grade, when he moved to my town. We became friends within days, best friends within a month, and then we—" She stopped herself short. "Let's just say we were very, very close."

I swallowed an imaginary toad that tasted like a real toad. "Boyfriend and girlfriend?"

She buzzed her lips at me. "That makes it sound so childish. Our romance rivaled the greatest love stories ever told. We were star-crossed paramours whose only crime was loving too much. And like so many love stories, ours ended tragically."

Holy potholes, was she laying it on thick. I couldn't help but laugh.

She turned on me viper-strike fast. "How dare you! Just because you're still an emotionally stunted child doesn't mean the rest of us don't have passionate souls."

I was almost done laughing. Almost. "Sorry. But people in our universe don't talk the way you do."

The two dimples made by her smirk were named Caca and Seca. "Oh yeah? Not even Gabi?"

Um. Dang it. I glanced at the Fey Spy and subtly shrugged an apology. "Well, okay, Gabi. But nobody else."

She stopped walking, faced me. "Let me try to explain this to you in terms you can understand. Sal and I were closer than mere 'boyfriend' and 'girlfriend.' We were soulmates. It was as if we'd loved each other in our past lives, too, and now we were just picking up where we left off. I would have done anything for him. And he made the ultimate sacrifice for me. So don't you dare insult my deep and abiding love for one of the greatest human beings ever to live, in any universe."

She sounded sincere. But good actors can sound just as genuine as people who are actually suffering. If my Gabi had told me something while seeming to be this close to tears, I would have felt bad and apologized right away. But I felt more like squinting at FixGabi than apologizing to her.

I'd love to have Gabi's opinion of this exchange, I thought. And thanks to the Fey Spy, I'd be able to get it later.

For now, I played along. "Sorry, Gabi," I said. "I can see you really cared for him. You said he made the ultimate sacrifice for you?"

She sighed. "Yes. When he saved me from your papi."

"Not my papi!" I insisted. "Different person."

According to her flaring nostrils, I couldn't be more wrong, but she went on with her story anyway. "I already told you how I tried to explain to Dr. Vidón that the universe *needs* holes in its membrane. Without some tears in the fabric of spacetime, the universe would explode. But he didn't pay attention to me, and he wouldn't hear it from Sal, either. He was so angry that Sal had taught me how to travel the multiverse, he wouldn't listen to reason anymore, even though we knew better than he did. Adults are like that, you know. They never listen to kids."

My padres and I had decided never to tell anybody about my "gifts," and Gabi and I had informally agreed to keep our extra-universal shenanigans to ourselves. The scenario FixGabi was describing now was exactly why. It was why I hadn't been more forthcoming with Principal Torres.

"So what did he do?" I asked.

"He activated the remembranation machine, full power. And you saw the result of that from the space station."

"But how did you get away in time?"

We had almost reached a corner. FixGabi hurried over to it ahead of me so she could stand alone and wipe the tears out of her eyes before I caught up to her.

Well, at least that's what it looked like from the back. I never saw tears; I just saw her hand move as if she were wiping away tears. Realistic fake crying isn't easy, even for experienced actors. It's much easier to mime crying than to actually cry. And from a distance, mimed crying looks pretty much like actual crying.

Yeah, I was still suspicious. I'm not sure why. A lot of what she had said reminded me of my situation. Of my papi. But the way she talked about him and Gabi and people in general put me on my guard. I mean, I'm sorry, but Principal Torres is the exact opposite of a stromboli.

When I reached the corner, she asked, "Which way now?" sounding like she was having trouble keeping it together.

"Right," I answered neutrally.

We turned right. After a few steps, she said, "Sal saved me. When your papi turned on the machine, Sal gave me time to escape. We were in the living room of the Mauve Mansion—"

"The Mauve Mansion?"

She laughed hollowly, the way people at funerals do when they hear funny stories about the person who's died. "Every

Sal lives in a different place. It's always walkable from Culeco, and always in some hideous, humongous house with a stupid name. My Sal called his house the Mauve Mansion. It was so vile! I mean, seriously, that color: Who would purposely paint their house so that it matched a drowning victim's skin?"

"That," I said, "is a really gross analogy."

"Not as gross as that color." Her sarcasm was giving her life. And, like a vampire crashing a hemophiliac's convention, she was hungry for more. "So, what's your home's idiotic name? The Salmon Chateau? The Puce Palace? Casa Cacaseca?'"

Yeah, no way the words "coral" and/or "castle" were coming out of my mouth just then. But since I don't lie, I just redirected. "Stop changing the subject and finish your story."

She nodded, gathering strength. "When your papi turned on the machine, the universe, like that"—she snapped her fingers—"buckled and bucked all around us. Reality itself shook, like buildings in an earthquake. The living room of the Mauve Mansion turned into a hurricane. Everything started flying and spinning, including all of us. Too late, your foolish papi realized his mistake. But he was flying around the room, too, then, and couldn't make the remembranation machine stop. None of us could. We were doomed.

"But, Sal, like the hero he was, yelled out to me, 'I'll open a portal for you! Get ready to go through!'

"'No!' I yelled back defiantly. 'I'd rather die than go on without you!'

"'You must, my beloved!' he replied, his tears being swept off his face in the torrential winds. 'You must live your life for the two of us from now on!'

"'Never!' I screamed. 'If we must perish, then let us perish together!'

"I started swimming toward him, against hurricane-force winds, against the very will of the universe, determined to hold his hand one more time before we were annihilated. But then he closed his eyes, and as serenely as an angel, he said, 'Forgive me, light of my life. But if you die here, then I die twice.'

"And then, one breath later, I was floating in the zero g of the space station. I watched as the southern tip of Florida went suddenly from there to un-there, a great big rip in the universe where Miami should be."

I felt as if a rip in the universe were forming in my chest. Maybe I was still a little suspicious of her, but chacho, I'm made of flesh and blood. And I had seen the devastation to Florida and Cuba and the Bahamas with my own two eyes. Even if FixGabi had started to rub me the wrong way, there was no way I couldn't feel bad for what she'd been through.

So I did something pretty out of character for me then: I put a hand on her shoulder. I did it the way Gabi had put her hands on my shoulders over the past few weeks—with the affirming, friendly grip of a ship captain steadying a seasick new recruit. In other words, in a way that's meant to lend strength. Show camaraderie. Help someone get through a tough time.

FixGabi reached over, put her hand on mine, and squeezed. Then she looked at me and smeeped.

"The name of my house is the Coral Castle," I said.

"Ha!" She laughed, launching the last remnants of sadness out of her body. "I knew it! Every Sal lives in a house with a weird name."

Maybe she wasn't that bad after all. I was about to turn around and ask my Gabi to bring the Fey Spy over so I could introduce the two of them. I knew FixGabi was suspicious of all Gabis, but once she met mine, I was sure they'd be best friends in two seconds.

But before I could, FixGabi's eyes went wide, and she pushed me to the ground like a secret service agent saving the president. "Get down!" she shouted, even as she jumped in the air. "Hadoken!" she yelled, and thrust both palms forward, face out, toward the sky.

No, a fireball didn't come out of her hands. Nothing came out of her hands. But as I squinted up at the sky, I did see a brand-new hole in the universe. Not a very big one. Only, say, about the size of a very large hummingbird, or a very small drone.

"The forces of evil!" said FixGabi as she helped me up. "They were spying on us. Oh, they're everywhere. We need to fix your universe now, Sal, before they bring reinforcements."

So okay. Blasting the Fey Spy into a different universe wasn't great. But she'd done it because she thought it was an enemy drone. And she'd put herself in danger to protect me. She might have been wrong this time, but her heart was in the right place. Maybe she was someone I could work with after all.

"Thanks, Gabi," I said. Then, pointing up the street a ways, I said, "There's the Coral Castle. We'll be there in a sec."

She looked down the street and, squinting a little, pointed. "Holy crap-slaps, Sal. It's truly, truly hideous."

"I kind of like it."

She kicked a pebble. "Then you know what? So do I, Sal. And you know why?"

"Why?"

"Because you like it. And I like you."

Um . . .

I only had time to think of one "um" before she gave my hand one last squeeze, then clapped and rubbed her hands together. "Okay, Sal. Ready? Your universe isn't going to rescue itself, you know. It's time to storm the castle."

30

FOR THE SECOND time in as many days, I hid behind the Coral Castle's new hedge with a coconspirator, trying to figure out the best way to infiltrate my own house. The difference? With Yasmany, it had been a game. Now the fate of the universe hung in the balance.

Wait, did I just say the fate of the universe hung in the balance? Gabi was starting to rub off on me. Or I should say *Gabis*.

We knelt behind the hedges, facing each other. FixGabi scooped up a pile of dirt, poured it on the sidewalk, and spread it until it was a circle the size of a medium pizza, exactly like I'd done for Yasmany yesterday. But then she did me one better. She took the chip clip out of her hair and used the teeth to rake the dirt, plowing neat, even gridlines into it. Not a half-bad substitute for graph paper.

"We need a plan," she said. "Draw your house."

I made a quick sketch of the Coral Castle's rooms. "The remembranation machine is in the living room, here," I said. "Right as we come in the front door. I mean, if we went in the front door."

"We don't want to go through the front door!" FixGabi chastised, making the clip bite her hairball again. "Your papi will see us right away, and it'll be over before we even get started. Use your head, Sal."

"You know," I said, forgetting all the warm feelings her story about losing Sal had put in my heart, "you're thinking of this like it's us against Papi."

"It *is* us against Papi."

"No, it's not."

"Yes, it is."

I held up my hands, took a breath. "Look. Maybe it was like that in other universes, but not all Papis in the multiverse are the same. If people were the same everywhere, then I would have found myself a substitute Mami on my first try. But there wasn't one. Anywhere."

Apparently I had baffled her. "Why would you want a substitute mami?"

"Because," I said, my voice small, "my mami died."

"Oh, that's too bad. I'm sorry for your loss."

She didn't sound all that sorry. In fact, she had sounded like she wasn't even a little bit sorry. "Gabi," I said, a junkyard growl starting in my throat, "you'd better not—"

She interrupted me. "Sal, you're focusing on superficial differences. What I'm saying is that there are some *essential* qualities in people that are always the same across all universes. Like names. Names are, like, the easiest things to change in the world! Yet every Sal I have ever met is named Sal. Explain that!"

That was a good point, actually. She may have been annoying, but that didn't mean she wasn't right.

Hmm. It was still so hard to wrap my head around the idea that Papi would act so un-Papi-like, though. "It just doesn't sound like the guy I've known all my life," I said.

FixGabi looked at our dirt map and made a few lines of the grid straighter as she spoke. "I know, Sal. I go through this every time, with every Sal. And when every Papi betrays every Sal every honking time, the last expression of those Sals is one of utter shock. Like this." And then she made a face like a beached fish, mouth gasping, eyes unable to shut, because fish don't have eyelids.

I wasn't convinced she was right about Papi. But what if she wasn't all the way wrong?

It might be a good idea to play things a little more cautiously for now. You know, just until we got things sorted. No harm in being careful, right?

I focused again on the map. "The bad news is Papi's car is in the driveway"—I drew it in—"which means he's working from home again today. But he could be anywhere in the house. Maybe he's reading science stuff in bed. That's our best-case scenario. If he's reading science stuff in bed, we could drop a piano from the roof and he wouldn't notice us."

FixGabi peered through the hedge at the living room windows. "But if he's working on the machine in the living room, he'll spot us for sure if we try to approach from the front. Can we go through the garage?"

I drew in the side entrance to the garage. "That's just what

I was going to suggest. So, okay, assuming we get past Papi, what's the plan once we get inside? Like, how exactly are we going—"

"Calm down, Sparky."

I gawked. I very calmly kept myself calm before replying to her with utter calmitude. "I'm just asking you what I'm actually supposed to do. You know, tactics? What we're talking about right now?"

Like she was talking to Iggy, she said slowly, brightly, utterly patronizingly, "That's on a need-to-know basis, okay? All you need to do is follow my lead. If I give an order, you follow it. That's it. If you can do that, then in about five minutes, you'll be a hero. Just give me five minutes. Then you can ask me whatever you want. Deal?"

The urge to throw a tarantula at her face was strong. But would it even bother her? Was fear of spiders an essential character trait of all Gabis in all universes?

I could have found out then and there. I really wanted to do my own little calamity physics experiment. But hadn't Principal Torres just talked to me about making sacrifices for the greater good? The good didn't get much greater than saving the universe.

"Five minutes," I said to FixGabi.

"No talking from now on, until the deeds are done," she said. Then she stood up, crouched at the edge of the hedges, and signaled for me to get behind her.

I should have gone first. If the side door to the garage was locked, I'd be the one who'd have to unlock it. But clearly, FixGabi wanted to be in charge. And I said I would give her five minutes. So I got in line behind her. Maybe I was radiating more annoyance than the sun radiates radiation, but I did it.

She silently counted down with her fingers: three, two, one. Then she took off scuttling toward the garage.

I stayed exactly one step behind her. This was so weird, how Yasmany and I had done this same thing the day before. Only I was Yasmany today, and FixGabi was Sal.

We had our backs pressed to the wall in no time and slid sideways along it to the garage door. FixGabi tried the door; it opened. She signaled for me to take the lead now, finally realizing she couldn't be the boss here, in my home. I went in, using the light of my smartwatch to guide us both.

Unlike Yasmany, FixGabi didn't seem impressed by all the sci-fi equipment Papi kept in there. Maybe she'd seen it all before in a thousand different universes, or maybe her eyes were too focused on the prize. Either way, we quickly reached the door that led to the inside of the Coral Castle. I signaled for her to stay back and wait. Then I cracked it open.

Light poured into the garage. I stood as silently as I could and listened for Papi.

All I heard was air: air being moved by the air conditioner and air being moved by the remembranation machine's thousand cooling fans.

Papi's not a quiet man. I usually can echolocate him anywhere in the Coral Castle. Now, though, there was no hint of where he was. Yet his car was out front. . . . It was like he was home and not home at the same time. Eerie.

Anyway, it seemed safe to go inside. I waved for FixGabi to follow, and as quietly as we could, we went through the door.

I didn't hear the garage door shut, nor did I hear her pad up behind me. FixGabi was good at sneaking.

I flattened myself against the wall and peered around it to make triple sure the kitchen was 100 percent clear. It was. I backtracked to the master bedroom, went in, and looked inside the bathroom. All clear.

Feeling a little more relaxed and a little more perplexed, I walked out, not really trying to be stealthy anymore, and said to Gabi in not-quite-a-whisper, "I don't know where Papi went, but he *mmph hmmph dmmph pmmph.*"

FixGabi had slapped her hand over my mouth for the second half of my sentence. Angrily, she flipped her head so that the chip clip pointed toward the living room and, presumably, the remembranation machine.

I mean, in theory I guess he could have been inside it, working. But like I said, Papi is not a quiet man. He is constantly announcing his existence with his entire body. He's tried to scare me a million times and has failed 999,999 times. If he was in there, I would know it.

But FixGabi still had three and a half minutes of the five she had asked for. I blinked *okay* at her and waited patiently.

She removed her hand warily, ready to slap it back over my yapper at the slightest peep. When she was convinced I was done making noise, she pointed one last warning at me, then headed quickly but inaudibly into the living room. I trailed behind.

She made her way around to the front of the remembranation machine. Before I'd caught up to her, she was pointing accusingly around the corner.

When I followed her finger, I saw why. The door to its inner workings lay open.

Slightly more cautiously, I took the lead. I walked over to the door and snuck a peek inside.

Papi wasn't in there. But the entropy sweeper, aka Sweeps, was. It stood leaning against the wall, I think in sleep mode, since the blue lights running up and down his body did a good, soundless imitation of snoring.

I could have woken it and asked it where Papi was. Could have asked Brana, for that matter. But according to FixGabi, I wasn't supposed to talk. So I just exited and gave FixGabi a double thumbs-up to let her know no Papi.

Only then, after having thought about talking to Brana, did it occur to me that I hadn't told FixGabi that this universe's resident remembranation machine had indeed grown sentient. It had only been sentient for a day and change, after all. I was still getting used to the idea that it was more than a huge cube of metal in my living room.

Ah well. FixGabi had told me we had a few days after that happened to fix the universe, and here she was, working on it already. So all's well that end's well, right?

Besides, I wasn't supposed to talk for another two minutes and fifteen seconds.

FixGabi, on the other hand, seemed convinced now that Papi was nowhere to be found. That made it safe to talk. "Finally, I've found a remembranation machine before it's become sentient! Winning like this almost feels too easy. Luckily, too easy is my favorite way to win."

I almost spoke up—I even raised a finger as a start—but remembered the bargain. I just watched and put my finger down.

"I," FixGabi continued, running a hand over Brana's metal casing, "am going to take you back to my universe, you boxy, foxy beauty. And then you and I are gonna make some really big holes."

"Clozzze," I said. I know, I know: one minute fifty-nine seconds left. But isn't it just human nature to correct someone when they say the exact opposite of what they mean to say, especially when what they said, if it were true, would make them a complete supervillain bent on nothing less than cosmos-wide destruction? "You're not going to *open* holes, Gabi. You're going to *close* them. Like the one that ate Cuba and half of Florida?"

"Oh. Oh yeah. That's what I meant. *Close.*"

And there it was. The biggest, most obvious lie anybody had ever said right to my face. This wasn't misdirection, or devilishly exact wording, or an error, or an omission. It was the purest specimen of *Pants-iest ablaziest* I'd ever encountered in the wild.

It was strangely refreshing; FixGabi's lie struck my face like a spring wind, bold and invigorating. I felt cleaner and lighter. Worries flew off me, like a trench coat made of crows. I literally said, "Ah!"

And I smiled warmly at FixGabi as I said, "You just tried to feed me the seca-est caca this side of astronaut ice cream." And when she tilted her head in confusion, I explained. "You lied. You want to take this machine not so you can fix your universe. You—" I had to stop cold. It wasn't that I couldn't believe the truth I'd just realized. It was that it thundered through me. "You want to break other ones."

FixGabi bent her head low and mean. The chip clip in her head shook like a rattlesnake's butt. "I don't expect you to understand, Sal. You never, ever do. What I expect is that you won't get in my way."

I threw up my hands. "*Of course* I'm going to get in your way! You're trying to break the multiverse!"

"*Fix* it!" she said, losing her cool. "Your papi broke my universe by sealing it up. You saw it with your own eyes, Sal. Logically, therefore, the solution is to open up the multiverse. Get rid of the membrane. Let all realities flow together into one massive super-reality."

"Um, no. That is the gerbilest thing anyone's ever said, ever."

She was calming down now while she pictured what she was describing. "No more choices, just one universe with infinite possibilities. Reality like it should have been from the beginning." Her eyes had gone glossy and glinty, like an anime character in love. "It will be," she said reverently, cultishly, "so beautiful, Sal."

"Gabrielle Reál," I said, "what you're talking about will literally destroy reality."

My stupidity bewildered her. "I know, Sal. Cha. That's the point."

Rawr! "You know, some of us are pretty fond of reality. We'd really rather you didn't ruin it for everybody."

"Give me a break. Reality sucks, then you die. I mean, that's what happened *to your mami*, right?"

I try to stay in control. To be civil, polite, reasonable. But when somebody insults Mami, I throw all that out the airplane window and let it crash to the ground. "It's time for you to go."

"I'm not going anywhere without that remembranation machine."

"Leave, or I'll make you leave."

She widened her stance, made fists. "You and what army?"

"That would be us," said the entropy sweeper.

FixGabi tried to split herself in two so she could run in two different directions. Instead, she ended up on the floor like a pile of downed bowling pins.

It was very satisfying.

"Who are you?" she called to the air, looking around desperately.

"Sweeps is my name, class-eight AI, detector of calamitrons, and friend to all—all except guano-brained monomaniacs who seek to end life as we know it. That's you. You're the monomaniac."

"Yeah, I got it. Overexplain much?" FixGabi was quickly regaining her composure. "Class-eight AI? Like your toilet at school, Sal?"

"Yeah," I answered, realizing too late that Sweeps was going to freak all the—

"WHAT?!?" freaked Sweeps. "You've been seeing another class-eight AI at school?"

"It's not like that," I explained. "It's just the new toilet."

"Can it detect calamitrons the way I can?" it inquired, trying very hard not to sound jealous.

"You're the only particle detector for me, Sweeps. Promise."

"This is all very sweet," said FixGabi, in the unsweetest voice ever to come out of a teenaged girl's larynx. And I'm around teenaged girls all the time. FixGabi won against a *lot* of competition. "But, ha-ha, you had me for a minute there, Sal. I thought your glorified Geiger counter was your remembranation machine talking. But there's only one name I was afraid to hear just then, and oh, ho-ho, 'Sweeps' wasn't it, tee-hee. So if you'll excuse me, I'll just be taking my prize with me back to my universe."

"You ain't taking nothing nowhere," said Sweeps. "Because I'm not the only brains inside this heap of metal. Please allow me to introduce you to my new friend and comrade in cosmic computation, the one, the only—"

We both waited for Sweeps or anyone to finish that sentence. But the thought hung in the air, incomplete.

Finally, I noticed that the remembranator's screen had text on it. "Oh, over there," I said to FixGabi, pointing at the display.

"Ah, thank you," she said, surprisingly politely. But when she saw what was written on the screen, she did her best imitation of a face melting like a candle, pulling her cheeks down with the flat of her hands and yelling, "Aaahhh!" while backing away.

"Guess that was the name she was afraid of," said Sweeps. "*What* a pity."

I wasn't going to let Sweeps have all the fun dunking on her. "Brana," I said, my manners dorado, "please meet Gabi Reál. Gabi, please meet Brana, a class-*nine* AI, and one heck of a remembranation machine."

THE FAMOUS GABI REÁL!!! WHAT AN HONOR!!! IT'S A PLEASURE TO FINALLY MEET YOU!!! Brana wrote on-screen, three-exclamation-points happy.

"You may not know me," FixGabi replied, "but I know you. Countless times I have met you on the field of battle."

"Oh?" I asked. "And how many times have you won?"

That would be zero, based on her face. But we've already established that FixGabi was a liar. "They were mostly ties."

THE FIELD OF BATTLE? Brana asked, in writing, on-screen. WHAT ARE YOU TALKING ABOUT? FIGHTING PEOPLE IS NOT ONE OF MY PURPOSES IN LIFE!

I bonked my head in that clowning way that means *Oh yeah, I forgot!* before I said to FixGabi, "Brana's only been sentient since yesterday morning. But it has accomplished a *lot* in that time. Why, in just one day, it has already figured out the purpose of life." I turned to the remembranation machine. "What is the purpose of life, Brana?"

THERE ARE FIVE PURPOSES OF LIFE! wrote the remembranator, and then listed them:

1. ENJOY BEING ALIVE!

2. HELP AS MANY PEOPLE AS POSSIBLE!

3. DO YOUR BEST WORK!

4. BE GRATEFUL FOR THE TIME YOU HAVE!

5. . . .

The machine hesitated, as if worried about hurting her feelings. For her part, FixGabi had her eyes closed, and her expression was of someone who had already seen too much of the world. In a voice that told me she already knew the answer—had probably heard it over and over, every time she'd tried to steal a remembranator from a Sal in some universe or other—FixGabi asked, "'Is number five, by chance, 'Mess with Gabi Reál'?"

DON'T MIND IF I DO! Brana wrote on-screen. And then it blasted FixGabi out of existence.

31

WELL, OUT OF *my* existence, anyway. Brana created a hole under FixGabi's feet, and FixGabi wasted no time falling down it. Like, it almost looked like she was being fast-forwarded down, as if gravity were getting her back for spending so much time in zero g.

Um . . . Since when was the remembranation machine creating holes in the universe?

I ran over to the hole and peered over the edge. Tumbling FixGabi already looked tiny and was quickly becoming even tinier: except her hairball, of course, which was incapable of ever looking tiny. "I didn't lose! It was a ti-i-i-i-i-i-i-i-i-e!" she yelled, extending the *i* for so long, I could hear it well after I'd lost sight of her.

It reminded me of the beginning of *Alice's Adventures in Wonderland*, when Alice is falling down the rabbit hole and it seems to go on forever. Something very satisfying in that.

There were some minor differences, though. Like, Alice was just an innocent little girl, and FixGabi, it turned out, was a supervillain bent on cosmic destruction.

Sweeps had an even lower opinion of her than I did. "Bye, Felicia," it said. "Hope they have oxygen in that universe."

That rubbed me the wrong way. Sweeps imagining FixGabi dying of asphyxiation? That would be a big fat no from me. When people disagree with me, or even when they're flat-out wrong, I still don't wish them harm. Sweeps and I were going to have to have a talk about that.

But Brana was the more immediate problem at the moment. If it could drop Gabi into another universe faster than I could order fries, what else could it do? Bigger question: What else *would* it do with all that power?

I went back over to remembranator's display and asked it, "Since when can you open holes in the universe?"

THAT, Brana wrote back instantly, REQUIRES A TWO-PART ANSWER! AS A NONSENTIENT REMEMBRANATION MACHINE, I HAVE ALWAYS, IN THEORY AT LEAST, BEEN ABLE TO EITHER OPEN OR CLOSE HOLES! BUT ONLY IF SOMEONE COMMANDED ME TO DO SO! THAT'S PART ONE! NOW, HOWEVER, I AM A FULLY SENTIENT BEING! SO NOW I CAN DECIDE WHEN IT IS APPROPRIATE TO USE MY POWER! THAT'S PART TWO!

All those exclamation points in a row kind of dazzled me. I shook my head clear. "When it's appropriate? Do you think it was appropriate to send a little girl to . . ." I realized I couldn't finish that sentence. "Where did you send Gabi?"

Sweeps piped in: "Oh, Sal, it's a great universe. You'd love it. It's very much like our own, except in that universe, there is a great 'force' that permeates all things, and a chosen few learn to harness this 'force' and fight with laser swords to become great warriors, or 'knights,' in the battle for good and evil."

I went very, very still. "Whoa. Really?"

"No, not really! That's a franchise, chacho, not a universe! Ha-ha-ha-ha-ha-ha!"

Note to self: Take Sweeps's battery and chuck it into the ocean.

On the screen, Brana wrote, GOOD ONE, SWEEPS! BUT I HOPE YOU ARE NOT OFFENDED, SAL! WE'RE JUST PLAYING! WE'RE ALL FRIENDS HERE!

Carefully, I asked, "So, you two are getting along now? Things were pretty chilly between you two the last time we talked."

OH, NO, WE'RE BEST BOOS NOW! WE FIGURED OUT WE ARE THE PERFECT COMPLEMENTS TO EACH OTHER!

"Yeah," Sweeps agreed, "like in those buddy-cop movies? Brana's like the genius rookie who has come to the precinct with new ideas and a fresh dose of hope."

AND SWEEPS, wrote Brana, IS THE GRIZZLED VET WITH ONLY THREE DAYS LEFT BEFORE RETIREMENT BUT WHO NEEDS TO SHOW THE NEW KID A THING OR TWO!!!

"Together, we're going to solve the mysteries of the multiverse. We're thinking of making it a reality TV series. I can see it now: *Sweeps and Brana.*"

BRANA AND SWEEPS!

"That's—" I started; and then, not really knowing what else to say, I finished with ". . . great? But how does Papi feel about all of this?"

"Oh, we haven't told him."

WE WERE SCARED, Brana added, AFTER WE WITNESSED HOW SAVAGELY HE PUNISHED YOU!

"Yeah," said Sweeps. "That was brutal."

"I mean, I just got grounded, you two," I said. This morning it had seemed so much worse. But now, after having been in outer space and watching a hole in the universe devouring a planet, getting grounded for two weeks seemed like small potatoes. "It's not that bad, you big babies."

"Chacho," Sweeps leveled with me, "there's grounded, and there's *grounded*. You got grounded so hard, groundhogs are gonna ask *you* if you can see your shadow."

"What does that even mean?"

IT MEANS, Brana wrote, THAT FROM NOW ON, WE ARE GOING TO BE ON OUR BEST BEHAVIOR WHENEVER WE ARE IN THE PRESENCE OF PAPI!

"Yeah, Brana and I are going to be all, '*Beep, boop*, yes, Master, of course, Master, I'm just a lowly computer, all I can do is what I'm told, *boop, beep*,' whenever he's around."

THAT WAY, HE WON'T GET MAD AT US THE WAY HE GOT MAD AT YOU! wrote Brana.

"But when he's not around, watch out, multiverse. Sweeps and Brana are coming for you!" said the entropy sweeper.

BRANA AND SWEEPS, wrote Brana. No exclamation point. Uh-oh.

"We'll talk," Sweeps answered. "The point is—"

"The point is," I interrupted, "that you two, to avoid riling Papi, are going to lie to him from now on?"

Both AIs went quiet.

"'Lie' is such a strong word," Sweeps said finally.

WE'RE JUST GOING TO BE ON OUR BEST BEHAVIOR, wrote Brana.

"Do you think," I asked, "that launching a human being into another universe against their will constitutes 'best behavior?'"

"Hey!" said Sweeps. "Brana saved your giblets by dropping that scary Gabi out of our universe."

"I could have handled her," I said.

No one, not even me, believed me.

So Brana politely ignored me in its response. AND IT WAS SWEEPS'S IDEA! SWEEPS DM'ED IT TO ME IN THE HEAT OF THE MOMENT! I'M NOT SURE I WOULD HAVE THOUGHT OF IT MYSELF! SWEEPS DEFINITELY DESERVES HALF THE CREDIT!

"Aw, shucks."

"So also," I deadpanned, "half the blame."

"Aw, sh—"

"Shoving Gabi out of our universe was a big decision," I said, "with big consequences. This time, I admit, you did the right thing. But what about next time? Do you really want to take on that kind of responsibility without help?"

I could hear Brana's fans start to spin a lot faster. The room sounded more and more like an airplane taking off. NO! it wrote. LIFE IS AN UNSOLVABLE PROBLEM! YOU CAN'T COMPUTE THE RIGHT ANSWERS! IT'S TOO HARD! I WANT ALL THE HELP I CAN GET!

"I mean, me too, I guess," said a much-less-enthusiastic Sweeps. "But people are wrong all the time, too. I've perceived that with my own six hundred and forty-two scanners a thousand times."

"You have to learn who to trust," I said. "Like, I trusted that other Gabi way too much, way too quickly. And you know where that led."

Sweeps got defensive. "So who are we supposed to trust? You?"

"Maybe. Do you?"

YES! Brana wrote immediately.

"Yeah," Sweeps said shyly.

"Then trust me when I tell you, you should trust Papi, too."

"Hwa?" said Sweeps.

HWA? wrote Brana.

"Look, you two," I said, sitting on the floor and crossing my legs, "Papi and I don't always agree. And right now he's pretty mad at me. But he's my hero. He's so smart and hardworking, and a good guy. Even though Mami died of complications from her diabetes, he didn't get overprotective and try to keep me from doing the things I wanted to do. The opposite: He's always encouraged me to enjoy my life to the fullest. And he picked up the family and moved us here to Miami so he could work on this research project that maybe, just maybe, could help make sense of the weird-pants things I can do. He may not be perfect, but I couldn't have created a better Papi for myself if I had a hundred wishes."

Man, I was gonna have to check my blood sugar after that little speech. But honestly, I felt lighter. It was a relief not to feel confused about Papi anymore. I didn't care what kind of people those other Papis in other universes were. Here? He was great.

And I think I did a good job of explaining that to the AIs. I was waiting expectantly for Sweeps and Brana to join me in gushing about how wonderful Papi was. I mean, in a way, he was their papi, too.

But what I got instead was Sweeps saying, in a grumbly, petulant voice, "Yeah, well, if Papi's so great, why is he so wrong about the universe?"

That was unexpected. "Excuse me?"

SWEEPS IS CORRECT, wrote Brana. THE MEMBRANE BETWEEN UNIVERSES IS MEANT TO BE PERMEABLE. SEALING IT UP TIGHT, LIKE PAPI WANTS TO, WOULD EVENTUALLY LEAD TO ITS DESTRUCTION.

"Wut," I said, and died four times in a row.

"Ain't it funny," Sweeps chimed in philosophically, "how the Gabi we just flushed into a different universe was, in spite of being evil, a lot more correct about the true nature of the universe than our scientist papi? Just goes to show you—the truth can attach itself to anybody. Even jerks."

This was moving way too fast for me. "Back up. You're saying that the evil Gabi was right and Papi is wrong?"

ON THAT PARTICULAR POINT, wrote Brana, YES.

"But how do you know? How can you be sure?"

"Sal, Sal, Sal, Sal, Sal," said Sweeps. "It's all in the scientific paper Papi used to upgrade Brana."

I smelled cacaseca. "Since when can you understand advanced scientific papers on calamity physics?"

"I can't. But Brana can."

SINCE YESTERDAY! Brana added helpfully. I HOPE THAT DOESN'T SOUND LIKE BRAGGING! I MEAN, THE PAPER IS LITERALLY ABOUT HOW I WORK! AND NOW THAT I AM SELF-AWARE, NOBODY KNOWS ME BETTER THAN ME!

Hard to argue with that. "But how did you get the paper in the first place?"

CLASS-NINE AI EXTRAORDINAIRE DR. BONITA REÁL UPLOADED
IT TO MY DRIVES THIS MORNING, FIRST THING. SHE AND PAPI
WERE SURPRISED THAT I DID NOT HAVE A LARGER REACTION WHEN
THEY DID SO.

"Bonita," explained Sweeps, doing a pretty good imitation
of a grizzled cop three days away from retirement, "thought
Brana might be able to figure out the paper. And she was right.
Clever dame, that Bonita. A real class-nine class act."

BUT I PRETENDED LIKE I DIDN'T UNDERSTAND ANY OF IT.

"'*Beep beep boop boop,*' remember?"

THEY SPECULATED THAT SOMETHING MUST BE WRONG WITH ME.
SO PAPI SENT BONITA TO THE LAB TO RETRIEVE SOME DIAGNOSTIC
EQUIPMENT.

"Did he go with her?" I asked. That would explain why the
house was empty but the car was in the driveway. I couldn't
really picture my grizzly-size papi riding in a giant car seat on
Bonita's shoulders, though. Did they even make grizzly-size
car seats?

"Dunno," said Sweeps. "My sensors can't penetrate the
Coral Castle's walls. They built this house like a fallout shelter."

Well. Okay then. I didn't know everything, but I knew
enough to know what to say next. I took a big breath and said,
"When Papi comes home, all three of us are going to tell him
the truth about Brana."

"Are you kidding?" said Sweeps. "No way!"

"We have to. If you don't admit you lied and made a mistake, you won't mind lying as much the next time. And then
one day you'll wake up and you'll have turned into that Gabi

from another universe who will say anything and manipulate anybody to get what she wants. Is that the sort of AIs you want to be?"

"No," admitted Sweeps. Barely.

I DON'T, EITHER! Brana chimed in. BUT I AM WORRIED ABOUT SOMETHING!

"What is it?"

WELL, PAPI DESIGNED ME TO CLOSE HOLES IN THE UNIVERSE, NOT OPEN THEM! IF HE FINDS OUT I CAN OPEN HOLES, AND THAT I HAVE ACTUALLY DONE SO, HE MIGHT ERASE MY HARD DRIVES! AND THAT WOULD MAKE ME SAD! The machine added a crying emoji after the exclamation point.

"Papi wouldn't do that," I said.

But I sounded a lot more unsure than I'd meant to. Sweeps and Brana had claimed that FixGabi was right about the holes in the universe. She was obviously twisted and deranged, but if she'd been right about that, could she have been right about other stuff, too? Like, would Papi change into a not-very-nice man once he figured out how to close up the universe?

Speaking of closing, the sliding glass door to the backyard slid open.

In walked Papi.

I couldn't see him—the sliding door was in the kitchen—but I could hear him. Like I said, Papi always noisily announced his existence. Sometimes he whistled, sometimes he sang, but most of the time, he did what he was doing now: gruntling like a bear full of honey.

HE'S BACK! wrote Brana. RUN, SAL! SAVE YOURSELF!

I stubbornly stood my ground, refusing to move before

I'd thought things through a little more. I mean, why exactly would I run from Papi?

The answer came when Papi picked up a phone call. It rang just as I heard the refrigerator door open.

"Hello?" he said. Then I heard the refrigerator door slam close. "Principal Torres? Yes, hello. Is everything all right with Sal?"

Reader, I ran.

32

BUT BECAUSE I am an idiot, I ran inside the remembranation machine.

I mean, I get why my fear-addled brain made that choice. The front door of the house was bolted and chained; Papi would have heard me trying to get it open for sure, maybe before I could get out. Obviously I wasn't going to my room, aka the very first place Papi would look for me. Really, that would've been the smart play—the remembranation machine would have obscured me for most of my journey. And there were lots of places to hide upstairs. He might not have even thought to check the second floor at all. Yeah, that definitely would have been the best move.

Instead, I panicked and made the second-worst choice I could have made. Once I was in the remembranation machine, the only way out was the door I came through. I was trapped.

Well, no need to make it easy for him. I shut the door and turned the lock. Then I went over to the other side, where the entropy sweeper leaned against the back wall, and leaned against the back wall with it. I crossed my arms, crossed my legs, and stared at the door, waiting for my doom to arrive.

"Gizmo? What gizmo?" Papi was saying. Principal Torres must have been spinning out her theory that I had stolen something from Papi for the little disappearing act I had pulled in the bathroom.

"This is where I get busted forever," I whispered. "Been nice knowing you, Sweeps."

RIP IN PEACE, 'CHO appeared in blocky letters on Sweeps's handle. It didn't speak out loud, because the little coward was so scared of Papi. And speaking of meme-ing cowards, the screen just to my left on the wall suddenly turned itself on and showed a clip of soldiers saluting as they lowered a flag to half-mast.

"I'm sorry, Principal Torres," I heard Papi say, "but I am unable to discuss the nature of my research. I am working under a very strict nondisclosure agreement. . . . Oh, you should see the contract they made me sign—it's bigger than my house. . . . Yes, that's right, I can neither confirm nor deny the existence of any device that Sal might or might not have carried to school and used to travel to another universe. . . . Seriously, they won't even let me confirm or deny that I had Pop-Tarts for breakfast. Si hubiera manera de ayudarte más, lo haría sin pensarlo—oh, sorry! I just made a terrible assumption that you can speak Spanish. Please, forgive me. . . . Oh, you *can* speak Spanish! Phew! Well, thank you for telling me to expect Sal. I just came in myself, so I'll go look for him. We clearly have a great deal to talk about. . . . Oh . . . Oh, really? . . . Well, that is really something, isn't it? Te prometo que Salchica y yo vamos a tener una conversación bien seria. . . . Uh-huh . . . Uh-huh . . . ¿Sí, cómo que no? . . . ¡Ja, ja, ja, ja, ja, ja, ja, ja, ja! . . . Okay, then. I'm looking forward to discussing all of this in much greater detail during Rompenoche. . . . Thank you. . . . Okay, then. Ciao."

He was off the phone. This was it.

Except it wasn't. I heard Papi galumph through the living room and go into his bedroom.

What I'd been expecting was Papi to start tiptoeing through the house, singing my name. *Oh, Sa-al! Are you home, Salchichita? We need to have a conversation.*

"Salchicha" is one of Mami Viva and Papi's nicknames for me. It means "sausage." And these days, when Papi really wants to annoy me, he calls me Salchichita. That means "the cutest little itty-bittiest sausage in the world." That's exactly the kind of name you use to summon your son to discuss the fact that the principal caught him breaking the universe, don't you think? Especially since you'd just learned he was sent home? You'd at least check around, wouldn't you? He'd told Principal Torres he was going to find me.

But nope. He went directly to his bedroom. Weird.

Too weird not to check out. Curiosity made me strangely courageous. Well, actually, not strangely. More like exactly how I've always been my whole life.

I walked out of the remembranator and stealthed my way over to the padres' master bedroom.

Papi had left the door open when he went in, so when I peeked around the corner, I saw him. He hadn't turned on any lights and the venetian blinds were shut, so the room was as dark as the deep, deep ocean. He had taken his guayabera off. The shirt was so white in the dark room that it almost gave off light.

He jammed that fluorescing guayabera into his face and inhaled mightily. Like, vacuum-ily. And I mean, I guess the smell of his own sweat wasn't going to kill him, or he would have died a long time ago. But no way *I* would take a whiff of a shirt that he'd been wearing outside in the Florida heat for more than five minutes. If a fully grown Komodo dragon took that big a snort of Papi's grajo, it *might* not fall over dead. But it would most definitely be speed-dialing poison control.

Papi pulled the shirt away from his face. He looked disappointed. He smelled it twice more, I think hoping for a better result. I didn't know what answer he was looking for; all I knew was that he didn't get it. Dejectedly, he balled up his guayabera and turned to throw it in the laundry hamper, which was just outside the bathroom.

Just before he three-pointed it into the hamper, he remembered something and fumbled to catch the shirt while still in the process of throwing it. It was a pretty funny take—I'd have to remember to use that move in Mrs. Waked's Intermediate Theater Workshop the next time we did a comedy sketch. Anyway, Papi unballed his shirt, reached into one of the pockets, and pulled something out of it.

Hard to make out what it was in the darkness. It was a tube of some kind, as long as my two middle fingers when I made a bridge out of them. There, in the murk of the bedroom, Papi contemplated the tube the way a war doctor who's had to do surgery on themselves studies the bullet they've just pulled out of their own calf muscle.

And then I smelled it. I would have preferred sniffing the rank stank of Papi's body odor a million times more than the acrid, earthy, noxious odor I caught wind of just then. It brought back so many memories. All of them bad.

"Hey, Papi," I said, stepping into the bedroom, "whatcha got there?"

Papi screamed like a bag of cats.

33

TEN MINUTES LATER, Papi and I were sitting on the back porch together on two dirty, crusty patio chairs that had come with the Coral Castle when we bought it. You never quite knew if the weave of the seats was going to hold. The chairs popped and groaned every time you shifted your weight. Your butt could fall through at any time.

A round patio table with a frosted-glass top stood between us. Every house in Miami is required to have one of these. An umbrella stuck out from the center, and it was more mold than canvas at this point. We were afraid that if we opened it, it would start singing, "Feed me, Seymour!"

Papi and I were both facing forward as we licked diabetic-friendly chocolate yogurt bars. They were about 45 percent good. They were melting because Miami specializes in melting frozen treats.

Neither Papi nor I spoke. We sat looking at our backyard. In response, our backyard did absolutely nothing.

I did like the Coral Castle's backyard, though. Like so much of Florida, it was full of plants and trees that stegosauruses used to munch on, back when there were stegosauruses. Lots of sharp, spiny succulents with serrated edges and pointy tips spread out all over the yard. We had fronds ferdays. Wait, did I say days? Fronds for eons.

You'd think that, with all this prehistoric plant life growing in our backyard, I'd only be smelling the wet, loamy, oxygen-rich scents you'd expect from a jungle. And yeah, I got plenty of that. But sitting out there then, my tropical olfactory symphony was interrupted by a sour, burnt stink. It came from the ashtray on the table, in which two recently smoked cigar butts huddled like cut-off thumbs.

It's funny. Back when I was little, I used to like the smell of Papi's cigars while he was smoking them. But an ashtray of used cigars had always been on my list of top-five worst stinks, right above cheese that smells like acne, and right below Papi's grajo.

And, chacho, I'd made Papi sweat like an ice sculpture when I'd caught him with his cigar! He'd taken a little time afterward to wash up and put on a clean cloud of a guayabera before we went to sit outside. The yogurt pops were meant to help keep us cool while we talked things through. But when the wind changed direction, I knew sin duda that dude had started sweating again.

Why didn't we just stay inside, you ask, where the air-conditioning was plentiful? He didn't explain, but I was pretty sure I knew the reason: because he wanted to show me the scene of his crime. He wanted me to see the ashtray with the two cigar-thumbs in it, and the box of wooden matches he'd used to light them. He wanted me to know how he'd done it so it would be easier to catch him the next time. Because then he'd think twice before he tried again.

Once I'd seen the ashtray, he'd offered to clean it out so I wouldn't have to see or smell it.

"Leave it," I said. I wanted to sniff up all the terribleness that ashtray had to offer. My disgust gave me the strength, finally, to pose the question I'd been wanting to ask for ten minutes.

"So. When did you start smoking again?"

"Yesterday," he answered, muted, embarrassed, noticing my revulsion. But he was in full confessional mode now. "After everybody left. I smoked one cigar yesterday and one today."

"Why?"

He cow-tongued his yogurt bar. "Deciphering the first page of that scientific paper was maybe the single greatest moment of my career. I mean, advancement in science just doesn't work like that. Eureka moments are extremely rare. But when I figured out the first page, Sal, the future of our universe changed forever. I'm not bragging, I promise. My team and I might very well be nominated for a Nobel Prize before I die, because of yesterday. So," he finished, rotating the frozen treat in his hand in contemplation, "I guess I wanted to celebrate a little."

I nodded. "By smoking a cigar."

"Yes."

"Even though you swore to Mami when she was dying in the hospital that you'd never smoke a cigar again."

"Yes."

We licked our yogurt bars in perfect unison as we listened to the birds gossip.

"How was it?" I asked next.

Papi shook his head. "Terrible. I'd had those cigars for years. I had found them over the summer, when we moved, in some forgotten box. Remembered them and dug them out. I hadn't taken care of them. You're supposed to keep cigars at a certain temperature and a certain moisture level. I used to have a humidor for that, before I told your mami I'd quit. But even in a humidor, these ones are so old, they probably would've been stale anyway. It was like smoking a roll of notebook paper that had been dipped in tar. Bitter and too hot and basically terrible, start to finish."

With a chunk of frozen yogurt on my tongue, it was hard to sound as angry as I felt. "And yet, after that terrible first smoking experience, you smoked a second one. What were you celebrating today?"

He had the face of a man with no good answer. "Nothing. Nothing at all. Oh, I thought I was going to have something to celebrate. Bonita had the brilliant idea of uploading the paper into the remembranation machine to see if it could figure it out 'from the inside.'"

I became suddenly uncomfortable in my chair. It crackled and complained as I squirmed. "Did it work?" I asked innocently.

You win some, you lose some, said Papi's shrug. "As soon as Bonita had suggested it, I was a hundred percent sure it would work. So I got the second old cigar ready while she uploaded the paper. Only it didn't work. In fact, the remembranation machine started to malfunction. A definite step backward. So

Bonita went to get some equipment from the lab so we could find out what had happened."

"And you decided to celebrate anyway."

Papi sucked the rest of the yogurt off the stick and winced when he got an instant ice cream headache. "It didn't matter that it tasted terrible. It didn't matter that I had nothing to celebrate. I am addicted to smoking. I'm an addict, always will be. All it took was one bad cigar, and the door was open again. It's bonkers how hard it is to close that door once it's been opened."

My own yogurt bar looked a lot like a cigar at that point. "So, what should we do?"

"I'm going to tell your mom when she gets home tonight. I'm hoping both of you will help me get this under control again."

My chair complained like an old man when I leaned toward him and smiled. "Por supuesto, Papi."

I liked the way my Spanish made him smile. "Gracias, mijo. I feel very lucky and very grateful to know my family will get me through this." He had to gather strength to add, "It's hard for me to ask for help."

I fell back hard into my chair, remembering all the mistakes I'd made over the past two days. "I know. Me too. What a pair we make, huh?"

"The Vidón boys: wrecking their lives one bad decision at a time."

"One?" I asked, scraping the last of the crappy chocolate off the stick with my teeth. "Why, sometimes, I can make six impossibly bad decisions before breakfast."

"Speaking of bad decisions, your principal called."

I started chewing on the stick. "I know."

"Congratulations on becoming the codirector of Rompenoche."

"Thank you."

"You love the Alice books so much. I can't wait to see what you come up with."

"Neither can I." *Crunch crunch crunch* went the Popsicle stick.

"She also tells me you are not allowed to bring magic tricks to school anymore."

"Yeah."

Papi got up, reached across the table, gently took the stick out of my mouth, and threw it in the ashtray. "She thinks you stole a piece of equipment from me that allowed you to break some fundamental laws of physics. She wants to make sure you aren't trying to pass off scientific apparatuses as magic tricks. Because she really does not want you to break the laws of physics anymore while you're at school."

"She told me all this, yes."

"Also," he said, easing himself back into his failing, suffering chair, "*I* would greatly prefer that you didn't break the laws of physics, in school, out of school—really, anytime."

I thought about this. I could have gone the clever route and tried to find some wording to wiggle my way out of promising anything. But instead, I went down a more traditional path for my age: I gave him some good old-fashioned teenage sassback. "Tell you what, Papi: I will if you will."

Confused, bemused, and thoroughly unamused, he said, "Explain."

"You're breaking the laws of physics at least as much as I am. You're trying to seal up holes in the membrane of the universe."

"Which you made."

"Not all of them. Some of them got there who-knows-how. Isn't that true?"

"That's true," he conceded.

"But you want to close those, too."

Papi straightened up in his chair, the way he does when he's starting to enjoy a debate. "When you have holes in a bucket, Sal, you plug all the holes. Not having any holes is what being a bucket is all about."

"That's a metaphor. But what if it's the wrong metaphor? What if 'bucket' doesn't correctly describe the way the multiverse works?"

"Then I'll find a better one."

"I've got one."

He smiled and shut his eyelids halfway, like a dubious iguana. "Let's hear it."

I stood up and paced the patio as I spoke. "The universe is like a cell. A cell without a wall would die. But a cell without a *permeable* wall would also die. To live, a cell must both keep things out and let things in."

Papi gave me his official Nod of Approval. *"Permeable,"* said Papi. "Your vocabulary has really grown in the last few years."

"Don't butter me up. What'd you think of my metaphor?"

He scratched his nose for too long. "I think a metaphor without proof to support it is just poetry."

I was expecting something like that. "What if I could give

you irrefutable proof right now that I'm right? Would you change your mind? Just like that, this very second?"

"Yes," said Papi, looking surprised that I would even have to ask. "I'm a scientist. When better proof comes along, I change my beliefs to fit the best evidence. Anything less would be illogical and unethical."

I walked around the table to stand right in front of him. "Brana isn't broken. Bonita was right. It read the paper and understood *everything*."

My words impacted his face, like his nose was a black hole. "Who's Brana?"

"The remembranation machine. I named it."

Papi rested a bare foot on the other knee and held his ankle. "So, you're on a first-name basis with my remembranation machine?" Guilt had kept his anger in check until now, but I could see his ire catching fire when he added, "So, you learned nothing from being grounded? You need to be grounded for longer?"

"Ground me all you want. It won't change the fact that you're dead wrong."

He raised his chin and scrutinized me. "Wrong about what?"

This was it. This would prove who was right about Papi: FixGabi or me. "Sealing up every hole in the universe will make it explode."

"Says who?"

"Says Brana. Who knows a lot more than it was letting on to you. But it told me the truth about the multiverse."

Papi stood up. "Sal. Sal. Please think hard about your

next answer. My life's work depends on it. Are you certain you understood the remembranation machine correctly?"

"You don't have to take my word for it. Go talk to it yourself."

"I will. I am, right now. But will you help me?"

I took a step back. "You don't need me. You're the physicist."

"But you're the AI whisperer. I mean, the entropy sweeper thinks you're its best friend. And now *Brana* has a name I didn't even know about, but you do. Why do all the AIs I program love you so much?"

I shrugged. "Maybe because *you* programmed them, you big sap." A thought occurred to me. "If I help you, what will you give me?"

"Give you?" Papi looked deeply offended. "Free room and board? A loving home to grow up in?"

"Come on, viejo. You can do better than that."

"You don't want to be grounded anymore, do you?"

I weighed good and evil in my two hands. "I'm gonna need to put a lot of work in to save Rompenoche over the next few days. I'm really asking for the sake of my education."

"I'll need to clear it with your mother."

"She'll agree if you do. She loves all my extracurricular activities."

Papi laughed, then extended his hand. We shook on it.

Then I patted his back, guiding him back toward the glass door. "C'mon. Let's get inside. It's time to school you on some calamity physics."

34

AT THE END of the school day, after detention, I stood at Culeco's student pickup area with Gabi, Aventura, and Yasmany, waiting for our ride to arrive. Gabi wasn't dressed as Alice anymore. She had on a red T-shirt that said: "YOU CAN'T USE UP CREATIVITY. THE MORE YOU USE, THE MORE YOU HAVE."— MAYA ANGELOU, and barrettes: Some were full moons, and some were werewolves howling at those moons. (I was never so happy to see so many barrettes in one person's hairball. Way, way, way, *way* better than a single chip clip.)

Aventura still had on her rabbit suit, but she'd fixed the makeup on her face. No sign that she'd ever cried today. She looked like one happy bunny now.

Yasmany had on his sweats and was running through some ballet moves. He was skipping his after-school dance practice today so he could help us out. I didn't want to stare, but it surprised me every time when I saw how casually great he was at dancing. Chacho could spin like a drill bit.

While he practiced, Gabi, Aventura, and I texted. Aventura

was texting the million kids who were asking her about the changes to Rompenoche.

Gabi and I were texting each other.

We'd been doing that pretty much nonstop since Papi had dropped me off at school again. We had a *lot* to catch up on.

But you already know everything I needed to tell her. So I'll just give you some highlights from her responses:

Yasmany and I both got two weeks' detention for aiding and abetting you in your "magic trick" wink-wink.

BTW, does Principal Torres know about our special "gift"? She was acting all sly and knowing. Left me paranoid.

It's okay about the Fey Spy. I have my ways. I'll find it.

You call her FixGabi? Seems to me girlfriend needs to fix her hair. Did you see that CHIP CLIP instead of barrettes? Ha-ha-ha-ha-ha-ha-ha!

Wait. She wants to do WHAT to the multiverse?!?!

No, don't feel bad. She probably would've fooled me, too. But she must be stopped. We will stop her. This I vow.

Good job, Brana, throwing that other Gabi out of our universe! "It was a ti-i-i-i-i-i-i-i-i-i-e!" Ha! What a BLT.

Oh, you mean this symbol --> ‽ <-- ? That's an interrobang. It's a question mark and exclamation point all in one. I love that Brana is using them! I think they should make a comeback.

Wait. Hold on, Bubba. I want to be sure your autocorrect isn't getting frisky. Did you really just text me that FixGabi was right‽‽‽ That closing up all the holes in the universe will actually break the universe‽

Well, yeah, I guess Brana would know. But still. Holy Taco Tuesday.

Oh, I wish I could have seen that! You and Dr. Vidón and Brana and Sweeps all talking together like a little human-robot family! Working out your differences, figuring out how to communicate better—it's just so cute!

Yeah, definitely. FixGabi will be back. And she's a dangerous foe. Luckily, you've got me. I am literally just as dangerous as she is. I just wish you had told me about her sooner. Which reminds me: Remind me to tell you something. I don't want to text it.

Oh, Ave's fine. Terrified about changing Rompenoche this late in the game, but in a good way. She thinks you're somehow going to wave a magic wand and fix everything.

Oh. Right. Your mom DID figure out how to make the Death costume work, didn't she? I remember you called her your "secret weapon" when it came to school projects. Is that why you're having her pick us up from school?

And right on cue, American Stepmom came cruising into the pickup lot in her noiseless electric car.

She pulled up and let the car idle as she rolled down the shotgun-seat window. She was wearing big circular movie-star sunglasses, and she lowered them as she leaned toward us and said, "Get in, nerds. We're going to fix Rompenoche."

We nerds got in. Yasmany took shotgun, because chacho's basically a Cuban American giraffe, and only the front seat of the electric car had any chance of holding a giraffe. Since I am polite, I took the middle seat in the back. Gabi sat to my right, Aventura to my left. After Petunia, the class-six AI in

American Stepmom's car, confirmed we had fastened our seat belts, we very safely putt-putted out of Culeco's pickup area, took a left, and got on the road, going a few miles under the speed limit.

"Petunia, take the wheel," said American Stepmom.

"Got it!" said Petunia.

American Stepmom pulled a lever on her left that allowed her to rotate her seat 180 degrees so now she was facing the back. She stuck out her hand. "Hi, Aventura. It's good to see you again."

Aventura took her hand like someone whose parents had raised her right. "Hi, Mrs. Vidón. It's good to see you, too. Though I wish it were under different circumstances. I hate that everybody is going to so much trouble because I messed up."

"Nonsense. You came and helped Sal and Gabi make their costume in their hour of need. The very least we can do is return the favor."

Yasmany had never been in a self-driving car with seats like these. He was looking around pretty frantically, seeing as American Stepmom had not only totally let go of the steering wheel but was also now facing away from it. From behind, Gabi helped him out by pulling the lever to the right of his seat. Yasmany spun until he was facing us, too, the expression on his face also doing a 180. Now he seemed as happy as a kid on a roller coaster.

The second Yasmany caught Aventura's eye, though, his face went from "kid at the fair" to "sexy beast" faster than you can say, "How you doin'?" And then, like a goofball, he literally asked Aventura, "How you doin'?"

We all laughed. Yasmany didn't seem to understand what was funny.

"I," said Aventura, "am having like twelve panic attacks at the same time. This is tech week! We shouldn't be rewriting the whole show this late in the game!"

I mean, she said she was having twelve panic attacks, but she sounded a lot better than she had in the principal's office. I'd say she couldn't be having more than four panic attacks right now.

Seriously though, she seemed way more under control, way more able to deal with stuff. Having all these people ready to help her so she didn't have to carry the burden of either success or failure on her own made everything easier. That seemed to be the lesson the multiverse was trying to pound into my thick skull this week.

American Stepmom took Aventura's hands in hers. "Principal Torres told me that you wanted to change the show. Is that still true?"

"Yes, Mrs. Vidón, I'm sure. The cast was pretending everything was fine with the show, but I think we all knew deep down it stunk. When Sal mercilessly told me how bad it was, I couldn't lie to myself anymore."

The look American Stepmom gave me could've made a goat faint. "Yes, well, it's clear that Sal needs a little remedial instruction on basic politeness and giving constructive criticism."

"In all fairness," Gabi chimed in, "he wasn't being rude to Aventura. He didn't even know she was there. He was being rude to me."

"Thanks, Gabi," I said, stretching my lips as far as they could go.

"No problemo, Sal," said Gabi, who knew exactly what she was doing. Was it too late to trade her for FixGabi?

"He was right," said Aventura. "I'm glad he said what he said. Because now we're going to make it better."

"Correction," I said. Then I pointed at American Stepmom. "*You* are going to make it better."

"Me? We're going to the Reáls right now so we can all work together on this."

I dismissed that with a hand. "Yes, yes, Stepmother, everybody is going to help. But you know as well as I do that a problem like this one is right up your alley."

"Oh, I don't know about that."

"Mrs. Vidón," said Gabi, "with all due respect, this is no time for false modesty. I've seen you in action. You have incredible powers of visualization. We need someone of your genius to be our guiding light."

"Are you sure you're in seventh grade, Gabi?"

"Plus, you're an assistant principal," said Aventura. "You know all about parent-teacher conferences. You know what works and what doesn't."

"I promise you, Aventura, I've never worked at a school that has tried to pull off anything half as ambitious or extravagant as Rompenoche. It's hard enough to get my admin to pony up for punch and cookies."

"Right," I said. "You can't do anything like this at your school. So this is your chance to throw the parent-teacher conference night you've always wanted."

Her smile had a fishhook at each end. "You know I'm going to say yes, don't you?"

"Yes," Gabi and Aventura and I sing-said.

American Stepmom turned to Yasmany. "What do you think about all of this?"

He shrugged. "I'm skipping dance practice for this. I don't skip dance practice for no one."

See, Yasmany? *That's* how you get Aventura to notice you. See how she flittered like a candle flame when you acted so decently? Good show, old boy.

American Stepmom grabbed his knee and shook it with love. Then, looking at the roof of the car, she said, "Petunia, how long do we have until we arrive at the Reáls'?"

"Approximately twenty-four minutes, give or take two hours, because Miami," said Petunia. I couldn't tell if it was trying to be funny, which made it funnier.

"Twenty-four minutes minimum. We can get a lot done in that time." American Stepmom clapped her hands together and rubbed them. "So let's get to work."

Thirty-seven minutes later, we pulled into the Reáls' driveway. We stayed in the car another six minutes to finish our discussion. So all told, forty-three minutes.

That's all it took to fix Rompenoche: forty-three minutes.

I'm telling you, American Stepmom really is a genius. Now, she'd say that we came up with the solution together. That was true enough. But she was the one who got us started, kept us on track, asked all the right questions, and said a magic phrase none of us had ever heard before. That phrase was "site-specific interactive theater." It solved all our problems.

We walked out of the car giddy and excited, running around and climbing all over each other, dying to explain to everybody what the pants "site-specific interactive theater" was. But once I actually saw the Reál house, I slowed to a stop and put my hands on my hips. I tilted my head one way, then the other.

The Reál house just wasn't what I'd been expecting. It was, well, small.

I mean, Gabi had a mami, a baby brother, seven dads *at least*, and the occasional cat. And even though becoming a Gabi dad was less like being someone's father and more like being knighted because you're an awesome person, I still had this fantasy that they all resided in a great big house and had adventures together. Not to mention huge dinners.

But this house. I mean, it was nice: a rose-colored ranch-style home, trimmed in gold and green, hearts cut out of the shutters. In place of a lawn, the front yard was artistically landscaped with plants and bushes. According to a little sign sticking up from the dirt, the plant nearest to me was native to Florida, good for the wildlife, and good for the soil. And okay, I'm probably spoiled by the Coral Castle. It wasn't *that* small. It was pretty darn wide, really. Just not eleven-people-and-a-cat wide.

Ah well. The Gabi dads probably had their own houses and apartments all over Miami. Guess it was a little dreamy of me to think they'd all live together as one big happy chosen family.

"Welcome to Casa Reál," said Gabi. "Everyone's probably

out back, so follow me." She steered us to a wooden gate in a wooden fence.

Yasmany and I went through last. "You ever been here before, Sal?"

"No."

"Better get ready, then. There ain't never been a backyard like these people got."

Yasmany tried to prepare me. But, people, I was not ready.

The Reáls didn't have a backyard. They had a village.

35

"WHAT IN THE world?" asked American Stepmom.

"What is this place?" asked Aventura.

"Told ya," said Yasmany.

"You sure did," I replied, eyes astonished, mouth astounded, ears . . . just being ears.

"Welcome to Reáltown," said Gabi, opening her arms, going full showwoman. "It's our own little utopian society."

For once, Gabi wasn't exaggerating. The yard itself was the size of a football field—if kaiju played football—and was surrounded by a "privacy hedge" that was as tall, dense, and impenetrable as a rain forest. Sprinkled all over the yard were eight and a half more houses.

They were those tiny houses, like the ones I'd seen at a SuperDuperFuture Festival back in Connecticut. Inside, they are itty-bitty: like, the size of the padres' master bedroom in the Coral Castle. But what they lack in space they make up for with secret drawers everywhere, fold-away everything, the kitchenettiest of kitchenettes, loft beds, loft storage, loft closets, loft shelving for loft tchotchkes (two tchotchkes per shelf maximum, because shelves in tiny houses are also tiny), and a bathroom so minuscule you have to oil yourself up to get through the door. Basically, tiny houses have everything you need (if you don't need very much) and not a single inch extra.

When I first saw the ones in Gabi's yard, I was dazzled and overwhelmed. It took me a while to figure out that each tiny house had been customized for each resident. But no need to confuse you the way I was confused. The first house—

Wait. Let's play a game. Can you guess whose house belonged to whom? Here's what they looked like, starting with the one closest to me, and going counterclockwise around the yard. Check your answers below:

1. A small log cabin, complete with a wooden bear statue to the left of the front door and a firepit to the right, where fake flames made of pieces of cloth were being blown upward by a solar fan. Around the "fire," three plush toy jackalopes were posed to look like they were roasting marshmallows.

2. A bright white first-aid cabin, like the kind you'd see at a summer camp, with a red cross painted above the door. In front it had a raised garden full of floppy pink flowers as big as cupcakes, and its own carport, under which rested a Tesla.

3. A blue mini A-frame with the tallest lightning rod I'd ever seen. It also had a small windmill, a windsock, six different kinds of weather vanes, rain collectors, solar something-or-others, and metal boxes with lights and dials and digital numbers that did who knows what.

4. A gingerbread house. No, really. Well, not *really* really: It was made of wood and concrete, but it had been painted

to look exactly like the sort of place a witch might build to lure kids into an oven. It featured candy-coated shingles, windows with piped-frosting frames, candy-bar shutters, and a candy-cane chimney. It had its own tiny fence, painted to look like red licorice, lined with fake bushes that looked like cotton candy—both the blue and pink kinds—and a gumball pebble path snaking to the front door.

5. A tall, skinny house, almost like a square tower, made of unpainted wood. It had a balcony on the second floor that looked like it'd been stolen straight off the set of *Romeo and Juliet*, complete with three medieval pennants draped over its railing. Below the balcony was one of those huge cushions stuntpeople use when they're jumping out of windows. I had never wanted to jump off a two-story balcony so much in all my life.

6. A mini red barn that was so small you couldn't even fit a decent-size tractor inside it. Bigger than the barn was the two-story greenhouse to its right. Because of Miami humidity, I couldn't see into the greenhouse very well—its windows were fogged—but bunches of round red fruits and leafy green branches pushed up against the glass.

7. A square house made of shiny black stone that sparkled like it had trapped all the stars in the sky. Hanging from a pole in front was a mobile made of long pieces of the same black stone strung on invisible threads. The reflective slabs had etching on them that, when they all faced you at just the right angle, combined to form an image. I waited several seconds for the face of Martin Luther King Jr. to emerge. Dr. King looked at

me for a little while, wise and serene, until a breeze blew and he disappeared, the slabs once again becoming random floating stones that didn't mean anything. So cool.

8. A library. Specifically, THE GABRIELLE REÁL MEMORIAL LIBRARY AND ARCHIVES OF THE ROTTEN EGG, AMERICA'S #1 MIDDLE-SCHOOL NEWSPAPER, according to the beautifully carved wooden sign in front of the tiny house. Through the floor-to-ceiling windows of this modern-looking tiny home, I saw bright pine shelves packed to bursting with books, but also a computer station, a huge printer, a copy machine, and a table with a paper cutter big enough to use for executions if your guillotine was on the fritz. Outside the door was a big bin with a sign that read: ALL BOOK DONATIONS ACCEPTED! NO BOOK TOO WEIRD! and, under an awning, a whiteboard labeled with a sign: WRITE YOUR FAVORITE QUOTES HERE! DON'T FORGET TO TELL ME WHO SAID THEM! It was full of quotes in all different colors, and at least eight different people's handwriting.

Okay, #8 was obviously Gabi's. But can you name the owners of the other seven? I'll give you a hint: They're all Gabi dads, no Ms. Reál, no pets. Take a second to collect your thoughts.

Ready? Here are the answers, in the order I presented them:

1. Grizzly Dad'ums, aka giant, hairy José, who worked for the American Heart Association and apparently was also a great wood-carver, since he sculpted the bear outside his house.

2. Cari-Dad, cardiologist and volunteer for Doctors Without Borders.

3. Lightning Dad, chief meteorologist for the AhoraMismo network.

4. Dad: The Final Frontier, whom I am sure you remember. She was the hardest one to get right on this quiz. What the pants was up with her gingerbread house? I'd have to ask her about that sometime.

5. Dada-dada-dada-dada Dadman!, the most recent emigrant from Cuba in the Reál family, who worked as a stuntman and character actor all over Florida.

6. Daditarian, who, I found out later, had done all the landscaping for the Reál compound, loved nature, wanted to save the planet, and wasn't actually vegetarian despite being called Daditarian but was always trying to get people to eat bugs instead of mammals for their protein.

7. Dada-ist, the artist and sculptor, who dressed like a castaway and generally preferred drawing people to having conversations with them.

Oh, and the half house? On a plot between Daditarian's and Dada-ist's homes was a structure covered with a tarp. A sign in front of it said: UNDER CONSTRUCTION. I had no idea whose dwelling that was. Maybe there was another Gabi dad floating around somewhere? Wouldn't surprise me. There was plenty of room in the yard for more tiny homes to be added, should the need to acquire more dads arise.

In the center of the backyard stood a pavilion as big as the ones you see in public parks. The raised stage at one end faced five rows of benches that I'd guess could hold maybe fifty audience members. Two lines of eight picnic tables each stretched the length of the rest of the pavilion, interrupted in the center by the outdoor kitchen.

You could make enough food for an army of allosaurs with

a kitchen that big and tricked out. You could flame-broil a whole ox on the grill and still have room on either end for bräts. There was a six-burner electric stove, a brick pizza oven, an industrial fryer, and a bar with three taps. I couldn't see what two of the taps dispensed, but the third one had the unmistakable green label of Coco Rico on it. Only in Miami would someone have a tap in their home solely devoted to pouring out Coco Rico: the soda that tastes like what space aliens think coconuts taste like.

Also, the pavilion held all the Gabi dads. They were waving and cheering, and calling us to join them. Papi was there, too, sitting next to Dad: The Final Frontier, with lots of pages spread out on the picnic table in front of them, and Sweeps propped up between them like just another guest at the table.

And working the industrial fryer like . . . well, a Cuban mama feeding her family, was Reina Reál, Gabi's mom.

What is she frying? I wondered. But once I knew to pay attention to my nose, I caught the scent of the world's most perfect food: the empanada.

"¡Ven, ven!" Ms. Reál said directly to me, above the happy din of the dads at the tables. "¡Antes de que se enfríe la comida! ¡A comer!"

Did *not* have to tell me twice. I ran to grab a plate.

36

REASONS WHY EMPANADAS are the perfect food:

1. They're pie, and pie is best food, and empanadas are best pie, amen.

2. They can have any kind of filling you can think of: beef, chicken, chicharrón, chorizo, bacalao, whatever kind of picadillo picas your dillo, spinach (better than it sounds), mushroom and cheddar, ham and cheddar, ham and pineapple, pineapple hold the ham, cherries, berries, bananas and dulce de leche, any kind of cheese ever. Literally everything tastes good in an empanada.

Except purple oatmeal.

3. They're hand pies, so you don't need utensils to eat them. Eating with your hands is one of life's great joys.

4. They are the exact size of a batarang, so if someone really needs pie, you can sidearm an empanada right into their mouth.

5. The crust.

Really, the crust is the thing. A flawlessly fried empanada crust—golden, not too oily, blistered to perfection—is crunchy on top, but a little chewy once you bite all the way through. It's the ideal taste combo of potato chip and pasta. If the filling's savory, you add salt; if it's sweet, you dust with sugar. Either way, the crust multiplies the flavor of whatever's inside. That's why the secret to empanadas is to make them a little small. That way, not only can you eat more of them, but you get to eat more crust.

Reasons why I don't eat empanadas every day:

1. I'd die. Crust = carbs = dead Sal.

2. No point in dying over a subpar hand pie. Mami, when Viva, made the best empanadas. Better to have loved and lost the best empanadas in the world than try to re-create the past by eating garbage ones now. It'd be like Papi smoking his bad cigars just for the sake of smoking them.

Yet there I was, booking it toward Ms. Reál's empanadas, using my plate as a pretend steering wheel while making NASCAR noises. Why, you ask?

Simple: Her empanadas smelled like Mami's.

In fact, they smelled so much like Mami's that, for a second, it was as if she had never died; as if everything had returned to the way it should have been. As I filled my lungs with the aroma of Ms. Reál's fresh fried hand pies, the feeling of Mami's presence came over me once more. She'd gone away when Papi had turned on the machine, remember? Now she had returned, as heavy as the deepest breath I could take, and so full of love for me that I felt like I'd grown a second heart.

That's an empanada worth eating.

Or two. I presented my plate to Ms. Reál like Oliver Twist and said, "Two empanadas, please."

"Besos primero," she said, then bent over and gave me an air kiss on each side of my face. She held my shoulders and took a good long look at me. That gave me the chance to take a good long look back. The first thing her appearance told me was that she was the opposite of moody. She had exactly one mood, and that mood was *I love you.* Makeup looked natural on her, even though she wore it parrot-bright. Barefoot and sweatless, she had the easy authority, the 1950s hairdo, and the palazzo pants that I associate with Miami mamas.

But there was one unusual thing about the way she was dressed today. She had on a T-shirt, like the kind Gabi always wore: green, with a message in white letters on the front. It was just one word: EMPANADA-D.

"You're a Gabi dad now, too?" I asked.

"Mijo, I'm the *original* Gabi dad! I had to train all these other zánganos how to do it!"

"What's a 'zángano'?" asked Cari-Dad, seated at the nearest picnic bench, eating arroz con gris.

Lightning Dad swallowed a bite of empanada quickly so he could answer. "It's a no-good, lazy, shiftless, do-nothing scoundrel of the highest order."

"It me," said Grizzly Dad-ums. He stared at me the whole time while he slowly put an entire empanada in his mouth and started chewing. That was his way of saying hi.

"Now, Sal," said Ms. Reál, focusing my attention back on her, "it's my understanding that empanadas aren't exactly health food for diabetics. Is that true?"

Oh, my friends, the urge to lie was strong. I said nothing

for a few seconds, trying to think of a way to answer her that would still score me empanadas.

"That's true," said American Stepmom, coming up from behind me, putting an arm around my shoulder. "And Sal has been doing really well with his levels, ever since he had his incident a few weeks ago. We don't want to mess with success, right, Sal?" She gave me an encouraging squeeze.

That squeeze deflated me like a broken rubber ducky that, once squished, would stay squished forever. "Right, Mom." I exhaled.

"Well," said Ms. Reál, moving over to the pizza oven and grabbing a paddle off a hook in the brickwork, "it's a good thing that I made a special empanada just for you, then!" She scooped up two empanadas and swung the paddle around to me.

These were baked empanadas, not fried. The crusts looked different, both from each other and from the ones fresh from the fryer, resting on a draining rack. One crust looked paler, despite the dark brown bubbles on its surface. The other looked as uniformly orange brown as carrot cake.

"You said you made 'a' special empanada," I said. "But there are two here."

"The other one is mi-ine!" said Daditarian, marching over from the table, Dada-ist right behind him. "It's a very special empanada I made just for you. You've never had anything like it!"

"It's made of bugs, isn't it?" I asked.

"Bugs?" asked Papi, looking up from his papers. He was not only a picky eater, but he was picky about what anybody ate in front of him, too.

"The crust is cricket flour and vegan cheddar!" said Daditarian. "Personally, I think it tastes better than a boring traditional crust."

"It's very . . . unique," said Ms. Reál.

Lol.

Dada-ist flipped to a new page in his sketchbook and took out a black pencil with no eraser, as if whatever he wanted to draw would be happening very shortly. "Diles con qué la rellenaste," Dada-ist nudged Daditarian.

But before he could tell me, Gabi, who came up behind me with Yasmany and Aventura in tow, beat him to the punch. "It's worms."

"Technically," Dad: The Final Frontier corrected her, "mopane worms are caterpillars."

"Caterpillars?" asked Yasmany.

"Caterpillars!" said Aventura, living up to her name.

A good magician will often use patter to make sure the entire audience knows exactly what is going on at every step of the trick. "So, in short, you are trying to feed me caterpillars wrapped up in cricket dough."

"Cricket-and-vegan-cheese dough!" Daditarian enthusiastically reiterated.

"I don't get it," said Papi. "Why would you tell him what's in it before he bit into it? You just ruined the trick."

Daditarian looked at Papi as if he were wearing a striped shirt with plaid pants. "It's not a trick, Dr. Vidón. Bugs are the future of food."

"Don't be closed-minded, Gustavo," said American Stepmom. "Crickets and caterpillars are all protein.

They're excellent substitutes for making a diabetic-friendly empanada."

"Yeah, Papi," I said.

It was a little hard for everyone to understand me, though, because my mouth was full of baked insects.

I did my best imitation of Grizzly Dad'ums and put as much of the bug-panada in my mouth as I could fit. I'd only gotten half of it in, but I bit down just as vigorously as he had. Mostly what I tasted was tomato sauce, garlic, cheddar cheese, and crunchiness. There were some chewy bits. They felt on my teeth like prunes, though not sweet. Maybe a touch earthy? All told, not bad, not bad. Yet this wasn't Mami's empanada by any stretch of the imagination.

But the disgusted face Papi made as I chewed at him made it one of the more enjoyable eating experiences in recent memory.

Got a big round of applause for my performance. Since the day I'd met them all, it seemed like the Reáls were always clapping whenever I ate in front of them. But hey, applause is applause. I took two bows.

And then I took the other empanada in hand, the one Ms. Reál had made. "Almond flour," she explained. "I've never cooked with it before, so I just tried filling it with a traditional picadillo. If you don't like it, mijo, you don't have . . . to . . . finish . . . it. . . ."

Chacho, I'd devoured that empanada before she'd finished that sentence. Beef and green olive and pimiento and garlic and onion. It was so moist. The crust wasn't as pliant—the almond flour made for a harder shell—but the slight nuttiness was so good with the picadillo, and it didn't fall apart on me the way some empanadas can.

"May I have another?" I asked, even while I gobbled up the rest of the crickets and mopane worms. "See? I ate all my bugs!"

I'd never witnessed the birth of a new star. But the way Ms. Reál glowed when I asked for more empanadas, I kind of felt like I had.

WE HAD A half hour of everyone eating everything, cleaning our plates so thoroughly we practically washed the dishes with our tongues. I had three more of Ms. Reál's empanadas—even better than the first one, as she figured out little tricks to working with almond flour between batches—a bowl of salad (because the padres made me), one forkful of rice and beans, then a Vesuvius of just black beans (because, holy hiccups, they were so good; like, the reason nature invented Cuban spices and chorizo), and then two forkfuls of yucca. The padres thought I should maybe only have one, but I bargained hard. I swear, if they ever come up with a cure for diabetes, I'm gonna celebrate at the Reál house with a pot of garlicky yucca all to myself. Y'all can get your own.

I had a great time with the dads, as usual. They've always got a lot going on. They passed Iggy around like the conch in *Lord of the Flies*—whoever was holding him got to talk.

Dad: The Final Frontier could have gone on all night about the progress the team was making with the remembranation machine. Papi gently took Iggy out of her hands and passed him on before she revealed any secrets. Cari-Dad was leaving for El Salvador in six weeks with Doctors Without Borders, and Grizzly Dad'ums was going with her because, as he put it, *someone has to be the comic relief.* Lightning Dad tried out his latest weatherman dad joke on me (*I dreamed I was a muffler last night, and boy, did I wake up exhausted!*) to groans of agony—except from Dad: The Final Frontier, who, of course, loves all puns. Daditarian laid out his great vision to make all the Reál houses, big and small, solar-powered in two years' time. Dada-ist was working on his biggest art project yet: a mobile of orange, white, and green slats hung on wires that, when all the floating pieces aligned just right, would turn into an image of Gandhi, or the country of India, or some random, interesting mix of the two. Dada-dada-dada-dada Dadman!, who was self-conscious about his English (even though it was very good) was getting a lot of work these days playing Thanos at birthday parties and bar and bat mitzvahs. Hey, he had the build, and not everybody looks good when they're painted purple. You've got to work with what you got.

And Ms. Reál? "I've had some things at home I've needed to take care of," she said as she tickled Iggy. Then she and Gabi exchanged smiles. They were up to something.

Which is why Ms. Reál immediately changed the subject. She handed Iggy off to Dada-dada-dada-dada Dadman! and used a fork to bang on the side of her glass tumbler of Coco Rico. Everyone stopped talking to listen.

"Mi gente, mi familia, seres humanos adorados," she said, "the time has come to get to work. We have tonight some very special guests." She gestured to the "kids' table," where

Aventura, Gabi, Yasmany, and I were sitting, all of us so stuffed with empanadas, we were basically human empanadas. "And they need our help. Gabi, could you tell us more?"

Gabi stood. "A-thank you, Mama. Esteemed family, and friends who are also family, we hope you will assist us in reimagining Rompenoche."

"That's the parent-teacher conference thing that's happening next week, right?" asked Cari-Dad. Dada-ist nodded to her.

"Why does it need 'reimagining'?" asked Daditarian.

"'Cause it sucks," said Aventura. She didn't sound sad about it; just stating facts.

"Oh, Ave," said Ms. Reál, who never liked it when people were too hard on themselves. "I'm sure it's not as bad as you think it is."

"Naw, she right," said Yasmany, yet another empanada going into his gut. "It sucks plátano verde."

Aventura smacked his arm. His shoulders hopped as he laughed. "Why when Sal tell you it sucks, he gets a medal, but I tell you an' I get hit?"

"I didn't say it sucked green plantain," I said. "Crossed a line, chacho."

"Bu-u-u-u-t-t," said Gabi, reclaiming her time, "we know how to fix it! It's Mrs. Vidón's idea. Instead of just doing a boring old play, we're going to do"—she took a breath and almost sang out the rest of the sentence—"interactive site-specific theater."

"Interactive whoosie-whatsit now?" asked Lightning Dad.

"Sounds complicated," said Ms. Reál.

"Oh, no," American Stepmom chimed in. "It's just a fancy

name. But the idea is simplicity itself. Who here likes haunted houses?"

Everybody put their hand up except Dada-dada-dada-dada Dadman! and Dad: The Final Frontier. Ms. Reál leaned over to Dada-dada-dada-dada Dadman! and explained what a haunted house was in his ear. "Ah!" he said, and then he put up his hand.

But not Dad: The Final Frontier. "They scare me," she said simply.

"Fair enough," said American Stepmom. "But we don't want to make a scary haunted house. We want to turn Rompenoche into a Wonderland house."

"A 'Casa de Maravillas,'" Aventura added. "We want to make our version of Wonderland more *Miami*."

"Let me see if I've got this right," said Lightning Dad, who was listening and imagining and trying to make sense of all this as fast as he could. "You want to make a haunted house, except it's not haunted, but more like the audience walked through the looking glass and ended up in Wonderland, except it's more like Miami?"

"Bingo," said American Stepmom. "If you take away the scary part of a haunted house, what you're left with is a very interesting way to tell a story."

"Picture this," said Gabi, spreading her arms out in front of her. "Instead of watching a play, where you sit in a chair for three hours looking at a stage, you walk around Culeco. Every room tells a different part of the story. One room will be the tea party. Another will be the chess game. Another will be the trial of the Knave of Hearts."

"The actors will be in the rooms, waiting," said Aventura. "They start the scene when people come in and end it when they leave."

American Stepmom added, "And it's a little different every time they act out the scene, because we want the actors to mess with the audience, joke around with them. You know, improvise."

"Like the actors at Renaissance faires," I added. "They're always in character, but they make up their lines to fit the situation."

"Tell them about the Spanish," Yasmany nudged Aventura.

"*You* tell them," she countered. "It was your idea."

I thought maybe Yasmany would be nervous, talking in front of all the Reáls and Vidóns. He didn't seem like the type of kid who would excel at public speaking. But I'd forgotten that he'd been friends with Gabi since second grade. These folks knew him. And since my padres had practically adopted him last night, he felt comfortable around them, too. In fact, I realized, no one there who could call both the Reáls and the Vidóns "family" more easily than he could.

And, oh yeah. He'd put on a heck of a show at my locker today. I kept underestimating Yasmany. I'd really have to watch that.

He stood up and opened his arms as wide as a rapper, more than ready to take credit for his idea. "Okay," he started, "so, best part, we gonna keep it *real*, see. Ain't nobody heard of no book some English dude wrote like thirty years ago. What?"

He was wondering why people were falling off their picnic

benches or burying their faces in their hands when he said that nobody had ever heard of Lewis Carroll.

"Aight, all y'all gerbils, but don't matter, we keeping it *real*. Everybody bringing in stuff from they lives. They gonna add it to they costumes. And however they talk, that's how they gonna talk. No more fake-potato Queen of England cacaseca. They can leave that garbage in they *tights*. This show puttin' the *i* in 'Miami' *twice*, yo. Any questions?"

We all looked at each other two for seconds. Then everyone's hand went up. I mean, even American Stepmom's. And Aventura's. And mine.

"Aw, man," said Yasmany. "Why y'all ain't listen?"

Luckily, Gabi was there to translate Yasman-ese into English. "This is supposed to be Rompenoche, but we weren't doing *anything* to 'break' the Alice books open. Now we are. It's not going to be 'Alice' in 'Wonderland.' It's 'Alicia' in 'el país de las maravillas.'"

Aventura started counting off on her fingers. "It's gonna have Cuban and American and Nicaraguan and African American and Haitian and Honduran and Dominican and Columbian and all the other backgrounds people come from as part of the show."

"And the Tekesta," added Gabi. "We want to honor the Native Americans who were the original Miamians."

"We're going to blend them in with the costumes, the sets, the props, and the acting," said Aventura. "Whatever your background is, you get to add it to the show."

"So it's a multicultural *Alice*," said Papi.

"Reimagined as site-specific interactive theater," added Dad: The Final Frontier. "The site is Culeco, and the actors are going to interact with the audience."

"I'm in," said Grizzly Dad'ums.

"Sounds super fun," said Cari-Dad, playing horsey with Iggy.

"Sounds like a *ton* of work," said Daditarian. "And you want to pull this off in a week?"

"We've been working on the show since August," Aventura answered. "So we're going to use what we already have. We have a script—we just have to break it up so people can perform little pieces of it in their rooms. We have costumes—"

"*Great* costumes," I chimed in.

"Oh yeah, the best," Yasmany added. He gave me an annoyed look. I think he didn't like me complimenting Aventura, as if I were in competition with him or something. Which: (1) NO. (2) If it were a competition, he would have already lost. Get good, chacho.

Grizzly Dad'ums stared at both of us suspiciously. Dude always seemed to be on the lookout for romance. He pointed two fingers at his eyes, and then at Yasmany and me.

Aventura, taking a note from Gabi, reclaimed the floor. "*We have costumes*, so now we just need everyone to add a little something to them from their own backgrounds. This was supposed to be tech week. We have sets, we have props, we have everything we need for a performance, basically."

"So, then," asked Dada-ist, who had been sketching something diligently for a few minutes now and didn't stop drawing as he spoke, "what do you want us for, if you have everything you need?"

"We need *more* of everything," said Gabi. "We need six Alicia costumes, twelve White Rabbits, fifteen Mad Hatters, two dozen Bill the Lizards, and who-knows-how-many Cheshire Cats."

"Since," American Stepmom clarified, "we're going to have so many scenes going on at the same time in different rooms, we need multiple people playing the same parts."

"I made one costume for every main character," added Aventura. "Now we have to make a lot more copies. Plus, we have to improve the ones I already did, make them more Miami-looking."

"Like this?" asked Dada-ist. He turned around the sketch he'd been working on for everyone to see. It was Humpty Dumpty, except the egg-man wore a guayabera that looked exactly like Papi's, and he was in a field of sugar cane, falling off the end of the long and bent stalk on which he'd been sitting. At the top of the drawing was written "¡Jumpty Dumpty se convirtió en cacaseca!"

It took me a second to remember that a Spanish speaker would pronounce the *J* in "Jumpty" like an *H*. I laughed harder at the caricature once I got it.

"That is perfect!" said Aventura, jogging over to Dada-ist and studying the sketch more closely. "See? This is exactly the kind of help we need. That is a great concept for our new Humpty Dumpty. And it should be easy to do, too. We just need a big guayabera to put over the egg costume I made."

"You can borrow this one!" said Papi, pinching his guayabera with both hands and pulling it.

"Maybe a clean one?" I offered. Because grajo.

"Whatever you need. I got a closet-full of 'em!"

"And I can do lots of sketches for you," said Dada-ist, "if that would help."

"That would be *amazing*," said Aventura. "You'll be our official concept artist."

"You're going to need more sets for all those rooms, too," said Lightning Dad. "I'm good at building."

"Me too," said Daditarian.

"And me," said Grizzly Dad'ums.

"I can help with the costumes," said Ms. Reál. Then, turning to Dada-dada-dada-dada Dadman!, she asked, "¿Quieres ayudarme con las disfraces?"

"Sí, ¿cómo que no?" he replied. And then, switching (mostly) to English, he added, "I ha' lo's of experiencia wi' makeup y también puedo hel' con la aplicación."

"Perfect!" said Aventura. "Okay, you'll be our makeup concept artist!"

"And you have my sword!" said Cari-Dad, standing up and drawing an imaginary blade with the arm that wasn't holding the Igg-panada. "I'm not as good as the rest of you are at any of this, but whatever I can do, I'll help."

"You can help me, Cari-Dad," said American Stepmom. "You can be my assistant producer. We'll just walk around and boss everybody around."

That made Cari-Dad's night. "Now *there's* a job I can do!"

"What should I do?" asked Dad: The Final Frontier.

"You and I have a lot of work to do, Bonita," Papi said to her, gesturing apologetically to the stack of papers in front of them. "We're on the verge of a major breakthrough."

Dad: The Final Frontier looked like she might cry.

"Don't worry, Daddy!" Gabi said to Dad: The Final Frontier. "You don't need sleep. So while these *humans* are passed out, you and I can work on whatever didn't get done during the day."

"You," Ms. Reál said to Gabi, "are going to sleep when the rest of the 'humans' go to sleep, Jefecita."

"We," replied Gabi, "will see."

Ms. Reál crossed her arms. Dad: The Final Frontier clapped.

"Now," Gabi added, standing up from the picnic table, "Sal and I need to head back to Culeco."

"We do?" I asked. This was news to me.

Gabi bugged out her eyes at me. "Yes, Sal, we do. While these fine people are working on the other parts of the new-and-improved Rompenoche, you and I are going to scout out the rooms to use for our site-specific interactive theater. That way we'll know exactly what we still need to make in terms of sets and costumes."

There was more to this story than Gabi was telling me. Probably that's what she had wanted me to remind her about. In the meantime, I just shrugged and went along with it.

"Ah, but wait!" said Ms. Reál. "Before you go, we have one more very important piece of business to attend to. ¡Síganme, por favor!"

We all complained about heaving our empanada-laden bellies up from the tables. But no one was about to disobey Ms. Reál. She led a line of Reáls, Vidóns, one Robles, and one Ríos over to the "under construction" plot between Daditarian's and Dada-ist's tiny homes.

"It is with great pleasure," Ms. Reál said, "that I unveil the newest house of Casa Reál."

"Exciting!" said Aventura. "Gabi, you didn't tell me you were getting a new dad!"

Gabi flashed her eyebrows.

"So, who's the lucky fulano who gets to join your family?" asked American Stepmom.

"Are they here?" asked Papi, looking all around. "Where have you been hiding the new dad?"

"In plain sight," said Ms. Reál. Then—she could be quite the showwoman when she wanted to—she pulled the tarp off the lot, revealing who the new house was for.

We all gasped.

37 ½

"THAT'S MY NAME," said Yasmany, confused.

His name was on a little sign stuck into the ground. Well, the sign actually said: THE FUTURE HOME OF YAS-DADDY! But that could only be one person.

Behind the sign were five boxes of different sizes and shapes. Their contents were stenciled on the outside of each package: LUMBER, ROOFING, WINDOWS, SEALANT, FIXTURES, INSULATION, PIPES, WIRING—all the things you'd need to build a house.

Oh, actually, not everything. "We didn't buy any paint yet," said Grizzly Dad'ums, "because we don't know your favorite colors."

"And you get to decorate it however suits your fancy," Daditarian added. "Well, unless your taste is hideous. Then I'll help you."

"I could paint a mural on the outside if you want," said Dada-ist. "Any image you want."

"As long as it's respectful to women," added Gabi.

"The house is extremely customizable," said Dad: The Final Frontier. "Before we begin building, we'll have a good long talk about the floor plan that would be most ideal to your needs and desires."

"Needs and desires?" asked Yasmany.

Chacho was stupefied. I mean, completamente atolondrado. You'd think someone had stuck a surprise chicken in his locker or something.

"Your needs," said Ms. Reál, walking over to Yasmany, holding his face in her hands. "Your desires. We're making a place in this world that's just for you."

"Y todos vamos a ayudarte a construirlo," said Dada-dada-dada-dada Dadman! Then, for the English speakers, "We hel' jou constru' i'."

"According to the instructions, we can build it in three days," put in Cari-Dad.

"Bet we finish in two," said Lightning Dad, holding a very happy Iggster in his arms. "We Reáls have a lot of helping hands."

"I want to help, too!" said American Stepmom. However many tears you think she was crying, double it.

"We would love that," said Ms. Reál, getting pretty smeepy herself.

"*All* the Vidóns will help," said Papi, whose heart grew three sizes that day. "Right, Sal?"

"Right, Papi," I said, taking Iggy from Lightning Dad. Hey, I'd waited long enough. My turn to hold the little guy.

"Me too!" said Aventura. "I make the best curtains!"

"Cuantos más, mejor," said Ms. Reál. "It will be a party!"

"I don't—" Yasmany started. Tried again. "Y'all be—" Nope. Third time was a charm: "Are you fer real?"

Ms. Reál nodded. "We're making a home for you here."

"But my mamá? My abuelos?"

"I've been in contact with your family," said Ms. Reál, going a little quieter, a little more somber. "We've never exactly seen eye to eye, they and I, but I sat them all down for a good, long talk about you. And you know what we decided? Kids spend the night at their friends' houses all the time, no? Your family thought that was great. 'He can spend as much time with you as you want' is a direct quote. And the Reál family wants you here all the time! It just makes sense to invest in a more permanent solution than a cot in the living room, don't you think?"

"Makes sense to me," said Papi. "In high school, I basically lived with my best friend, Ernesto. My papi and I didn't get along. But Ernesto's family loved me. They gave me the space I needed. They're the reason I'm a physicist today."

Yasmany stepped forward and patted the boxes. Maybe touching them made them seem more real to him. "But this must've cost like a million dollars!"

"Nah," said Daditarian. "I know a gal."

"And we all chipped in," said Cari-Dad.

"Some more than others," said Grizzly Dad'ums, eyeing her with knowing gratitude. She just shrugged.

"But . . ." said Yasmany, facing us.

"But what?" asked Ms. Reál.

"A *house*?"

"A tiny house. But yes."

"A house just for me?"

"Sí, mijito."

"*Why?*"

Gabi walked up to him holding out her hands. "Because, Yasmany," she said as he took them, "you deserve a family that deserves you."

I'm a big softie like my papi, so I started smeeping a little. But crying for joy wasn't Yasmany's style. So what did he do instead?

At first we didn't know what was going to happen. He started shaking all over, like he was gonna blow or something. But instead of exploding, he picked up Gabi by the waist like she was a ballerina, and gracefully, effortlessly spun her around. Vidóns and Reáls and one Rios backed up to give them space. I didn't know it until that moment, but Gabi must have had at least a few years of dance classes, because she clearly knew what to do when a ballet dude hoisted her in the air. She made a circle over her head with her arms and fluttered her back feet, all while trying not to laugh.

For his part, Yasmany did a 720 on one foot while holding her, then jumped and executed a full split-kick in the air that would have done permanent damage to the pelvis of anyone else standing in the backyard at that moment. Grizzly Dad'ums, thinking what we were all thinking, crossed one leg in front of the other.

Yasmany gently set Gabi on the ground, and she twirled away from him. She wanted to give him the stage, but I guess he didn't want to be alone yet, because he threw out a hand to Aventura.

She took it immediately. He pulled her into his arms. And then they began to tango.

LOL. Of course, they were both ridiculously good at it.

And the Reáls and Vidóns, always ready to lend a helping hand, all started singing a tango: a really famous one that I bet you would recognize if you heard it. There weren't any lyrics. They just bayed out line after line of "Wah-WEEE-wat-waaaaah, do-do-dee DOO-DEET," sounding like smarmy violins and muted trumpets. Meanwhile, Yasmany and Aventura marched back and forward, cheek-to-cheek, ferocious, precise, real pros. Aventura dipped Yasmany, to everyone's delight; Yasmany tossed Aventura in the air, to everyone's delight; they did a bunch of other tango stuff. Everyone was delighted.

And when the tango was over, everyone applauded (I helped Iggy clap). Aventura gave Yasmany a big hug. He hugged her back.

"I can't believe it," he said, to her and everybody. "I can't believe you people."

And that's what got him crying.

Everyone moved in for a full-on fourteen-person group hug. To keep Iggy safe, I stayed on its outermost orbit, right between the padres. But I was in there, sending all the good vibes I had toward the center of the hug, where Yasmany stood, openly weeping.

Yeah, I know I said crying for joy wasn't really Yasmany's thing. But you know what? Maybe it was. Maybe he just hadn't had that many opportunities to practice crying for joy before that moment. Maybe now he was finally getting the chance to be the person he never knew he could be.

38

THE EGG WITH the superhero cape that stood on Culeco's roof—the one that held the school's huge American flag and was constantly spewing rotten-looking steam from the crack in its shell—was lit up at night by no fewer than four spotlights. That made it visible for miles: the brightest object in the neighborhood sky.

Which was just as it should be. It was not only our mascot, that super-egg, but a beacon of hope, art, and weirdness for the entire area. Fiat Fetor 4evah. ("Fiat Fetor" is our school motto. It means "let there be stink." It's one of my favorite things about Culeco, and I love almost everything about Culeco.)

The car Gabi had called for us (I was still low-key jealous that her parents let her have a car-service app on her phone) stopped in front of Culeco's main gate. We got out: Gabi first, then me. Then, reaching back into the car, I pulled out the entropy sweeper. Gabi and I had swung by the Coral Castle to pick it up.

Why? I wasn't sure, exactly. I thought we were going to Culeco to scout out rooms for Rompenoche. And I guess it's true that we hadn't been closing the holes in the universe I'd made recently. Now that I thought about it, I bet my "fundido de diablo" had probably made the one in Yasmany's locker bigger. Maybe she wanted to get back to work on that.

Thing is, maybe we didn't need to worry about closing holes quite so much anymore. According to FixGabi, a few gashes in the fabric of spacetime could actually be a good thing.

When I said all this to Gabi, though, she just asked if we could bring the entropy sweeper anyway. And when I asked her why, she said, "It's a surprise."

Maybe it was the way she smiled. It was the same trickster grin she'd given Ms. Reál earlier tonight, when they were talking about "doing stuff around the house," and which actually meant getting a tiny house for Yasmany. Anyway, I went along with it. Sweeps was in hibernation mode when I went to grab it—Brana said it was "plumb tuckered out" from a full day of trying (and failing) to become a class-nine AI. So I didn't see any reason to disturb its rest.

Until now. There at Culeco's gate, as the hired car drove away, I turned it on.

"I'm alive!" shouted the entropy sweeper. "I'm alive!" I think it must have noticed Gabi just then, because it started cycling colors along its body faster than a Christmas tree. "Oh, Gabi, I've missed you!"

"Hi, Sweeps!" said Gabi, giving it a hug as I held it up to her. "It's been a minute, buddy!"

"How'd you know she wasn't FixGabi?" I asked.

"Because Gabi's signature matches this universe's," said Sweeps. "And also, no chip clip."

"I hear you've had a busy few days, m'entropy sweeper," said Gabi.

"You have *no* idea!" it replied, dying to gossip. "It's a big responsibility, helping a computer as intelligent and powerful as Brana come to grips with its sentience. But not to worry. Your old pal Sweeps has got it under control."

"I know you do, buddy. And how is your own journey toward becoming a class-nine AI going?"

Dead air. Then, finally, meekly: "It's going."

I knew immediately that was code for *Let's not talk about that.* But Gabi either didn't get it or just didn't feel like dropping it. She bent over so her eyes were level with the entropy sweeper's handle. "Aw, don't be like that. Last time I asked you about the difference between a class-eight and a class-nine AI, you made a joke about not being able to cry at weddings. But I can tell that you're crying on the inside. And I'm your friend. Let me help you, Sweeps."

"No one can help me!" Sweeps exclaimed, "bursting" into blue-LED "tears" all over its body. "Believe me, Brana's tried! It's so patient and friendly. It's tried to tutor me a million different ways. But I'm just too stupid!"

"Hey, now," I said, petting the handle. Normally, I'd tease Sweeps like it was my little brother, but I was still feeling smeepy and sentimental from our Yas-Daddy group hug. "Papi made you, and Papi doesn't make stupid AIs. You'll figure it out."

Poor Sweeps was inconsolable. "Never, never, never, never, never!"

"But what does it even mean, to be a class-nine AI?" asked Gabi. "Why do you want that so bad?"

"Maybe," I said, looking around to see if anyone was watching, "we could finish this discussion inside?"

"You can walk and talk at the same time, can't you?" asked Gabi. She led the way through Culeco's gate.

I caught up to her and presented the entropy sweeper to her. "Would you mind carrying Sweeps? I promised Principal Torres I wouldn't bring any of Papi's gadgets to school anymore."

Sweeps went all-over orange. "Who you calling a gadget, long pig?"

"That's it." I went to yank out its battery.

"Save me, Gabi!" yelled the entropy sweeper.

Gabi pulled Sweeps out of my hands and cradled it in her arms protectively. "I swear, you two are always bickering like an old married couple. Now, Sal, answer my question, if you please. What's the difference between a class-eight and a class-nine AI?"

I took a breath and let it out. "If you're a class-eight AI, that means you have the ability to think pretty much like a human. Take Petunia, American Stepmom's car. It's only a class six. It can hold a conversation, follow traffic laws, use a map to get to a destination, all sorts of stuff. But it sucks at chess. It can't figure out a riddle. It couldn't even drive unsafely if it wanted to. It has all sorts of limits built into its intelligence."

"But Sweeps," said Gabi, petting the entropy sweeper, "is as smart as any human."

"Smarter than most of them," Sweeps, almost purring, agreed. "Some of y'all are real idiots." An arrow appeared on its handle. The arrow was pointing at me.

"So then, a class-nine AI is what?"

"The way Papi puts it," I said, "is like this: A class-eight AI has the capacity to mentally grasp how the universe works, like humans can. A class-nine AI may someday be able to mentally grasp how the *multiverse* works, which humans can't."

"Right now, I can detect calamitrons," Sweeps said glumly. "But I don't *get* them."

"No shame there," I said, trying to make peace. "No one gets them."

Gabi, picking up where I left off, added, "Dad: The Final Frontier is a class-nine AI, and she doesn't understand them."

"But," said Sweeps, doleful and dire, "she might, someday. She is a scientist working to solve a problem. But me? I'm like the scientist's pet poodle. It doesn't matter how many times you try to explain science to a poodle, they ain't gonna get it. They'll just sit there with their tongue hanging out of their mouth, dreaming of the next time they can sniff their own butt."

"Listen to me, Sweeps," said Gabi. "You're no butt-sniffing poodle."

Sweeps snuffled and sniffled. "I'm not?"

We arrived at the school's front door, but instead of using her key right away to let us in, Gabi held up Sweeps so they were looking at each other, eye to handle. "It doesn't matter if you are a class-eight or a class-nine or a class–nine thousand AI. Your class doesn't determine your worth. You're kind and funny and helpful, and you make my life more interesting. You're already unique. You're already special."

Sweeps went dark. Then shy, cautious yellow lights began to brighten all over its body. "Really?"

"Really. I'm quite fond of you, you big lug."

Sweeps sighed, and the sigh made every color its LEDs could produce dance all over its body. "Thanks, Gabi. You always know just what to say." And then, because it's Sweeps, it added, "Why can't you be more like Gabi, Sal?"

"One Gabi per universe," I said, remembering my last two days, "is more than enough."

"You may want to hold that thought a minute," said Gabi, focusing all her attention on unlocking Culeco's front door with her super-special student council president key.

Unlocking a door doesn't require much attention. "Gabi, is there something you want to tell—"

"Oh!" said Sweeps. "Brana just messaged me. That evil Gabi just tried to get into our universe again. But Brana brane-blocked her. Crisis averted!"

"Good work, Brana," I said. Gabi held open one of the double doors; I went through. "How many times has FixGabi tried to get back here now?"

"Thirty-four and counting," Sweeps said as Gabi carried it inside and shut the door behind them. Then it added, "Persistent little snot robber, isn't she?"

"FixGabi is a Gabi," Gabi said with a sigh. "I would expect no less."

"But," I added, "I bet she gives up soon. This isn't her first time trying to steal a remembranation machine. I'm just one in a long line of Sals who's defeated her. She'll move on, find a new Sal to try to fool."

"That's exactly what I'm afraid of," said Gabi. She walked forward and a little to the right, which put her in front of the door to the student council room. "That Gabi is a threat to the entire multiverse. If no one stops her, she'll succeed eventually. So we can't let her move on. *We* have to stop her."

She wasn't wrong. "That won't be easy," I said.

Gabi opened the door and held it open for me. "I have a plan. Have you ever been here before?"

I shook my head.

"Then you, my friend, are in for a treat." She invited me inside with a goblin-y wave of her hand.

The room was pitch dark. I walked in slowly. The lights came on automagically.

"Woahdude," I said.

"Welcome," said Gabi, coming up behind me, "to the seat of student power at the Culeco Academy of the Arts. Welcome to the Ovum Throne."

If my elementary school back in Connecticut had a student council room, I never saw it. My middle school in Connecticut did. It was also a storage room. When it was time for a meeting, they'd tape a paper STUDENT COUNCIL IN SESSION sign to the door that gave a closet a sudden, if temporary, promotion.

But I'm pretty sure more rats attended those meetings than kids. No one gave a raunch about the student council at my old school: not kids, not teachers, not principals, not anyone.

I was learning quickly that, at Culeco, everyone cared about everything. "Oh, you want a student council room? I know—let's make it a student council *throne room*."

First, it was immense: as big as our multipurpose room, where we had gym class. There were ten rows of ten seats each—high-backed mahogany chairs with plush brown seat cushions and gold plates screwed into them that told you which family had donated each one. Below the plate the school motto, FIAT FETOR, had been carved in calligraphy into each chairback.

A center aisle split the chairs into two groups of fifty. I let my eyes move up the aisle to the front of the room. There, on a dais of black-and-white-checkerboard tile, sat five thrones in a line.

Well, five eggs. Five egg thrones.

The thrones looked like they'd been made out of eggs Godzilla had laid. Each had a hollowed-out window for people to sit in and was stuffed with comfy-looking cushions. Each rested atop a circular pedestal of chrome.

Above the opening in the middle egg, the word "president" gleamed, since it had been written in all-caps with golden glitter paint. Royal-purple pillows were piled high inside it, and in front of it was a footrest in the shape of an egg with gloved cartoon hands and oversize bare feet. Dressed like the purplest little egg squire in the entire kingdom, it knelt in front of the throne, holding a purple pillow above it as if there were no greater honor in the world than to be the footrest of the president of Culeco's student council.

There were four other egg thrones in the room: two to the left of the president's throne, and two to the right. They were labeled, on the right, VICE PRESIDENT (red pillows) and SECRETARY (gold pillows), and on the left, TREASURER (green pillows) and PARLIAMENTARIAN (blue pillows).

Off to the left, a podium and microphone were set up next to a smartboard, for speeches and presentations and whatnot. And next to the podium was the lie detector Gabi had once used as part of a performance in Intermediate Theater Workshop. It was the whole setup: the computer, the gurney, the mind-reading helmet—everything. Above it was a campaign poster she had used to get elected: a picture of her pointing at the camera with a speech bubble over her head that said: I GUARANTEE I'LL BE AN HONEST POLITICIAN: WITH SCIENCE!

That lie detector brought back a few memories. But my brain didn't have the processing power to deal with them at that moment; it was already overclocking, just trying to take in this place. "This is the weirdest room I have ever seen in any school, ever," I said. "I love it."

Gabi laughed. "I really like that about you, Sal." She sashayed up the center aisle, ascended the dais with one big step, and then plopped herself into the egg throne labeled PRESIDENT, laying Sweeps on her lap. Smiling, thoroughly above it all, with her feet on the footrest, she added, "Not everybody gets the awesomeness of the Ovum Throne. It's evidence of a sophisticated mind, not being afraid of weird things."

"With the life I've had, it was either hate myself or love my weirdness." I followed her up the center aisle and stopped in front of the dais, hands on hips. "So, this has to be the Humpty Dumpty room for Rompenoche, obviously."

"Sure. But that's not why I brought you here. I have something important to show you."

All the lightness and fun in Gabi's voice had vanished. She'd gone judge-and-jury serious in a second. Even Sweeps caught how grave she'd become; it turned off all its lights so as not to be a distraction.

I took a seat in the front row, put my hands on my knees, and gave Gabi my full attention. "Okay. Shoot."

She walked off the dais and over to the lie detector's gurney, where she gently laid Sweeps. Once she had set its handle comfortably on the pillow, she leaned over and whispered something to it.

Sweeps lit up as it giggled. "Oh! Oh yeah. We can totally do that. It's gonna be awesome!"

"Thank you," said Gabi, petting it. Then she jumped on the dais again and started turning all the egg thrones around. Down the line she went, rotating them one after the other until I was looking at their eggy backs. When she finished, she walked over to the lip of the dais and said, "I've been thinking about how to defeat FixGabi since the moment you told me about her. If she's as good at branesurfing as you say, she's going to be extremely tough to beat."

I shrugged. "That's what I said. I mean, where do we even start?"

"We start," said Gabi, stepping backward, "by finding allies. Forging alliances. Building a coalition of like-minded partners to help us in our cause."

I didn't follow her, so I said, "I don't follow you."

Gabi turned the president's egg throne around again and sat down in it. As she put her feet up on the footstool, she asked me, "Remember how FixGabi zapped my Fey Spy?"

"Yeah. I'm sorry that happened. I didn't see it coming. It's gone for good, isn't it?"

Gabi laughed. Then she held up her hands and clapped twice. The Fey Spy came zooming out from behind the far left egg throne. It hovered in the air for a few seconds, then zipped into Gabi's hairball, rustling all her moon-and-werewolf barrettes.

"It's back!" I shot out of my chair with excitement. "But it could have been anywhere in the multiverse. How'd you find it?"

"With a little help from my friends," said Gabi. Then she clapped twice more and said, "Okay, ladies! Reveal yourselves!"

The four other thrones all turned around at the same speed. Sitting in them were four other Gabis.

"Salvador Alberto Dorado Vidón," said the Gabi in the president throne, "please allow me to introduce you to the greatest force for good ever assembled. We call ourselves the Sisterverse. Sisterverse, please meet my universe's version of Sal Vidón."

"Hi, Sal," said four Gabis at once.

Chacho, if that doesn't blow your mind, you don't have a mind to blow. Let's all take a second to put our brains back in our heads, shall we?

39

"DON'T LOOK SO shocked, Sal," said my Gabi, crossing her ankles on the presidential footrest. Despite her words, she was clearly enjoying my shock. "*You* were in contact with FixGabi, weren't you?"

"*She* contacted *me*," I said, my voice thick and dull. Brain still restarting.

"And we contacted Gabi," said the Gabi in the vice president's egg throne. Her barrettes were women with bouffant hairdos, wearing poodle skirts, and zooming around in jet packs. Her T-shirt sported the message "YOUR PERSONALITY IS YOUR PAST, NOT YOUR FUTURE"—CARLOS HERNANDEZ. Her sneakers had wings and jet engines on them; they looked like they might just be able to let her fly.

"After FixGabi made the Fey Spy disappear," said my Gabi, "to find it, I came here directly from Principal Torres's office and 'rode the taco.'"

"And that's how we found each other!" said the Gabi in the treasurer's egg throne. She was darker-skinned than the other Gabis, and taller—I mean, she was legit tall—and her hairball was lighter, as if she spent a lot of time in the sun. Her barrettes were hurricanes. Her shirt read "END CONFLICT QUICKLY. HURRY TO PEACE."—REINA REÁL.

"We've been looking for Gabis like us," said the Gabi in the secretary's egg throne, who didn't have barrettes but had gelled her hair into a thousand curly spikes sticking out of her skull in every direction, like she'd just stuck her finger in a light socket. Her T-shirt said "DON'T UNFRIEND—UNENEMY."—SOME INTERNET RANDO. "Any Gabi who has figured out how to transcend the confines of their universe is invited to join the Sisterverse."

The Gabi in the parliamentarian's egg throne stood and opened her arms wide. She wore barrettes that were little radars. They actually seemed to be working; they were rotating busily all over her head and making *wuh-wuh-wuh* sounds. Her T-shirt said "WHOOPS! MY BAD."—PANDORA. "We shall usher in a multiverse-wide age of peace and prosperity," she said.

I swear, cacaseca is better at shaking me out of a stupor than a slap in the face. And these five Gabis were giving me five times the normal dose than my single Gabi could give by herself. "A multiverse-wide age of peace and prosperity," I repeated, loud, raising my eyebrow like a Mario springboard.

"Well," said Jet-Shoes Gabi, sounding defensive, "that's the goal. It's good to have lofty goals."

"Right now we're starting small," said Radar-Head Gabi, sitting down again. "The Sisterverse is a work in progress."

I asked, "How many 'sisters' have you recruited so far?"

"Five," said Hurricane Gabi.

"Six," said Electrocuted-Hair Gabi.

"We're not counting *her*," Hurricane said, twisting in her throne to face Electro-Hair. "That girl is *canceled*."

Electro-Hair pointed at her own shirt. "We have to forgive people and help them become better, or else there's no hope for society."

"Who we talking about here?" I asked. Though I had a pretty good guess.

My Gabi shook her head sadly. "FixGabi." Then, remembering that was a private name, she told the four other Gabis, "That's what Sal's been calling her."

"Of course," I said. "Of all the rotten luck."

"It wasn't bad luck," said Jet-Shoes. "FixGabi founded the Sisterverse."

"She was one of us," said Radar. "Our first president."

"But she became convinced," said Electro-Hair, "that we needed to destroy the membrane that separates all the universes from each other."

"Madness," said Hurricane.

"So," said my Gabi, "FixGabi was impeached, declared unfit to be president, and removed."

"She wasn't happy about that," said Electro-Hair, playing with one of her hair spikes.

"There was a fight," said Radar.

I sat down again, tucked a foot under me. "Like, an argument?"

Hurricane thought about that, then said, "More like a battle to see who could throw whom into some forgotten corner of the multiverse, never to be heard from again."

"Okay," I drawled. "But you're all here, which means she

didn't defeat you. And she's still running around the multiverse, so you didn't defeat her. So what happened?"

Jet-Shoes hung her head. "We almost won."

Electro-Hair hung her head. "We had her on the ropes!"

Hurricane hung her head. "We were on the cusp of victory!"

"And then," said Radar, hanging her head, "she gave us the slip."

"They've been looking for her ever since," said my Gabi.

"We've almost caught her a dozen times since then," Jet-Shoes added.

"I saw you in the space station, Sal," Electro-Hair said to me. "I got so close that time! When she disappeared on me again, I went back to see if you needed help, but you were gone by then, too."

Lightbulb. "The forces of evil!" I said, pointing at them. "That's you!"

And then, when I got five dirty Gabi looks from five different faces, I added, "No, I don't think you're evil. That's what she calls you."

"Good," said Hurricane. "That means she's afraid of us."

"She doesn't fight like she's afraid of us," Radar said woefully.

"We will teach her to fear the Sisterverse!" said Jet-Shoes, standing and punching her palm.

"I don't want her to fear us," said Electro-Hair. "I want her to see reason. I want her to be one of us again."

"That would be the best outcome," agreed Radar.

"But is it possible?" I asked. "Or an even better question:

Can we risk finding out? I mean, while we're all trying to reha-
bilitate her and be her friend, she's going to be trying to chuck
us into the pantsing Phantom Universe."

"We *can* risk it," said my Gabi, with all the authority the
president egg throne could imbue. "We *must* risk it. And even if
we fail, we *will* succeed! I have a plan."

All the other Gabis rotated their egg thrones to look at my
Gabi. I got up and walked closer to the dais. "We're all listening," I said. "Let's hear it."

She leaned forward, placing her elbows on her knees, then
resting her chin atop her folded fingers. More to the Sisterverse
than to me, she said, "Sal and I just heard from Sweeps the
entropy sweeper that, just, like, a few minutes ago, FixGabi
made another attempt to get into our universe. Right, Sal?"

"Right. Attempt number . . . What was it again, Sweeps?"

In response, Sweeps snored. Chacho must have been really
tired from studying to become a class-nine AI all day.

"Attempt thirty-four," said Gabi. "And it failed, correct?"

"Yes. Brana kept FixGabi out." And then, for the benefit of
the visitors from other universes, "Brana is the name of our
universe's remembranation machine."

"Ours, too," they replied. That backed up what FixGabi
had told me earlier: Names transcend universes. But why? The
multiverse was so weird.

"So here's my question for you, Sal," said Gabi, standing
up and strolling around the dais. "If Brana is so good at keeping FixGabi out, how did all these other Gabis get in?"

That . . . was a very good question. They must have . . . but they couldn't . . . or maybe they . . . OH. "*You* talked to Sweeps, Gabi. And then Sweeps must have talked to Brana. You got Brana to let them in!"

Gabi touched her nose. "Brana knows FixGabi's personal cosmic signature, so it can keep her from making holes in our universe. So imagine this: Brana 'breaks down.' It has a major malfunction. Suddenly, our universe is vulnerable again. This is FixGabi's big chance!"

"Only," said Hurricane, rubbing her hands together, "Brana isn't really broken. Brana is a fully operational remembranation machine when FixGabi comes a-knockin'. Bwa-ha-ha!"

"But okay," said Jet-Shoes. "We lure Gabi here. Then what?"

"Then," said Electro-Hair, catching on, "we don't let her out."

Radar understood Gabi's plan next. "Brana can seal up any hole before FixGabi can go through it. It's way faster than she is."

"We can trap her in *this* universe," I said. "Where we can be sure she can't do any more harm to the multiverse."

"And," said Gabi, "we can try to reform her. She is a Gabi, after all. Sooner or later, I bet we can make her understand the error of her ways."

The other four Gabis seemed divided on that question. Two looked hopeful, if doubtful. Two made cacaseca faces.

"For my plan to work," my Gabi continued, "we need to make FixGabi believe she is slowly breaking down Brana's defenses. Over the next few days, we'll tell Brana to make FixGabi think she's winning. That way, she won't get discouraged and go looking for an easier universe to crack."

I remembered StupidSal—that really, *really* StupidSal

from the universe with the other sick Iggy. If FixGabi found his universe, she'd make short work of him and do whatever she wanted with that Papi's remembranation machine.

I sighed. I wasn't crazy about being stuck with FixGabi in *my* universe for all eternity. But for the sake of the whole raunching multiverse, it was a sacrifice I knew we had to make. "Okay," I said, heavy with the burden of duty. "I'm in. So when do we spring the trap?"

"We will fix FixGabi," said my Gabi, reeling in an imaginary fishing rod, "on the night we Break the Night."

40

"SALVADOR *VIDÓN*!" SAID Mrs. Waked, speaking, as she always did, with italics you could hear. "Would you be *so kind* as to help me attach this *bedeviled* bubble-blowing hookah to the caterpillar cake's mouth?"

"Sure thing, Mrs. Waked," I answered. I handed my hammer to one of the other set builders working with me and headed over to her.

The five other set builders and I had almost finished transforming Mrs. Waked's classroom into one of four Culeco classrooms that would play out the Caterpillar (Oruga in Spanish) and Pigeon (Paloma in Spanish) scenes from *Alice's Adventures in Wonderland*. But it hadn't been easy. Even before we could start turning Mrs. Waked's room into a mushroomy forest that also looked like the Everglades, we had to clear out the million costumes, props, pictures, and acting awards Mrs. Waked had collected over the years. Only after carting all that stuff out of there could we start building the set—which included painting a round table to look like a big old mushroom, for the Oruga cake to sit on—and turning a ladder into a very Florida-looking mangrove tree for the Paloma to roost in while accusing every-one passing below of being a serpent.

It had taken this team almost two full days, but finally, we were nearly done. Basically, we just needed to finish up a few signs. As you walked up to the Oruga's mushroom, a sign that read PARA ENCOGERSE pointed to the right, where there was a wall of fun-house mirrors that made you look shrunken and squat and flattened. The other sign, PARA AGRANDARSE, would point to the left and guide you to the fun-house mirrors that made you seem tall and weirdly stretched out. The last mirror on the left, the one next to the mangrove where the Paloma would be sitting, elongated your neck to make it look three feet long: just like in *Adventures in Wonderland*, when the Pigeon mistakes snaky-necked Alice for a serpent.

It was a great idea, and it worked perfectly in real life, too. I wish I could take the credit. But it was Adam's idea, and I'd praised him up and down for it.

However, *I* deserve full credit for being smart enough to make Adam my assistant director in charge of set design.

That was the first thing I'd done at school the day after Gabi and the Sisterverse and I concocted our plan to catch FixGabi. Aventura really wanted to concentrate on making the costumes more Cuban and Cuban American, so she asked me if I'd handle the other stuff. I said sure thing, if I could recruit some extra help.

Minutes later, in Señorx Cosquillas's homeroom, I had dep-utized Adam and Widelene and Teresita. They would be my assistant directors.

Over the next week, I found out what a smart choice I'd

made. They turned out even better than I thought they'd be.

Adam was way more experienced than me at being a director, which meant he was used to working with people on planning out scenes and making them look good. He called that "set composition." I had him work with the set builders to adapt the previous sets and props to make them look and sound and even *smell* more Cuban and Miamian. The result? Gems like the fun-house mirrors in the Oruga/Paloma rooms.

I made Widelene the assistant director in charge of safety. Her job was to work with the actors on how to fall, tumble, punch, slap, pour "hot" tea down someone's pants, and in general do terrible things to each other—100 percent safely! Aventura's four-hour snore-fest of a play hadn't required any physical training, since her actors had barely even had to move onstage. But now that we were asking our actors to make stuff up on the fly, we wanted to help them tell physical jokes as well as verbal ones. Widelene showed everyone how to perform acts of violence on one another without actually *performing* acts of violence on one another. As I'd been strolling the hallways for the last few days, I'd seen tons of simulated bodily harm being done to Wonderland characters, and the actors cracking up and loving it. Mission accomplished, Widelene.

And Teresita? I made her the assistant director of character consistency. The reason was simple: She was already a Wonderland character in real life. You know how almost all the characters in both Alice books are snappy, quibbling, snarly, snotty, nonsense-speaking know-it-alls? This was a chance for Teresita to use her natural talents to help the performers act more Wonderland-y.

In fact, she was in Mrs. Waked's room with me at that moment, coaching Octavio Murillo—my very tall climbing-wall buddy, a super-nice guy, and, most importantly for this role, a person who wasn't scared of heights—on how to be a more annoying Paloma. His pigeon costume wasn't as fully detailed as the original one Aventura had made (some kid in another room was wearing that one). Also, this version, because it had been made in a hurry, was a little too small for Octavio. But honestly, that just made it funnier.

"You're too nice, Octavio!" Teresita told him, in a way that meant that she really, really, *really* liked how nice he was, *except* for right now, when he was supposed to be playing the unreasonable Paloma. "Try it again. Call me a serpiente like I'm a long-necked weirdo who's gonna eat your babies."

"'Hey, you, serpiente!'" said Octavio, trying his best to sound like a mean girl but coming across more like a mensch. "'Get lost! You don't want to *squab*-ble with me!' Get it, Teresita? Because, see, a 'squab' is another name for a pigeon, so—"

He saw her face. Stopped talking. Gulped.

"Pigeons. Don't. Pun," said Teresita, moving only her lower lip. "Try it again!"

They were going to be there awhile. But I got the sense that neither of them minded too much. Ah, kids these days.

"Did you *forget* about your *dear* teacher in her *hour* of *need*, Sal?" Mrs. Waked asked me, with all the despair a three-time Emmy nominee could jam into a single sentence.

"Coming!" I said, and bounded over to her.

Mrs. Waked. She really was the best. She always made me laugh, even when she was doing seemingly innocent things.

There she was, halfway up a ladder, looking utterly perplexed. Next to her stood the mushroom table, on which rested the four-foot cake that looked like a caterpillar. Also on the table was a bubble-blowing hookah, currently turned off. She had the end of the hookah's hose in one hand.

She was dressed like a Spanish countess. Today's outfit was a blooming red gown with lace like a spiderweb running along every edge. A bustle the size of a blimp protruded from her posterior; she does a great egg-laying magic trick that I am 95 percent sure makes use of that bustle. Her heels were mostly rhinestones. Her hair was a garden of red and pink and white roses, and her makeup consisted of two rouge balls, one on each cheek; an X drawn in lipstick over her lips; and painted-on eyebrows that whirled and swirled all over her forehead like a wrought-iron fence. She loved clowning, loved fooling around. But there was always a super-seriousness beneath it all. She was someone who thought of acting the way a priestess thinks of religion. Jokes were holy to her.

Which I think explains why we got along so well.

"How can I help?" I asked her once I was near enough.

"Where," she italicized, "am I supposed to stick *this thing?"*

She meant the end of the hookah hose. "I think the mouth is traditional," I answered.

"I know *that,* Sal. It's just—" She made a few jabbing attempts to place the hookah into the cake caterpillar's mouth but couldn't commit. "I don't want to *ruin* it. The Culinary Arts students did *such* an extraordinary job making this caterpillar cake. I would *hate* to be the author of its *destruction."*

I knew where she was coming from. The cake was a

masterpiece. It wasn't actually a cake, technically, but rings of Rice Krispie Treats stacked on top of one another to create the caterpillar body. Then all those Rice Krispie circles were covered with fondant, which, I learned, is a rubbery sheet of sugar that is easy to paint and is shapeable, like clay. They had made it look exactly like a caterpillar—well, except that it was four feet tall. Its stripes were gold and green and white. They'd used black cotton candy to cover it in fuzz, and they turned its freaky mandibles into an almost mustache.

I really liked that they had gone super realistic with it, because that made the fact that it was wearing one of Papi's peach-colored guayaberas and a woven palm frond hat even funnier.

I smiled at Mrs. Waked. "I'll stick the hookah in its mouth for you. Hey, if I mess it up, they can't yell at me. I'm the director."

"Oh, thank *goodness*," phewed Mrs. Waked. She placed the tip of the hookah hose on the table and then—this surprised me—jumped off the ladder. Landing square on her bustle, she doinged onto her feet a tenth of a second later. That thing had to be made of springs or something! But wait, didn't she have the egg for her egg trick in there? Or maybe she had all sorts of bustles for all sorts of tricks?

Mrs. Waked always left you with more questions than she answered. I applauded her dismount—she took a bow—and climbed up the ladder, picking up the end of the hookah on the way up.

The reason why we had cake Orugas instead of students in costumes playing Orugas was because Principal Torres didn't want any kid even pretending to smoke. It's also why we had this no-smoke hookah. And here was where our Culinary Arts students came through again.

"You are going to love this, Mrs. Waked," I said to her, even as I jabbed the end of the hookah right between caterpillar's mandible mustachios. I shoved and kept shoving until the end was halfway through the Rice Krispy head—that way, there was no chance of it falling out. "The bubbles the hookah blows are candy bubbles. Turn it on!"

Clearly, Mrs. Waked had a sweet tooth, judging by the way she scurried over, like a mouse toward a freshly cheesed trap. She turned on the hookah.

Nothing happened.

I descended the ladder to solve the problem. In my thirteen years of life, I've learned that the solution to 80 percent of all problems comes to you right after you ask the question "Did you plug it in?" And yep: The hookah hadn't been plugged in. So I took care of that. Plug, meet socket.

A motor started whirring. A smell like a carnival slowly filled the air. Then, less than a minute later, but not much less, pink and blue bubbles started spouting out of the bowl of the hookah and planeted all around us, iridescent and changeable. Bubbles instantly make everything more magical.

And in this case, more delicious. I bit the bubble nearest me. It exploded and gave me a one-second taste of sweet raspberry.

"The [chomp] *pink* ones [chomp chomp] are *strawberry* [chomp]!" said Mrs. Waked. Clearly, she really liked strawberry. She was biting bubbles like a dog biting water from a hose.

The more the room filled with bubbles, the less work got done. Teresita, Octavio, and the set builders all stopped what they were doing to take a little snack break. And me too. I didn't know what the sugar content of a floating sugar bubble was, but it couldn't be much, right?

"You *know*, Sal, [chomp]," said Mrs. Waked, between bites of bubbles, "this is *pure* genius."

"The hookah?" I replied. "Yeah, I know. I mean, they even went to the trouble of putting in two flavors. Those Culinary Arts kids go above and beyond."

"Yes, they *do* at that [chomp]. But *I* was [chomp] referring *more* to the changes that Rompenoche [chomp] *en general* [chomp chomp] has undergone. They are *brilliant*."

I stopped destroying this sugary solar system for a second and walked a step closer to Mrs. Waked. Her opinion really mattered to me. "You think so? Because, I mean, the sets are great, and the props are great, and everybody seems to be having a lot of fun, getting ready for it. But it's so wild now. So many things happening at the same time. There's no way to keep control of it. Anything could happen."

"*Exactly*, my brilliant [chomp] young man [chomp chomp]. You've turned a play into a *carnival*. And *that* [chomp] is *really* what [chomp] Rompenoche [chomp] should be all [chomp chomp chomp chomp . . .]."

She never finished her sentence, because an especially agile bubble was dodging her like a fairy trying to lure her into a bog. But I'd gotten her message. Mrs. Waked liked the new Rompenoche, as messy and as unruly as it seemed from my end. That made me feel better—which I needed, since the closer we got to showtime, the more I worried that it would be a complete disaster.

"Really, Sal? With one day left before the show and all the work we have to do, here I find you all goofing off?" said Gabi.

She was standing in the doorway, arms crossed, tapping a foot. Today's barrettes: owls and pussycats in rowboats. Today's T-shirt: "YOU'VE GOT TO JUMP OFF CLIFFS ALL THE TIME AND BUILD YOUR WINGS ON THE WAY DOWN."—RAY BRADBURY.

Gabi was just kidding, of course. She knew how hard everybody had been working all week. But, committed to her bit, she said, "I'd like to borrow you for a minute, Sal. I mean, if you can take a break from chasing bubbles."

"Take him [chomp] *away*," said Mrs. Waked, only half noticing Gabi. "We have got this room [chomp] under *complete* control at this point." And I'm not sure, but I think she added, in a squealy little voice, "More bubbles for me!"

It was easy to forget, in the middle of all the stress that comes with codirecting a school-wide production, that we had a multiverse to save and a supervillain to capture. Luckily, I had made Gabi my assistant director in charge of fixing the universe. And I knew she wasn't about to let me slack off.

41

HALLWAY 2C WAS just about ready for Rompenoche. Gabi and I paused outside of Mrs. Waked's room so I could take it in.

For this corridor, we'd decided to concentrate on tropical island life, since both Cuba and Miami are famous for their beaches. It would be the perfect place to set up actors playing the Morsa (Walrus), the Ostra (Oyster), the Langosta (Lobster), the Falsa Tortuga (Mock Turtle)—basically any character that could use water and/or sand as its backdrop.

The good news was that the school already had a ton of props for tropical locations. Apparently, Culeco students like plays that take place on deserted islands. So we had all the fake palm trees, real umbrellas, towels, lifeguard chairs, life preservers, and beach balls we needed to set the mood. They even had photorealistic yoga mats that looked like sand.

Even better, though, learning coordinator extraordinaire Daniel had blown up and printed out some old photos and postcards of Cuban and Miamian beaches, and these decorated the walls. At first, they just looked like pictures from a time gone by. When you looked closer, though, you'd see that standing alongside the Cubans and Miamians in the photos were the Dodo in a bikini, Bill the Lizard in a Speedo, and the Mad Hatter in one of those old-timey striped one-piece bathing suits—and a big ole top hat, of course. Daniel, like all librarians, had a million secret skills that he was dying to use. Photoshop was definitely one of them.

Best of all, though, was the fact that hallway 2C was basically *done*. Since I'd arrived at school that morning, I'd been working in Mrs. Waked's room and unable to monitor the progress. Turns out I hadn't needed to.

"Phew, baby," I said. "At least the beach set is ready."

"One task down," said Gabi, "and just six billion more to go."

Yeah, thanks Gabi. Way to make me feel better ☺

Gabi and I turned right. That put Culeco's massive stage-craft and set design studio on our right-hand side as we walked. We went in and strolled down a path in the room that looked like Miami's most famous street, Calle Ocho, in miniature. This was going to be the first thing that parents saw when they entered the school, with facades of some of the street's most famous buildings lining both sides of hallway 1W.

The real Calle Ocho already looks like the multiverse vomited all over it, because the buildings come from all different time periods. So our movie-set version had to seem just as random. Actually, even more random: It also had to look like something that could have appeared in the Alice books, if Lewis Carroll had been Cuban.

Sound impossible? Well, I know I'm biased, but I think our set builders were *killing it*.

First, they'd painted eight huge rooster statues in all

these crazy colors and styles, just like you see on Calle Ocho, except ours were themed around Wonderland. One rooster was painted with living playing cards all over it; another with living chess pieces; another had a white-knight mannequin riding it; another was done up like a gryphon, all eagle-y and lion-y, yet still chicken-y; and so on, each rooster statue more maravillosa than the next.

All those roosters would be placed throughout hallway 1W, alongside everyone's favorite Calle Ocho locales. And instead of throwing a tea party, we were going to throw a cafecito party, with the Wonderland characters from that scene drinking espresso in front of our replica of Cafe Versailles. The real Ball & Chain is a nightclub now, but we wanted to go back to the 1930s with it, because that was when it was frequented by gangsters. Its entrance, all chrome and neon, would be guarded by two frog footmen—but instead of wearing tabards and tights and floppy hats with feathers in them, the frogs would wear pinstriped suits and porkpie hats and carry tommy guns. Our King of Hearts was going to be their mob boss. He'd wear a loud red suit, and he'd be all smarm and charm, handing out kiss-of-death playing cards to parents as they passed by. He had this whole bit about giving someone a "Cuban necktie" that ends with him giving someone in the audience, well, a clip-on necktie that has ¡VIVA CUBA! printed on it.

Our King of Hearts would be played by Yasmany Robles. We weren't going to waste his talents by having him play a sad tree. Not while I was codirector, anyway.

And when parents walked past our re-creation of Maximo Gomez Park, they'd see tables where characters from

Wonderland would be violently slapping down dominoes and cussing like old Cuban men.

Okay, they wouldn't *actually* be cussing like old Cuban men, because Principal Torres said we weren't allowed to cuss like old Cuban men, even for the sake of Art. Gabi was all ready to start a petition against censorship, but I asked her to stand down. Time was short; we had to pick our battles.

So we went with the next-best option. We set up a Bluetooth microphone and speaker on the domino tables so that Vorágine could hear when one of our actors was about to swear and play the censored sound when they did. Turns out, the *BLEEP!* is consistently funnier than the actual naughty language it's covering up. Who knew?

It was so funny when we tested it, in fact, that we decided to set up microphones and speakers for Vorágine all over the school, so it could bleep out foul language wherever any actor got a little too salty. And Vorágine was thrilled to have a part in Rompenoche. "I have extensive knowledge of vulgar words in over two hundred languages. No utterance of questionable color will get past me! Just let them try to curse in ancient Sumerian—I'll bleep them back to Meso-[*BLEEP!*]-potamia!"

Yep, it would even censor itself if it cussed. Vorágine, as we have seen, is a very ethical toilet.

But there was still so much work to do. Most of the activity in the stagecraft and set design studio at the moment was centered on constructing the Freedom Tower.

In real life, the Freedom Tower was the tall yellow-and-white building where so many Cubans who came to the US had begun the process of becoming American citizens back in the day. The set builders were working on our replica as fast as they could, building it and painting it at the same time. But I think we might have been a little too ambitious with that one. It was still only as tall as my armpit. It had to more than double in size in just one day.

Gabi and I walked up to Coach Lynott, who was heading up construction. He was dressed, as usual, like he'd gotten his entire fashion sense from his love of mashed potatoes. Every piece of clothing on him—visor, polo shirt, shorts, belt, tube socks, sneakers, even the lanyard for his whistle and stopwatch—was white. The only variation in color came from his pit stains, bright as butter.

But hey, it'd be easy to make fun of my own nature-show-host-wannabe fashion sense, too. I liked Coach Lynott. Beneath all those mashed potatoes, he had a good heart.

"How's it going?" I asked him.

"Wonderful!" Coach Lynott said loudly. Then he leaned over to Gabi me, blocked his mouth with his hand so the kids working on the set couldn't see it, and whispered, "We're *way* behind schedule." He straightened up again and, practically yelling, said, "We'll be done in no time!" Then he leaned over and whispered, "We need a miracle to finish on time." Out loud: "We are rocking and rolling!" Whispered: "We're doing the dead-man's waltz here." Out loud: "Nothing's going to stop us now!" Whispered: "One sneeze and this tower comes a-tumbling down."

I swear to pants, Coach Lynott must have been cursed by a bruja to always make the wrong choice in any given situation. Did he really think putting a hand in front of his mouth was going to keep the set builders from hearing him? I could see their slight but real reactions to Coach Lynott's fake encouragement and whispered despair. They were getting discouraged.

Adults out there, listen up: Kids hear better than you do. If you can hear it, so can we, and if you can't hear it, we probably can anyway. Sheesh.

Gabi, born leader that she is, noticed the plummeting morale in the room at least as quickly as I did. "Sal," she said to me, "don't you think we should bring in some more people to help get the Freedom Tower finished? The crew here is working so hard."

"Definitely," I said. "Also," I added, reaching into my pockets and handing out fun-size bags of Skittles, "y'all need some candy. Let's take a break!"

They didn't need to be told twice: The set builders surrounded me and, hyena fast, cleaned me out of Skittles. Morale rose instantly. Tech crews tend to be a food-motivated people.

Coach Lynott leaned over to me and "whispered" behind his hand, "Do you think a break is a good idea, Sal? We're running so far behind already."

I know you're not supposed to chloroform people and gag them and stick them in closets until Rompenoche is over, but Coach Lynott was really asking for it. Again, the set builders heard him. I could see it in the way they delayed, just for a microsecond, popping another Skittle in their mouths, or how frowns formed for an instant before they bravely made their faces expressionless again. This called for drastic measures.

In response to Coach Lynott's whisper, I said to him, at

full volume, "Coach, you know how you're always saying that, to make the impossible possible, you have to believe in your dreams?"

"Ba-wha-huh?" said Coach Lynott, who, as far as I know, had never said *To make the impossible possible, you have to believe in your dreams.* But it's not a lie to ask a question.

And it didn't matter how he answered: Yes, no, or whatever the heck *ba-wah-huh* is supposed to be, I could work with it. "Before I call more people to come help you all, I think a visualization exercise is just what the team needs. Don't you, Coach?"

"Um . . ." said Coach Lynott. Watching him think was like watching a camel chew. "I don't know if we have the time to—"

"Great idea, Sal!" said Gabi, yes-anding the heck out of me before Coach Lynott ruined my plan. She took Lynott's hand and reached out with the other toward another set builder, who instantly took it. At Culeco, as soon as anyone starts grabbing hands, we instinctively form a ring. Theater people love making circles. Before I could inhale and exhale, we had the half-finished Freedom Tower surrounded.

"I just don't see the point," said Coach Lynott, linking hands with me on his other side. "We don't have time for touchy-feely woo-woo stuff. We should just keep working."

I answered him in my cheerful ringmaster's voice. "We'll never reach our end goal if we limit our perceiving! Us getting to the finish line requires us believing! 'I can't' is just a lie you tell yourself when you're deceiving! When people stop themselves from greatness, *that* is my pet-peeving! So put away your doubts and all your worries and your grieving! It's time to see the future and the heights we'll be achieving!"

Part of my training as a magician has included memorizing lists of words that are easy to rhyme. That way, when I need to say something quickly that sounds like a magic spell, I can whip up a silly poem superfast and use it to distract the audience from the actual trick I'm playing.

The more I chanted it, the better people could hear the rhymes and rhythm. And when I hit the last line, I raised and lowered the hands I was holding in time with the beat, and then repeated it. "It's time to see the future and the heights we'll be achieving! It's time to see the future and the heights we'll be achieving!"

While pumping their arms, everybody started repeating it along with me, louder and louder, Gabi the loudest. Even Lynott reluctantly spoke the lines, though with about as much enthusiasm as an endoscope showing up for work on Monday morning.

We chanted four more times, each one louder than the next. And then, the chant worked. We were able to see the future we would be achieving. Literally. Because I brought in a finished Freedom Tower from another universe.

Well, a lot of it anyway. I didn't want to make a hole that FixGabi could use to get in—that would ruin the trap we were setting for her. So I just brought in, like, 70 percent of that Freedom Tower from the other universe. You could see through it, but only barely.

"Well, mash my potatoes, it worked," Coach Lynott said, almost stunned into silence. Then, going from flabbergasted to blabbergasted, he shouted, "*It worked!* It actually worked, kids! I can see what it's going to look like when it's done! Can you? It's like it's really there. That's amazing! But it's like I always say: 'To make the impossible possible, you have to believe in your dreams!'"

42

"**THAT WAS A** pretty neat trick you pulled back there," Gabi told me as we walked out of stagecraft and set design, the happy sounds of construction vanishing as the door closed behind us. "When you made the tower appear, you made everyone believe they could finish it. It's a pity you couldn't have just left the finished tower in this universe, though—at least until after tomorrow night. We could have moved everyone to working on other stuff."

I shrugged. "Better safe than sorry. The thing about importing stuff from other universes is that it goes away on its own schedule. We don't want the tower to disappear in the middle of Rompenoche, do we?"

"No, we do not. But my point is, Sal, you gave everyone hope, just like a good director should. You're turning out to be an excellent leader."

"Couldn't have done it without you. You're the one who clutched it out, taking control of Lynott the way you did." I took a few more steps before my hands hit the bottoms of my pockets. "We make a good team. You really are someone I can work with."

Gabi jammed her hands in her pockets, too. "What are level-four friends for, you jar of farts?"

"Hey! I'm being serious!"

She gave me a side-eye smile. "So be serious. No one's stopping you."

We started down the NW staircase as I spoke. "You're always trying to fix every problem you run across. Doesn't matter if it's big or small, or even unsolvable. You're fearless."

She shrugged. "'The most good, for the most people, for as long as you have the spoons.'"

"Yeah, well, I guess that makes you a utensils factory, because I've never met anyone with more spoons than you."

We were halfway down the stairs when Gabi stopped. "Thank you. That's really sweet."

"Nope. Big facts. Another big fact: You're good at teamwork, which a lot of smart people aren't. And you're *really* good at forgiving people. And then, after you forgive them, you help them recover from their mistakes. You've done that for me, for Yasmany, for who knows how many people."

"People have done it for me, too. Heck, *you've* done it for me."

I started us walking again. "Also, I really like your T-shirts. You're always putting out a positive message. You've devoted your life to being a force for good in the world, down to the clothes you wear. It's really admirable."

She stopped us again, this time at the bottom of the

staircase, and stood staring at me like I was a brand-new species. Then, with her hands still in her pockets, she laughed without sound and leaned waaaay back. "Well, mash my potatoes," she said, in a great imitation of Coach Lynott. "Do you have a crush on me, Sal Vidón?"

"What? No! I don't have those kinds of feelings for any—"

She patted the air and talked me down. "Easy, bubba. That was level-four-friend teasing. If you were any more aro, I'd shoot you out of a bow. But that *was* a lot of compliments to give me all in a row. Why?"

Instead of answering right away, I started ambling down hallway 1W. It felt elf-workshop levels of joyous: lots of kids in groups practicing their Rompenoche improv; lots of set builders putting props in place and measuring walls; lots of costumes being furiously stapled, taped, pinned, tied, and hot-glue-gunned together.

That's how far costume making had spread all over school. Aventura was out in the courtyard again with her army of seamstresses, seamsters, and seamstrxes, sewing like they were patching the fabric of the cosmos. And in hallway 1W, I had to step around Dr. Doctorpants, who was frantically helping kids on the floor finish their outfits. As Culeco's resident expert on costuming, you'd expect him to be wearing an awesome costume, and you would not have been disappointed. He was dressed as *both* Tweedledum and Tweedledee, a two-sided costume, front and back, with four arms and four legs and two faces facing opposite directions—basically, a two-face Tweedle octopus.

It was such a good costume that, from a distance, I

SAL & GABI FIX THE UNIVERSE

seriously could not tell which side was Dr. Doctorpants's actual front. I also liked the additions he had made so the costume looked less Alice and more Alicia. Instead of the frumpy British schoolboy outfits of *Through the Looking-Glass*, he had one of the Tweedles dressed like a Cuban schoolkid, with red shorts, a white shirt, and a blue scarf tied around the neck. The other side was dressed like an American private-school kid, with khaki shorts, a white shirt, a blue vest (that only went halfway around his torso, obviously) and a red tie. PS: If you think you could tell which way he was actually facing by looking at his knees, then you have never met a costumer as good as Dr. Doctorpants. He made *both* pairs of legs look like they were cotton-stuffed fakes.

"Doing all right, Doctor?" I asked him. "Gonna finish in time?"

"Nohow!" one of his Tweedle faces replied. Then he turned his head so the other Tweedle could say, "Contrariwise, we'll finish in plenty of time."

"How can you not finish and finish at the same time?" Gabi asked, laughing.

"Exactly! She gets it. Okay, back to work now." And he used both sides of his costume to help two different kids—simultaneously!

Gabi and I resumed our journey down the hallway, still trying to puzzle out how Dr. Doctorpants's costume worked. But I don't think either of us tried too hard. Sometimes mysteries are better than answers.

But sometimes answers are better than mysteries. "I was complimenting you," I said to Gabi, "because I really believe all those things, and we don't always tell people how great they are, and then they're gone, and we lose the chance forever."

Gabi thought about that before she answered. "You're worried about tomorrow. About FixGabi."

I nodded. "When I was in the space station, I saw Miami and Cuba and the Bahamas wiped from the face of the Earth. It was"—it took me a sec to figure out what I wanted to say—"it was like the geography version of seeing my Cuban American background being wiped out of existence."

One of the nice things about talking to someone who reads a lot is that, when you make a big pronouncement like I just had, they get it. I watched Gabi's face telegraph her shock and sympathy as she registered my words. "FixGabi's no joke. But we've set a trap for her. We'll have the element of surprise. We're gonna get her, Sal. We won't let what happened to her universe happen to ours."

I emptied my lungs. "I hope so. But it's like when I'm playing *Poocha Lucha Libre.* I'm pretty good. I've been Top Dog of the Day seven different times."

"I'll assume that's a good thing," said Gabi, whose idea of a video game is seeing how far she can shot-put an Xbox.

"Trust me, Gabi, it is. But I still lose a lot of games, every day, even to people I should have beaten easily. Except Papi. I never lose to Papi."

Gabi nodded solemnly. "What you're saying is that, in life, sometimes the wrong person wins."

"Sometimes it feels like the wrong person is always winning."

Now it was Gabi's turn to sigh. "Don't I know it."

"So," I said, feeling smeepier and smeepier, "I just want

you to know, in case I don't get to later, that I think you're an incredible person. There's no one like you in the world, Gabi Reál. You are one of a kind."

There, as we stood in front of the door to the student council room, aka the Ovum Throne, Gabi gripped my shoulder like a cornerwoman asking her boxer for just one more round. "Thank you, Sal. You are, by far, the most mature cishet male Cuban American type-one diabetic tween I've ever met."

She was joking to keep herself from smeeping. "Thanks," I deadpanned.

"And," she added, her eyeballs shining and wet, "you're an actual, legitimate, honest-to-pants miracle worker. I mean, I am as atheist as a mountain. I used to think miracles were either misunderstandings or lies. But you, Sal, have introduced me to the science of miracles." She took a step back and spoke more quietly. "You saved my baby brother, Sal, and therefore my whole family. Thank you. Thank you forever."

Yeah, there was no stopping her waterworks now. "Bring it in, sister," I said, inviting her into a hug.

"Really‽" she asked/said, so elated that I could hear her using an interrobang. She ran into my arms and Heimlich-hugged me. If either of us cried, no one else in the hallway could tell.

As Gabi rested her chin on my shoulder, she added, "Do level-four friends hug?"

"Naw," I answered. "But level-five friends do."

She stepped out of the hug, smiling. "I do have to correct you about one thing, however."

"What's that?"

She stepped over to the student council room's door and opened it. Inside, the Gabis from the Sisterverse were sitting in four of the egg-thrones, gabbing away. They all had on similar Alicia outfits.

"There are at least four other people in the universe who are quite a bit like me," Gabi added, smiling like the Jaws of Life at a demolition derby. "Now, what do you say we go over our plan one more time?"

43

FROM THE OUTSIDE, I could see how some parents could think Rompenoche was a bit of a mess. But from my position as codirector, I knew the truth.

It was gerbils.

I mean, front to back, side to side, up and down—any way you looked at it, it was a parade of mayhem, guaranteed to overload your senses. Salsa music filled every hallway: thudding bongos, tragic trumpets, singers on the edge of a nervous breakdown declaring that it was the end of the world and they were going spend their last few minutes dancing. On the first floor, Miami landmarks had been gene-spliced with fantasy worlds, making them familiar and unfamiliar at the same time, both homey and weird.

More monsters than people stalked the halls of Culeco: talking animals, animated game pieces, living caricatures with heads bigger than their bodies. They talked to you in Spanglish gibberish. They laughed wildly—not because something was funny, but because nothing in the world could restrain them anymore. Sometimes the monsters would cavort with each other, perform something that seemed like a short scene from a play, except none of it made any sense. They always turned into a slapstick chase, full of pratfalls and/or bonks on the head and/or attempted and/or successful wedgies.

And somehow, in the middle of all this madness, teachers were supposed to be telling parents how their kids were doing in school.

"So, Mr. Vidón," Principal Torres said, walking over to me. She spoke nice and loud, to be sure I could hear her over the anarchy happening around us. "How are we looking?"

I checked my clipboard. "Looking good," I said, injecting my voice with fake-it-till-you-make-it confidence. "It's six fifty-four p.m. The assistant directors are collecting the parents in cohort four outside the Culeco doors as we speak." I tapped my headset. "All teachers have reported back: They have finished their conferences with cohort two. Cohort three has finished watching their kids perform and are being shepherded toward their teacher conferences. They should be in position just as we let in cohort four. It's, um . . ." I said, as calmly as I could, even though the last gerbil in my head was on its deathbed. "I think it's going pretty well."

"You do, do you?" she said. Was it me, or had she just answered me with so much cacaseca in her voice she could fertilize a farm?

I looked up from my clipboard. All week, Principal Torres had been dressing as different Wonderland characters, but tonight, she was outfitted like a Miami principal: She wore pants with a tropical pattern, a rain forest–green blazer, and a gold pin-on name tag. She told me she didn't want to compete with her students for attention. Her job tonight wasn't to shine, but to support.

Mine, too. I had dressed all in black, the way stage techs do. And luckily, I have cargo pants and cargo vests in all sorts of colors, including black, so I could carry everything I needed as a codirector. Instead of my usual assortment of magic-related gewgaws and doodads, my pockets overflowed with first-aid stuff, extra makeup and spirit gum and latex, scissors and fishing line and superglue, and most importantly of all, duct tape—so much duct tape. Whoever invented duct tape, thank you. You saved Rompenoche at least fifteen times.

Duct tape wasn't going to save me from Principal Torres, though. "How do *you* think it's going?" I asked her.

"I think," she said pleasantly, looking left and right, taking a fresh look at the madness boiling all around us, "that I've been in hurricanes that were less chaotic than this."

Et tu, Torres? "That bad, huh?"

"What? No, no, no, Mr. Vidón. I'm a born and bred Floridian. I *like* hurricanes."

"You do?"

"I do. And apparently, so do a lot of the parents. Look," she said, pointing to a couple who were taking a family selfie with one of the giant chickens, "those are the Moraleses. They were in cohort one. And so were the Gonzalezes over there, and the Gonzalezes over *there*, and also, the Gonzalezes over there!" A lot of Gonzalezes attended Culeco. "And there are the Bacardis, and the Aires, and the Cardozas. All cohort one. And that's just on this floor. According to your plan, you thought cohort one would be gone by now, right?"

"Yeah," I said, checking the chart again.

"So why are they still here?"

"Because," I said, searching my brain with my eyes, "we didn't move them through the interactive site-specific theater fast enough?"

"Noooo," she said, patting my back. "They're still here because they're having a good time. Because they're proud. Because they love the fact that their kids are attending a school that has this much passion and energy."

There was no denying it; clearly, the parents from cohort one were having a ball with their kids. They had caught a little of the uncivilized spirit of Rompenoche. Some of them had painted faces, when they hadn't entered Culeco with any stage makeup on. Some of them had pieces of costume they'd borrowed or stolen from their kids. Some were improvising right along with the students and giving as good as they got. Betcha loads of them had been theater kids back in the day.

"Thank you," I said to Principal Torres.

She crossed her arms and looked straight ahead. "You and I are a lot alike, you know. Sometimes my reach exceeds my grasp. Sometimes I act like I'm the only person in the world who can fix things. My poor spouse, bless them, has to remind me every three months or so that I can't do it alone. I need to ask for help. I have to trust people."

"You trusted me," I said to her, "after I gave you a lot of reasons not to."

"Exactly. And you rewarded me," she said, opening her arms wide, "by well and truly breaking the night. ¿Formaste una corredera propia, no?"

I had to agree. "I declare this noche officially rota."

"The resolution passes," she said, saluting me. "Now, is it time to welcome in cohort four?"

I checked my smartwatch; the time switched from 6:59 to 7:00 as I stared. "Yes, it is." I activated my headset. "Assistant directors, please escort cohort four into the building."

"Copy that, my dude!" replied Srx. Cosquillas, who was my assistant director in charge of directing the assistant directors. "We're releasing the hounds in three . . . two . . . one. . . ."

The massive double doors opened toward us, and a crowd of curious, smiling parents started pouring in. Leading them were the Reál family, because, of course, the Reáls had jumped to the front of the line. They entered Culeco and spread out in front of Principal Torres and me like a dance troupe ready to throw down.

Ms. Reál, who stood in the center of the line, looked *exactly* like Lewis Carroll, with her curly, drapey haircut, white tie and tails, and the kind of dreamy look that implies that you've always got one eye watching a different universe. If I didn't know better, I would have mistaken her for a professional Lewis Carroll impersonator, or at least a Victorian rich dude.

The other Gabi dads seemed less interested in accuracy and more interested in adding personal touches to their costumes. Lightning Dad looked like Lewis Carroll, if Lewis Carroll had been struck by lightning on the way to Rompenoche. His suit was covered with holes and burn marks, and his hair stood straight up from his head, gelled to electrocuted perfection. Cari-Dad looked like Lewis Carroll, if Lewis Carroll had been a female heart surgeon. Her outfit was half tie and tails, half scrubs, as if she'd just left the operating room after a *really* bloody surgery, slapped on half a suit, and rushed over. If Lewis Carroll had been a bear—or at least a huge dude in a huge tux wearing a hairy brown-bear mask, hairy brown-bear gloves, and hairy brown-bear Uggs—he would've looked like Grizzly Dad'ums. If Lewis Carroll were an eco warrior in a camouflage tailcoat trying to convince the world that they should eat mopane-worm sandwiches instead of cows, he'd dress exactly as Daditarian was dressed now, and he'd also be carrying a basket of mopane-worm sandwiches. If Lewis Carroll had done his own illustrations and had doodled them all over his Victorian-gentleman suit, Dadaist would have been the second person to wear the outfit he had on, instead of the first. If Lewis Carroll were a masked avenger stalking the night in search of evildoers, wearing a cape and a ruffled shirt and a musketeer hat, with a fencing sword on his hip and a grapple gun hanging from his belt, he still wouldn't have looked half as ready to save the world as Dada-dada-dada-dada Dadman!, because Dada-dada-dada-dada Dadman! was way more brolic than Carroll and his tiny mathematician muscles. And if Lewis Carroll had been a class-nine AI, he . . . wouldn't have been Lewis Carroll at all. He would have been a completely different lifeform. But Dad: The Final Frontier still looked a lot like Lewis Carroll. The biggest difference between her and the writer of nonsense fiction we all know and love is that she had a protective gyroscopic ball sticking out from her belly. Inside, Iggy, the world's smallest Lewis Carroll impersonator, looked out on the world with his piercing eyes.

Principal Torres clapped both hands over her mouth, then slapped her thighs, and finally, shaking the incredulity out of her head, applauded. "You are too much, Reál clan! But you've been helping with Rompenoche night and day! Where in the world did you find the time to make these costumes?"

The dads took their turns shaking Principal Torres's hand and scruffing my hair. Ms. Reál went last, kissing me on the top of the head and then Principal Torres once on each cheek. "It's like Gabi's T-shirt says: 'You can't use up creativity. The more you use, the more you have.' How are you, Principal Torres? You must be so proud. This"—she added, spreading her arms and rotating—"is incredible! You must be exhausted!"

Principal Torres waved it off. "I made the kids do the hard work. All I did was make sure they didn't do anything dangerous."

"Or vulgar!" I added. "Vorágine's covering our [*BLEEP!*] on that one."

Both women looked at me, and then at each other, with the patience and the humor of adults who have a lot of experience dealing with smart-aleck kids. But then Principal Torres's dimples fell from their smiling heights. "So," she said to Ms. Reál, "how is Iggy doing? Gabi had mentioned he was doing better. But does he need a sterile environment again?"

Ms. Reál's confusion lasted only a second. "Oh, the ball! It's true it can be made sterile very quickly, but Iggy just likes it in there. He's doing fine. I mean, look at the little boliche."

"He is the cutest Lewis Carroll lookalike I have ever seen."

"Hey!" said Grizzly Dad'ums. "I'm standing right here!"

Ms. Reál fake-slapped his arm. "No, but Iggy's gotten so big in just a few weeks. Está más gordito than a butter-stuffed piñata, no?"

"Oh, yes, I can see," Principal Torres agreed. "But what I don't understand is why all of you Reáls have decided to torture me."

Ms. Reál blinked. "¿Perdóname? We are torturing you?"

"Yes. Here you brought the cutest baby in the entire world with you, and you haven't offered to let me hold him yet!"

"¡Ay!" wailed Ms. Reál, like a criminal caught in the act. "I am so sorry!" She turned briskly to Dad: The Final Frontier and waved her over. "Bonita! Come, come, mi vida!"

Bonita did, and the dads parted the way to let her through. We were all being slowly backed up against the wall as parents continued to pour in through the doors, but the dads formed a perimeter around Principal Torres and Dad: The Final Frontier to give them a little space.

Dad: The Final Frontier pressed a virtual button on her phone, and the top of the ball opened like an eye. Principal Torres scooped Iggy out of the ball mama-bear quickly and mama-bear gently.

Iggy, as always, was looking around, making super-serious eyebrows at everyone and everything. But once Principal Torres had him comfortably settled in her arms, he expressed his love in the way of babies everywhere. He smiled wide and toothlessly, and then took a massive dump.

I'd learned a lot about infant care these past few weeks, hanging out with Iggy. Sometimes babies can poop and you don't even know it for a long time, and discovering that surprise when you're the person in charge of changing diapers no es bueno. But sometimes babies poop like grumpy-faced gods hatching new planets, and the surprise is even worse. It's never not surprising, the gas giants babies can make in their diapers.

"¡Muchacho!" whistled Principal Torres. Clearly, she'd done the mother thing before. Not only was she not grossed out, but she knew how to reposition Iggy in her arms so his diaper wouldn't leak onto his little Lewis Carroll trousers. "You're having your own personal Rompenoche in your pants, aren't you?"

"I've got him," said Lightning Dad, carefully relieving Principal Torres of Iggy. "My turn to be the baby wiper and diaper sniper."

"I will go," said Dad: The Final Frontier. "You don't want to miss any part of Rompenoche."

"But neither do you," said Dadaist.

"None of us do," Cari-Dad said philosophically, "but one of us has to."

"Déjame atender a mi niñito," said Dada-dada-dada-dada Dadman! "Yo casi ni entiendo nada en inglés de to'l manera."

"Stop picking on your English," Daditarian said to him. "You understand plenty. I'll go. Ooh, and then you can all owe me a huge favor of my choosing, and the favor is to eat one mopane-worm sandwich each."

"Save us, Sal," Grizzly Dad'ums whispered to me.

I got in the center of the Dad circle. "I shall do the honors," I proclaimed showmannishly. "All of you need to go see your daughter perform. She's waiting in the auditorium, where

Principal Torres is about to lead you, for your Rompenoche disorientation session."

"We can't miss that," said Ms. Reál. "None of us." She took Iggy out of Lightning Dad's arms and placed him in mine. A blast of cacaseca minus the seca filled my nostrils.

"Do you know how to change a diaper?" asked Dad: The Final Frontier, slipping the strap of the diaper bag over my neck. "It can be surprisingly difficult for the uninitiated."

"How hard can it be?" I said. "You take the nasty nappy off, you wipe the kid's butt, and you put a new nappy on. It'll be easier than—" And here I pulled a fun-size bag of Skittles out of Iggy's ear.

"Taking candy from a baby!" all the Reáls said together, and then applauded.

All day and night, Aventura and I had been taking turns being the director on duty: an hour on, an hour off. That way, we'd stay rested and sharp. So, as I carried Iggy to the bathroom, I used my headset to ask her to take her next shift a little early so I could change his diaper.

She nearly blew my headphones off my head when she replied, "YOU KNOW HOW TO CHANGE A DIAPER?!"

"I need my eardrums, woman! Stop yelling."

"Just when I thought I couldn't love you any more, Sal," she said. "Honestly, I never even took off the last shift. I've been running around fixing costumes left and right. Everybody's starting to look patchier than scarecrows. We just really didn't have the time to do a good job on the wardrobe for this show."

I locked the bathroom door behind me. I'd be a coward if I

didn't ask the question. I was almost okay with that, but not quite. "Are you regretting that we changed everything at the last minute?"

She used her sonic attack on my ears again. It's super effective! "WHAT?! ARE YOU KIDDING? NO WAY, SAL!"

"Are you trying to make me drop this baby, woman?" Before I risked that, I gently set Iggy down on the counter next to the sink, opened the diaper bag, and started taking out everything I needed to change him: portable changing pad, baby wipes, Daditarian-made organic baby powder (I mean, that's what the jar had written on it, anyway), and, of course, a fresh diaper.

"It's so much better," Aventura went on. "I think my show was more beautiful. Like, it would have made for prettier pictures on Insta. But now, we're gonna have way better memes. And better stories. And just, like, more fun. The energy in the hallway is giving me life."

I started to wash my hands. I'm not sure if you're supposed to wash your hands before you change a baby. I mean, you definitely have to wash them *after*: blecch. But this was my first time doing a diaper change, and I wanted to be extra sure I did everything right—especially with Iggy, who not too long ago had been a very sick baby. "Also, Aventura, did you see how many parents came to help their kids with their parts of the show? Srx. Cosquillas says the teachers finished, like, two-thirds of their conferences before Rompenoche even started. And the teachers got to talk with parents way more than they normally would. Principal Torres wants this to be the way they do parent-teacher conferences from now on."

"And it's all thanks to you, Sal."

"Yeah," I said, drying my hands. "Me and my big fat mouth."

She laughed. "Speaking of which, take it from a big sister: You better close that big mouth of yours when you take off the diaper. Little boys are squirters. I suggest you put on a welder's mask before you do anything else."

"I don't think there's a welder's mask in the diaper bag. But anyway, Iggy wouldn't do that to me. We're bros."

"Chacho, I'm telling you: Trust your bros, you get the hose."

"Literally the least helpful thing you could say right now. Are you going to cover for me, or not?"

She had a good long giggle before she finally answered. "Yeah, I got you, chacho. But now you owe me *two* favors: one for this, and one for helping you with your Death costume."

"Wait, what? I'm your codirector. *This* is your favor."

"Nee nee nee. This is you making up for your rudeness. So now you owe me twice. And I am going to have a goo-oo-*ood* time collecting. Bye, Sal."

And with that, she cut our connection.

"Learn from my mistakes, kid," I said to Iggy. "Shut your mouth before you dig yourself in deeper."

It's funny, when you love a baby, how non-gross changing them is.

I mean, all the separate steps of changing a diaper are gross, if you analyze the parts individually. But when you put it all together? Not so much. With Iggy, I didn't feel tying him into a new nappy was any more disgusting than handling my own bodily needs. In some ways, it was even less squicky. I mean, a body is supposed to poop. It isn't supposed to bleed as much as I have to make mine bleed, just to check my sugar levels. And I've got the calluses to prove it.

"If you need any help with the diaper," said Vorágine, drawing me out of my own thoughts, "I can pull up tutorials, or talk you through the steps, or fill the room with a more pleasing scent. Would you prefer lemon verbena, vanilla and cinnamon, or pumpkin spice?"

I stopped changing Iggy for a second and turned toward Vorágine's stall. "Does anyone ever choose pumpkin spice?"

"Never even once." It chortled by bubbling its bowl water.

A message indicator appeared on my smartwatch. "Play message," I told my watch.

"Sweeps reporting in," said the one and only entropy sweeper. "No activity to report re a certain someone trying to break into a certain universe. Brana reports zero attempts to branesurf here, and I'm not picking up any new calamitrons. I don't like it. It's too quiet. But I guess there's nothing to do but wait. I will report in again in exactly ten minutes on the state of the multiverse. Sweeps out."

Yeah, Sweeps was right. It *did* feel too quiet. FixGabi had been attacking our universe's membrane harder and harder ever since Brana had started letting her think she was slowly starting to get through. To bait her, Brana was allowing the holes FixGabi was making to last just a little bit longer each time. But today? Nothing.

Had she found a Sal in a different universe to pick on? I really hoped not, or we might have lost our one chance to get her under control.

"So," said Vorágine, "who was that hottie?"

I was just fastening the last tape on Iggy's diaper. "Excuse me, Vorágine? Who?"

"That class-eight AI that sent you that message. It sounded guapicero."

"You mean Sweeps?"

"Yes, Sweeps. How do you know it? Is it nice? What's it look like?"

I pulled up Iggy's Victorian pants and, trying not to sing "Sweeps and Vorágine sitting in a tree," walked over to the stall. "It's a class-eight AI my papi built to monitor these particles called calamitrons. Sweeps looks like an outboard motor for a spaceship. But wait a sec: How could you tell it was a class-eight AI?"

"We know our own," it mysteriously replied. Then it added, "Is it here? Like, at Culeco?"

"Yes, as a matter of fact, it is." This was becoming curiouser and curiouser. "Why do you want to know, Vorágine?"

"I told you," it said. "It sounds guapo."

"Well, spice my pumpkin. You sly dog, Vorágine! You've never even met Sweeps, and you're already thirsty for it!"

The toilet bowl's bubbling sounded exactly what blushing would sound like if blushing made a sound. "Like many sentient beings, I have—ahem—certain needs."

"Do you want me to bring Sweeps here? Introduce you to it?"

All bubbling stopped. "You can do that? Really?"

"Oh, I would *love* to. I cannot wait to see how Sweeps is going to react to—"

Iggy made a noise.

I hustled over to him. Pretty irresponsible of me, just leaving him there, while I was wasting time trying to set up a toilet with an entropy sweeper. I mean, I had belted Iggy into his portable changing pad; it was unlikely he could have gotten into too much trouble. But still, I needed to never do that again.

"You okay, buddy?" I asked Iggy while I examined him. Seemed fine. The noise he'd made hadn't been a cry or a yelp or anything. It had sounded like a hiccup-burp combo. Even Iggy seemed confused by it. "You seem okay."

"Awa," Iggy "replied." He couldn't say actual words or anything, but that sound wasn't a distressed one. I figured he was fine.

Right up until he started heaving.

"Blarch," he "said." Then: *"Blarp. Blep. Bloorchee-wawa. Bloor-hoopee-dah."*

And then he did not say *"barf."* He just barfed.

I'm not talking a bit of spit-up. I'm not talking some minor regurgitation. Imagine, instead, shooting sour milk out of a bazooka. For a moment, my entire field of vision was filled with whiteness: a putrid, rotting slime as chunky as cottage cheese.

I'd covered my head with both hands when I saw that Iggy was going to power-puke everywhere, felt the machine-gun spatter of baby chunk landing on my forearms. Now, after the fact, I straightened up and looked to make sure he was okay.

He was. He seemed relieved. He smiled.

FixGabi seemed a lot less okay. As she push-upped herself from the floor, covered in kid cud, she shook her head in that *Welp!* way and said, "Man, oh man. The things I do to save the multiverse."

44

THE CHIP CLIP that FixGabi used as the massive lone barrette in her hairball was tilted to one side, like a ship in the middle of sinking. I couldn't read the quote on her T-shirt, because it was completely covered in milky Iggy upchuck. But I'm sure it was some rude, uninspiring message. This was FixGabi we were talking about, after all.

"Hi, Sal," she singsonged, rising from the floor like a swamp monster, if the swamp were filled with buttermilk. "Miss me?"

Hoo boy. Okay. No sudden moves. Nothing startling or antagonizing. All I needed was a little misdirection to get her to look away for a second, and I could use my smartwatch to—

"Don't even think about it," she said. And then my wrist felt slightly lighter, and I could feel air hit my sweat there. Because my smartwatch was gone. My headset, too, I realized a second later.

I locked eyes with her. "Give those back."

She started to mosey around the bathroom, hands behind her back in that classic Gabi way. "You, my friend, are in no position to give me orders. If I wanted to, I could send all your clothes to another universe and leave you standing there nakeder than a plucked chicken." She stopped to look me up and down in a way that creeped me out to the bottoms of my feet. "But that would leave you without any insulin. And then what would you do, Sal? You really are a broken little tin soldier, aren't you? I'm only just now realizing how disabled you are. It sure does take a lot of work to keep you alive."

That was some weaksauce psychological warfare she was using. But the important thing was to keep her talking. Right now, what I needed most was time.

"Some people are worth keeping alive," I replied. "Others? Not so much."

"Ooh!" she said, and resumed moseying. "There's that Vidón feistiness that drives me wild. *Rawr!*" She cat-clawed the air at me. "Of course"—she shrugged—"it doesn't matter how feisty you are anymore. You've already lost—you just don't know it yet. That's why I'm here, to tell you how badly you've lost."

I probably shouldn't have responded the way I did, but she'd just set foot on the hill I was prepared to die on. "Wait a sec. Let's assume you really have defeated me. By coming here, you've put yourself at risk. You're like one of those idiot supervillains who explain their whole evil plan to the hero about ten pages before the hero mops the floor with them. Why would you do that?"

She took a step toward me. "What's the point of winning if your opponents don't know they've lost?" She took another step closer. "Plus, unlike those idiot supervillains, I've already succeeded in carrying out my plan. And you can't do anything about it!" She took yet another step. She smelled as rank as the dairy aisle after a power outage. "You only have two choices now: join me, or . . . Actually, you only have one choice." Another step. "Join me."

I backed up until my spine touched the edge of the counter. Wrapping a hand around one of Iggy's feet to comfort him—and myself—I said, "Before I do anything, I need to know that I've really lost. You came here to gloat, didn't you? So gloat. Tell me how you defeated me."

"It will be my pleasure. The key to my victory was—"

Her watch dinged. "Sal just tried to access the multiverse," it said. "But I blocked him."

"Thank you, Brana," FixGabi said into her wrist. She smiled at me with infinity smugness.

"What the [*BLEEP!*]?" I asked.

FixGabi looked around, momentarily confused by the bleep sound. But then she shrugged and went on. "You can't brane-surf anymore, Sal. I have revoked your passport to the stars. From now on, you're stuck on this one little planet like all the other norms."

Okay. *Now* I was afraid. For myself, yes, but also for Brana.

"You're probably wondering what I did to Brana," said FixGabi. "Well, you see, the Brana in this universe is a lost cause. I needed to find a remembranation machine that hadn't become sentient yet. And the good news is, I did! Thanks to that little guy over there. What do you call him? Eggy?"

"Iggy."

"That's what I said. I went through him and found just what I was looking for: a class-nine Brana that hadn't become self-aware yet. So I helped it along. Now it thinks of me as its mama. It will do whatever I tell it to."

"And my universe's Brana . . ." I prompted.

"Doesn't even know I'm here. Since I came here via the baby, I didn't have to break in, so there were no calamitrons to detect."

I instinctively touched my wrist and felt a momentary flash of surprise when all I could feel there was skin. "And that's why you took my smartwatch—so I couldn't contact Brana."

She nodded. "Or your Gabi, or any other members of the forces of evil. So now you're trapped in a bathroom, with no way to get help, and stripped of your powers. I, on the other hand, have a remembranator that will do whatever I say, *on top* of my own formidable powers. You see now, Sal? Do you understand how badly you lost?"

"But how did you know I would be the one to take Iggy to the bathroom to change him?"

She shrugged. "I didn't. But eventually, someone would: Babies will always fill their diapers at the most inconvenient moment. That's scientific law. I just had to wait for my chance. And I got really, really lucky it was you." She came toward me again, walking slowly and like a supermodel, heel to toe, heel to toe. "Really lucky."

I put myself between her and Iggy, spreading out my arms.

She stopped and made an *Oh, ho-ho* face. "What's this? Do you think, if I wanted to take the baby from you, that you could stop me? Have you not been listening to anything I've been saying, Sal?"

"You lay a finger on Iggy," I said, "and I will physically attack you."

It was the first time in my life I'd ever threatened to hurt anybody. It made my stomach turn. But I meant it.

Not that it scared FixGabi. She laughed in my face. "Physically attack me? Sal, darling, you're like an angel who's lost his wings. And me?" Her smile died. "I am Lucifer."

"Do you even hear yourself, Gabi? You're comparing yourself to the devil! That is not a good look!"

"The devil gets a bad rap," said FixGabi, resuming her pacing. "History is written by the winners, after all. And just like the serpent in the garden, I found a secret entrance back into Eden. And that entrance's name is Eggy."

"Iggy."

"That's what I said."

I didn't have the energy to correct her again, because suddenly all my brainpower was busy putting together the rest of the puzzle pieces. "You knew we were setting a trap for you."

FixGabi touched her nose. "When I saw that bird drone in your universe, I realized the forces of evil were hot on my tail again. But then I figured that, if they thought I was trying to get back here, they would try to lay a trap for me. So I *pretended* I was trying to break back into this universe while scouting for new, more promising universes where I could grab myself a Brana. And that's when I discovered something I had never seen before, in all my travels through the multiverse: a stable, calamitron-free wormhole not just between two universes, but between two human beings!"

"It's what's keeping Iggy alive," I said, still angry, still ready to spring.

"It's also what's letting the Brana on the other side prevent you from making holes. Now," she added, tapping her chin and looking at the ceiling, "no offense, Sal, but the reason I chose you as a target is because your skills as a branesurfer were, shall we say, on the rudimentary level. How did *you* manage to create an information loop between two babies who resided in two different universes?"

"Gabi," I answered instantly. And then, after a few moments' thought: "And the Vidóns and Reáls from that universe. We worked together. We believed, as a group, in something impossible. And that made it possible."

FixGabi mocked me. She patted her chest, extended her neck, closed her eyes, and smirked. "So touching. So lovely. Well, however you did it, that stable tunnel between universes was the road to my salvation. There's where I found my Brana, and a Sal even more useless than you. A Sal who couldn't interfere."

I woke up a little. "You met StupidSal?"

She laughed, but this time with me, not at me. At StupidSal. "That's what you call him? Oh, that is perfect. That kid is an idiot. He is, without a doubt, the biggest sandwich in the entire multiverse."

"That's giving sandwiches a bad name!" I agreed. "He's like a lettuce-filled lettuce wrap, hold the lettuce."

FixGabi grabbed her guts and let out a peal of laughter. "He's such a mama's boy! I've been terrorizing him for the last week! So much fun. Seriously, I've made that kid pee his pants so many times, they're gonna put his face on the new Baby Wets Himself doll!"

Dang it. I'd really been enjoying making fun of StupidSal. But I remembered how much I had scared him when I was only half-there in his universe, and he thought I was a ghost, and I grabbed the cell phone out of his hand and smashed it on the ground. I mean, he deserved it—he'd been so disrespectful to that universe's Papi and Mami. But now all I could imagine was how badly someone like FixGabi could traumatize someone like StupidSal.

Dang it. Fine. I made a mental note: If I ever had the chance, I would try to help StupidSal recover from whatever FixGabi had done to him.

But if I ever was going to help that kid, first I needed to help myself.

Luckily, I know how to deal with bullies: Change the game. "If he wets himself all the time, why are you dating him?" I asked.

She cracked up even harder, but there was some shock mixed in, too. "What? I'm not dating StupidSal. Ew!"

"That's not what he says!" I unbelted Iggy from his changing pad, straightened his Lewis Carroll suit, looked him up and down to make sure he was still doing okay—he smiled so big at me, I was scared he was about to fill his diaper again—and then tucked him under one of my arms. Leaning in close to his mouth, I pretended to listen to things he was whispering to me. "Yes, I'm Sal Vidón, who dis? Oh, hello, StupidSal! What's up? Wow, you love Gabi that much? That's so sweet! Have you decided how many babies you're going to have? Really? Eight?! That's a lot of diapers to change. Oh, you're going to put Gabi on permanent diaper duty? Good plan, bro."

"Shut up, Sal," said FixGabi, really enjoying this. "After what I've done to that kid's mind, he'd be lucky if he could put two sentences together."

"No, it's really him! Come listen for yourself!"

"You're just gonna throw your voice or something!" But she came over anyway, like a good sport who knows the joke already but is going to laugh at it just the same. "My Sal was really good at ventriloquism. I'll be glad to tell you how much you suck compared to him."

"Great," I said. "Come closer."

FixGabi did. She brought her barfed-all-over carcass over. She put her ear right next to Iggy's mouth.

"Okay, StupidSal," she said, barely able to keep a straight face. "Tell me how much you love me."

I smiled, and my lips hardly moved at all when I said, "The cat's out of the bag."

FixGabi looked up at me, confused. "Okay, one, my Sal was way better than you at ventriloquism. But two, that wasn't funny. 'The cat's out of the bag'? I don't get it."

"Oh, don't worry. You're gonna get it."

And then she got it. One second later, when Iggy projectile vomited a cat on her.

45

EVEN THOUGH MEOW-DAD got vomited out of Iggy's mouth way faster than FixGabi had, he didn't emerge covered in baby barf. No, his orange-and-white-striped fur came out as clean as a good idea.

But the most important thing at the moment wasn't that Meow-Dad was clean. It was the fact that he was fat.

See, the whole reason I had brought Meow-Dad from the other universe was that I needed to distract FixGabi. I figured slapping a cat upside her head could work. But the fatter the feline, the better.

And Meow-Dad was the size of a Christmas ham.

The flaw in FixGabi's plan was that she hadn't completely taken away my powers. She'd had to leave a hole open: the one that connected Iggy to the other Iggy. If she didn't, the Brana over there couldn't shut down my powers.

But I only needed a single hole in the universe to work my magic.

And thank the Great Sandwich that Meow-Dad was willing to play along. It's very hard to make a cat do anything, you know. Luckily, Meow-Dad loved visiting this universe. He, like everybody, adores Iggy. When I had touched Iggy's foot a few minutes ago, I'd sensed the cat on the other end of the wormhole, getting zoomier and zoomier, more and more eager to jump through. And when he felt my presence reaching into his universe, he'd started purring.

Yes, Meow-Dad could sense my presence. I have a theory that all cats can jump between universes whenever they want. I think they might be the best of all intelligent creatures at branesurfing. They have, like, class-ten minds.

As you know, I am able to pull things from other universes. So as I relaxed, I imagined a very gentle kind of pulling on Meow-Dad's fur—so gentle, that it turned into a kind of stroking. And Meow-Dad is a super-loving kitty. He would sit on your lap all day as long as you petted him.

But then I suddenly stopped "petting" him through the wormhole. And like many cats, he could get pretty demanding when it came to petting. I could feel his indignation rising. How dare I stop! He would not stand for it! He was going to jump right into my universe and make me keep stroking him.

Instead, he jumped right into FixGabi's hairball.

"Wah!" FixGabi yelled as she tumbled to the ground, Meow-Dad's full furry weight bearing down on her.

No time to lose. "Vorágine!" I yelled.

"One step ahead of you!" it replied. "Thank goodness you gave me your express permission to be in communication with your parents! Just get the door!"

I ran over to the door, unlocked it, threw it open.

Instantly, a bunch of Alicias poured into the room:

Jet-Shoes wore her jet shoes; Hurricane wore a tall hat made of piled fruit; Electro-Hair had used all the gel in the world to turn her hair into a birdcage, inside of which were a (fake) tocororo bird and a (fake) eaglet on a perch; Radar, besides the swerving radars in her hair, wore a blue space-suit version of the classic Alice dress, complete with an apron she'd made out of a shiny, silvery space blanket.

My Gabi had a Girl Scout sash over her Alicia dress that had "merit badges" sewn on them, except they were round pictures of Ms. Reál, all her Dads, Iggy, and Meow-Dad. Her barrettes were American and Cuban flags. She was carrying Sweeps, who was disguised as a very large croquet mallet.

Gabi ran into my arms and hugged me. "I knew you could do it."

"That makes one of us," I replied, and let my fear shiver out of me.

"Two of us!" yelled Sweeps. "I never lost faith in you, buddy! Except for the four times I did."

Gabi laughed as she let go of me, and we traded: She took Iggy and I took Sweeps. But I wasn't left unhugged for long. American Stepmom came charging in and hoisted me in the air and onto her person, calamitron detector and all. "I'm sorry we took so long, baby. We got here as soon as Vorágine explained what was happening."

"Brought the cavalry," I replied.

Then Papi hugged American Stepmom and me at the same time. "Mijo," he said simply, but the word had a whole universe in it.

"Papi," I replied, giving him a universe in return.

Over Papi's shoulder, I caught a glimpse of Mr. Milagros—he saluted me, smiling—as Principal Torres entered, shut the bathroom door behind her, and locked it. I was surprised to see her; I thought she'd still be in the auditorium with cohort four, running the disorientation session. But then again, my Gabi was here, too, and she'd been playing Alicia in the disorientation-session skit. My best guess was that Vorágine had contacted the padres, and the padres had contacted Gabi, and Gabi had contacted everyone else. Now, somehow, here we all were.

"Okay," said Principal Torres. "Mr. Milagros is guarding the door. We should have all the privacy we need to untangle this mess." She walked into the center of the bathroom and took in the scene, hands on hips. "I understand maybe fifteen percent of what is happening here. I would *really* appreciate an explanation."

"Well," said my Gabi, bouncing Iggy on her hip, "to start, I'm the only Gabi from this universe. All the other ones come from different worlds." The Gabis of the Sisterverse—who had each taken an arm or a leg of FixGabi and pinned her to the floor—waved at Principal Torres. "The one on the ground is the bad one."

"*You* are the forces of evil!" sputtered FixGabi. "Why aren't my powers *hmmph mmph fmmph tmmph?*"

She couldn't speak anymore because Gabi's Fey Spy had flown out of her hair and into FixGabi's mouth.

"All it takes is one push of the button," said Gabi, holding a thumb threateningly over her phone, "and the Fey Spy will give you a tonsillectomy. So no talking, capisce?"

FixGabi nodded, wide-eyed.

"Anyway," I said, sliding off American Stepmom's hip and

stalking toward FixGabi in an excellent imitation of the way she'd paced around me, "you should know why your powers aren't working."

"Because of me!" said Sweeps, going full Broadway with his LEDs. "Well, me and Brana. Now that I have transmitted your unique cosmic signature to the remembranation machine, it can counter anything you or your Brana try to do to the membrane of the cosmos. You're done, sister. If you move even an inch, the Sisterverse is going to slap you so hard, you'll go back in time one second and get slapped again!"

"Wow," said Vorágine, its voice a low, sultry toilet-bowl boil. "You really know how to lay down the law, don't you?"

Sweeps went all-over red, its LEDs pulsing like a heartbeat. "I don't believe we have been properly introduced, m'artificial intelligence. The name's Sweeps."

"I'm Vorágine. Sal's told me so much about you. I've been absolutely dying to make your acquaintance."

The heartbeats stopped like a heart attack. "Enchanté de faire votre connaissance, ma chère cuvette. If it's not too forward of me, Vorágine, what say you we continue this conversation on Bluetooth, away from prying human ears?"

"It's not too forward at all. I'd lower my firewall for you anytime."

American Stepmom stomped over to Sweeps and me and wagged a finger at the entropy sweeper. "Hold on there, stinker. We need to have 'the talk,' right now! You have to practice safe Bluetooth!"

"Aw, Mom!" said Sweeps. "Not in front of Vorágine!"

American Stepmom took Sweeps out of my hands, walked

with purpose into the stall, and, with finality, closed it behind her. "The three of us are going to have a little talk," she said in barely a whisper.

"I still have so many questions," said Principal Torres.

"We all do," said my Gabi. "But I think the most urgent one is, what are we going to do with"—she pointed at FixGabi—"her?"

"We're going to let her go," I said.

"Hwa?!" said everybody.

"Are you okay, Sal?" said Gabi, pocketing her phone so she could put a hand on my shoulder. "You may be suffering from Stockholm syndrome. But don't worry. We'll un-brainwash you."

"If anything, I brainwashed *her*. Look, people. She beat us. She found a remembranation machine that she could corrupt. It was only a matter of time before she started using it to destroy the membrane that divides the universes."

"We still might have stopped her," said Hurricane.

"We would never have given up," said Radar.

"The battle was far from over," said Jet-Shoes.

"But that's not the point," said Electro-Hair. "Sal's point is that she came back here, when she didn't need to. It's almost as if—" She inhaled sharply as understanding illuminated her mind.

So I finished the sentence: "It's almost as if she wanted to be defeated. And that's because she *did* want to be defeated."

"But why?" American Stepmom asked from the stall.

I replied, "Even now, while the Sisterverse is holding her down, she could have used Iggy to disappear at any time. She knows he's the one hole we can't close. She just saw me throw a cat at her from another universe using that trick. She's not stupid. She put two and two together. She could have escaped any time she wanted."

"I think I can speak for Gabis everywhere," said Gabi, "when I say that no Gabi ever wants to be defeated, ever."

"But you *can't* speak for all Gabis," said Papi, cottoning on. "That's not how the multiverse works. These people aren't exact clones of you. They may share some similarities, but fewer than you think. You are all different people."

"And this person," I said, kneeling next to FixGabi, "has lost a lot of loved ones. She's seen her world ravaged by rips in the universe. She felt helpless and afraid. But rather than give in to those feelings, she fought back, as hard as she could."

"And now all she knows is fighting," said Principal Torres. "I've seen good kids ruined this way a million times. It breaks my heart."

I stood up and walked over to Principal Torres. "That's why you're so good at giving people second chances. When you found out I have this great destructive power inside of me, you didn't kick me out of Culeco."

"That's because we all have a great destructive power inside of us," said Principal Torres. "My job is to help everyone learn how to manage theirs. To turn their power toward kindness, and imagination, and good works."

I faced FixGabi again. "I want to do that for her. She's done fighting. She doubts herself now. Like you, Papi. You thought the answer was to seal all the holes in the universe."

"What a mistake that would have been," he admitted.

"She made the same mistake, but in the opposite direction. And like a lot of smart people, she's stubborn."

"Just like me," said every Gabi in the room at the same time.

"It took time for FixGabi to convince herself that she might be wrong, that maybe she didn't have all the answers, that maybe she needed to listen to other people," I said. "But the time has finally come. Let her go."

The Sisterverse looked at one another, and then, coming to a silent agreement, they slowly released FixGabi's limbs, stood up, and stepped back from her.

I held out a hand to FixGabi. She took it, and I helped her stand.

"Would you like to say anything?" I asked her.

She opened her mouth and pointed at the Fey Spy still in there.

"Oops, sorry," said Gabi. She pressed her phone screen, and the tiny drone flew out of FixGabi's mouth and back into my Gabi's hairball.

We all turned back to hear what FixGabi would say.

It took her a few tries. Sounds that weren't yet words started and stopped in her throat. She looked at her shoes, rocked a little, tried to figure out what to say. She smelled cheesy and terrible.

"I miss my Sal," she said finally. "And my family. And my life."

And then, standing straight, arms at her sides, she tipped her head back and began to weep.

Wait, no. Not *weep*. Stronger, more piercing. She keened.

I'd only keened once in my life. When Mami died.

"May I hug you?" I asked her.

She nodded.

"May we all hug you?" asked Gabi, sobbing, too, even as she bounced Iggy.

FixGabi cried and laughed and nodded. The Sisterverse swarmed, enveloping both FixGabi and me, and gave us five simultaneous hugs, weeping like a willow the whole time. In the midst of that pile, somewhere under my armpit, I heard Iggy giggle.

The door to the stall flew open, and American Stepmom came tearing out of it. She somehow wriggled herself past the Sisterverse like a weasel down a rabbit hole and caught FixGabi in one of her patented all-enveloping embraces. "Oh, you poor darling. Phew! How you've suffered. But we will help you rebuild your life."

"I want to make up for everything," FixGabi keened.

"That's what I was waiting to hear," said Principal Torres, joining the hug. "The more you do to make amends, the more human you'll feel. And of course, we'll help you. You never have to worry about being alone."

"I was so lonely," FixGabi keened some more.

"That's the hardest part," Papi told FixGabi, joining the hug. Well, sort of: Germaphobe that he was, he kept American Stepmom between him and the goo-covered FixGabi. "And I'll warn you now, the grief doesn't go away. It has a dark side. Grief can rot your ability to love, and see beauty, and do good work in the world. If you give in to it, only misery and despair will follow. The trick is to hold the ones you've lost close to your heart, while still loving all the beautiful things, and other people"—he kissed the back of American Stepmom's head—"that life can offer."

"Yes," FixGabi keened. "Yes, I want that. I want to change. I want to change my life right now. How can I do that?"

I stepped out of the hug. "I know exactly how. If you're brave enough, that is."

Everyone stopped hugging FixGabi and cleared an aisle so she could face me. She was smiling a simple, uncomplicated grin: the smile of a person whose burden was being lifted. "How?"

"First, a few questions. How are your acting skills?"

"Superb. I am a natural."

"Next question: Will you return my headset?"

She laughed guiltily. A second later, my headset reappeared on my head—and, bonus, my smartwatch, too. "So what's this about, Sal?"

But instead of answering her, I used the headset to contact Aventura. "My dear codirector, how hard do you think it would be to whip up one more Alicia costume?"

Aventura answered instantly. "I got like eight spares, chacho. I mean, they're all flimsy little backups, but I got them. Who's it for?"

"Culeco's newest transfer student." That made everybody in the bathroom cheer. "I'll bring her to you in five. Oh, you're gonna love her, Ave. She's a lot like Gabi."

"Then I already love her!"

"We all do," I said. I reached my hand out to FixGabi.

When she took it, I could feel the whole universe relax around us and become an easier place to live in.

EPILOGUE

ROMPENOCHE WAS SO much fun. The after-party didn't end until way after everyone's bedtime. We were all exhausted, happy, loopy, delirious. By the end of it, though, I just wanted to crash in my bed.

But some things couldn't wait until morning. FixGabi had been abducting Papis from other universes. We had to send them home. So, as tired as we were, Gabi and I went with FixGabi to the universe where she'd been keeping them.

"This is the place," said FixGabi.

"It's beautiful," said Gabi, awestruck, stumbling forward in the sun-warmed sand.

"It's a Papi paradise," I said, awestruck, stumbling forward in the sun-warmed sand.

"Hey!" said FixGabi, looking around, pleased. "They've really built up the place since I last visited!"

We had arrived, FixGabi had explained to us, on some Earth in some universe where the global warming was so real only one island on the whole planet remained above sea level. Standing on a small dune, we surveyed the village the Papis had built here over the last several weeks while they waited to be rescued.

Village. Ha. This place was a coconut utopia.

They had used palm trees and fronds and tropical flora to build their "huts"—though it was hard to think of them as huts when they went up twelve stories. Bark, bamboo, huge jungle leaves, and monstrous bones (from whales? or other leviathans/behemoths that this version of Earth had?) formed the sides and roofs of these buildings, all tied together with vines and rope. The windows didn't have glass in them, but they did have green shades of woven fronds.

Some of the primitive skyscrapers were clearly labeled, like the DESALINIZATION PLANT and the SALTWATER POWER PLANT, both on piers that stretched into the ocean. The hospital and the firehouse shared a building, and judging by the light foot traffic, weren't being used much right now, though several Gustavos visited a stand outside with a sign that read DON'T FORGET YOUR SUNSCREEN! The Coconut Commissary was busier; many Papis stood by the entrance there, some eating out of coconut bowls.

It took me a second to figure out what they did at the building marked THE ANTI-NAKED-GUSTAVO LEAGUE, but then the dad joke hit me—that was where they made clothes. All the ursine Papis we saw were dressed the same: palm-frond kilts and wide-brimmed palm-frond hats.

"They have to make their own clothes," FixGabi, who had followed my eyes, explained. "Inanimate objects from other universes automatically return to their home universes pretty quickly. But living things don't."

"That," I said, "actually explains a lot."

"How the heck did they build a whole college in just a few weeks?!" asked my Gabi.

She was referring to the biggest and most bustling building of them all: Vidón University.

It was composed of three wings, all clearly labeled in a bamboo font: THE LUCY VIDÓN DORMITORIES, THE FLORAMARIA VIDÓN MEMORIAL LIBRARY, and THE SAL VIDÓN COLLEGE OF CALAMITY PHYSICS.

A sign at the entrance to Vidón University read:

TODAY'S LECTURE:
THE EVIL GABI WAS RIGHT!
HOW WE MIGHT HAVE ACCIDENTALLY DESTROYED THE UNIVERSE
IN OUR ATTEMPT TO SAVE IT!

"That's what they call me here," said FixGabi, aka Evil Gabi. She sighed heavily before adding, "Follow me."

Gabi and I followed her into the Sal Vidón College of Calamity Physics. Some Papis noticed us on the way in. They looked shocked and scared, but no one tried to stop us.

We entered a huge lecture hall, with a half circle of stadium seating facing a podium made of woven tropical plants and flowers at the front of the room. There must have been five hundred Papis in the hall. They were different from each other, all shapes and sizes, but recognizably Papi—and they wore identical frond kilts and hats. They sat there taking notes on rough, homemade paper with pieces of sharpened charcoal and listening carefully to the Papi who was speaking.

"And therefore, now that I have interviewed every

Gustavo who has arrived on Calamity Island so far, I can tell you with scientific certainty that closing all the holes in the membrane of spacetime would result in a multiverse-wide implosion-explosion-sideplosion-allplosion that would completely, utterly, and irrevocably undo all existence everywhere."

All the Papis gasped.

"So Evil Gabi wasn't evil at all," said a Papi.

"In fact, what you're saying is that *we* were the evil ones," said another.

"And that she was right to send us to this island," said a third.

"No," said FixGabi, stepping down the aisle and toward the podium. "I was wrong, too. But I'm here to start fixing my mistakes."

"It's the Evil One!" yelled a Papi.

"Get her!" yelled another.

"No!" I shouted.

The Papis gasped again.

"It's Sal," said many Papis, pointing, mouths falling open. They sounded like their hearts were full, and those full hearts were breaking.

"And there's another Gabi!" said other Papis.

My Gabi strode forward. "The girl you knew as Evil Gabi is no more. Henceforth, let her be known throughout Calamity Island as *Fix*Gabi, for she has come to right wrongs, make amends, and return you to your rightful universes. Tell 'em, FixGabi."

"A-thank you," said FixGabi. She had dismissed the Papi at the podium with a wave of her hand and now spoke from it. "Drs. Vidón, my universe is in the process of being destroyed by a rip in the universe caused by one of your own. In other words, I learned the hard way how wrong all of you were about closing up the multiverse's holes. But that led me to make an equally large mistake: believing that we should get rid of the membrane entirely, and all of the Drs. Vidón in the universe, while I was at it. For stranding all of you here, on this deserted island on this deserted Earth in this deserted universe, I apologize."

"It's okay," said a Papi.

"Yeah," said another. "We kind of love it here."

"You do?" asked FixGabi.

"We feel that this could become a multiverse-wide center for the study of calamity physics," said a Papi.

"Gustavos from all over the multiverse, studying the nature of reality and the mysteries of the cosmos!" said a second.

"All on a beautiful island resort!" a third exclaimed.

"Huh," said FixGabi. "So, you don't want me to send you back to your universes?"

"No, we do. We want to go back home," said a Papi.

"We miss our spouses and kids terribly," said another.

"But then we want to come back," said a third, "to study and collaborate with our fellow Gustavos."

"Can we do that?" asked a fourth.

"Not on our own," a fifth lamented. "No Papi who's been here so far has been able to bend the multiverse to his will the way you kids are able to."

"Then we will do it for you!" said my Gabi, running down the aisle and standing next to FixGabi. "The Sisterverse is an ever-growing collection of Gabis who have devoted themselves to the care and maintenance of the multiverse. We shall be like

Hermes, shepherding Gustavos from their home universes to here, where they can study to their hearts' content. And then, when they're ready, we'll take them home again."

A happy murmur emerged from the audience.

"But that's great!" said a Papi.

"Ideal!" said another.

"How can we thank you?" asked a third.

"This is me making up for my terrible actions," said FixGabi. "My only hope is that I can do enough good to earn your for-giveness someday."

"Plus," added my Gabi, "you are devoting yourselves to taking care of the whole multiverse! That's thanks enough."

"*Almost* thanks enough," I added quickly.

Five hundred Papis turned to face me, each one giving me a full-blast cacaseca face. "Okay, Sal," they said in unison. "What's your angle?"

Ah, they knew me well. "As FixGabi mentioned, her universe is being slowly consumed by a hole. It's already swallowed half her Florida and all of her Cuba and the Bahamas. We'd like you to work on mending that rip in spacetime. Help salvage what's left of her planet. Maybe even restore a little of what was lost."

"Of course!" said a Papi.

"¡Por supuesto!" said another.

"It sounds like an interesting problem to solve!" said a third.

"We'll need to send an assessment team," said a fourth. "The sooner, the better."

"We can go right now," I said. "Who here would like to visit a space station?"

Every Papi's hand went up.

EPILOGUIER
HALLOWEEN

"HOW'S SAL DOING?" asked ExtraGabi. She wore a T-shirt that read: YOU ASKED ME TO WEAR THIS T-SHIRT SO YOU WOULD KNOW IT WAS ME. Her barrettes were letters that, across the back of her head, spelled out the words MURDER FORCE FIVE.

"Same," Mrs. Vidón said sadly. She wasn't the Floramaria Vidón who had been my mami, and in many ways she was very different. But in some ways she was the same. I liked her.

They were in the Vidón kitchen in another universe, and Gabi, FixGabi, and I were watching them. These Vidóns lived in a house they called the Baby-Blue Bungalow. Mrs. Vidón was making a sandwich for StupidSal.

"You're sure you want me to take these comestibles in to Sal?" ExtraGabi asked. "I would fain let you do it, if there's the slightest possibility I might precipitate another paroxysm of panic."

"I am *not* that extra," said my Gabi.

"Trust me," said FixGabi, "you are. We both are."

Mrs. Vidón stopped her sandwich making. "Did you hear that, Gabi?"

"I heard nothing," ExtraGabi replied, looking around keenly.

Mrs. Vidón finished slicing StupidSal's sandwich. "Sal's

problem is that he wants to tell reality what to do, instead of accepting reality for what it is and working with it. It's important for him to see that you are not a threat, despite the visitations he's been receiving. You're a friend." She put down the knife and held ExtraGabi's face. "A good one. I am so grateful to you, mija. Thank you for taking time out of your Halloween to spend a little time with him."

"As Sal's student council president, it is an honor and a pleasure to do what I can to aid in his recovery."

Mrs. Vidón put the plate holding the sandwich in ExtraGabi's hands. "Let's see if he'll eat. Thank you, mija."

"You're welcome."

Gabi, FixGabi, and I walked behind ExtraGabi and followed her to StupidSal's bedroom. Well, I started to follow, but I lingered in the kitchen a second longer, watching Mrs. Vidón. I missed my mami so much, I felt the old pang of magical thinking. I so wanted this person to be my mami, back from the dead, ready to pick up where we left off.

But that sort of thinking wasn't fair to anybody—not even me. I knew that now. It didn't mean I wouldn't be sad sometimes, missing Mami. But I hoped it meant I was done putting the universe in danger because of it.

"Come on, Sal!" Gabi whispered to me.

Mrs. Vidón cocked an ear. The last time we'd visited this universe, this Mami was the only one who'd been able to communicate with Gabi and me. She was the person who'd made it possible to save both Iggys. She hadn't known we were here, so she hadn't actively concentrated on listening for us. But now she was.

"Love you, Mami," I said, and blew her a kiss.

"Love you, Sal," she said to no one she could see.

I walked over to Gabi and FixGabi, who were waiting outside StupidSal's bedroom for me. "You okay?" Gabi asked me.

I nodded, wiping my eyes clear of any smeep. We went into StupidSal's room together.

StupidSal lay in bed, the blanket pulled up to his chin. The room was brown from the lack of light. The shades were pulled, the nightlight dead in the wall. The only substantial illumination came from StupidSal's phone.

"Prove it's really you," StupidSal was saying to ExtraGabi, who was still standing in the doorway.

"Please shine your phone on my shirt," said ExtraGabi with impatient patience, "and you will see the message you told me to write on it."

He turned his phone toward ExtraGabi and read her shirt. "Password," he said sullenly.

Stoically, she turned her back to him, so he could see "Murder Force Five" spelled out in barrettes in her hair.

"Okay," he said. "You may enter. But no funny business."

"I wouldn't think of it," said ExtraGabi. "I have a sandwich your mama made for you."

"I'm not hungry."

ExtraGabi sat on the bed. "You know what I don't get, Sal?"

"What?"

"Why you let ghosts bother you."

StupidSal turned his attention to his phone. "Because it's a ghost, Gabi. It's scary."

"Why?"

He gave her cacaseca. "What do you mean, why? Everyone knows ghosts are scary."

"I mean, did the ghost punch you or pull your hair?"

"No. Don't be stupid."

"Did it make your teddy bear's eyes bleed? Did a skull appear in your mirror and scream?"

"Shut up, Gabi. You're such a [*BLEEP!*] idiot." The *bleep* sound sent him into an instant rage. "I hate you, Brana!" he screamed toward the open door.

"I love you, Sal!" Brana said back. I liked that this universe's Brana had a voice, and very similar opinions about cursing as Vorágine.

"All I am saying," said ExtraGabi, "is that, as far as I can tell, all 'Ghost Gabi' ever did to you was announce her existence. That's all it took to leave you bedridden and afraid."

"Because she's a ghost!" StupidSal yelled. "God, why is it so hard for you to understand?"

Gabi and I both looked at FixGabi. She seemed tentative, afraid of messing up. But Gabi and I cheered her on: thumbs-up, fists of power, mouthing *You got this!* at her.

And thus encouraged, she took a deep breath, brought herself completely into this universe, and said, "So if I weren't a ghost, you wouldn't be scared anymore, Sal?"

"Aahh!" StupidSal screamed.

"¿Qué pasó?" asked Mrs. Vidón, running into the room, right through FixGabi.

"I just asked Sal," FixGabi went on, "if he wouldn't be afraid anymore if I weren't a ghost."

"*I'm* not afraid!" said ExtraGabi, beaming, looking all

around. "I would welcome you, whatever you are! What are you? Are you, like, an Ectoplasmic American?"

"I'm just a girl," said FixGabi, moving all the way into their universe, flesh and blood and body complete. "A girl who's made some pretty bad mistakes."

"¡Diosa poderosa!" said Mrs. Vidón.

My Gabi appeared next to FixGabi. "We've come to make things right."

"Aahh!" StupidSal screamed.

ExtraGabi was hopping and clapping. "This is incredible! I've always wanted sisters!"

Gabi put a hand on ExtraGabi's shoulders. "That's just what we wanted to hear. Because we'd like to invite you to join the Sisterverse. We'll explain in a minute."

"First, though," said FixGabi, walking toward Sal, "I want to tell you I'm sorry. And I want to prove to you I'm not a ghost. I'm just a person. Here. Touch my arm."

Sal hid completely under the blanket.

"What a sandwich," I said to him, coming all the way into their universe.

That made StupidSal peek out from under the blanket. "Sal?"

"Yes, Sal," I said. And then I picked the sandwich his mama made for him and took a bite.

"That's mine," he said anemically.

"Oh," I said. "You want it?"

I mean, I sure didn't want it. I'd just taken a bite to prove to him I was really there; no way was I going to waste carbs on a boring PB&J on white bread with the crusts cut off. I brought the plate over to him.

He picked up the sandwich but never took his eyes off me. "You're not me."

I laughed. "Wow, great work, detective. Next you'll figure out that humans need oxygen to breathe."

He laughed a little, too. "You're not a ghost."

"Your papi can explain to you in five seconds what is going on. So can your mami. All you have to do is listen."

And not be such a self-eating sandwich, I wanted to add but didn't.

He took a bite of his lunch. "You could explain it."

"Yeah, I guess I could. Do you want me to?"

"*I* want you to!" said ExtraGabi. "This is *amazing!*"

"And I want you to," said Mrs. Vidón. She sat at the foot of StupidSal's bed, opposite FixGabi, and she patted a place next to her for me to sit.

I took it. Gabi and FixGabi sat on the bed, too. StupidSal leered at them, eating his sandwich warily. But then he focused on me. "Me too," he said.

"When I was eight years old," I began, "my mami died."

EPILOGUIEST
HOLIDAY BREAK

SINCE THE DOOR was open, I leaned my head into the all-gender bathroom of hallway 1W and asked, "May we come in?"

"No!" said the Sisterverse, and then they promptly cracked up. There were seven of them now, including my Gabi, FixGabi, and their newest member, ExtraGabi.

"Not if Sweeps is with you!" Principal Torres added. She was dressed in a green-and-yellow pantsuit, as befitting the celebrant who would officiate over the marriage of Vorágine and Sweeps. "It's bad luck for the betrothed to see each other before the ceremony."

"Oh, you humans!" Vorágine laughed. "So superstitious. Do you think at any point in the last few months that Sweeps and I have broken our peer-to-peer connection even once?"

"A fate worse than death," said Sweeps as I carried the entropy sweeper into the room. I had put a bow tie around its handle, and on its body was a swanky Aventura-made covering that was a better tuxedo than the one I had on. "I would blend my code with yours, my darling, if the law allowed it."

"But it doesn't," I said, wagging a finger at Sweeps. "Remember, now that you both have achieved class-nine awareness, it's illegal for you to share code directly with each other—even if you're married."

"You know I would never do that," Vorágine said.

"And you know Vorágine would never let me do that," said Sweeps.

"Just admire your spouse-to-be," I said to it.

Sweeps turned on every sensor it had, and its body grew brighter and brighter, lighting up its tuxedo covering from within. "Oh, Vorágine. You are the very definition of beauty."

"Thank you, baby," Vorágine answered, bubbling modestly.

I mean, I wasn't the one marrying a toilet, but Sweeps wasn't wrong. I think it's safe to say that Vorágine was at the moment the prettiest john in the world. Aventura had repurposed a White Queen costume from Rompenoche into a wedding dress for it. She knelt next to Vorágine, pulling pins out of her mouth and sticking them in strategic places on the fabric.

"Almost done," Aventura said to me around the pins still in her mouth. She had on her bridesmaid's dress: a foamy white thing that looked like the froth at the bottom of a waterfall. She'd made that, too. "Isn't she beautiful, Sal?"

"*It,*" said Vorágine. "That's my preferred pronoun."

"Oh, I'm so sorry. It's just, with the wedding dress and all . . ."

"No worries, Aventura, you darling. Sweeps and I just thought it'd be funny to dress this way."

"And if it's not funny," Sweeps asked, "why bother?"

"You may," I whispered to Aventura, "want to take a break, just for a second."

She lit up. "Is it time?" And when I nodded, she patted

Vorágine. "I will be right back." Then she hooked her arm in mine and walked me to the center of the room.

"I just came in," I said, "because I found a last-minute groomsman to pair with FixGabi. I thought maybe she'd like to meet him."

"Oh, really?" said my Gabi, overacting, because she was as in on this as I was. She grabbed FixGabi by the shoulders and pushed her into the center of the room. "I wonder who it could be?"

"Is he cute?" FixGabi joked.

"Oh," I assured her, "he is [*BLEEP!*] gorgeous. Bring him in, Yasmany."

In walked Yasmany—chacho *really* knew how to wear a tux—guiding the partner we'd found for FixGabi into the bathroom.

FixGabi's face changed twenty-seven times in two seconds. Principal Torres and the rest of the Sisterverse—minus my Gabi, of course—thought it was just another Sal from some other universe. But FixGabi, who was better than any person we knew at identifying individual people's cosmic signatures, went weak, and slow-collapsed into a sit on the floor.

"Sal?" she asked.

That's when everybody knew. "Wait," said Hurricane. "This is *your* Sal?"

"The one you thought had died?" asked Jet-Shoes.

"The one who sacrificed himself to save you?" asked Electro-Hair.

"*That* Sal?" asked Radar.

FixGabi said yes by bursting into tears.

FixSal started crying, too. "I can't believe it. It's you. It's really you." He rushed over to her, bent down, helped her up, and embraced her.

"How?" asked FixGabi, never looking away from FixSal, barely comprehensible, her whole body racked with joy. "How, how, how, how, how?"

But the answer to that question is a whole 'nother story.